The Lost
Mata Hari Ring

Elyse Douglas

COPYRIGHT

The Lost Mata Hari Ring
Copyright © 2018 by Elyse Douglas
All rights reserved

COVER DESIGN   KEN KENYON

COVER ART   MATA HARI (IMAGE: PUBLIC DOMAIN / MEDIADRUMWORLD.C)

COVER PHOTO   SHUTTERSTOCK - HEDJIK'S

ISBN-13: 978-1513634326   BROADBACK
ISBN-10: 1513634321

TO THE READER

Wherever it was appropriate, and served the plot, the dialogue spoken by Mata Hari and Pablo Picasso were taken directly from quotes, letters, diaries and postcards. Although most of the novel follows the historical record about Mata Hari's life from 1916/1917, certain changes were made for convenience of character, time and plot.

For Neelima, always the Muse,
whose mysteries are timeless.

ACKNOWLEDGEMENT

We would like to express our gratitude to Hans Groeneweg, Lid projectgroep Mata Hari, of the Fries Museum in Leeuwarden, Friesland in the Netherlands, for his invaluable help as we researched the life of Mata Hari and her daughter, Juana-Luisa MacLeod.

THE LOST
MATA HARI RING

CHAPTER 1

With a certain unease and reluctance, twenty-nine-year-old Tracey Peyton Rutland entered Maynard Hopkins' private, sunny office on East 78th Street. Dr. Hopkins closed the door softly behind her, clearing his throat.

"Good morning. May I take your coat?" he offered.

Tracey shouldered out of her long, stylish winter coat, peeled off her leather gloves, stuffed them into her coat pocket and handed the coat to the doctor, who hung it in a closet.

A tall, thin man in his middle 70s, with stooped shoulders, Dr. Hopkins had clear, steady eyes and thinning white hair, combed sideways. He wore a crisp white shirt, dress pants, and spectacles that lent an impression of intelligence and wisdom.

After closing the closet door, he turned to her. "Ms. Rutland," he said in a thin tenor voice, "can I get you anything? Water? Tea? Coffee?"

Tracey gave him a quick, friendly smile. "No, thank you. And please call me Trace, Dr. Hopkins. It's short for Tracey."

He nodded in agreement, noting Trace's slight southern accent. He indicated toward his plush leather couch. "Please sit down so we can have a little talk before we begin."

It was a rectangular office—a private room connected to his 24th floor two-bedroom apartment. Trace lowered herself onto the couch and folded her hands on her lap. As she took in the room, she saw an ornately carved oak desk, with an open laptop computer and papers neatly arranged on it. A vase of fresh flowers bloomed next to a gold-framed color photograph of a broad-faced older woman, whose smile was generous, eyes dark and hair a silver gray. There were floor-to-ceiling bookshelves, filled to capacity; floor plants, all green and healthy; and silver-framed engravings on the exposed walls. They featured familiar photos of the Brooklyn Bridge, the Empire State Building and the 42nd Street New York Public Library. Trace's eyes finally rested on the psychiatrist's couch, with its black leather upholstery and ebonized wood claw feet. Was that her ultimate destination?

Dr. Hopkins drew up a ladderback chair and sat opposite her, a legal pad, some typed pages and a pen at the ready. "And how are you, on this chilly January morning, Trace?"

"I'm well, Dr. Hopkins, thank you."

He adjusted his glasses. "You were referred by Dr. Margaret Cummins, is that right?"

"Yes."

"And she is your primary care physician?"

"Yes."

"And you are a dancer, singer, actress?"

"Yes."

Dr. Hopkins produced a thin smile. "Have you been in any shows I might have seen? I'm quite fond of the theatre."

Trace tried to keep the pride out of her voice. "I've been in *The King and I* and *On the Town*, and I played Christine in *The Phantom of the Opera* for about a year. I've also done some TV, a movie for *Netflix*, and had a few minor parts in other feature films. I also had a part in a TV series two years ago called *Happy Ever After, You Fool.*" She smiled. "Believe it or not, it was a family drama."

"Well, that's very impressive," Dr. Hopkins said, with a lift of an eyebrow. "It sounds like you're doing quite well in your chosen profession."

Trace smiled, demurely. "I hope so. I'm between shows right now. I'll be starting rehearsals for a new musical in a few weeks, in February."

As she spoke, Dr. Hopkins studied her in earnest. Trace Rutland was a very attractive young woman, with long, honey blonde hair, startling blue eyes, a delicate mouth and high cheekbones. Her figure was fine, waist thin, neck long and elegant, skin white and radiant. When she'd entered, he'd guessed her height to be about 5 feet 10 inches, only three inches shorter than he. Yes, Trace would be a striking figure on the stage.

He shuffled some of the typed pages, found what he was looking for and drew one out, quickly perusing it. "On the questionnaire you filled out, you stated that you saw a psychiatrist for about two years... a Dr. Alma Steinmetz?"

"Yes, that's right," Trace said, unfolding her hands and picking a piece of lint from her V neck, emerald-colored sweater. She then readjusted herself on the couch, tugging gently at her tight designer jeans, feeling an acid stomach.

Dr. Hopkins lifted his eyes. "Over the phone last week when we talked, you said Dr. Steinmetz was a more traditional psychiatrist. That is to say, her treatment recommended lifestyle changes, in addition to pharmacological treatment and group therapy. You stated that she did not use hypnotherapy."

"That's right. But after two years, I didn't feel like we were making much progress. Also, I stopped taking the medications she prescribed, and that went against Dr. Steinmetz's recommendations. So, I decided to make a change. Dr. Cummins told me that you have had some success in treating patients with psychosomatic symptoms and insomnia, and that you sometimes use hypnotherapy."

Dr. Hopkins nodded. "Yes, in some cases. But I also prescribe medications, Trace, depending on my patient's symptoms."

"I'd rather not take any medications right now, Dr. Hopkins. When I take them, I feel out of touch with myself, and I don't perform as well. I feel dizzy sometimes and, I don't know, sort of strange."

"Did Dr. Steinmetz try adjusting your medications?"

"Yes, but I had almost all the same reactions each time. I've never tolerated medication very well."

"All right, Trace. Fine."

Dr. Hopkins sat up a little straighter and nodded again. "So you have persistent nightmares and often feel pains in your chest, is that correct?"

"Yes."

"Have you undergone testing for these complaints?"

4

"Yes. I have had every test there is, from EKGs to X-rays, CT scans, blood tests, and angiograms. I've taken sleeping pills for years, but then I stopped because I was afraid I was getting addicted, and then I started drinking wine to help me sleep. When you do eight shows a week, you have to sleep or you're just dead on Monday, your day off. As it is, I have to sleep all day on Monday, just to have the energy for the next week's performances."

Dr. Hopkins observed her as they spoke. Trace's hands would form fists, then she'd relax them for a time, then form the fists again. He wondered if this was some relaxation technique she'd learned or if it was related to nerves. He also observed a muscle twitching near her left eye. Her beautiful eyes did look glassy from fatigue, although her expert makeup job hid most of the lines and signs of weariness.

Trace's eyes ventured toward the windows. She saw a shaft of sunlight illumine the beauty of the Doctor's oak desk. Her face changed into sadness.

"Dr. Hopkins, I'm getting desperate. I can't keep going on like this... always tired, always frightened I'm going to fall asleep and have the same nightmare. I've had it, on and off, since I was a girl. When I have that nightmare, I jerk awake and I can't go back to sleep. It's just so terrifying. Sometimes when I'm on stage dancing or singing, I feel a hot searing pain in my chest, and it nearly knocks the wind out of me. I almost fainted the other night on stage. I just have to find some way to cope with all this, without taking pills. Sometimes I feel like I'm going to crack up. I don't want to get addicted and I don't want to become an alcoholic, because the only way I can fall asleep now is to drink three glasses of wine every night."

Dr. Hopkins pursed his lips and leaned back. "Trace, how often do these nightmares occur?"

Trace faced him. "Maybe four times a month, sometimes less, sometimes more."

"And it's the same nightmare—I mean to say—the events are exactly the same in each nightmare?"

"Yes, pretty much. Sometimes I'll see more events and faces, sometimes less, but it's always pretty much the same."

"And when did you first recall them occurring…approximately at what age?"

Trace lowered her eyes in thought. "I guess I was about five or six. Mom or Dad used to rush into my bedroom because I was screaming. I'd tell them about the nightmare and they'd comfort me and tell me it was all just a dream, and to go back to sleep."

Trace continued. "The nightmares went away for a while when I was in high school, but they returned again when I started college. I lost roommates, because I would wake up screaming in the middle of the night. I finally had to get my own room. The university doctor prescribed some medications and they suppressed the dreams for a while, but I always felt a little out of it, and dreamy. I had boyfriends who called me Space Girl."

Dr. Hopkins scribbled notes, nodding absently as he wrote and listened. Finally, he lowered his pen and crossed his long legs. "Trace, have you ever been treated with hypnotherapy?"

"Once, about four years ago, when I was in Los Angeles. I was working on a movie, and the nightmares got really bad."

"And how did you respond to it?"

"I guess I'm not a very good candidate. I felt relaxed, but I didn't go very deep. I remembered a few things from my childhood, but nothing much more than that."

Dr. Hopkins noted her response on his pad, and then he lifted his eyes toward the ceiling, as if in thought. "Trace, can you tell me about your persistent nightmare? Are you comfortable doing that?"

Trace licked her lips, eyes blinking rapidly. She sighed, hesitating. "Yes..." she said, glancing away toward the windows again. "But sometimes it makes me a little sick to talk about it. That's why I don't talk about it. Talking about it just, I don't know, hurts, and it's scary."

"Okay, Trace. Have you talked about it with other doctors?"

"Yes... Dr. Steinmetz and I worked to identify certain aspects of it. She believed the dream held buried parts of myself...the shadow parts of myself, that I didn't want to face."

"Did you improve? Did the nightmares subside?"

Trace shifted uncomfortably and raked fingers through her lush hair. She shrugged. "Maybe. The nightmares went away for a while—maybe a month or two—and I thought they were gone—but then they came back. They always come back, and sometimes they come in a kind of kaleidoscope of images and memory, all spinning around."

"Okay, I see. Trace, I want you to relax and take a few deep breaths. Would you like some water?"

"No... I'm fine."

"Okay, just sit back with your hands at your sides and, when you're ready, I want you to close your eyes and tell me about your nightmare. Is that all right? Can you do that?"

Trace nodded, and Dr. Hopkins saw tension form around her mouth and eyes.

"Just take a few deep breaths, Trace. Relax."

She did so and closed her eyes.

Immediately, Trace saw images and motion. She smelled a foul odor, felt cold and frightened. She began to shiver.

"Are you all right, Trace?"

Trace felt a cold hand of resistance pushing her away. But she was desperate for help. She struggled to follow the images as shadows fled down dark, dank hallways, and angry sinister faces jutted out from walls, shouting her name. She struggled to pierce the darkness and push through the terror, but she couldn't.

Her eyes popped open. "I can't," she said in a trembling voice. "I just can't. It makes me sick and scared. I can't."

Dr. Hopkins lowered his voice to a comforting whisper. "It's all right, Trace. It's fine. Just relax now. Just take some easy, comfortable breaths."

They sat in a long pulsing silence. Outside, Trace could hear the murmur of the City, distant taxi horns, a helicopter passing over, the wings of a pigeon flapping by.

Dr. Hopkins uncrossed his legs and leaned forward. "Trace, I'd like to try hypnotherapy now, if you are agreeable."

Trace looked at him with nerves and hope.

"Okay…"

"I want to hypnotize you, to do some gentle exploration. Now I realize you've done this before, but I would like to try it again—but only if you feel comfortable with that."

Trace flashed him a brief twitch of a smile. She lifted her shoulders and let them slowly relax.

"Well…that's why I'm here, Dr. Hopkins, to try to get at this thing and release it. I just hope it works better than last time."

Dr. Hopkins smiled reassuringly. "Let's give it a try. I believe it might help us understand you better. Of course, it may not. As you know, not everyone responds to hypnosis."

"Right, but I'm willing to try," Trace said. "I'll try anything."

Minutes later, Trace was lying on the black leather psychiatrist's couch, covered by a light cotton blanket, her eyes open, focused on the white ceiling. Dr. Hopkins had lowered the lights and closed the draperies to shut out the late morning sun.

He returned to Trace and adjusted his chair so that he sat beside her. He quietly led her through a series of relaxation techniques that allowed her to go deeper within, until her eyes fluttered closed and her breathing deepened.

"How do you feel, Trace?"

"Good…warm."

"All right, very good. Now let's go even deeper."

Trace's breathing was slow and even, her body peaceful, her mind quiet. It was as if she had dropped below the surface of a calm lake, drifting down into a peaceful awareness, not asleep, but hovering softly on the periphery of consciousness, where all the static of her everyday conscious mind was dwindling away.

"All right, Trace, I want you to listen to the sound of my voice and only my voice. No other sounds will disturb or distract you. Okay?"

"Okay…"

"What is your full name?"

"Tracey Peyton Rutland."

"Where were you born?"

"In Lexington, Kentucky."

"Okay, Trace… I want you to drift back and see yourself as an eight-year-old child. Go to a beautiful day and to a pleasant memory, and just tell me what you see and feel."

Trace cleared her throat, and when she spoke, her voice took on a girlish quality.

"I'm…well, I'm outside on a hot, sunny day. Bobby and I are down by the pond, diving and swimming off the wooden pier. Bobby is doing cannon balls and he flaps around like a wild duck, cackling and making quacking sounds."

"And who is Bobby, Trace?"

"He's my older brother. He's so silly. He makes me laugh. He makes me scream with laughter, because his legs are so skinny, and he makes ugly faces at me."

"Okay, Trace, very good. Very nice. How do you feel?"

"I feel good. I'm happy. On the patio, my mother and father are sitting in chairs, sipping iced tea out of big, frosted glasses."

Trace smiled. "It is such a wonderful day…except for the pains in my chest. I started feeling them again this morning, after I had that bad dream. It was really scary."

"Oh? And why are you feeling pains there, Trace? Are you sick?"

"No, I'm not sick at all. It's just that sometimes after I have that bad dream, I feel pains in my chest for a while."

"Did you tell your parents about the pains and the bad dreams?"

"Yeah…"

"What did they say? Did they take you to see a doctor?"

"Yes, my father is so good to me. He's taken me several times, but the doctors don't find anything. They say it's probably stress because I work so hard at being a good dancer. I want to be a dancer and singer someday. I love dancing."

"Okay, Trace, very good. Now, Trace, I want you to just relax and drift back to an earlier time. What I want you to do, and please listen very carefully… What I want you to do is to go to the source of that pain you feel in your chest. I want you to tell me where you were the first time you felt this pain in your chest. Okay, Trace. When I count to three, I want you to go there. Understand?"

"Yes."

"One... Two... Three. Go there now. Where were you? What were you doing? Okay, Trace, go to that very first time—that event—and tell me what you see."

Trace swallowed, and her head shook, her face suddenly filled with alarm. "No....No. I...."

"It's all right, Trace. No harm will come to you. I want you to simply stand aside from the event, and just watch it as if you're watching a movie. You will not feel any emotion or fear. You will just be observing. Can you do that, Trace? You will be safe."

Trace's eyelids twitched, and her breath quickened. "I...well, I just...No, not... over there. That place. No. I'm not going over there. No!"

"Just relax, Trace, everything is fine. You are perfectly safe. Now, gently, go to the first time you felt the pain in your chest, and tell me what you see."

The silence lengthened, and Dr. Hopkins saw Trace's hands poke out from under the blanket and form fists.

Dr. Hopkins gently tapped Trace on the center of her forehead and said, "Go there now, Trace."

Trace began to tremble. When she spoke, her voice was low, hoarse and angry.

"Je ne peux pas le croire. Même en ce moment! Je n'ai rien fait de mauvais."

Dr. Hopkins stared in confusion. "What was that, Trace? What did you say?"

The voice was strident. "Qui est ce que c'est, ce Trace?"

Dr. Hopkins stiffened, bewildered. "I only speak a little French. Will you please speak to me in English?"

"Monsieur, don't you understand? I am not this Trace, whoever that is. I am not—and do not call me

12

by this name. Don't you understand, you fool? I did nothing wrong. They are sending me to my death!"

CHAPTER 2

Visibly shaken, Dr. Hopkins reached for a glass of water and took two quick sips. He gathered himself and leaned in closer, almost whispering.

"Relax, Trace," Dr. Hopkins said, fighting for calm, his own voice quivering. He reached for a tissue and dabbed at his damp forehead.

"I want you to rise above what is going on. Do you understand? You won't feel fear or pain. You will just watch what is happening, like an observer, and calmly tell me what is happening, in English. Do you understand? Please speak in English."

There was a long pause, as the stress lines around Trace's mouth and eyes relaxed.

"Yes, I understand."

"Okay, good. Fine. What is going on now?"

Trace's voice lowered and sounded mechanical.

The voice began in French again. "Ils arrivent me cherchez. Je veux écrire trois lettres. Je dois les écrire."

"English, please. Can you please speak to me in English?"

"English?" the voice, sounded distracted. "They are coming for me. I want to write three letters. I have to write them."

Trace began to shake, the emotion returning.

"Relax, Trace," Dr. Hopkins said. "Just relax and observe."

"Do not call me Trace, Monsieur."

"Okay. How old are you?"

"What does that matter now, Monsieur? Do not ask such a question to a lady. It is rude."

Dr. Hopkins didn't understand what was happening. Nothing like this had ever happened to him before. Of course, he'd read about such things—regression leading into past lives—but he was not a believer. He did not believe in reincarnation. So, had he tapped into a multiple personality? He considered himself to be a scientist and a doctor, and as a scientist, he had to continue this line of questioning to understand and learn what exactly was going on.

"What is happening now?"

"I'm scared. So scared."

"Where are you?"

"In my cell."

"Cell, what cell? Where are you?"

"I'm in prison, Monsieur, in prison."

Dr. Hopkins removed his glasses. "What prison?"

"Prison Saint-Lazare, in Paris."

"Paris?" Dr. Hopkins asked, struggling to keep the emotion out of his voice. "What year is this?"

"What year? 1917, of course."

Dr. Hopkins sat frozen for a minute, his pulse rising. "Paris, 1917? Are you certain?"

"Of course, I am certain. Bien sur, I know what year it is, Monsieur. It is October 15, 1917. Of course, I know this day, of all days."

"Okay... Okay, just relax now. Okay..." Dr. Hopkins was flustered, but he had to go on. "Okay, fine. Can you please tell me your name? Your full name?"

"Margaretha Geertruida Zelle."

Dr. Hopkins' eyes flitted about as he searched for the right questions to ask. He stammered. "All right. Fine. All right. How old are you?"

"Why do you ask such a thing again? I am 41 years old."

Dr. Hopkins faltered, then pushed on. "You are 41 years old?"

"That is what I said, Monsieur," she said, caustically. "Why do you keep asking me what I have already told you?"

"Okay, fine. And... And you say you're in a cell in the prison Saint-Lazare?"

"Yes, I told you that. Yes. Where else? It is a lice-infested, rat-infested hell hole. But it doesn't matter anymore does it, Monsieur? I'm soon to be killed for nothing. Nothing! Do you hear me? I am innocent of these ridiculous charges!"

"Okay. Please continue to tell me what is happening."

"Sister Leonide is with me, and my lawyer, who was once my lover."

"And who is your lawyer?"

"Edouard Clunet. He looks so much older now than his 74 years. He is too distressed to speak. He tried his best to save me but that pig, the military prosecutor

16

Capt. Pierre Bouchardon, had it in for me anyway, didn't he?"

"Okay, okay, what is happening now? Please describe all that you can."

"From the meager wardrobe that they let me keep in this rat prison, I am wearing my pearl-gray dress with a wide skirt and lace cache-corset at the bosom. I'm wearing my tricorn felt hat and a pair of buttoned shoes. I had to cut my hair short because of the prison rules, but I will still hold my head high with dignity. Those bastards will not see me cry. The Baptist prison chaplain is about to baptize me."

Trace took in a deep, bracing breath.

"Please go on..." Dr. Hopkins said, his own breathing coming fast.

"Sister Leonide is clasping me by the shoulders and holding me close. Her eyes have filled with tears. She is so good and so kind. I tell her, 'Don't be afraid, Sister, I have lived, and I know how to die.'"

Dr. Hopkins broke in. "Okay, relax now and remember that whatever happens, you are just observing it. You will not be harmed. You can leave that scene at any time."

"And go where, Monsieur? There is nowhere to go. It is time, you know. Time to go. I throw a blue coat over my shoulders. Now the male warden is taking my arm. I brush him away, that pig! I tell him 'I am not a criminal.'"

Dr. Hopkins again wiped his sweaty brow. "Please continue. Please go on."

"I have accompanied the execution party down the steps to a ground-floor office. I want to write three letters."

"Letters to whom?"

"The most important one is to Juana-Luisa, my dear little Nonnie. Oh God, how I love her. And how wrong I have been. I have been so wrong about my little Nonnie."

"Who is Nonnie?"

"Don't you know, Monsieur? Nonnie is my daughter. She is 19 years old now, and she is a beautiful girl. I have heard she looks like me. I have prayed to God that He let me see her one last time. I have prayed to the Blessed Virgin that she send Nonnie to me. It has been my biggest sin, you see. I left my little girl, and now I will never see her again."

"Where is Nonnie now?"

Trace's voice was choked with emotion. "She is with her father, in De Steeg. If only I could see her once more, then I wouldn't mind dying so much. If only I could make my peace with her and tell her how much I love her. How I had hoped she would write to me when she heard I was here, but she didn't. I received no letters from her. She must hate me, Monsieur, and I shall never rest in my grave knowing that I have hurt her so badly."

"Can you write to her now?" Dr. Hopkins asked.

"Yes, they will let me. I must also write to my lover, Captain Vadime de Masloff, and to the Baron de Marguerie. None of them came to see me. I thought— I believed to this last hour that Nonnie would come to see her mother one last time. I thought Vadime would come. I thought he loved me. But now I am alone…left all alone. What have I done to be left so alone during my last hours?"

Emotion returned to her voice. "Why didn't Vadime come? Why didn't my daughter come? Was I so bad a woman?"

Dr. Hopkins swallowed. "Relax, now. Please, take a few breaths and relax, and when you're ready, continue to tell me what is happening, in English."

"Are you going to watch, too, Monsieur, like all the other scoffers?"

"No, I'm not. Please continue."

"I write my three letters and I hand them to Monsieur Clunet. He promises me they will be posted. I tell him, the letter to Nonnie must be delivered, and he assures me it will be. Outside the prison, I see the crowds. They are silent, watching me. In the street, the drivers crank the cars. A gendarme leads Sister Leonide and me to a large sedan. We are soon on our way, and as we pass through the silent streets, my head is held high. It is about half-past five in the morning and the sun is not fully up. How desolate and sad the world looks. How sick inside I feel. We are arriving at the old castle-palace of Vincennes, onto a wide field used for cavalry displays. As my car bumps across the muddy field, I see troops assembled. I must take a breath. It won't be long now. I am terrified, but I will not show my terror to anyone. The automobile stops, and I am the last to leave the car. I hear a bugle call, and the soldiers straighten their uniforms and form up."

Trace paused, licking her dry lips.

"Relax, now," Dr. Hopkins encouraged, in a whispery voice. "Just relax and continue when you are ready."

"The stake is clearly visible. It is the limb of a young tree that was just thrust into the ground. Around me is a parameter of trees, mostly beech and poplars. It is cold. I am told it is nearly freezing. I see the firing squad—12 soldiers of the 4th Zouave Regiment— standing there, waiting, in two rows of six, white vapor puffing from their mouths. I am told they are the sole survivors of a regiment that was butchered at Verdun. How tragic that was. This war is a butchery. A savage hell of a thing that will kill us all."

"Did you say firing squad?" Dr. Hopkins asked, his voice rising.

"Of course. They are waiting for me, Monsieur. God is also waiting for me. Let me continue now. Let me finish this, my last day on Earth. I see the journalists but, for once, they are keeping their distance."

Dr. Hopkins ran a shaky hand across his face. "Okay, okay. Continue then."

"As we draw level with the Zouaves, I kiss Sister Leonide and give her the coat from my shoulders. A sergeant major comes to lead me, but I turn my back on him and walk to the stake alone. Then I turn around gracefully, to face the Zouaves. I am handed a glass of rum, the same amount given to soldiers before battle. I drink it. It tastes good sliding down my throat. I hand it off, and the chief military court clerk, a captain, reads the sentence of my death. A sergeant major loops the cord around my waist, and he is about to bind my wrists to the stake."

I shake my head. "No need for that," I say, curtly. "Let's get on with it."

"Now I am standing with Sister Leonide at the stake and she is whispering prayers. The air is very cold now, and the sun is just about to break up over the horizon. I hear a command: 'Sabremain! Presentezarmes!' Their sabers flash, pointing at the mostly cloudy sky. Now I stare at the men in my firing squad. Most of them have downcast eyes. They know I am innocent. Those lovely men in those perfect Zouaves uniforms know I am not a criminal. Yes, they are sad."

"Father Arbaux speaks to me but I do not hear his blessing. A handsome French officer approaches me, carrying a white cloth. Ah, yes, this, of course, is the blindfold. They want me to hide my face from them. They do not want to see me accusing them with my eyes."

"The blindfold," the officer whispers to Sister Leonide. He hands it to her.

"I look at my lawyer, my sad old lover, and I say, 'Must I wear that?'"

Maitre Clunet turns his weary eyes to the French officer and says, 'Madame prefers not.'"

"The officer says, 'It makes no difference,' and so he strides away, not looking at me. It seems so absurd, so dramatic, like some silly play I am a part of. No, but it is real, Monsieur. It is real, you can be sure of that. Now that the time has come, I am not afraid to die. I watch the weeping nuns, standing near Sister Leonide, and I see Maitre Clunet walk away. His shoulders are slumped and his footsteps slow. I feel so alone now. So awfully alone, like the loneliest person in the world. Now, it is my hour of death. My heart hurts. It is beating so wildly, thumping so loud in my ears. I will not show my fear. I lift my chin in defiance and stare down these men. Then I give them just the hint of a smile."

Trace trembled, her eyes twitched. "I see the Zouaves lift their rifles to their stubbled cheeks. There is a sublieutenant, and he turns his face toward me, his expression very grim. It is a likable face. At another time, perhaps we would have been lovers, who knows? I return his stare and I say, in a voice that all can hear very clearly, 'Thank you, sir.' Now I lift my hands and blow them all a kiss. My final kiss to them and to this world."

Trace licks her lips again, her face slick with sweat. Dr. Hopkins is conflicted. Should he let her go on or should he stop her? He decides to let her finish, and then he will bring her out of hypnosis swiftly.

Trace continues, her voice quivering, reflective. "I am a woman who enjoyed herself very much; sometimes I won, sometimes I lost."

Trace is shaking now. "I hear a sharp, loud command and the twelve men assume rigid positions at attention. There is another strident command, and their rifles are at their shoulders. I see each man gaze down his barrel at me—the target. I am the target. In my head I shout 'Oh, God, come to me and receive me!'

"I see the sublieutenant's sword extended in the air. I watch, breathless as the saber sweeps down. In my head I scream out, 'Nonnie, forgive me!'

"Eleven shots explode. Loud! Ahhhh! I feel a hammer fist to my heart. Oh God, please come for me!"

Dr. Hopkins cut in. "Leave that place, Trace. Leave it now. Do you hear me? You are free. Leave. Now! You will feel no pain."

Trace's body went limp, her mouth slack, eyes wide open. One arm dropped over the edge of the couch and hung still.

Dr. Hopkins shot up. "Trace. Trace! I'm going to count to ten and when I reach ten you will wake up. Do you hear me? Do you?"

There was an icy chill in the room. Trace did not respond, despite Dr. Hopkins' repeated counting.

Suddenly, Trace shut her eyes and began to speak, in a strange and bewildered voice, as if she were on a far-off hill.

"I see my body. I see it. What is this? I am above my body, looking down at it. Am I dead? How can it be? Is that me down there?"

Dr. Hopkins struggled to steady his voice. "Trace... where...where are you?"

Trace did not move a muscle.

"I see it. The sun is up. It flashed on the burnished blade of the saber just as the officer yelled 'En joue!' The saber fell, and I heard the sound of the rifle volley ring out. I saw flames and tiny puffs of greyish smoke pour from the muzzle of each rifle. I saw it. I felt the thud of impact, the pain in my chest. But then there was no pain. No pain at all. But here I am above it all. I see my lifeless body down there. I am just a heap of skirts. Is that me? Am I still alive? I see the crowd, heads down, nuns weeping. They are weeping for me, Mata Hari's last performance."

Dr. Hopkins' felt an icy chill run up his spine. "What? What did you just say? Who are you? You said you are Margaretha. Who are you?"

Trace sighed. "Who am I? I am Margaretha, Monsieur, but you will know me as Mata Hari, the famous exotic dancer and lover of officers."

Dr. Hopkins staggered back down into his chair, searching the room for any explanation. None came.

Trace continued. "Of course, I am Mata Hari, Monsieur. Everyone knows Mata Hari, even if no one came to help me, including my lover, Captain Vadime Masloff. But none of that matters now. Now, I must go see my dear Nonnie. I must tell her how sorry I am. I must go to her and tell her that I love her with all my heart. I will not rest until I see her again."

"Mata Hari?" Dr. Hopkins asked, incredulous. "Are you saying, you were Mata Hari?"

"Were? Monsieur, I am Mata Hari. Of course, I am. The only one. You must know me. Everyone knows me, and they will remember me. I am, and always will be, Mata Hari!"

CHAPTER 3

When Trace phoned him, Cyrano Wallace was in his formidable house in the Berkshires. Cyrano was a wealthy, influential man in state politics and finance. His family was from old East Coast money, and his deceased wife, Constance, had been a generous patron of the arts, her passion leaning more toward the classical arts, especially opera.

Cyrano was seventy years old, a cautious and taciturn man, rather blunt and candid, and known more for his no-nonsense approach and practical manner than for his tact and diplomacy. He was not one to beat about the bush, and he'd never been particularly gifted at humor, nor at the social graces. Constance had been the diplomat, the mediator, the vivacious hostess.

Cyrano had grown even less social in the last few years, due to heart problems and the death of his wife, to whom he had been extremely devoted. At her death, he had been quoted in the New York Times as stating, "I was desperately in love with Constance, and it is a loss from which I will never fully recover."

On January 15th, Trace had used a connection to help her approach Mr. Wallace. Rodney Caldwell was a Broadway producer Trace had dated two years before. Though the relationship hadn't worked out, she and Rod remained friends.

Rod had had some dealings with Cyrano and Constance a few years back, when Cyrano contacted him as a possible producer for an opera which Cyrano and Constance had commissioned for the New York City Opera, an organization Constance supported.

Unfortunately, the opera had not yet come to fruition when the New York City Opera filed for bankruptcy in 2013, and a year later, Constance became seriously ill. The title of the opera was Mata Hari.

When Trace called Mr. Wallace, he had not been warm or welcoming.

"I see very few people these days, Ms. Rutland," he'd said gruffly, "and only those I've known for many years. Rodney said you had some questions about my wife's Mata Hari collection. What is it you want to know?"

Trace cleared her throat and began the patter she'd prepared. Obviously, she couldn't tell the man the truth of why she was calling.

"Mr. Wallace, I'm an actress, and I'm going to be playing Mata Hari in a soon-to-be-produced play. I'm interested in seeing your wife's collection so…"

Cyrano cut her off. "Why? What good is seeing it going to do you? You can see most of what Constance has online. You can also go online to the Fries Museum in the Netherlands and see most of their exhibition there. As you young people know, the internet brings everything in the world to your laptop or cell phone screen."

"Yes, yes, that is true, Mr. Wallace," Trace responded nervously, "but it's not quite the same as actually seeing Mata Hari's personal possessions in front of you. I read somewhere that your wife—who had great interest in Mata Hari—once said that those personal possessions helped to bring Mata Hari to life."

Silence. Trace waited, pacing her apartment, the phone cradled between her neck and her shoulder. "Mr. Wallace, I promise I won't stay long or be any kind of a burden. I would be so grateful."

Trace heard him sigh deeply into the phone. It made a little hissing sound.

"All right, Ms. Rutland. I will have my butler lay the items out for you. You can view them briefly. Please do not—and I stress—do not bring anyone else with you. Do you understand?"

"Yes, Mr. Wallace. Thank you."

On Saturday, January 20th, Trace drove her rented, late model Prius along the Massachusetts Turnpike, turning left onto a two-lane road, driving past fieldstone walls, stately homes and a white church with a rising white spire. She drove on, observing clumps of modern townhouses and condominiums nestled behind majestic firs and pines, feeling the rise of nerves and the familiar acid stomach. She swallowed two Tums as she turned onto Route 23, following her GPS until she was on the other side of Lenox, where Mr. Wallace's house lay, secluded behind a grove of trees.

She turned left onto a winding asphalt road that rose and fell across rolling fields, still glistening with an inch of early afternoon snow, and craned her neck to see the obscure turn-off just ahead.

Minutes later, she pulled into the curved gravel driveway and parked in front of a classic and magnificent Colonial Revival Style house. Trace shut off the engine and sat in the stillness for a time, taking in the grand old two-story home, with its symmetrical façade, side porches and sunrooms on both sides. The entrance was centered and accented with a portico and Greek-style Corinthian columns. She was impressed.

As she studied the side-gabled roof with narrow eaves and the hipped roofs and dormers, Trace recalled her encounter with Dr. Hopkins only the week before. She'd been a nervous wreck ever since.

Both she and Dr. Hopkins had been shaken that day. He could not entirely believe what had happened, and his startled eyes and pale color revealed a man who had witnessed something both troubling and extraordinary.

Trace had had to sit on the couch for nearly a half hour, sipping tea and watching dancing patterns of light play across the walls, before she was able to finally stop shaking. For long minutes, she felt as though she wasn't entirely anchored in her own skin. She'd remembered everything that had happened back in 1917—every scent, every face, every emotion—and it was as real as anything she'd ever experienced in her present life.

She had asked Dr. Hopkins for an explanation. In a distracted and aloof way, he'd lifted his hands, unable to offer anything other than to say "I'm not the right therapist for this kind of thing, Ms. Rutland. It's not something I'm comfortable with or understand. I can recommend another therapist, if you wish."

Trace wished he'd been more helpful and supportive. After he'd brought her back to full consciousness, he'd withdrawn his attention, and she felt she was left dangling on the precipice of a terrifying experience, having no idea how to proceed.

For two days, she'd slept and called out for food. She'd gone for walks and ignored friends, emails and texts, even those from her agent. If anything, the regression—or whatever it was—made her feel even more lost and vulnerable. How could it be true? How could she have been Mata Hari in a past life? She knew who the woman was, but not the details.

Didn't most people who believed in reincarnation, or past lives, believe they'd been some famous person or the other? Cleopatra, Queen Elizabeth or Marilyn Monroe?

Still, something had happened. She couldn't deny that she had gone through a kind of doorway into a shocking and chilling experience. She had actually felt herself as that woman, Mata Hari. She saw her hands, felt her sweat, her panic. She smelled the awful stench of that dank and depressing prison, and she felt the heaviness of those clothes she was wearing.

And what about Mata Hari's daughter, Nonnie? Trace had felt the overwhelming guilt and the agony of loss Mata Hari had felt over abandoning the girl, and of not being the kind of mother she should have been. Trace had felt all of it, painful, deep and strong.

Right after her experience, Trace realized that, throughout her life, she'd had dreams in which a young girl swam up from the depths of a deep blue pond and waved to her, calling and beckoning Trace to dive in and join her. Trace found the whole past life thing unnerving, but she recognized now that that girl was Nonnie, presumably her daughter in a past life. Whenever she recalled that lovely face—Nonnie's face—she longed to reach for her, to touch her, to be with her.

Trace had also felt the sense of betrayal by her lover, Captain Masloff. Why hadn't he come to see her in prison? What had the woman done to be so abandoned?

And how was it that she had spoken French so fluently and so easily? It had been so natural and available, so immediate and effortless on her tongue. Although she'd taken two years of high school French, she'd forgotten most of it.

By the third day, Trace knew she had to act. She had to find some way to free herself of the angst, doubt and confusion she was feeling. Dr. Hopkins had recommended a woman therapist, but Trace wasn't ready to go through all that again, at least not yet.

By Wednesday, she was at her laptop, exploring everything she could find about Mata Hari, reading blogs and articles about the woman and her time. Trace knew something about the First World War because of a play she'd performed in, but what she read now shocked and astounded her. What she'd experienced under hypnosis had, in fact, been true. History had happened just as she had experienced it.

Trace broke out into a cold sweat, and the shakes started again. Was it possible that she could have been Mata Hari? It was absurd. It was one thing to hear and read about reincarnation, and it was another to actually experience it, front and center.

But then her nightmares had returned with a force— and the nightmares had played out what she had experienced during her regression. Trace was a mass of nerves, pacing her one-bedroom apartment, desperate for some kind of help.

Back at her laptop, Trace learned that Constance Wallace had purchased some of Mata Hari's personal possessions at an auction back in 2010, and something in Trace snapped. An idea struck. She had the sudden, insatiable urge to see those items—to touch them, feel them and put them on. It became a compulsion—an obsession.

That's when she'd traced Constance Wallace to Rodney Caldwell, and the Mata Hari Opera.

Now, Trace emerged from her car, shut the door and started toward the house, her feet crunching along the pink gravel. She mounted the brick stairs under the portico and stood tensely before the large oak door. Her emotions were in turmoil. She was perspiring, despite the quick, cold wind. She lifted the knocker and let it go.

A few moments later, the door slowly swung open. A pleasant-faced man with short, gray hair and still, dark eyes, wearing a dark suit and blue tie, stood smiling.

"Ms. Rutland?" he asked, in a soothing baritone voice.

"Yes," Trace said, with a smile.

"I'm Andrew, Mr. Wallace's butler. Please come in."

Andrew stood aside, and Trace entered a white marble foyer with stained glass windows and a gleaming, multi-tiered chandelier.

"May I take your coat, Ms. Rutland?"

Trace slipped out of it.

After Andrew deposited her coat in a side closet, he returned, indicating toward a room to the right. "Mr. Wallace has arranged the collection in the library. This way, please."

Andrew ushered her across the entranceway, past a curved sweeping staircase leading to upper rooms, across oriental rugs, to two polished hardwood doors. Andrew slid one door open and nodded for Trace to enter.

The library was an astonishingly luxurious room, with thick patterned carpets, dark wood floors, and cherry wood floor-to-ceiling bookshelves holding leather-bound books, hardcovers and books with antique bindings. There were two richly carved reading tables with fringed tablecloths and Tiffany lamps. One held a large antique ocean globe. Trace took in the burgundy leather upholstered chairs, a plush leather couch, and a generous fireplace. Tall windows let in a wealth of natural light, a shaft of it alighting on a claw-foot table covered by a cream satin tablecloth, where the Mata Hari collection was clearly displayed. Caught by it, she stared. Trace took in a quick breath to calm her nerves.

Andrew stood by. "Can I get you anything, Ms. Rutland? Some tea perhaps?"

Trace couldn't pull her eyes from the awaiting collection. "No... no, thank you."

"I will stand by then, if that is all right, according to Mr. Wallace's request?"

Trace turned, distractedly. "Yes, of course. Fine."

Andrew stepped back to the entrance doors and stood at ease.

Trace approached the Mata Hari display haltingly, feeling her pulse in her neck. She swallowed away a lump, and gently placed her purse on a chair nearby. Gathering herself, she advanced, first lifting her eyes to the ornately framed oil painting of Mata Hari that hung on the wall above the collection.

Trace's eyes narrowed on the image of the woman, who had billed herself as a Hindu artist, draped in veils—which, during her dance, she artfully released from her body.

Mata Hari stood tall, in a seductive pose, against a moody, cloudy background, the large Hindu god of Shiva clearly visible. The dancer had luminous olive skin and luscious blue-black hair. She wore an elaborate jeweled headdress that was both dramatic and perhaps a bit ridiculous. A flowing diaphanous gown revealed an exposed stomach, and her rather small breasts were covered with brassiere-styled beads.

Mata Hari stared back at Trace with dark, flirtatious, smoldering eyes and the hint of a seductive smile. The painter had captured the beguiling spark in her eyes, and Trace could actually feel the desire in them, and the magnetic lure of the sensual dancer.

Attached to the lower picture frame was a brushed gold nameplate with the quote: I will be celebrated or notorious—Mata Hari.

Trace had read that Mata Hari helped turn the striptease into an art form that captivated audiences across Europe, and she had finally won over the critics. Trace's eyes were suddenly drawn to an old newspaper spread out on the table to the immediate left of the collection. There were Post-it arrow markers pointing to quotes. Trace leaned and read a review that a Viennese reporter of Mata Hari's day had written about the dancer. "Slender and tall with the flexible grace of a wild animal. Her face makes a strange foreign impression."

Another smitten newspaper writer described her as being "so feline, extremely feminine, majestically tragic, the thousand curves and movements of her body trembling in a thousand rhythms."

There was a brief biography of Mata Hari in a second newspaper. Trace was captivated.

Margaretha Geertruida Zelle was born on the 7th of August 1876 in Leeuwarden, Netherlands. At age fourteen her mother died and her father, who owned a haberdashery and who invested heavily in oil stocks, went bankrupt. She attended an all girls' school and, after a still-unclarified sexual episode with a teacher, she was suspended from school. She spoke fluent French, English, Italian, Dutch and German.

She left school and fell in love with a military captain. In 1895, they married and moved to Indonesia. The marriage was not a successful one. He was an abusive alcoholic, and she had sexual encounters with military officers, whom she desired more than other men. Their son died due to poisoning, and there are still some questions surrounding his death, as well as the near-fatal poisoning of her one-year-old daughter. Her husband blamed his wife for not keeping a better eye on the boy, and when they moved back to the Netherlands, they divorced.

Mata Hari posed as an exotic Eastern princess, trained in sacred and sexual temple dances, an identity that was well-suited for her exotic beauty and society's current romantic inclinations. Her erotic dances and her delicate, revealing costumes soon made her celebrated as the most sought-after and most desirable woman in Europe. For nearly ten years, she became the glamorous mistress of many powerful and important men. Mata Hari danced before wild, enthusiastic crowds in Paris, Vienna, Madrid, Berlin, Milan and Rome, inspiring admiration, jealousy, hatred and vicious condemnation.

Trace was filled with excitement as she looked the collection over. The objects seemed somehow familiar, and they seemed to stare back at her, glowing in the silver afternoon light. There were Chinese marble sculptures, opera glasses, two fur necklets, silver cutlery and some old money, French Francs, one banknote reading Bon de Monnaie Un Franc. There were also several five Franc notes, neatly stacked. An open scrapbook lay to the right of the items and Trace stepped over, carefully leafing through photographs, newspaper clippings, playbills and calling cards from Mata Hari's years of performing in European capitals.

But the item that caught her eye—no, seized her eye—was a ring. A remarkable ring—a stunning ring—an emerald sapphire with a glossy gold band. It sparkled and dazzled, and the light danced in it like a constellation of stars.

Trace was transfixed. Her eyes seized it, heart pounding. A shiver of desire startled her. In a sharp flash of recognition, it seemed only natural to reach for it. It was hers, after all. Yes, it was hers!

A deep, commanding voice from behind stopped her. She jerked her hand back, pivoting to see a man at the entry doors. Andrew was gone.

The man spoke in a low, resonating voice. "That ring is a rare, natural green faceted oval sapphire, 6.40

carats. It cost me a fortune, but Constance wanted it. I outbid two museums for it."

Trace saw a broad, white-haired man with steel gray eyes and a forceful mouth staring at her, sizing her up, his gaze leveled on her.

"You must be Ms. Rutland?"

Trace struggled to shake the mist of old memory from her eyes, but a part of her was still wedged in the past, recalling the ring, remembering the ring. Craving the ring.

CHAPTER 4

Trace finally brought her full attention back to Cyrano Wallace's library. She fought for control of herself. "Yes... Yes, I'm Trace Rutland."

"I'm Cyrano Wallace, Ms. Rutland. Forgive me. I hope I didn't startle you."

"No... No. I... Not at all. I was just admiring your collection."

Cyrano was dressed in dark slacks, a white shirt and a blue blazer, with a red silk handkerchief blooming from his jacket pocket. As he entered the room, he moved with an aura of power and authority, obviously used to being in charge. He approached, extending his big hand, and, as they shook, Trace felt Cyrano's piercing gaze, full of fire and, surprisingly, warmth.

"Welcome to my home, Ms. Rutland."

"Thank you for allowing me to come."

He shoved his hands into his pockets and glanced about. "I hope you're enjoying the little collection."

"Yes, very much. Where did you get the scrapbook? It's captivating."

"I purchased it from a Hollywood producer. I have no idea where he found it. The album, and everything else you see, will be donated to the Fries Museum in the Netherlands when I die. They have a very impressive collection of Mata Hari's things."

Trace turned toward the ring. "And I love the ring," Trace said.

"So I see. Well, it is the most remarkable piece of the collection, although I'm also fond of the opera glasses. Constance brought them to the opera a couple of times and showed them off to her envious friends. She loved doing that. She loved the ring, too, but she never did slip it on. I asked her to several times, but she wouldn't. She always refused."

"Why? It's so beautiful."

"I don't know why. She once said it wasn't hers to wear. She said it should never be worn by anyone except Mata Hari. I said, 'Mata Hari is long dead,' and do you know what she said to me?"

Trace waited, eagerly.

"Let me preface her response by telling you that Constance believed in astrology and the occult. She believed that old things have power. I thought it was silly, but I never told her so. Constance was a wonderful woman, Ms. Rutland. I am not a sentimental man, but she often made me so."

Trace smiled. "It sounds like you had a very special relationship. It's rare these days."

Cyrano smiled, pleased. "I hope so, and I believe so. Well, anyway, when I asked her to wear the ring she said, and these are her exact words, 'The invisible world lies all around us like a shadow. There it is, the still present past, only a breath away.'"

Trace thought the words were moving and provoca-
tive.

Cyrano leveled his half-hooded eyes on her, measuring her. "Do you want to put the ring on, Ms. Rutland?" Cyrano asked.

Trace stepped back from it, now self-conscious. She
was firmly back in her body, and once again perplexed
and troubled by that peculiar feeling of having been
lodged between two worlds.

"No...No, I don't want to put it on."

"You know, the ring was lost for a time. There were
two photos of it, and many collectors spent years trying
to track it down. I'm still not entirely certain how it
came to auction. I was told by a reliable source that an
old lover of Mata Hari's owned it. The story goes that
he sold it to a jeweler in Paris when times got bad, and
then it was locked away for years, only to be sold again
sometime in the 1960s to a private, anonymous collec-
tor. Our auctioneer didn't know or didn't tell me how
he'd come by it. But it has been authenticated. I saw to
that. The initials MH are etched inside the band, small,
but they are there. In one of her letters, Mata Hari mentioned receiving the ring as a gift, describing it in detail.
A man she called Maurice H gave it to her. Maurice H
was most likely Captain Maurice Herbaux, an officer in
the French Army, who was from a wealthy family, and
who had fallen in love with Mata Hari as early as 1912.
He was killed in 1915, at the Battle of Neuve
Chapelle."

Trace studied Cyrano. She thought him a handsome
man, a virile man, even in his 70s. He did not seem
threatening or condescending, as she had imagined he'd
be.

"Well, take your time looking Mata Hari's things over, Ms. Rutland. I'm sorry if I disturbed you."

"Not at all," Trace said. "Again, I'm truly grateful you let me come by."

Cyrano turned to leave, then paused. "You said you are an actress?"

"Yes… I'm an actress, dancer, singer. A triple threat, as they say."

Cyrano nodded. "You look like a dancer. Do you sing well?"

"I'm a fair singer. Not exceptional."

"Dancer?"

"I love to dance. I started when I was four."

A slight smile formed at the corners of Cyrano's mouth. "Are you performing now?"

"I start rehearsals for a new Broadway show next month."

"A lead?"

"The second lead. The part requires a lot of dancing. Some singing, and some good scenes, I'm told."

"It sounds like a good part. Perhaps I'll travel to New York to see you. What is the show called?"

"Daydreams."

"Ah… interesting. Over the phone, you had mentioned a role as Mata Hari."

Trace dropped her gaze. In a small voice, she said, "I lied about that, Mr. Wallace, and I'm sorry."

"And why did you lie, Ms. Rutland?"

"I was afraid you'd turn me down unless I came up with some direct connection… Some compelling reason for wanting to see your Mata Hari collection."

"Well, you're honest. That's refreshing."

"I am sorry. I shouldn't have done that."

"Oh, it's of no importance, really. Oddly enough, Ms. Rutland, you could have said most anything. I liked the sound of your voice. I've always been a good judge of people, often by just the sound of their voices. I detected great tension in your voice, Ms. Rutland. I also detected something else—a certain passion for Mata Hari."

Trace turned toward the collection. "I do love the collection, Mr. Wallace."

Cyrano turned to leave, then stopped and turned back to her. "Ms. Rutland, why don't you stay to dinner."

"I don't want to be any trouble. And I should probably get back."

"We could discuss the collection, and I can tell you some interesting things I've learned about Mata Hari. I think you might enjoy it. I guarantee dinner will be excellent. My chef is one of the best around these parts. I eat rather early, about six o'clock. What do you say?"

Surprised by his offer, she took a minute to respond. This was not the man she thought he would be. He possessed an ineffable quality of the familiar. She felt at ease, comfortable in his presence.

"Are you sure I won't be interrupting anything, Mr. Wallace?"

"Not at all. Meanwhile, I'll have Andrew bring you some tea and snacks to hold you over. Now, you just take all the time you want with the collection, and if you need anything at all, you let Andrew know."

Trace nodded.

"It was a pleasure meeting you, Ms. Rutland."

"And you," Trace said, with a slight bow.

"I'll see you at six then. Good afternoon."

After Cyrano was gone, and the library was loud with silence, Trace turned her attention back to the ring. It flashed in the light. It seemed to beckon her, and she moved closer to it.

CHAPTER 5

Cyrano Wallace was already seated when Trace arrived, feeling grossly underdressed in fitted designer jeans, a blue top, white sweater and boots. She'd worn her hair up and swept back from her forehead, revealing her yellow gold, hooped earrings. They were her favorites, a gift from her father last Christmas.

It was a formal dining room, with mauve colored walls, richly patterned oriental carpet, and a long mahogany dinner table, with matching chairs and custom wood paneling.

Andrew held the chair for Trace as she sat to Cyrano's right, under a crystal chandelier. The walls held 18th-century landscapes, and portraits of 18th-century women looking out with cool, placid eyes, dressed regally, with stylish, elaborate hairstyles. The room was understated elegance; good taste at its best. Trace noted the pleated pearl-colored draperies drawn back from French doors, revealing a dormant fountain and private garden beyond, illuminated by soft patio lights.

"I hope you're hungry," Cyrano said.

"Yes, I am a bit hungry," Trace said, sitting stiffly, looking about. "This is a lovely room."

"Constance decorated it. She was good at design and decoration, as she was with most things. She had plans to design a Mata Hari room, but she became ill, and it never happened. So, did you enjoy the Mata Hari collection?"

"Yes, very much. I found two books about her in the library. I hope you don't mind that I removed them and read parts. I replaced them carefully."

"Not at all, Ms. Rutland. I'm glad you made yourself at home. Do you prefer red wine or white? For dinner, you have a choice of sea bass with fennel salad, parsnip puree, and orange beurre blanc, or grilled guinea hen with celery root fregola—fregola is a kind of pasta—and black truffle vinaigrette, if that helps you decide."

"Red please."

"Pinot Noir, from Burgundy?"

"Yes, fine."

After Andrew opened the wine and decanted it, he poured Cyrano a taste. He smelled, swirled, tasted and nodded his approval. Andrew poured for Trace, finishing with Cyrano. Trace took a sip and was pleased by its lively cherry fruit and dry finish.

"Do you like it?" Cyrano asked.

"Yes, very much."

"It was one of Constance's favorites. I hope you'll forgive me for speaking about Constance so much, Ms. Rutland, it's just that I still feel somewhat lost without her."

"Not at all, Mr. Wallace. Most people never find that kind of love."

After the vegetable/ginger soup arrived, Cyrano talked about the house, which he'd purchased in 1981; about his New York City condo on Fifth Avenue, and about Constance's love of the theatre and opera.

"We stayed in New York much of the time during the opera season," he said.

After a brief pause, he lowered his soup spoon and said something that surprised Trace.

"We had a daughter just about your age, Ms. Rutland. Her name was Allison. She was the outdoors type, who loved skiing, white water rafting and hiking. She was a risk taker, not unlike myself when I was a young man. Sixteen years ago, while on a hiking trip with friends in Hawaii, Allison slipped on a narrow path and fell to her death."

Trace stopped eating. "I'm so sorry, Mr. Wallace."

He waved a hand to dismiss it. "The only reason I mentioned it is—well, it's been a long time since I had dinner with a pretty, young woman. My daughter was quite pretty, you know, and though Constance hoped Allison would become a singer, Allison could barely carry a tune. She was more interested in environmental things. She had a real thirst for life. Are you married, Ms. Rutland?"

"No, I'm not."

"And where are you from? Somewhere in the South, I think?"

"Originally, Lexington, Kentucky. I've lived in New York for a little over eight years."

"Yes, I hear a slight southern accent. Did you enjoy your childhood?"

"Yes, it was fairly normal. We lived in a big old house with big rooms, winding back staircases, and

45

deep closets I used to hide in. I would spiral down the circular banisters, play with the Ouija board—or the talking board as I called it. I loved playing in the attic, my favorite place."

Trace swirled the wine, and stared into it, reflecting, comfortable talking about herself with Cyrano, and there were few people she ever discussed her childhood with.

Cyrano sipped his wine, his eyes sparkling with pleasure, a pleasure he had not felt in a long time. "Go on, Ms. Rutland. Please continue."

The wine had made Trace a little high, and she was enjoying herself.

"That old attic seemed endless. There were boxes filled with musty old books, diaries, newspaper clippings and letters, and heavy trunks in the corner, packed with old clothes. But the creepiest, and most fun of all, were the wide-eyed antique dolls that sat on an old, lopsided table. They had been my grandmother's, and some dated as far back as the early 1900s. They had these dull, milky eyes that gazed out like death, and I knew they watched my every move as I crept along, stooping under the low-beamed ceiling."

Andrew removed the soup bowls, and then refilled their glasses with more wine before leaving the room.

"Well, anyway, I'm babbling on here. I don't usually talk this much."

"I'm enjoying it, Ms. Rutland. May I call you... is your first name Tracey?"

"Yes, but I go by Trace. My father used it when I was a kid and it stuck."

"Trace is a good stage name," Cyrano added.

"Yes, there aren't many of us."

After Andrew served Trace the sea bass and Cyrano the hen, they ate for a time in silence.

"Trace, why did you want to see the Mata Hari collection? Was there some burning reason, I mean, if it wasn't about using it as research to play the role of Mata Hari?"

Trace chewed, thoughtfully, considering her answer. Could she tell him the truth? She probably could have told his wife, Constance, but she didn't feel comfortable mentioning the hypnotherapy session she'd had with Dr. Hopkins to Cyrano Wallace. He seemed too much the pragmatist. She also didn't want to lie.

"I heard about Mata Hari and became interested. It's a strange and moving story in many ways. Certainly tragic."

Cyrano reached for his glass of wine. "Constance thought that Mata Hari was innocent of the French espionage charges, believing she was a scapegoat of sorts."

"According to what I've read," Trace said, "Mata Hari made some bad choices. She shouldn't have returned to France in 1917."

"Yes, that's true, but she was an impulsive woman. She also claimed to be the daughter of a British lord and an Indian princess, which, of course, was a complete lie. And then she was the lover of the Crown Prince of Germany, and the German spy chief. That didn't help her any with the French military authorities."

Trace nodded. "But in some ways, I think she was a prototype of a 20th-century liberated woman—like Madonna or Lady Gaga."

Cyrano nodded, pensively. "Yes, perhaps. But the fact is that she was executed for passing military secrets to the Germans."

"Do you think she was guilty of that?" Trace asked.

Cyrano laid his fork aside, steepled his hands and leaned back. "Well, I always like to look at the facts. Constance and I often kicked the facts around. It became a kind of game with us, especially when we commissioned the Mata Hari opera. Okay, so, what do we have? Mata Hari was arrested twice and questioned by M15 and Special Branch in 1915 and 1916."

"That was the British Secret Service, wasn't it?" Trace asked.

"Yes, that's right. Among other things, Mata Hari was accused of betraying the existence of the British secret weapon, the tank. Tanks were new in those days. Tanks took the Germans completely by surprise when they were first used on the Somme in the autumn of 1916. Her French accusers also claimed that she'd delivered allied shipping into the hands of the U-boats, or German submarines, who sank them, thus directly causing the deaths of at least 50,000 soldiers. What is interesting, however, is that none of these accusations came up at her trial."

Trace was riveted. "Why not? It's just weird. I read that one of the stories they included was that she often bathed in milk. What did that have to do with spying?"

"Yes, that's right," Cyrano said. "But you must realize the time and place when all these events happened. The world was at war. The First World War. It was a time when there wasn't enough milk for children, so it would have seemed callous and heartless for this famous and indifferent woman to have taken milk baths. But the French military was interested in painting her as a German spy, so this false story would have quickly turned the French public against her. It was the worst kind of publicity for her. But there is no evidence, whatsoever, that Mata Hari ever did take milk baths. What is perfectly clear is that she did love to live in style. When she was briefly arrested by the British in 1916, she was traveling with ten trunks of luggage, containing, among other things, eleven pairs of shoes and thirty-three pairs of stockings."

Cyrano lowered his hands, his eyes filled with thought. "As you may have read, Trace, Mata Hari had a particular liking for men in uniform. Military men. It was a weakness, I'd say. If you'll pardon me for saying this, Trace, she once said that she would rather 'sleep with a poor officer than a rich banker.' I think this weakness—along with her curious lack of practical worldliness, and an incredible naiveté —helped lead her to her death."

They resumed eating, and Andrew entered and poured the last of the wine. Trace reached for her napkin and blotted her lips.

As Cyrano was speaking, Trace had begun feeling the intrusion of unwanted memories. They arose from some dark place deep within, and flashed across her eyes, like old dreams—some in shadow, some sharp and clear—faces appearing, fading. It was disconcerting, and she began to perspire.

Cyrano noticed her sudden change of mood. "Is everything all right, Trace?"

Trace stared ahead at nothing, eyes still. "Yes…It's just that I remember some things, but they get all mixed

49

up and I can't put it all together. Just pieces here and there, like a jigsaw puzzle."

Cyrano saw the faraway look in her eyes, as if she were lost in a memory. "What are you trying to put together, Trace?"

He noticed that Trace's eyes seemed to glaze over. Her back stiffened and she raised her head, shifting her posture.

"Well, you see, I separated from my husband in 1902 and I was granted custody of little Non, our daughter. But then he refused to pay the legal allowance, and I had no money and so few choices. I didn't want to give her back to him, but I didn't know what else to do. So, I reluctantly returned Non to her father and left for Paris. I thought that all women who ran away from their husbands went to Paris."

Cyrano's eyes sharpened on her. She had changed. She seemed peculiar and oddly distant. Her voice had deepened, and she had a slight accent, but it wasn't a southern accent.

Cyrano sat rigidly still. He found her behavior bizarre and perplexing. Why was she suddenly speaking in the first person, as if she were Mata Hari? Was she performing? Acting? He couldn't help but be captivated.

Trace continued in her new, lower voice. "When I finally settled in Paris, I yearned for my Nonnie. My husband wanted to reconcile but I couldn't go back to him. He was so abusive, you know. One Sunday afternoon, crazed and deranged, he came close to murdering me with a breadknife. I owe my life to a chair that fell over and which gave me time to find the door and get help. You see, my husband suffered from what one doctor called tropical frenzy. Others called it sadism."

Cyrano watched her turning her hands, her eyes moving, searching the ceiling and the walls. She didn't seem to see him, or even be aware of him. Then who was she speaking to? She was an incredible actress—or was she? Was the girl unbalanced? Was she on medication, and the alcohol was affecting her adversely?

Cyrano hesitated. Should he stop her?

Trace gazed ahead, sightlessly. "You see, without Nonnie, I felt lost. I could get by well enough in Paris, but I wanted my child. I tried to earn money by giving piano lessons and teaching German. I applied to work as a lady's companion and as a model in a department store. I did all that, yes. But I couldn't make enough money, so I did what was less respectable but more lucrative. I sat as an artist's model for Montmartre painters such as Edouard Bisson and Victor Guillonnet. I made important theatrical contacts."

Cyrano didn't stir. He watched. Trace was a beautiful young woman, with an aura of magnetism. He'd seen it right away. Now her eyes glowed in a strange, detached way, as if she were looking off into distant worlds.

Trace continued. "I had to re-invent myself again, you see, as an exotic oriental dancer, disguising my real identity. I took the name Mata Hari, which means 'eye of the day' in Malay."

Trace smiled, thoughtfully, with an inward stare. "Yes, I liked that name. I liked it very much. And when I danced, I fell in love with the world, and the world seemed to fall in love with me. Oh, yes, the world did indeed fall in love with me."

CHAPTER 6

Cyrano let Trace continue, watching her closely.

"I didn't have any dance training, so I just improvised. I had studied Indonesian culture and traditions, including dance, and so my act was an imitation of oriental dances."

Trace smiled with pride, lifting her chin. "I wriggled gracefully in front of a statue of Shiva, as I seductively removed my veils. It was such fun, and I felt so powerful and erotic. I knew that the audience was excited by me. I could feel it. I was a great commercial success and I appeared in many European capitals. Gradually, I was accepted as an artist, rather than as just an exotic dancer. Did I have lovers? Of course, and why not? I was highly paid. As I said at my trial, 'I am a courtesan. I admit it. A spy, never!' I have always lived for love and pleasure."

And then, as if a curtain had dropped, Trace's eyes closed, her head fell forward and her shoulders slumped.

Somewhat shaken, Cyrano leaned toward her. "Trace, are you all right?"

Trace's eyes popped open. She jerked erect, as if touched by a live wire, and snapped out of her dozing vision. Her troubled eyes flitted about, as she struggled to reorient herself. Finally realizing where she was and what had happened, she blushed, still feeling weirdly disordered.

"Yes... Yes, I'm fine," she said in her own quivering voice. She quickly sought to recover, realizing she'd slipped away into that other world—a very real and astonishing world—a world that seemed to be slowly . taking her over. She fought panic, as she realized that when Dr. Hopkins had regressed her, a doorway to the past had been flung open, and she didn't know how to close that door and lock it.

She struggled for composure. "Yes, I was just remembering... I mean, I was remembering what I read today. It was so compelling. I felt like I was actually there, experiencing it all."

Cyrano sighed, smiling away his nervous concern, reaching for his almost empty wine glass. "Well, you certainly are a good actress, Trace. You completely captured me. What a performance. You really should perform in that Mata Hari play. Even your voice was changed. You completely lost your Southern accent and took on a sort of European accent. Very impressive."

Trace inhaled a breath to help cool her agitated mind. She reached for her wine and downed the rest at one go. Cyrano passed her an uneven stare.

"Are you sure you're feeling all right, Trace?"

She fixed her gaze on him, feeling the pressing need to continue. "It's just that I feel her life so deep inside me, Mr. Wallace. When the First World War began,

Mata Hari was in Berlin about to start a new show. She was expelled from there because of the war, and the German authorities took all her money and several of her fur coats. She returned to the Netherlands in 1915. While there, she was first approached by the Germans to return to Paris as a spy. She agreed and accepted 50,000 francs—but only to get back what the Germans stole from her. This was all true," Trace said with pointed authority. "All true. But no one seemed to believe her about that, or no one wanted to believe her. She never gave any serious thought to spying on the French. It was a ridiculous idea to her."

The wine began to soothe her nerves.

"Yes, Trace, all that is true, as I recall it," Cyrano said, taking over, placing his folded hands on the table. "Mata Hari made two trips to France in 1915 and 1916. Both times, she was closely watched by two rather clumsy and bumbling inspectors from French counter-intelligence. After six months of surveillance, they produced no credible evidence that Mata Hari was spying."

Trace looked at him firmly. "No, they didn't. But on her second visit, she fell in love with a 21-year-old Russian officer, Captain Vladimir de Masloff, of the Special Imperial Russian Regiment, stationed on the Western Front."

Trace stopped, her eyes going vague again, as if she were seeing something playing out before her.

Cyrano lowered his voice and continued. "As Constance often said, Mata Hari's relationship with Captain Masloff seems to have been the one true love of Mata Hari's life. She was 40 or 41 years old at the time.

This affair may have contributed to her arrest and subsequent execution."

Trace nodded. "Yes... Yes, she was truly in love with Masloff. Funny...I don't know what finally happened to him. I should know that."

"Well, Trace, I did some looking into that a few years ago," Cyrano said. "He returned to Russia, got married and vanished in the chaos of the Russian revolution. According to recorded history, he was never heard from again."

Trace's face suddenly filled with urgent thought as she turned to Cyrano. "Did Constance truly believe that Mata Hari was innocent of espionage?"

Cyrano considered the question. "She came to me once, very upset. She'd done some research and even hired professional help. She learned there were over 1,000 pages of documents that were 'presented' to the judges at Mata Hari's trial. Nothing in them proves that Mata Hari was spying for the Germans in 1916. Some, in fact, directly suggest that, by then, she was a spy for the French, which is what she claimed. The military judges reached their verdict based on a summary which gave wholly misleading accounts of the evidence. As a matter of fact, the prosecutor, André Mornet, admitted 30 years later that 'there wasn't enough evidence to flog a cat.' Her judges took only 45 minutes to return a guilty verdict and sentence her to death. Newspapers reported that Mata Hari exclaimed, 'C'est impossible.' It's impossible."

Trace's eyes were remote, staring, a smoldering anger rising in them. "Yes... That's what she said, 'C'est impossible.'"

Cyrano reached for his crystal water glass, leaned back, and sipped at it.

"So, here's the picture, Trace. We have an extraordinary woman who re-invented herself many times over. She symbolized the independence and hypocrisies of turn-of-the-century Paris, but she failed to understand that the world had changed in 1914, when the First World War began, and soldiers were being slaughtered by the thousands in Belgium, northeastern France, Alsace-Lorraine and western Germany—what was known as the Western Front. I think she firmly believed, even until the day of her execution, that her magnetism and fame would somehow get her through the whole spy mess, and she'd be set free. Constance believed that Mata Hari's curious mixture of worldliness and arrogance proved to be her undoing."

Trace felt an inner fire building in her chest. Her thoughts returned to the Mata Hari ring in the library. She felt the compulsive need to see it again—to touch it. To wear it. Her spine straightened with defiance. Yes, she wanted to show everyone that she was the owner of that ring. She wanted the entire world to know that she had never spied for the Germans, and that she had been set up to die by those scheming men because they were incompetent cowards.

Trace could feel Cyrano watching her intently, his eyes firm, trying to understand.

"I think you should stay the night, Trace. You look tired and stressed, and more snow is predicted. I have plenty of room in the house, and you can get a good night's rest, and leave after breakfast."

Trace's thoughts clung to images of that ring—the Mata Hari ring. "That's very nice of you, Mr. Wallace. I am feeling a little tired from the wine."

"It's settled then. We'll have a glass of Port, and then I'll ask Andrew to make up the guest bedroom for you."

Trace gave him a brief glance. "You've been very kind to me, Mr. Wallace."

"Call me Cyrano, Trace. We're old friends now. It's done me good to talk about Mata Hari again, the way Constance and I used to talk about her. You've given an old man a very pleasant evening."

After Trace said good night to Cyrano, Andrew led her out of the dining room, down the hallway and past the library doors. As they mounted the stairs, she glanced back over her shoulder toward the library, and her mind began working on a delicious thought: late in the night, she'd return to the library and slip on the ring. Her ring.

Trace lay in the soft canopied bed, covered by a warm down quilt, hovering between sleep and the strange splendor of memory. She heard galloping horses, the sputtering motor of a single-engine airplane, and the distant booming of artillery, all sliding in and out of her head. She felt a silky veil sweep across her face; felt its whispering softness against her skin.

Then she saw his face: The broad, square face and dark mustache of the French counter-intelligence chief, Georges Ladoux. A sinister face. A sneering face. How she hated him.

In 1916, he had tried four or five times to convince her to spy for the French. She finally agreed to go to Belgium and seduce a senior German officer in return for a million francs. She needed the money. She even told Ladoux she needed the money, so she could settle down with Vadime Masloff and give up her other paying lovers. This information was recorded in the documents prepared for her trial but was deliberately omitted during the trial and in Judge Bouchardon's summary—the summary which accused her of spying for the Germans.

Trace felt the start of tears—old stinging, angry tears—and they began to pump out of her. She turned and buried her face into the pillow and wept.

Why had she been so stupid? She had been arrested when she returned to Paris in February 1917. She should have never gone back to Paris. She should have gone home to the Netherlands to see Nonnie and to wait out the war. But she didn't. Instead, she foolishly played into the hands of French counter-intelligence, the French military and the French government. They seized on the opportunity to turn her—a wanton and promiscuous woman, and perhaps a dangerous seductress and foreigner—into a wicked master-spy. They killed her as a deflection, as a scapegoat to cover up for the incompetent French generals' mismanagement of the war, and for the 350,000 needless French deaths on the Western Front.

With her face still buried in the pillow, Trace fell into a light, anguished sleep.

CHAPTER 7

Trace left her bed at 2:23 in the morning, the green light of the digital clock casting an eerie glow in the dark, unfamiliar room. She'd hardly slept. Her dreams had been filled with dark images and half-remembered faces that swam across her consciousness and bullied her.

After he'd shown her to her room, Andrew had brought her silk pajamas and a bathrobe, both folded and looking new, as well as a pair of slippers.

Now, Trace slipped into the robe, belted it, found the warm, fur-lined pink slippers and padded across the deep carpet toward the door. She opened it, poked her head out, and peered into the dimly lit hallway, waiting, listening for sounds. All was quiet and still.

Her face was filled with determination and confidence as she moved across the blue and beige hall carpet toward the stairs that led to the library below. She quietly descended the stairs and made for the closed library doors. Again, she paused, straining her ears and eyes. It was as quiet as a cave, except for the distant sound of a grandfather clock, ticking away at her like a warning. As if making a tsk, tsk sound. As if to say, "No, No."

At the library doors, she gently reached for the right wooden door handle. She tugged. It didn't squeak but opened and slid easily across the rollers. Trace slipped inside, quietly sliding the door closed behind her.

She stood still, allowing her eyes to adjust to the murky darkness. Vague images and shapes slowly began to emerge. Was the Mata Hari collection still there, or had Andrew removed it to a safe in another part of the house?

Anxious, with a high pulse, she started for the display table where the collection had been. Dread and excitement beat away at her as she approached, moving gingerly.

She began to remember things, to see things, like old ghosts rising from buried graves. In the quiet night mood, the past seemed close, like a breath. Like a loud thrumming heartbeat.

Outside on the patio, a garden light leaked into the slightly parted draperies, just enough to illumine the Mata Hari collection in all its enchanted mystery, casting a hazy glow on the Mata Hari painting, and on the warm, bewitching eyes of Mata Hari.

Trace's eyes widened on the objects: the Chinese marble sculpture, the ornate opera glasses, the two fur necklets, the silver cutlery and the old French Francs. Slowly, deliberately, her eyes moved along the table until they settled, with swelling pleasure, on the ring. There it was, alive and waiting for her, an old friend.

A shaft of the outside lamplight struck it, and the ring broke into prisms of dancing emerald fire. Trace's throat tightened. She felt an extravagant emotion of terror, recollection and hope.

Her trembling hand reached for the ring. Again, it beckoned her on, as if some unseen energy were reaching back for her, gently tugging her hand, drawing it forward. As she took a shallow breath, her index finger briefly brushed the emerald's fire. She jerked back her finger, feeling it burn, as if she'd touched a hot stove.

A fragile, impulsive and inner darkness brought startled tears. She suddenly recalled, in great detail, Mata Hari's children—or had they been Trace's children? Her mind reeled and tangled, again tumbling about in the past and the present. In her mind's eye, she saw her sweet children's faces very clearly. She heard their manic cries when they had been poisoned. How she regretted all that had happened to them. She should have been a better mother. She shouldn't have been so self-absorbed. She shouldn't have gone off to Paris to become the doomed and silly old woman who stood there panicked and small before that firing squad. It should never have happened.

Her dear son, Norman, was struck down by that damned doctor—an overdose of mercury poisoning. He was only two years old when he died. Dear Juana-Luisa, Nonnie, was given the same overdose of mercury but, by some miracle, she had pulled through. She had only been one-year-old. Why did the doctor administer the mercury? Because her husband, Captain Rudolf MacLeod, had caught syphilis overseas before they were married, and he'd neglected to tell her. Yes, he hadn't told her that, the bastard. Their children were given the mercury as a precaution against the syphilis.

She should have never married Rudolf. Never. They'd met through a newspaper ad. She'd answered, including a photo of herself—something that wasn't done so much in those days. There was no Instagram in the early 1900s.

The article read: Captain in the Army of the Indies, on leave in Holland, seeks wife with a character to his taste. The man was Captain Rudolf MacLeod. He was handsome enough, even if he was 20 years older than she. He had a splendid mustache. Three months later, they were married.

Trace breathed out a jet of air, as she recalled Constance's words to her husband.

"The invisible world lies all around us like a shadow. There it is, the still present past, only a breath away."

Trace felt those words strike her in the heart, nearly punching the breath from her. She had the obsessive need to pick up that ring and slip it on. And, despite a rising alarm that went off in her head, she reached for the ring.

With a determined, crazed expression, she fumbled and trembled, and slid the burning ring onto her middle finger.

Silence.

She stood dead still, staring at it, transfixed. A stab of pain knifed through her chest. She called out, reaching for the nearest chair to brace her fall.

From behind, she was startled by a voice. With effort, she turned, squinting. It was Cyrano Wallace.

"Trace? Is that you? What are you doing?"

His ghostly figure stood before the dark library doors.

Trace tried to open her mouth to speak, but she had no voice. She could only make a strange wheezing sound. The pain in her chest struck again, and she doubled over in agony.

"Trace!" Cyrano called, breaking toward her.

Trace lifted her head, astounded to see blue glittering sparks of light falling from the ceiling like snow. She became lost in a childlike wonder and, despite her pain, she was mesmerized by the dazzling spectacle, the lights encircling her, increasing in density and blowing about the room like a frenzied snowstorm, the cool flecks bathing her, tingling her face like snowflakes.

Cyrano had vanished. The room had vanished.

Then came a low bong of steeple bells, loud in her ears, and the cry of distant songbirds. She was lost in a rolling, blue, misty fog. She blinked about, her hands still pressed to her pained chest.

The blue, scintillating sparks quivered for a time, and then shot off like shooting stars converging, then exploding into a brilliant flash—like the flash of a massive flashbulb.

The floor opened up, and she dropped into a spinning void. Terrified, she screamed, reaching, her limbs flailing helplessly as she plunged down into infinite darkness.

She heard a whooshing sound, felt a cold draft of wind. When her fall was swiftly broken, in a helpless panic, she struggled to right herself. Before she could, she was shot, like an arrow, through a long, endless tunnel that whirled in a rainbow of colors.

Timeless minutes later, she saw a towering wooden door racing toward her. In a desperate reflex, she covered her face with her hands, believing a collision was imminent.

To her astonishment, as she approached, the door dissolved into blue icy flecks, and she was flung ahead, passing through puffy white clouds, sparkling sunshine and thousands of tiny bubbles, like the bubbles in a glass of champagne.

She heard a voice, a woman's voice, like an echo in her head; "These are the bubbles of time... Yes... these are the bubbles of time."

Gasping for breath and struggling for balance, Trace tumbled through the scattering bubbles, her body tense, fists clenched. She cried out for help, and just when she felt her heart would explode with unspeakable pain and fright, everything stopped and went black.

Trace awakened gently, eyes sticky, body aching and fatigued. She was lying on a comfortable tufted pink chaise, still dressed in her silk robe, pajamas and matching slippers. Where was she? She lifted up on an elbow and glanced about, her eyes widening on the elegant room.

It was a large, stunning French Renaissance style room. The ceilings soared, the heavy gilded mirrors gleamed, the two fireplaces were made of white marble, and the carpets were a lush gold and red with delicate patterns. Trace took in the French-style winged back sofa and chairs, a love seat and gilded, intricately carved French settee with matching pillows. She turned to her left and saw a golden harpsichord, with four pink silk-upholstered chairs arranged around it.

Above was a mezzanine library and balcony sitting room. She saw stone columns, an arched gallery and peaked chapel windows.

She sat up, kinking her neck, struggling to orient herself in this strange and magnificent room. Suddenly remembering what had happened, she glanced down at the ring—the emerald Mata Hari ring. It was there, still on her finger, the pulsing light still alive, and glittering.

What had happened? She tried to swallow away a lump, as her mind raced and worked to think and match memory with reality.

It was quiet—strangely quiet—as early morning light streamed in from the upper windows. Trace stood slowly, as if to ensure she didn't break into pieces. Had she had another nightmare? Was she still dreaming now? It seemed real—this room, this light, her aching body—but her nightmares had often seemed real too. She'd often awakened from them confused and disoriented. She shook her head as if to clear it, then took a step, feeling wobbly and dizzy. Slowly, she started toward the windows to look out, to learn where she was.

It was a breathtaking view. She saw an unraveling, vivid green, manicured lawn and artfully carved winding hedges. A quiet lake was in the immediate distance, as well as an oak and chestnut forest, with a kind of French chateau far to the right, mostly obscured by trees.

Trace craned her neck up to inspect this chateau, seeing rows of wrought iron balconies, curved and curled into delicate tendrils. The tall upper windows were opened to the day, like doors. What season was this? It felt warm.

With effort, she turned from the window back to the room. She strained to reconstruct what had happened to her. The last thing she recalled was standing in Cyrano's library, staring at the ring. She'd slipped it on and heard Cyrano's voice. Then he'd just disappeared, and she'd seemed to be tossed off a cliff into an abyss.

Trace's frantic eyes searched the air for answers, and she wrapped herself with her arms for some security. What had happened? Where was she? Why couldn't she awaken from this crazy dream?

She heard footsteps. Twisting toward the sound, she suddenly froze as the footfalls grew louder, closer, echoing. When the golden doorknob turned, she held her breath, waiting in an agony of anticipation as the tall door swung open.

CHAPTER 8

They stood staring at each other: Trace, tall and statuesque, honey blonde hair mussed, skin white from fear, blue eyes wide, heart pounding in the startled silence.

The woman who stepped inside the room was tall and exotic, her olive skin glowing. Her raven black hair was swept up on her head, but curling tendrils flowed down to her shoulders. She wore an embroidered chiffon peignoir, with pink trim and ruffled sleeves, that accented her curvaceous figure and small breasts. She glared at Trace in dark suspicion, looking her up and down, her eyes finally coming to rest on the emerald ring.

Neither spoke. The seconds were strained and fragile. Trace was unable to move or speak, as her jumbled mind labored to decipher the incredible scene before her. In that staggering moment, a storm of terror and emotion awakened her to the impossible—that she was seeing the living image of herself as she had once been so many years ago, in a world long submerged in the deep river of time.

In that ominous timelessness, as Trace stood taut and trembling, she was both a witness and a participant, both a ghost and alive. She was two apparitions—both lost in a world of flickering shadows.

Trace was looking at a handsome woman in her late 30s, no longer a girl but settling into maturity. There was an uncanny magnetism to the woman, an indescribable allure, a powerful aura about her that made the hair on the back of Trace's neck stand up.

The woman alarmed and unsettled her. Trace knew this woman—knew her from nightmares—knew her from childhood daydreams—knew that she had breathed the same breaths in that past life regression.

Trace intimately knew the low, sonorous timbre of her voice; the proud impetuous spirit; the powerless strength and raw terror she'd felt in prison while waiting for the call of the firing squad. Trace stared at the woman in a hypnotic wonder.

Was this a new kind of nightmare? A trick of the mind? A gothic joke?

The equally-startled woman finally spoke to Trace in French, and Trace strained to understand what she said.

"Who are you? What are you doing here?" she asked curtly.

Trace tried to speak, but failed. She couldn't form a single French word. The language simply wasn't on her tongue. Only English words came to mind.

The woman glowered at the ring, her voice low and accusing. "Where did you get that ring? It's mine. You stole it."

The woman took two aggressive steps toward Trace, and then stopped short, unsure.

Trace's brain locked up. She could feel herself slipping away, could feel her rubbery legs wobble, her blood turn cold. The wild experience of falling into the abyss and landing in this vision or nightmare had stunned and weakened her. Her vision was blurred, her voice thick and hoarse.

Trace spoke in English. "No, I didn't steal it. I didn't."

The woman's eyes narrowed. She responded in English, in some kind of accent, not quite French or Dutch, but a mix of the two.

"English? You speak English? Who are you?"

Trace forced out. "I'm an American."

The woman's eyebrows lifted in surprise. "What? An American?"

"Yes."

"How did you get in here? Who are you?"

Trace searched for an answer. None came.

"Where did you get those clothes? They are hideous."

Trace glanced down at herself, still unable to feel anchored in any reality. She had to say something, even if it was a lie. "A friend..."

"What kind of friend?" And then her face changed, as a new thought struck. "Are you Edward's girlfriend? Did he bring you here and put that ring on your finger, as some kind of joke?"

Trace was at a complete loss for words.

"Speak up, or I'll have you thrown out!" the woman barked.

Trace nodded, finding her desperate voice. "Yes... I'm Edward's girlfriend."

The woman relaxed, releasing a sigh. "Well, why didn't you say so? Why all the silence? What is your name?"

Trace's eyes flitted about. "Trace."

"What? Trace?"

"Yes, Trace Rutland."

"I've never heard of that name. It's a strange name." The woman thought about it and nodded a grin. "But I like it." Her chin tilted up. "I like the strange and the different. Yes, I like the name."

The woman started toward Trace, walking easily, with a gentle sway of the hips, the chiffon gown whispering against her as she walked.

She stopped a few feet away. The two women's eyes met, and locked. An electric spark startled them both. They fell silent, again, staring, exploring the depths of each other's eyes, as if seeing into fathomless depths and timeless worlds. As Trace fell into Mata Hari's eyes, she could hear echoes of old conversations, see snippets of scenes and impressions from Mata Hari's childhood; she saw images of the time she'd spent in the Dutch Indies with her husband and children.

Mata Hari finally broke the spell, glancing away, blinking. "We have met. I know it. Yes, I know you. We have met. Yes?"

Trace shut her eyes, to help clear her head. "No…"

"You seem so familiar," Mata Hari said, warily. She pursed up her lips. "I'm Mata Hari," she said, proudly.

Trace nodded. "Yes, I know."

That pleased her. "When did you arrive? Last night with Edward?"

Trace didn't know what to say. "Yes… last night."

"Vadime told me Edward was coming, but this is the first time Edward has brought a girl. Has he finally come to his senses and dropped that silly fiancée of his?"

"...I don't know."

Mata Hari studied Trace. "Where did you meet Edward?"

Trace stared down at her slippers, avoiding Mata Hari's eyes, afraid of them and what they held. Trace wanted desperately to wake up from this damned dream. She wanted to run away, but to where? She didn't know where she was, and it was ridiculous not to know where you are, or how you got there.

The last thing she recalled was being in Cyrano Wallace's library in Lenox, Massachusetts, slipping the ring on her finger—and feeling strongly compelled to do so. Trace glanced down at the ring. What strange magic lay coiled in the ring? Where had the flying hours gone?

"You do recall where you and Edward met, don't you?" Mata Hari said, jarring Trace from her thoughts.

Mata Hari pursed up her lips again. A spicy thought occurred to her, and she smiled.

"Or even more interesting, maybe you don't remember. I have had such encounters. To tell the truth, there are many officers I knew quite well and later I didn't recall where I had met them. I found that exciting. I think I was a better lover because of it."

Trace was exhausted. She couldn't pretend what she didn't know, and she didn't have the strength or will to fight. "I don't know where I am," Trace said, in a hopeless whisper.

71

At that moment, a door on the opposite side of the room swung open and a tall man entered. When he saw Trace, he ventured forward, unsure of what he was seeing. He stopped short. He had a pencil thin mustache, good shoulders and a chiseled handsome face. He wore a brown, knee-length jacket, striped trousers and shiny leather boots. His white shirt was minus the wing collar, giving him a jaunty look. His shiny chestnut hair was combed back smoothly from his forehead, and his sleepy gray/green eyes widened and blinked a couple of times when they found, and then fixed on, Trace, as if he couldn't believe what he was seeing.

He gazed at Trace, struck silent by her serene, unquestionable beauty and gorgeous mass of glossy, honey-blonde hair.

Mata Hari's eyes swung toward Edward. "Edward. Why is everyone up so early, and dressed?"

Edward rubbed his sleepy eyes, and then slapped a hand over his heart for theatrical effect. He spoke in a loud, dramatic voice, as if reciting Shakespeare.

"My God! I believe I'm having palpitations of the heart," he said, with a very British accent. "Oh, my dear Mata Hari, where did you ever find such a lovely creature? Has she descended from the Gods, from Mount Olympus? Is she perhaps Athena, the goddess of wisdom and military victory, or is she, in fact, Venus incarnate? Pray tell me, dear Mata Hari, where have you found this incomparable, delectable and gorgeous creature?"

"Where have I found her? Don't be silly, Edward, you found her, and she is yours, although she doesn't remember where she met you, which I find absolutely fascinating. You must tell me and Vadime the entire story when he wakes up."

Trace stood as still as a statue, dumbstruck. She inhaled a steadying breath and looked at Edward with pleading eyes. Edward squinted a look at her, his eyes penetrating and actively watchful. There was a slow exchange of hope—Trace hoping for his play-along recognition of her—and Edward, that she would find him as attractive as he found her.

Edward laughed and went to Trace, with a cheery smile. As he drew up to her, his eyes caught hers and he winked, took her by the shoulders and pulled her into his arms for a long, passionate kiss.

Trace caught a whiff of his sandalwood aftershave, as he pressed his lips against hers. A shocking wave of stinging desire electrified her, awakened her, melted her. When he released her, wrapping a long arm around her shoulder, drawing her intimately close, Mata Hari laughed, very pleased.

"Oh yes, I can see you two are lovers. Take her back to bed, Edward, and you two sleep as late as you want."

Mata Hari approached Trace, with her hand extended. "Please take off the ring and give it to me."

Trace, still reeling from the wet, warm kiss, couldn't move.

Looking at the ring and Mata Hari's waiting hand, Trace was conflicted. The ring had power. No doubt. There was some strange power contained in the ring that had sent her back into time. That was obvious. Or had her fragile mind finally shattered, and she was slipping helplessly into insanity? If she gave up the ring, would she be trapped and helpless? Would she ever be able to regain her sanity and return home?

Mata Hari waited. "Please give me my ring, Trace."

Haltingly, Trace obeyed, gently sliding the ring from her finger, instantly feeling vulnerable, caught in a chilling web of time.

Mata Hari took the ring, staring at it pensively. "I've always felt this ring would bring me luck just when I needed it. I still believe it will save me from all harm, even when all my friends, family, and lovers flee."

Edward spoke up, keeping his curious eyes on the ring. "It looks like a rare beauty, striking and unusual. Who gave it to you, Mata Hari?"

Mata Hari smiled, sadly. "Captain Maurice Herbaux. He loved me so much, you know. He was a good lover and a rich man. Yes, a good and tender lover, and he looked so handsome in his uniform. He was killed only a week after he gave me this ring—killed in 1915 at the Battle of Neuve Chapelle. The last time I saw him, he presented it to me, saying, 'May it always keep you from harm. May it always protect you. Believe in it, chérie.'"

Now in a low mood, Mata Hari turned and strolled toward the same door she had entered from. She looked back over her shoulder with a bland smile. "You two do look like lovers, you know. Go now, and make love. That is what life is all about, you know—especially now with this awful war exploding our hopes and dreams, and killing so many of our good and handsome officers."

As soon as the door clicked shut, Edward released his arm, clicked his boot heels together, and snapped a crisp salute. "May I present myself. I am Captain Edward Kenyon Bishop, of The Royal Flying Corps No. 11 Squadron, at your service, madam. Should we obey our good hostess, the unrivaled and notorious Mata Hari, and return to my room to make love?"

Despite Edward's breezy exterior and handsome face, Trace saw a weary sadness in his eyes, and it touched her. He couldn't have been more than 25 years old.

"Thank you for saving me," she said, softly.

He lowered his saluting hand, looking her over. "Did I hear Mata Hari call you Trace?"

"Yes...my name is Trace Rutland. It's a nickname my father gave me. My real name is Tracey."

"And you are an American? Well, yes, of course. I hear it. How utterly astonishing."

"Why astonishing?"

"I have met a number of American flyers, but not so many devastatingly attractive American women dressed in, well, for lack of better words, such eccentrically stylish sleeping attire. Where on earth did you ever find such garments?"

Edward's eyes were penetrating and actively watchful, and Trace sensed they took in more than they gave out.

She absorbed another wave of fatigue, and she nearly fainted. "Captain... would you do me one more chivalrous thing?"

He gave a little bow. "Anything, Miss. Rutland. I presume it is Miss Rutland? Not Mrs. Rutland? Pray, say it be so, or my panting heart shall wither with the heaviest sorrow," he said theatrically, with a forced arch of his brow.

"Yes, it is Miss Rutland."

He grinned, a devastatingly attractive boyish grin.

"I'm so delighted to hear it, dear Miss Rutland."

"Captain..."

"Edward, please."

"Edward. I'm exhausted. I need to sleep. I need to try to figure some things out, but I must sleep before I faint. Is there a room somewhere where I can sleep... alone? Separately?"

His smile was brief, but warm. "Yes, Miss Rutland. I will conduct you there, and assure you that your virtue will remain intact and safely protected, as long as is humanly possible for me to do so."

Trace didn't know if it was the absurdity of the moment, her utter exhaustion or just some sudden impulse, but she lifted a hand and ran her fingers gently across his warm, smooth cheek, pausing to touch his lips. He shut his eyes, overcome. When he opened them, he looked at her differently, solemnly and tenderly.

"What a touch you have," he said, in a low, intimate voice that stirred them both.

Trace's heart quickened, moved by his sudden vulnerable expression and his masculine handsome face. Even though she was exhausted and off balance, her attraction to Edward was swift and disturbing.

Without words, Captain Bishop led Trace out of the room and down a long, carpeted hallway to a partially opened door. He stopped, indicating with a hand.

"This is my room. Sleep as long as you like. Use anything you need."

Trace met his eyes. "Will you be around when I wake up?"

"Yes, Miss Rutland, you can count on it."

Trace hesitated, his kiss still impressed upon her lips, his scent lingering. She stepped inside and silently closed the door.

Immediately, there was a light knock. Trace opened it, peeking out. "Yes?"

"After you sleep, Miss Rutland, will you tell me from which gilded, heavenly cloud you descended?"

She stared at him for a moment, considering his question. "Perhaps you can tell me where I am, Captain Bishop."

"Oh, my dear Miss Rutland, you break my heart. You must be more intimate with me and call me Edward. May I call you Trace?"

Trace felt as though she might faint. She struggled to stand. "Yes… Fine. Where am I?"

Edward's eyes explored her eyes and lips. "Trace, you are just outside of Chantilly, at a Chateau owned by the Marquis de Beaufort, an old lover of Mata Hari's."

Trace sank in height. "Chantilly? In France?"

"Yes, in France."

Edward tilted his head slightly, looking for a joke. Instead, he saw she was troubled.

"Yes, Trace. You are in France, about 40 minutes from Paris. Where did you think you were?"

Trace nodded, dazed and resigned. "What month and year is it?"

Edward stood a bit taller, concerned now. "Are you quite all right, Trace?"

"No, I'm not. I am not quite all right at all," she said, more forcefully than she meant to. "What are the month and date, Edward?"

He was serious now. "It's Saturday, June 28, 1916."

Trace's eyes went vacant, her body wilted. She slowly shut the door, turned, and leaned back against it, unable to move. She was at the end of all thought.

CHAPTER 9

Trace awoke in a wide, four-poster bed covered by wine-colored velvet fabrics, each with fine, crystal studded detailing. She felt like a queen, awakening in a world of castles, class and powdered wigs.

Outside the open windows, she heard birdsong and distant voices. She heard a hum of mumbled words, and then a break into laughter. She raised up, instantly awake, searching the room, sure she'd been dreaming—praying it had all been imagined: Mata Hari, Edward and a chateau near Paris.

She examined the place, seeing a stunning antique Louis XVI style paneled room, gilded with silver leaves; furniture of red velvet chairs, a cream color settee, a towering, delicately carved armoire, gilded mirrors and mantle clocks, and a four-foot marble statue of Apollo in all his muscled glory near a white marble fireplace.

The wood floors gleamed, partially covered by an extravagant royal blue and gold fringed carpet that must have been over 100 years old. The smooth walls contained 18th-century landscapes and portraits of elegant royal ladies, dressed in flowing silk dresses, showing off jewels that shimmered, shouting out wealth and privilege.

This was no dream. She had not imagined it. She was stuck in the glue of another world, and she sank back down into the bed, willing herself to fly away.

The voices outside persisted, and her curiosity took over. Sun streamed in from the partially opened yellow silk draperies, and a gentle wind blew in, fluttering them.

She threw back the red, wine-colored satin sheet, swung her feet to the floor and pushed up. Still a little unsteady on her feet, she meandered toward the window and squinted out.

Below, on a pink stone patio, she saw Edward, Mata Hari and another man, who was dressed in a dark uniform, all seated around a table, sipping wine, with a silver tray of cheese and fruit before them. Was the other man Captain Vladimir de Masloff, the officer in the Russian Army, and Mata Hari's 21-year-old lover? But he looked so young—just a boy.

She drew back from the window and eased down to sit cross-legged on the cool wooden floor. She closed her eyes, and for a long time she just breathed in and out, until her spinning mind became controlled and still. Learning to survive in this time would be paramount, until she could learn why she was here and how she could return.

As absurd and insane as it was, she had to consider the fact that when she looked at Mata Hari, Trace was actually looking at herself as she once was—Mata Hari in 1916.

A searing thought struck, one she knew occurred to all time travelers. If she had time traveled to the past, would she, by her choices and actions, alter the future? Her future and the world's future?

During her life as Trace, she'd struggled nearly every day with nightmares and pain. She had been close to losing her mind. Could this journey to the past be a kind of saving grace? Could she plot to change what had happened to herself in the past as Mata Hari, and thus save herself in the future?

Maybe she could influence and encourage this Mata Hari to make better choices and thus prevent the mess she'd made of her life. Maybe Mata Hari could reconcile with her daughter, Nonnie, and have a meaningful and loving marriage with Vadime, and escape her awful death.

Then what was she, Trace? A kind of living, breathing ghost, haunting this world of 1916, searching for redemption for what she'd done in the past?

Outside, she heard more laughter. She was startled when she heard Edward speak her name. She raised to the window and, hiding behind the draperies, she drew them back and peered down.

Mata Hari held a wine glass poised at her lips. Vadime was smoking a cigarette and Edward held a pipe, staring off toward a sprouting fountain, water glistening in the sunlight.

"I think something rather traumatic has happened to Trace," Edward said.

"She has such a strange, far-away look in her eyes," Mata Hari said. "Frankly, it unnerved me to look into them. Will you be taking her back with you tonight, Edward?"

"I can't wait to meet this Trace," Vadime said, in a thick Russian accent.

Edward continued. "I've been thinking that perhaps she has a kind of memory loss. She seems kind of distant and dazed. I know a doctor in Paris I can take her to. I've seen soldiers from the front who have lost their memories. They call it shell shock. They don't know who they are or where they come from."

"Well you should know what's the matter with her, Edward," Mata Hari said. "You brought her."

Edward cleared his throat, as if he'd lost himself in reverie, forgetting he had vouched for her, pretending he knew her. "Well, yes, of course I did, Mata Hari, but something has changed in her since she's been here. She doesn't seem to recall certain things."

"Maybe it's the way you make love to her," Vadime said, with a chuckle. "Be more gentle, man. You're too passionate with the girl."

Mata Hari and Vadime laughed. Edward did not.

"You never did tell me where you met her," Mata Hari asked. "She told me she didn't recall, and I don't think that is so flattering for you, Edward, when a girl can't recall where she has met a handsome British flyer war ace."

There was a brief silence. "We met in Paris," Edward said, so softly that Trace just barely heard him.

"Paris is a big city, Edward. Where in Paris?" Vadime asked.

He stuttered. "Oh, well… you know at the Boulangerie Patisserie in Montmartre. She was with some friends."

"And, of course, you fell in love with her right off, didn't you, Captain Bishop?" Vadime said.

"Yes, Captain Masloff, my friend. At first sight, I indeed did fall in love with her. And I can tell you, without any doubt, that it is a love you feel just one time in a lifetime. It's an odd kind of feeling, and I'm not sure I can quite put it into words."

"Why Edward, I have never known you to be so romantic," Mata Hari said. "Otherwise, I might have seduced you."

"You tried, Mata Hari. Don't you remember?" Vadime said, with a laugh, "but my dear friend, Captain Bishop, is engaged to a very proper English girl, and he turned you down."

"How rude of you to remember, Vadime. I was merely teasing Edward. So, have you told your British fiancée about this Trace Rutland, Edward, and your sudden gushing love for her?"

Trace backed away from the curtain, feeling hot outside and cold inside.

"Some things a gentleman doesn't discuss. Anyway, as you know, Mata Hari, we pilots are living on borrowed time, and so life becomes more heightened and much more precious to us. We must take love where we can find it. Isn't that right, Captain Vadime?"

"I'm afraid so, my dear friend."

"Mata Hari, did Captain Masloff tell you that we are about to embark on a new offensive? This is all hush-hush, of course, but there are no Germans around, are there?"

"Don't speak of such things, Edward," Mata Hari said in a scolding voice. "I detest unpleasant things, and I especially detest this war. It has taken all the joy out of Paris."

"Nonetheless, my sweet," Vadime said, "Captain Bishop is right. We flyers are like puffs of smoke in this war. So many of our comrades have perished, and they continue to perish every day in the skies above France."

"Let's stop all this depressing talk. I'll have no more of it," Mata Hari said, jutting out her jaw. "From now on, we talk only of pleasure, good times and making love. That is all. Meanwhile, Edward, go check on your lovely girl. You must wake her up and prepare her for dinner. There is so much I want to ask her."

"And I must see this girl who has captured your heart so quickly, Captain Bishop."

Trace heard Edward's chair push back, scraping across the stones. She backed away from the window. He was on his way. What now? She had no clothes, no makeup, no money. What in the world was she going to do? She stood like a deer in headlights.

When the inevitable knock came, Trace was in the marble bathroom, staring at a gilded porcelain clawfoot tub, with gold fixtures and a rack of snow-white fluffy towels. After a bath, what would she put on?

The knock on the bedroom door was persistent. She left the bathroom and stood in the middle of the floor with her hands on her hips, hoping for a confident look.

"Is that you, Edward?"

"Yes, Trace. Are you up?"

"Yes..."

"May I come in?"

She had a thought. "Just a minute."

Trace swiftly buttoned the top two buttons on her pajamas and reached for her robe. After she'd belted it with a tight tug, and finger combed her hair, she took some deep breaths and returned to her previous confident pose.

"Come in, Edward."

The door opened slowly and when Edward appeared, she felt a little tremor of desire. He was coatless, his white shirt rolled up at the elbows, revealing strong forearms and a wide chest. But it was his lips that captured and held her for a short hypnotic moment. They were full and sensuous, and his mouth slightly parted as if waiting for her kiss. The man was certainly appealing, but she quickly brushed the thought aside. She had no time for anything even slightly romantic.

"How are you feeling, Trace?"

"Much better, thank you. I was just going to take a bath, if that's all right. Do you need to use the room for anything?"

He didn't seem to hear her question. He just stared. "You are such a beautiful woman, Trace," he said, smiling into her eyes. "You are telling the truth, aren't you? I mean to say, that you are not married?"

It was a simple question, but a direct one. For some reason, it unsettled and thrilled her. Edward oozed charm and class—an old-world gentlemanly approach and polish that, against her will, unwrapped her defenses and relaxed her.

"No, I'm not married. Are you?" she said, staring with a challenge into those bottomless gray/green, glittering eyes of his.

He looked toward the windows, with a slight frown. "Shall I tell you the truth, Trace, and risk losing you?"

"Do you have me?" Trace said, knowing how it sounded, bold and flirtatious.

He met her direct gaze, and he squared his shoulders.
"I'm engaged to a girl back home in England."
"And does this girl back home have a name?"
His expression pained. "At the moment, does it matter?"
"To me it does. Yes."
He gave her a quick nod. "All right then. Her name is Elizabeth Ashley Pemberton."
"Well now, that's a very long name, isn't it? A classy name. Must be rich. I bet you're rich, aren't you, Edward?"
That amused him, and he shut the door behind him, not taking his eyes from her as he did so. Trace liked the sudden intimacy, and the flirtatious play. It was refreshingly distracting, and she needed as much distraction as she could get.
Edward cleared his throat. "Bishop Manor is a stately home in North Yorkshire, England. The first Bishop Manor was built in 1756 for the 3rd Earl of Carlisle, a relative. Yes, Trace, I come from a wealthy family. My father is a member of Parliament. My mother is descended from royalty."
"And I bet Ms. Pemberton descends, or shall I say ascends? Yes, ascends sounds so much better, I think. Does Miss Elizabeth Ashley Pemberton ascend from royalty as well?"
He waggled a finger at her. "You are making fun of me, Trace."
She grinned. "Yes, I am. Is Miss Pemberton from a wealthy family?"
"Her family had wealth. Actually, at present, she has more title than wealth."
"But you love her?"

He gave her a sharp, cunning gaze. "You keep toying with me, Miss Rutland."

"...Yes, Edward, I am, and I must have irritated you because you just called me Miss Rutland."

"I'm not at all irritated with you. Intrigued by you, yes. Infatuated? Definitely. Completely undone by you? Oh, yes. Now that I have told you about me, what can you tell me about you," Edward said, slipping his hands into his pants pockets and rocking on his heels.

Trace considered the question with care. "If I recall my family tree, John Rutland came from Lincolnshire, England in 1763, and settled in North Carolina. Two of my distant descendants fought in the Revolutionary War to rid the colonies of the bloody British and help establish the United States of America. So, it seems, Captain Bishop, that your family and my family were once enemies."

Edward smiled. "It is so good of you to point out the obvious, Miss Rutland."

"Are you being sarcastic, Edward?"

"Yes, I am. So where were you born?"

"Lexington, Kentucky."

He brightened. "Ah, yes, Kentucky. I know about Kentucky. My family has a stable of horses, and one of our trainers, a rather curious chap with a very curious accent, is from Kentucky."

"Was his accent like mine?"

"Not as charming, I can assure you, Miss Rutland, Trace. And how and why did you come to France and, more importantly, how did you end up here with Mata Hari?"

Trace dropped her gaze. "I can't tell you that right now, Edward. Maybe later. In the meantime, I'm going to level with you."

"Level with me? What a curious thing to say. Is that an American expression?"

"Yes. Edward, it is American. Okay, so I have no clothes, no money and nowhere to go. Can you help me?"

A slow, pleasurable smile creased Edward's lips. "Miss Rutland, you are the most bewitching, attractive and fascinating woman I have ever met. Rest assured that you can place yourself entirely in my care for as long as you may wish. And I hope that it will be for a very long time."

CHAPTER 10

At dinner, Trace wore one of Mata Hari's extravagantly designed dresses, a full length, red wine Edwardian style dress, with silky chiffon and cappuccino satin.
It was finished with silver embroidery, silver beading
and handmade flowers and lace.

Mata Hari had stopped by Trace's room to present it
to her, with smiling pride and probing curiosity.

"I had it made in Paris, in 1905. It should fit you
well. I have gained some pounds since then. Vadime
says he finds the pounds sexy, but I find that I can no
longer fit in these old gowns that hold such fond memories for me. So goes life. I think it will look lovely on
you."

After Mata Hari left, Trace carefully slipped into the
dress, touching the silver beading and satin, awed by
the feel and style. For a second, she had a flashback—
recalling wearing the same dress to a dinner party in
Paris, in her past life as Mata Hari. Suddenly dizzy,
Trace dropped to the couch with a bounce to catch her
breath, and to shake off the memory.

Later, Trace slipped on the matching gloves and turned stiffly to face the mirror, nervously surprised. It was a regal and elegant dress and it fit her well, taut in the waist, clinging gently to her hips. She had never worn such a richly designed and textured gown in any Broadway show. It was truly an original.

When Edward returned from a walk, entered the room and saw her standing before him in the soft light, he breathed her in and sighed with pleasure. His eyes lingered on her, the red berry lips, the curly voluminous hairstyle, the regal posture. A small smile formed at the corners of his mouth.

"Miss Rutland, you look as though you just have stepped out of a dream."

Trace wanted to say You have no idea, but she didn't.

At dinner, Edward sat across the table from Trace, and as he spooned his soup, his lively eyes stole flirtatious glances toward her. Mata Hari had also lent Trace a French enamel pearl and gold locket pendant with a gold chain, a gift from the Marquis de Beaufort, or so Trace had been told. He'd been a lover when Mata Hari had danced in Paris in 1907.

Mata Hari wore a long bobbin lace gown that helped hide some of the tummy weight, while accenting her hips and modestly covering her breasts. Her makeup was light, but her lips were very red, and her dark intelligent eyes took in everything, missing nothing, including Edward's obvious attraction to Trace. But Mata Hari was cautiously watchful and, at times, her dark eyes seemed to bore a hole through Trace, as if she were struggling to crack the mystery of her.

Edward and Vadime wore their military uniforms, Edward looking especially lean, muscular and striking in his green gabardine jacket with leather brown shoulder straps, broad belt, and royal flying corps khaki wings badge. In the light, the luster of his eyes was a greenish gold, his chestnut hair combed back from his forehead, his bearing regal and straight. To Trace, this man was a definite "turn on." A masculine fantasy come true; the type of man that did not exist in her time, but a man she'd dreamed of in the deepest and most secret core of her heart. She tried to swat away her attraction to Edward, but whenever she was with him, there was a familiar tug at her heart, as if she'd known him before. She felt an opening of emotion, a letting in of desire and hope.

And yet, as she sat there at the dinner table, she also felt as though she had stepped onto a movie set, and she didn't know the plot, the character or her lines. She seemed to be wavering in and out of a reality that was both enthralling and frightening.

During dinner, the conversation wandered and rambled, but the men always brought it back to the war and to flying.

"You know, my dear Captain Bishop," Vadime said, "we always face German pilots who have much better aircraft than we do. They have more speed and a higher ceiling, and they have a better training system."

"Yes, Vadime, and the weather is also a significant factor on the Western Front, with the prevailing westerly wind favoring the Germans."

"But of course, Captain Bishop," Vadime said, sliding his soup bowl aside. "So, the most important thing in fighting is the shooting, then come the tactics, and last comes the flying."

Edward thought about that. "Yes, Vadime, you are right about that. In nearly all the cases where I've seen planes shot down, it was during a dogfight that was very short in duration. The successful machine gun fire occurred within a minute after the fight began."

"Enough about war, you flying soldiers," Mata Hari said. "You talk about war as if it were a woman you are about to make love to, when you have two beautiful women right here before you, wanting to be made love to. Now, not another word about war and flying those damned flimsy machines."

Mata Hari turned to Trace. "My dear Trace, please tell me what you have been doing with yourself while in France."

The French waiter, dressed in black tails and white tie, leaned toward Trace with a silver tray that held plump pheasant breasts, covered with crispy ham and dripping orange sauce. Not being used to serving herself, she fumbled the serving spoons, finally managing to drop the breast onto her porcelain plate with a little bounce.

After the party was served, Trace prepared herself to answer the question she knew was on everyone's mind. Where had she come from, and how had she dropped in from out of nowhere?

Trace needed all her acting skills to tell the story she'd worked on and polished while taking a bath. Fortunately, she'd had a dancing part in a Broadway musical two years before, called Woman at the Front. It was set during the First World War, and even though the show closed after only 80 performances, Trace had learned some important facts about World War I.

The musical's story had been loosely based on a real person, Lena Ashwell, an actress, impresario and suffragette, who had bravely and brazenly fought the War Office to travel to France to entertain the troops. The War Office did not share her views on "entertaining troops." As far as the generals were concerned, soldiers made their own amusement: playing cards and dominoes, and writing letters, interspersed with playing a little football. The generals felt that the men did not need women causing a raucous sensation, and complicating matters behind the front lines.

But Lena Ashwell persisted, finally winning a wealthy patron's support. So, Lena and a troupe of women and men actually did travel to Europe. In 1915, the first concert tour got underway, with 39 concerts in two weeks.

Trace remembered parts of Lena Ashwell's story and managed to recall lines from the show, bits and pieces of monologues and songs' lyrics. From these, Trace had put together a story—a convincing story she hoped, one she had rehearsed, both in her head and aloud—and now she was about to share it with her curious and waiting dinner guests.

"So, why did you come to France?" Edward repeated.

Trace calmly lifted her crystal wine glass and took a swallow of Chardonnay, drifting into performance mode.

"I came with Lena Ashwell, to perform for the French troops behind the lines."

Silence. The candles, burning in the silver candelabra at the center of the table, flickered and danced.

"Who?" Mata Hari asked.

"Lena Ashwell. I'm sure you've heard of her. She grew up in Canada and attended The Royal Academy of Music in London. She's an actress and suffragette." Trace had worked hard to remember to tell Lena's story in the present tense.

"And what are you?" Mata Hari asked, her eyes narrowing. "An actress? A suffragette?"

"I'm an actress, dancer and singer."

More silence. Edward stared, dumbly, not moving, not blinking. "An actress?"

Trace knew what that meant to these people. During the course of rehearsing Woman at the Front, Trace had learned that in 1915, being an actress and dancer was looked upon by polite society with disapproval and suspicion. At that time, actresses were considered loose women, who drank champagne all day long, languished on sofas, and received bouquets from countless lovers, who patiently waited in lines at the stage door to present themselves, hoping for a night of love in return for money and favors. In other words: Mata Hari's own way of living.

Trace took another sip of wine, wanting to get buzzed and relaxed as soon as possible.

Vadime spoke next. "My dear girl, you certainly must stir the hearts of those soldiers. I for one would love to see you perform."

Mata Hari glowed with jealousy. "Miss Rutland, who are your current admirers? Generals? Marquis? You must have many, with that thick blonde hair and those red lips."

Edward lowered his disappointed eyes to his food. He laid his fork aside and blotted his lips with his linen napkin, as if his appetite had fled.

Though she fought it, Trace turned defensive, her tone edgy. "I have no admirers, Mata Hari. I worked very hard to become an actress, singer and dancer." Now Trace launched into the meat of the story she'd rehearsed.

"Life behind the front line is not easy, I can assure you. We often find ourselves wading knee-deep in mud towards candlelit huts, barns or tents. We carry heavy props and musical instruments and costumes, only to find that the stage is covered with a pile of suitcases, which we must move to set up for the performance, after having had little or no sleep. But the men—those good and weary, and sometimes sick and wounded men—who have seen the horrors of war—eagerly await our performances. In those smoke-filled rooms, jam-packed with soldiers, we perform, and they're excited and thankful for it, and they applaud the songs and the recitations with such laughter and enthusiasm that it brings tears to our eyes."

Edward leaned back in his chair with renewed interest, his hands in his lap.

Trace continued. "At the base camps, we often spend time after concerts with the wounded, sometimes sitting quietly, singing to just one man. Over time, I believe we have proved our worth, and now, there is an increasing demand for what is known as 'firing-line parties.' We are now being invited to many base camps to perform."

Trace set her wine glass down, firmly, as a kind of punctuation, a period, to end her dramatic speech.

What she'd said had all been true—it had happened just the way she'd spoken it, as the entire cast of the musical had learned during rehearsals from the writer of the show.

The dinner guests quietly went back to eating. Trace felt satisfied that at least she'd made them aware of the women and men who were currently performing in France. Of course, she also hoped they'd believe her, and she'd survive another day.

After another brief silence, Edward began to applaud, and Vadime soon joined in. Finally, Mata Hari smiled, warmly, tapping a spoon against her crystal glass.

"Brava, Miss Rutland," Mata Hari said. "Brava to you and those brave women."

Edward raised his wine glass. "And to the brave soldiers who fight for us all."

Their glasses chimed as they touched.

Trace let out a little breath of relief. For now, she was okay.

Vadime said, "My dear Captain Bishop, I believe you have found a girl with, as I hear the American pilots say, 'A girl with moxie.'"

Trace turned her eyes toward Edward, and although she saw his eyes shining at her, she could also see that those eyes held more questions. Questions that he'd surely want answers to in private.

After dinner, they retired to the library, where the men had cigars and cognac and the women, glasses of port. Trace, not used to the stinking smell of cigars, nearly gagged when Mata Hari left to retrieve one of her scrapbooks of photographs, newspaper clippings, playbills and calling cards from her years of performing in many European capitals. They sat in elegant chairs as Mata Hari turned the pages slowly, reminiscing, commenting on photos of her in seductive poses and suggestive costumes. Trace masked her astonishment when she realized she was looking at the same scrapbook she'd seen at Cyrano Wallace's library, as part of his Mata Hari collection, far into the future.

"I haven't really danced since 1915, you know," Mata Hari said. "Maybe I'm getting too old. Although," she pointed to a newspaper clipping in her scrapbook, "look at that. Look at how The Daily Telegraph of London described me only last year. "I'll read it out loud, so everyone can hear. This reporter says I'm 'mahogany in color, rather tall, aged between 35 and 40, a very pretty woman.' End quote."

Vadime applauded. "And yes, my dear, you are a very pretty woman."

"Hear! Hear!" Edward said, raising his glass so he and Vadime could clink a toast.

Mata Hari sighed. "Oh well, this damned war has spoiled everything. The salons and the theatres all play those silly patriotic shows now. They don't want me."

Edward spoke up. "But Mata Hari, they do help keep up the people's morale."

"Good plays and popular reviews would do a better job of it, Edward."

"You should go back to dancing, my love," Vadime said. "It would be good for you, and the public."

"I tell you, they don't want me anymore, Vadime. You know that. The world is changing, and not for the better. I'm sure you saw that awful pamphlet that sold more than 75,000 copies in one week, written by 'A Little Mother,' which basically states that women were 'created for the purpose of giving life, and men to take it.'"

"What a bunch of bullshit," Trace said, without thinking.

All startled eyes in the room stuck to her.

Edward managed a smile. "My, my. Is that American slang?" he asked. "That word?"

Trace blushed, looking down.

Vadime spoke up in her defense. "My dear Captain Bishop, I have heard the Australian troops using that very word. Miss Rutland must have picked it up during one of her troop entertainments."

"Well, I like the word," Mata Hari said, with an emphatic jerk of her chin. "It's so...alive with meaning. I have never heard of it. Bullshit! Yes, I like it, and I will surely use it. If it's good enough for those brave Australians, then it's good enough for Mata Hari."

The conversation soon fell into the trivial, and as the clock ticked on toward eleven, Trace worried about where she was going to sleep. If they shared the same bedroom, would Edward try to force himself on her? And what was she going to do in the morning? Where would she go?

The dinner party finally concluded near midnight, when Edward wrapped a possessive arm around Trace's shoulders and said, "Well, my friends, it's late, and I for one am exhausted. Thank you, Mata Hari, for a wonderful evening. Trace and I bid you both a very good night."

Trace stood stiffly, with a tight smile, feeling the pressure of Edward's hand on her arm. "Yes, thank you for a lovely evening. Good night."

Mata Hari fixed her attention on Trace. "What are your plans, Miss Rutland? Where will you go? Will Edward take you away on Monday?"

Trace looked at Edward for help. She didn't realize he was leaving on Monday. "Well, I…I didn't know Edward was leaving so soon."

Vadime took Mata Hari's hand. "Yes, Miss Rutland. Captain Bishop and I are due back at the airfield. We have sorties to fly on Tuesday, over the Western Front. There will be a lot of action."

Mata Hari spoke up. "If you're not returning to entertain the troops, Miss Rutland, you could always stay here with me. I could use the company when Vadime is away."

Edward spoke up quickly. "That is kind of you, Mata Hari, but Miss Rutland is going to Paris. She'll be staying at the Hotel Elysee Palace."

Trace shot him a side glance. "I am?"

"Of course, my darling. Don't you remember? We discussed it in some detail driving up here."

"Well, if you change your mind, Miss Rutland, you are welcome to stay with me," Mata Hari said.

With his arm linked in hers, Edward and Trace left the library, strolling down the long hallway that led to their bedroom. Trace remained silent until they entered the bedroom and Edward shut the door behind them. They were very alone, with only the ringing sound of insects outside.

Just as she turned to speak to him, Edward took her shoulders, pulled her into him and kissed her. She felt the stirring sensation of his lips. She nearly relaxed into his arms, but she fought it, pushing him away.

They stood staring, Edward's eager eyes exploring her, she stepping back, her expression cool.

"Is there another bedroom I can stay in, Edward?" she asked.

"No."

"Aren't there plenty of rooms in this house, or chateau, or whatever it is?"

"Yes, but Mata Hari will know, and our lies will be discovered."

"I'll tell her we had a fight."

Edward sighed. "Miss Rutland, I apologize for that kiss...Actually, no, I don't apologize for it—it was quite wonderful—but I apologize for springing it on you like that. I didn't intend to. It's just that I've been wanting to kiss you again, ever since that first time, and the impulse simply took me over."

"I am not going to sleep with you, Edward," Trace said, firmly.

"My, but you are very direct, aren't you, Miss Rutland? It's quite all right, I promise you. I will not compel you to do anything you do not want to do. I will sleep on that couch or settee or whatever it is, and you can have the bed. I assure you that I am an English gentleman."

Trace eyed him suspiciously. "I wonder. Somehow, I doubt that."

Edward held a hand over his heart. "You have my word of honor, Miss Rutland, that I will not make any further advances...that is, unless you ask me to."

"I am very tired, Edward. I just want to sleep."

"Then I will watch over you."

"No, please, just stay on the settee... and sleep."

He gave a little bow. "Yes, Miss Rutland. As you wish."

Trace used the bathroom first, appearing once again in her 21st-century pajamas and a silk robe. She hurriedly climbed into bed and slid under the sheets.

She was fast asleep by the time Edward left the bathroom, turned off the light and crept quietly to the couch. As he lay in darkness, his mind spinning out romantic possibilities, he sat up.

"Miss Rutland, what shall we do tomorrow? We'll have a whole day and night together."

He heard a little tearing snore, and he grinned. "Ah, the lady snores. How wonderfully human she is. And I thought she was all goddess."

As he lay there, feeling, thinking, it took all his willpower not to leave the couch, cross to the bed and slip under the sheets beside Trace. He was sure he could coax her into lovemaking. He'd seen the sparkle of attraction in her eyes. He'd felt her heated desire for him.

From his point of view, Trace Rutland was the most attractive and magnetic woman he had ever met. As he lay there, he began to sense a difference in himself. Since he'd met Trace, a new kind of fear had emerged. As a hard rain began to fall, and flashes of lightning strobed the room, he became freshly aware that he could very well be dead on Tuesday.

It was that cold fear of dying—of leaving the world—that impressed him more than ever. Yes, he could die, never having had the opportunity to get to know Trace, of having a relationship with her.

Yes, he wanted that now. He wanted that very much. He wanted them to laugh and touch and explore, and grow to know each other, to make love and, as crazy and rash as it sounded, perhaps even to marry. It was an irrational thought. He had only just met the girl. What would his father, Sir Alfred Kenyon Bishop, say?

Was it the war that made him feel so boyishly reckless and spontaneous—the fact that he could die at any time? He was not by nature a rash or impulsive man, but the possibility of imminent death does change a man. He'd seen the change in others: Brits, Americans, Australians, French and Canadians. Death is no respecter of men, of class, race or nationalities.

He'd seen so many men shot down in flames, plunge to the earth and die. He had been scared to death countless times, with a sickening stabbing fear, a fear that swelled and pounced and twisted happiness into dark mockery. Live today, tomorrow you're dead, my boy.

But on that stormy night, Edward faced a new kind of fear: a raw, tearing, ice cold fear.

Had Trace appeared at the right time in his life? Or was it all wrong? Had he met the woman of his dreams—this lovely, lively girl he could imagine spending the rest of his life with? The thought thrilled and terrified him.

The vision of a glowing, joyful life with Trace, complete with children and happy old age, seemed both plausible and preposterous. After all, he lived in a daily kind of hell, amidst the near certainty of dying in a bloody war that likely wouldn't end for years. How could he even consider a courtship, a relationship, a marriage? He certainly hadn't given it much thought where Miss Pemberton was concerned.

But with Trace, everything was different. He knew, instinctively, that a life with Trace would be a wonderful, unpredictable and endless adventure. So, what was

"And I'm sure that you're a total romantic. Anyway, I'm not going to Paris to live in a hotel."

"But it's a beautiful hotel, and it will be easier for us to see each other. Don't you see? Vadime and I will be flying near Vittel, not so far from Paris. It's a resort area, but there's an airbase near there. I can get away sometimes and meet you in Paris."

Trace sought to change the subject. "When did you start flying, Edward?"

He placed his hands on his hips. "Are you deliberately trying to change the subject, Trace?"

"Yes, Edward, but I still would like to know."

Resigned, he gave a little shake of his head. "I received my wings in May of this year. I joined the 13th Squadron RFC in France, and I flew reconnaissance missions before I was posted to the 11th Squadron, a fighter unit. There you have it."

"And what kind of airplane do you fly?"

"Does that really interest you, Trace? I don't know any woman who gives a good tinker's damn about what sort of airplane I fly."

"Does Miss Pemberton give a tinker's damn about what airplane you fly?"

"Are you jealous of Miss Pemberton?" Edward asked, a hint of a smile forming. "I hope you are. Please say that you are."

"I'll bet you're not quite as forward with Miss Pemberton as you are with me, Captain Edward Bishop."

"And you would be right. When I am around you, I have great difficulty keeping my eager hands and my thirsty lips off you, Miss Rutland. I will tell you truthfully—though you may not believe me—that I have never felt quite so anxious, nervous and bold around any woman, until now. Until I met you."

"And when you're around Miss Pemberton, Captain Bishop? Do you feel the same about her?"

Edward's features brightened. "Then you are jealous of Miss Pemberton," he concluded with a broad, sunny smile. "How delightful. How splendid."

"You didn't answer my question."

He turned playful, giving her a teasing smile. "And what question was that?" he said, searching the sky. "Now, let me see. Oh yes, what air machine do I fly? That was it, wasn't it?"

"You know it was."

He lowered his gaze on her, a humorous glint in his eye. "Well, if you must know, it's a Nieuport 1, with a Lewis gun mounted on the upper wing."

"Oh, well, a Lewis gun. I'm quite speechless, Captain Bishop, not that I know what a Lewis gun is."

He became animated, acting out his words. "Now picture this, Trace. When you attack an enemy airplane, you must have finesse. You must be tender, yet fully engaged. Do you understand? You see, I, personally, get below and behind the thing, and when it feels just right, I fire my Lewis machine gun, which is a .303 caliber weapon, upward, into the enemy's underside. It is quite effective."

Trace felt the rise of sexual heat. She knew he was being boldly suggestive, but she didn't mind. She found it a delicious turn-on.

Trace thought it ironic that in her entire life, she'd never met a man who excited her with such force, allure and pleasure as Edward did—and right from the start. But she couldn't give into her sexual fantasy, even if she wanted to. Having a sexual fling would surely throw her old and new lives into total chaos. And she still wasn't entirely convinced that what she was experiencing was even real. It was possible that she was trapped in some mesmerizing dream or hallucination, although hourly, this theory was fading.

She still didn't feel balanced or confident or even sane. Fortunately, her rational mind told her that the last thing she needed—at least for now—was to fall into a hot, sexy affair with Captain Edward Bishop, although her body was crying out for it.

And then Edward moved in close to her, and she caught her breath. Was he going to kiss her again? She hoped so.

Edward looked deeply into Trace's eyes, the sunlight bright and bold on her face and hair. He saw a dark-blue rim around her iris, and a blend of pale blue and white rays inside the iris.

He sighed out his words. "My dear Miss Rutland, you do me in, absolutely."

A minute later, he drew back, as if startled. "Are you betrothed to anyone? Not married, I know. But are you betrothed?"

Trace laughed at his formal choice of word. "Betrothed?"

"Yes? Are you? Tell me you're not. Please tell me you are not."

"But you are, Edward... that is, betrothed to Miss Pemberton."

"Not that again," he answered, petulantly, throwing up his hands in frustration. "Why do you keep bringing that woman up?"

"That woman?" Trace said, batting her eyes, mockingly. "Why Edward, Captain Bishop, may I remind you that you are, after all, betrothed to her."

Exasperated, he placed his hands on his hips, looking away toward the distant band of trees. Both he and Trace watched a jittery yellow butterfly flitting across the lawn; a bird skimming the surface of the pond, darting about in hot pursuit.

Edward's expression turned somber. "That bird has good flying skills. He'll get that poor fleeing insect."

Trace moved closer to him. "Don't think of war right now, Edward. Not on this lovely day."

He turned to her, nodding. He lowered his voice to a conspiratorial whisper. "I'm not in love with Miss Pemberton, Trace."

"Then why be betrothed?"

He shrugged a shoulder. "Family. Name. All of that. I know you Americans think it's silly and old-fashioned, but we English have a deep, rich history built on family and titles. Even in politics. Well, you wouldn't understand."

They stood silently under the glowing yellow day. Finally, Edward faced her fully. "Who are you really, Trace, and where did you come from?"

"I told you."

He stared at her earnestly. "Mata Hari didn't invite you here and yet, you were here. I didn't bring you, and yet you were here. If I hadn't vouched for you, what would you have done?"

Trace looked deeply into his worshipping eyes. "I don't know, Edward."

"So, will you tell me who you are, and how you appeared here? Truly?"

It was a bizarre moment. Trace should have felt frightened and worried. Instead, her mind flitted away like a butterfly, and she thought of her friend, Kelly Richards, from college. They had been as close as sisters for a time. Kelly was killed in a car accident during their senior year in college. Her boyfriend, Evan, had been shattered. He came to Trace the following night, a picture of agony and grief. They'd spent the night crying and reminiscing about Kelly, and Trace recalled how much she'd wished that someone loved her as much as Evan had loved Kelly.

As Edward stood there waiting for her answer, her mind was a swirling jumble of past and present—of fleeting faces, fragments of conversations, heightened emotions and childhood memories.

"Trace? Miss Rutland?" Edward asked, bringing her back from the inner world of the far and near past. "Where have you been? You seemed so far away."

Trace smiled, ruefully. "Yes, Edward, I was far away. Can we just walk for a while and not talk?"

They strolled off around the pond.

"You're not going to tell me how you got here, are you?"

"No, Edward, I'm not. At least, not now."

They spent the rest of Sunday in a variety of outdoor activities. First, they found a rowboat and drifted away on the pond, Edward rowing, Trace languishing under one of Mata Hari's pink parasols, feeling very much like a woman in a 19th-century painting. They picnicked on the far green hill, and roamed paths that curved through tunnels of sun-drenched trees. They did some bird watching and wandered in silence, simply enjoying each other's company. They also shared childhood stories, which Trace altered, as needed, to place them before 1900.

That evening, the quartet met for a formal dinner, consuming two bottles of Champagne and two red Burgundies, while Mata Hari shared stories of her many travels and adventures; Vadime spoke sentimentally about his Mother Russia, and Edward waxed poetic about his lovely home in England, Bishop Manor.

Trace had stayed mostly silent, grateful to listen and enjoy Edward's masculine voice and dashing uniform. His eyes often strayed toward her, clearly trying to make a connection, and he had made a connection. Trace was often flushed with pleasure and adrenalized with desire for him. It was a new experience for her to feel such an overwhelming attraction to a man. It made her feel giddy, foolish and contemplative.

They spent another night in the spacious room, apart, but it wasn't easy. In the hallway, outside their room, Edward stopped abruptly, took her by the shoulders and kissed her long and sweet. As she inhaled a cooling breath, he raised his hands in surrender.

"Once we pass through that door, Trace, you have my solemn word as an officer and a British gentleman, that I will not touch or kiss you... that is, as I have said, repeatedly, unless you wish me to do so."

She looked him boldly in the face, feeling both weak and vibrant with passion. "I wish it, Edward, but not here, not now, and not like this. We deserve better... our own private place. Tonight, we keep apart and sleep alone."

He saluted. "I don't like it, but I will obey your direct order. Your wish is my command, fair lady."

The next morning, Mata Hari, Vadime, Edward and Trace left the chateau and descended the grand stairs to the chateau's circular driveway and center fountain, its arching water sparkling, catching the late morning sun. They strolled to Edward's 1914 Saxon Model A Roadster that he'd had shipped in from England. They muttered things in half whispers, as the festivities and the play of love faded into the grim reality of parting. Now, it was a world filled with unease and fleeting smiles.

Edward took Trace's arm and led her away to privacy. Mata Hari and Vadime embraced, their expressions filled with heavy sorrow.

Edward placed both hands on her shoulders, peering deeply into her eyes.

"I don't want to lose you, Trace. Will you be here when I return?"

"When will you return?"

"I don't know. As I said yesterday, a new major offensive is about to begin."

The wind picked up and stirred the trees, and the sharp morning sun glinted off Edward's car, lighting up his hopeful eyes.

"But we must write to each other, Trace. You know we must."

She nodded.

It was disheartening and confusing to be without answers, Trace thought, as she studied Edward's solemn face. Was Edward a phantom—a fleeting face—a passing dream? Was he leaving her for the last time? He was going off to war, to fly in one of those rickety little airplanes that she'd seen in old photos—those small fragile flying machines that looked like unwieldy toys a kid glues together, and then breaks when he's angry. How could anyone fly in them, much less survive, weaving and diving bullets in aerial combat?

She was startled by a sudden grinding feeling of dread and despair. She'd only met Edward, but there was already a strange invisible bond between them. She'd felt it at his first kiss. Now, she might never see him again.

Who knew what the next days would bring? Who knew if she might suddenly return to her own time in a day or two, and be standing in Cyrano's library, struggling to make sense of what had happened to her?

"I have left some money for you, Trace," Edward said, quietly. "I placed it in the pocket of that very impressive silk robe of yours. Buy yourself some clothes, shoes, makeup and whatever else you need. If you need more money before I return, ask Mata Hari. I'll pay her back."

Trace's eyes misted with tears. She looked at him earnestly. "Edward... please come back. Don't take any chances and don't try to be a hero."

Her words pleased him, and he smiled warmly. "What a splendid thing to say. What a lovely and wonderful thing to say, Trace. Yes, I will come back, and when I do, I will kiss you for hours at a time."

"What a romantic you are, Edward. Guys like you don't exist in my time."

He turned serious. "And what time is that?"

She was silent. He leaned in and kissed her, his lips sensual and warm, and as he kept his lips pressed to hers, he ran a hand through her thick, luscious hair. Trace was soon lost in a hazy daydream of pure pleasure, wishing they had the time to make love. Her body suddenly ached for him.

"You must write to me, Trace. Promise?"

"I already promised."

"You have the address I gave you?"

"Yes, Edward. I have it, and I will write to you."

"And if you leave, you will tell me where you go so I can write to you?"

Trace nodded. "Yes, Edward, as soon as I find a place, I'll send you the address."

As the Roadster growled away, Mata Hari and Trace waved, both downcast, watching the car fade into a small speck in the shimmer of sunlight. Silence surrounded the chateau and grew loud with birdsong and the gurgling fountain. Where there should have been peace in the soft afternoon air, Trace felt conflict and confusion.

Mata Hari clasped her hands together, as if closing the chapter. "Well now, Miss Rutland. We must prepare for the Marquis de Beaufort. He will be here this evening."

Trace turned to her, surprised at the abrupt change. "He's coming here? Tonight?"

"Why yes, this is his chateau, after all."

"How long will he stay?"

"Oh, two or three days. He is an old lover, who still likes me in his bed. He's quite virile, although not as strong as he once was, of course. But he has lots of money."

Trace tried not to show her astonishment. Instead, she looked at Mata Hari with quiet eyes, trying to read the woman, straining to understand why she, Trace, was here.

In that brief silence, Trace felt a shift going on inside, like tiny stabs of awakening agitation. An image of Juana-Luisa, Nonnie, slowly took shape in her mind, and Trace suddenly yearned to find the girl. In her nightmares, Trace had felt the nagging guilt for not visiting her daughter. As Mata Hari, it had been one of her last memories just before the bullets ripped into her body.

Before she'd arrived in 1916, Trace had searched online and found a photo of Nonnie's tombstone, with the inscription Onze Non (Our Non) and the dates May 2, 1898—August 10, 1919. Trace had felt crucified as she'd stared at that computer screen.

As Trace followed Mata Hari up the steps, she asked, "Mata Hari, do you know where your daughter is?"

Mata Hari whirled about, eyes wide, face pinched in suspicion. "How do you know about Non, my Nonnie?"

Trace was ready with a planned answer. "Edward told me about her. She sounds like a lovely girl."

Mata Hari's eyes lowered as she swallowed away something, and Trace knew exactly what it was: she was trying to swallow away guilt.

Mata Hari's voice was low and sad. "Non is 18 now. She was born in Indonesia, you know, and yes, she is a lovely girl and a very smart girl. She did very well in school. I had legal custody of Non, and my ex-husband was required to pay child support. He never did. She was living with my relatives at the time. I was trying to make money, so she could come and live with me. Once, when her father was visiting, he just took her, and did not give her back."

Mata Hari's eyes teared up. "I did not have access to the resources necessary to get her back, so I had to accept it. About two years ago, I desperately wanted to see my daughter again. I wrote a letter to my ex-husband, requesting a meeting." She paused, lifting her chin. "I am famous, you know," she said, with pride. "My face is on packages of cigarettes, and on the cans of Dutch biscuits. My face is on so many things."

Mata Hari stared down, and some of her pride melted away into gloomy reflection. "Perhaps I am too famous, in all the wrong ways. I was told that Juana-Luisa had grown tall and beautiful, and some say she resembles me."

Mata Hari shrugged. "MacLeod, my husband, seemed open to my seeing my dear sweet little Non, but it never happened, even at a time months ago when we were both living in The Hague. I don't know why. I just can't remember why I didn't see her then."

Trace remained silent for a minute. "I would love to meet her."

"Meet her?" Mata Hari said, sharply. "You will never meet her."

"Is she still living in The Hague?"

Mata waved a hand to end the conversation, turned and started up the stairs to the front door that was promptly opened by a servant. Mata Hari pivoted. "She lives in De Steeg, and I shall never see her again."

And then Mata Hari strutted off inside, head held high.

Trace clenched her jaw in determination. Maybe Mata Hari would never see her Non again, but Trace certainly would. She only hoped that Edward had left her enough money to travel.

And then another jarring thought rattled her. If she did meet Non, would she also have to meet Rudolf MacLeod, Mata Hari's ex-husband—Trace's ex-husband? She shivered, recalling him from her research, and from her dreams. Would she remember him? How would he respond to her? Would he know her?

Trace turned back to face the arching water of the fountain. In order to travel to The Hague and then on to De Steeg, she would surely need a passport or travel papers. Could Mata Hari help her with that?

Trace was suddenly filled with excitement and purpose. It was time to make a move—time to change her past for the better, forever.

CHAPTER 12

On Wednesday, July 2, 1916, Captain Bishop and Captain Masloff were in their cockpits, ready to fly another sortie against the Germans. Since they'd already flown six that day, they were tired and their nerves on edge. The Battle of the Somme had begun the day before. It was intended to help accelerate a victory for the Allies—the British and the French—against the Germans. By the end of the first day, 21,000 British and 8,000 Germans were dead. Many French would die in the months that followed.

Edward and Vadime had been badly shaken that first day, seeing so many of their friends go down in flames. New, inexperienced pilots arrived for breakfast, and Edward and Vadime wondered how many would be dead before dinner. They were both fighting fear, dread and depression.

On that bright Wednesday afternoon, Edward sat in the open cockpit of his Nieuport 11. He was positioned just behind and below the upper wing of the biplane's wings, a machine gun fitted in the center of the upper wing.

A mechanic, with great hoops of sweat under the armpits of his gray coveralls, stood by Edward's two-blade propeller, gripping it, waiting for the pilot's command. When Edward displayed thumbs up, the mechanic gave the propeller a downward thrust. The 80-horsepower piston engine sputtered, coughed and shuddered to life, gray puffs of smoke billowing away.

Captain Vladimir Masloff was seated in the airplane to Edward's left. His mechanic also turned a crank, sparking all the plugs. As the first pistons fired, the propeller slowly whirled and roared to life. The mechanics of both planes quickly yanked away the two-wheel chocks and backed away, out of the prop wash.

Moments later, their planes and eight other Nieuports bounced across the shimmering grass, ready for takeoff. Edward was dressed in sheep-skin high boots, warm pants, a white shirt, a leather coat and a motorcycle cap and goggles. He was wedged into the cockpit, hand on the control stick, running his water-cooled engine up for the usual two or three minutes.

Then he wrapped and tied his white scarf around his neck, flinging back its flapping tail. Edward wore the scarf for two reasons: his engine was prone to leak oil that could splatter on him, and rain and fog could accumulate, so his goggles had to be wiped clean.

Despite his fatigue, he grinned broadly at Vadime, more to bolster his courage than for dramatic flair, and enthusiastically returned Vadime's thumbs up.

They were off on another sortie to meet the Germans. Edward turned his airplane into the wind and opened up the throttle. The plane crept forward, slowly, gathering speed, engine growling. Vadime was beside him, his face grim and determined. He also wore a leather cap and goggles.

To his relief, Edward could feel the roar of the engine pulling itself forward across the grassy field, every rib, strut and wire vibrating in unison. As the engine bit into the air, grass rippling in his engine wash, Edward was confident the mechanics had done a thorough job preparing his machine for yet another battle.

Edward met the lift of the plane with the gentle pressure of the joystick, and he raced down the field with Vadime close behind. The plane left the ground, dropped, bounced, surged up again and lifted over the tops of trees into the hazy, afternoon sky. At 500 feet, the ten biplanes gathered into formation and started toward the front lines, about 20 miles away.

The planes sailed over patchwork fields and farms, and the jagged rows of meandering trenches, where British soldiers lay crouched, tensed and waiting for the whistle blow to signal it was time to break from the trenches and charge the Germans, who waited in their opposing trenches with rifles, hand grenades and machine guns, aimed and ready. There would be much death and suffering, only minutes away.

The formation of biplanes slowly gained altitude, finally reaching 15,000 feet. As the squadron flew with about 20 to 30 yards between each airplane, Edward's head was in constant motion, searching for the black specks that were enemy fighters. His plane swayed and danced in the gusting currents as he glanced over at Vadime and set the throttle, making sure he was in position for the attack.

Vadime lifted a hand and grinned, signaling he was ready for battle.

Ideally, Edward and the squadron wanted to be flying above the enemy, but nearly always, the German fighter planes were better machines and their pilots easily maneuvered them above, allowing them to attack in the glare of the sun.

Edward's plane, made of wood, wireframes and fabric, felt good under his control, his engine chewing up the air, his white scarf snapping in the cold, rushing wind.

Again, he glanced up and down, searching the sky for enemy planes. It took long practice and constant watchfulness to guard against a surprise air attack that could come from any point in the sky.

Edward suddenly jerked erect. There they were, ten or twelve black specks about two o'clock high, diving down on the Nieuports from out of the sun.

Edward waved at Vadime and pointed at the attacking enemy. He'd seen them too. Both pilots reacted fast. Edward banked left and dived, as two German Triplanes, one a yellow Fokker, the other a red Albatross, raced after him.

As the yellow Fokker closed in on him, Edward heard a burst of machine gun fire. He fell into a practiced maneuver, flying in a zig-zag course, making it hard for his enemy to shoot accurately. Edward felt the bullets whizz by his head and shoulders as he weaved and dipped, struggling to escape.

As a last resort, he pushed his airplane into a sharp dive—gaining speed—eighty-five, ninety, ninety-five. A hundred and five. It was now or never. Edward opened the throttle. Nothing happened. He cursed, shut it, opened it again. Finally, a sputter. A cough. The plane was screaming and vibrating like crazy.

Would he be able to pull up? Uttering a silent prayer, he yanked back on his control stick. He broke the dive and shot up, wind rushing by, his breath coming fast. Had he shaken off the yellow triplane? Edward swiveled around with wild triumph, watching as his yellow adversary fell away, already closing in on another target.

Edward had barely survived the attack and the dive, and despite the frigid air, he was sweating, his heart kicking in his chest.

After gathering himself, Edward found a German Albatross—a bold black cross painted on the side of its fuselage. He dived, zooming in after it. As the distance between them narrowed, the plane grew large in Edward's sights. The German pilot must have seen Edward's approach. He began to circle, ten times to the left, ten to the right. Edward and the German danced, dived, swayed, struggling to get behind and above the other. Edward realized his opponent was no beginner. This was a skilled and experienced pilot, maybe even a German Ace, with many kills.

The sky became filled with airplanes in a free-for-all, life-and-death struggle, all diving and twisting, picking targets and firing 30 or 40 rounds in quick, lethal bursts. Every pilot was taut and alert, twisting around to ensure no one was on his tail, lining up to fire at him as he fired at the airplane in his sites. There was no time to focus. It was just snap shooting—a burst here—dive away, check your rear, find another veering, weaving target, fire another burst. Run. Dive.

All the flying formations soon fell into chaos, as planes dived and wheeled, as pilots fought for their lives. Planes approached head-on, guns blazing, planes diving on the tails, both sides locked in mortal combat. Edward watched an Albatross chasing a Nieuport. A quick burst from the enemy punctured the Nieuport's gasoline tanks. The plane burst into flames, shot up, corkscrewed away and then plunged to the Earth. Edward felt an icy terror. Was that Vadime? Edward had no time to think. Two Germans were lining up on his tail. Edward threw his plane into a dive, as bullets zipped past his head, chewing into the fabric of his left wing. Still they pursued him, guns blazing.

He knew it often took only five or six rounds to down an enemy aircraft, so he took evasive action and hoped a bullet didn't find him. He craned his neck, desperate to escape his pursuers. Battle was raging all around him and planes were taking hits, pilots killed, slumped over in their cockpits, their planes trailing smoke, tumbling from the sky.

Edward banked right and left, his eyes wide, the cold air rushing past his face. And then, as luck would have it, he spotted a heavy band of clouds just ahead. Still taking evasive action, he fled toward the clouds. Another burst of bullets ripped into his right wing, just as he entered the thick foggy protection of a cloud. Gulping in breath to cool his frayed, burning nerves, he grabbed the tail of his white scarf and desperately wiped his goggles clear. Lost in a white cotton world of peace, he heaved out a heavy sigh of relief.

Where had all those German planes come from? The British and French were greatly outnumbered—at least two-to-one. He continued to take in gulps of air to calm himself, to gather himself, to stop his throbbing fear.

Moments later, Edward broke through the clouds to the other side and blue sky returned. He twisted about, searching the skies. He'd lost the Germans, but as he gazed down and below, he saw that the battle was still raging on. He peeled off left, dropped to 3,000 feet and started back to join the fight.

The dogfight lasted 20 more minutes. Edward fought on at 300 and 400 feet until his ammunition was low, and his gun jammed. He searched for Vadime, and when he didn't find him, he darted back up into the sky and ran for home.

Back at the airfield, he landed, taxied to a stop and cut his engine. Still shaking, he pushed out of the cockpit. When his mechanic hurried over, Edward jumped to the ground, peeling off his flying cap and goggles.

"Have you seen Captain Masloff? Did he make it back?"

The mechanic's expression was grave. "Captain Masloff crashed about a mile away. Rescue left about ten minutes ago. I don't know any more than that."

"Which way?"

The mechanic pointed left. "As far as I can tell, he went down just over the trees near that farm we pass when we drive back from the pub."

With his legs still shaking and his face slick with sweat, Edward bolted for his car, vaulted in and cranked the engine. He unraveled the white scarf from his neck, flung it into the back seat, and sped away into a cloud of dust.

CHAPTER 13

On Thursday afternoon, July 3, a telegram arrived at the Chateau Beaufort. Fabrice, the very upright butler with salt and pepper hair and a slight limp, delivered it to Mata Hari, who was languishing on a pink settee, reading a newspaper and sipping a glass of Champagne from a crystal flute.

She looked at Fabrice with a sudden, watchful anxiety. Hesitating, she finally lifted the telegram from the offered silver tray, reached for the gold letter opener, also on the tray, and sliced the envelope flap open. After a bracing pause, Mata Hari drew out the telegram and read it.

Outside, Trace was wandering along the stone pathways that led between thick trimmed hedges and flowering gardens. At the fish pond, she placed her hands behind her back and watched the orange and silverfish slither under lily pads and disappear into the shadowy depths.

She sat on a white marble bench, presenting her face to the sky, her eyes closed against the warming sun. She was fatigued and emotionally weary. Being on overload for days was taking its toll, as were the constant psychological and emotional shifts from present to past.

As Trace sat there resting, feeling the soft silky wind moving across her face, hearing glorious birdsong, she was comforted by the peace of it all, and by the gurgling sounds of nearby fountains. The air was cleaner in this time, there was no doubt about that. She'd noticed that from the beginning, while she took her first walk with Edward. The air was alive and caressing, the distant horizons so wonderfully in focus, the colors vibrant and exhilarating.

And she had also noticed that flowers smelled sweeter, food tasted fresher, the butter and bread seemed to sing with flavor, and the fruit exploded into ripe sweetness at the first bite. The coffee was dark and rich, without acidity, and the wine was simply the best she'd ever tasted.

Granted, Mata Hari demanded the most expensive clothes, food and wine, but even at that, Trace had noticed a dramatic difference. Despite the violence of war and the same volatile human emotions that plagued her time, the air, the food and the water were less damaged and polluted. The earth seemed healthier.

As Trace sat on the bench and experienced that simple peace, some of the cobwebs of her mind cleared and she was able to focus. The silence was heavenly—being far from the constant monitoring of her cell phone, the 24-hour bombarding news cycle, and all the cacophony of 21st century sounds assaulting her ears.

Inevitably, her mind returned to her problems. What was the way forward? Mata Hari had been good to her, and very generous. She had supplied her with clothes, shoes and jewelry and, on Trace's behalf, she had appealed to the Marquis for a passport for Trace. The Marquis, a portly, florid-faced man with a waxed white mustache, bushy eyebrows and a very bald head, had looked Trace over with obvious lusty pleasure, and then readily nodded his consent.

"I dare say, we can come up with something for the lovely girl," he said.

He turned to Mata Hari, took her hand and kissed it. "How can I deny you anything, my dear Mata Hari, when you bring such extraordinary beauty and passion to my lovely chateau? Of course, I will do all I can to help this beautiful creature procure a passport. I have some influence at the American Embassy, and I am a friend of the Ambassador, Mr. William Graves Sharp. Why, only two weeks ago, I attended a dinner where he was in attendance. Yes, I'll see what I can do."

He turned back to Trace with an ingratiating smile. "You will have to go to Paris, to the American Embassy, but I think I can safely say we can arrange a passport for you. It may take time, of course. Nothing in France is hurried, especially these days, during this war."

Trace had felt encouraged, but also skeptical that the Marquis really had so much influence. After all, in this time, Trace had no past, no birth certificate and no relatives, at least none that she was aware of.

That same night, after dinner, and after the Marquis had retired to Mata Hari's bed, no doubt waiting anxiously for her to join him, the two women sat alone in candlelight. Mata Hari waited until the fruit tart was served and the coffee poured before she lifted her serious eyes, narrowing them on Trace.

"Are you spying for the Americans, Trace?"

Trace had just sipped coffee from her flowered dem-itasse cup. Stunned, she nearly spit it out.

"What?"

"You can tell me. It will be our secret."

"No...No, of course, I'm not a spy."

"Then what happened to your passport? Why do you need to get another?"

"I told you. I lost it someplace when I was perform-ing near the front."

"And I don't believe you. You just happened to meet up with Edward in Paris at some bistro? No, I don't think so. I saw how he stumbled and fumbled out his answer that first night. He was trying to cover for you and we both know it. I saw that frightened look in your eyes. I also saw him fall instantly in love with you—a first sight love. No, Edward had never seen you before, but you instantly captured his heart and, I dare say, his loins. I'm a lot of things, Trace, but I am not a fool. I have traveled all over Europe and have been with many men. I know all the looks of fear, the looks of lust, and the many looks of love. Edward had defi-nitely never seen you before."

Mata Hari tapped the ends of her fingers together, her eyes fixed on Trace. "So, that brings me to my next question. How did you get into this chateau, why were you dressed in that odd, erotic ensemble, and why didn't you have a trunk or any clothes?"

Trace frantically searched for a plausible answer. No words came.

Mata Hari waited, fingers tapping. Finally, she reached for her demitasse. She took a dainty sip, two fingers shining with jeweled rings, not allowing her eyes to stray from Trace's worried face.

"Did the Marquis' son bring you here? I know it wasn't the Marquis himself. He didn't recognize you either."

Trace was trapped. She couldn't tell the truth, and she didn't want to tell more lies. Mata Hari was sharply perceptive and intelligent, and although Trace was a good actress, she had to come up with some plausible answer, one that Mata Hari would believe.

"Something happened to me, Mata Hari. I don't know what. That morning...when I arrived, I woke up on the back lawn, near the flower garden. I don't know how I got there. I don't remember how I got here."

Mata Hari considered this, with some skepticism. "What is the last thing you remember?"

"Being somewhere in France, near a battlefield in my tent, trying to fall asleep."

Mata Hari shook her head, took another sip of her coffee and looked away.

When she faced Trace again, her jaw was fixed. "Then where did you get my ring? Tell me that. How was it that you were wearing my emerald ring?"

Trace was flummoxed. Her mind raced for an answer, and she could only come up with a flimsy one. "I found it lying on that white, marble-top pedestal table. The one near the piano. When I entered the room, sunlight flashed on it and it drew my attention."

Not satisfied, Mata Hari searched Trace's face. "That ring was in its proper silver jewelry case in my bedroom. I had not worn it in weeks. Your explanation makes absolutely no sense at all. In fact, what you say and who you are make no sense."

Trace offered only a weak smile.

"I don't know what to think of you, Trace. I have to say that you are the strangest woman I have ever met. You just seem to have dropped in from thin air. And you are different somehow. I can't quite put it all together, but you seem both familiar and yet distant and frightening to me. Half of me wants to throw you out, and the other half of me wants you to stay. I'm just not sure I can trust you, and trust is a much-needed commodity during this dreadful war."

"You can trust me," Trace said. "Please believe that. You can trust me."

As they returned to their dessert, Trace knew that Mata Hari wasn't convinced.

Back on the marble bench with the afternoon sun on her face, and a chorus of birds in the nearby trees serenading her, Trace wasn't surprised when Mata Hari approached, her footfalls striking the stone path in quick, surging steps, disturbing the peaceful afternoon.

Trace already knew what had happened. Captain Masloff had been wounded. She'd read about it before she'd arrived in the past. She'd also had vague memories and dreams about Vadime Masloff. There were many things about Mata Hari, her family and friends, and her life that Trace couldn't recall, although she sensed that all those memories existed just below the surface of her conscious mind.

So here and now, Trace would have to pretend to be shocked and surprised, and she would have to offer comfort, which of course she wanted to do. But there was more. What about Edward? Had he been injured or killed?

Trace shot up, seeing the alarm on Mata Hari's face, as she stood before her, the telegram still clutched in her trembling hand.

In the bright sunlight, Trace could see the age lines forming around Mata Hari's eyes. She could see the first unavoidable signs of sagging skin forming on her face and neck. Trace could clearly see that Mata Hari's indulgent lifestyle had taken its toll. She was no longer that young, exotic beauty. In this light, Trace saw a woman growing old before her time, and even the expert makeup job and the expensive clothes couldn't mask it. Mata Hari appeared older than her 40 years, and she surely knew it. How much longer could she live off the riches of men, who would pay her handsomely to be their mistress, when there were so many young and beautiful women to choose from, even if they weren't as famous as Mata Hari?

In Trace's time, of course, a bit of Botox or Juvéderm would have helped Mata Hari smooth out her wrinkles or plump out her face. But that world—the world of the future that had been her world—was now a dream world. This time—this world—was now Trace's world. This was the real world.

Traces shuddered. How utterly frightening it was to be trapped in the agonizing prison of this time, seeing a deteriorating image of herself from a life lived so long ago. No wonder people couldn't, and shouldn't, remember their past lives.

Again, the urgent questions arose. How could Trace save her past self, and yet stop what was meant to be? And if she couldn't change history and stop the inevitable—the very things that caused those terrible nightmares in the future—then why the hell was she here?

Again, Trace heard a still small voice deep in the secrets of her mind: "Nonnie. You must go see your daughter, Nonnie."

Trace looked at Mata Hari with the soft eyes of compassion. "What has happened?"

"Miss Rutland. Trace. Vadime has been shot down. He's badly injured. He has lost sight in both eyes. He's in a hospital in Vittel. I must go to him. Will you come with me?"

"I'm so sorry, Mata Hari. So very sorry. Is there any news from Edward?"

Mata Hari held up the telegram. "This is from Edward. He said Vadime barely escaped death. He wants you to come with me. His airfield is not so far from the hospital. Will you come, Trace?"

Trace stared into the distance, her thoughts tangling. She'd known this urgent moment would take place, and she'd agonized about it ever since she'd arrived in this time.

Trace knew that Mata Hari, as a civilian of a neutral country, the Netherlands, would not be allowed near the battlefield to see Vadime. Her repeated requests to the French authorities would be persistently denied until she met with the French Secret Service and agreed to become a spy.

This one meeting—this event—would be the beginning of the end for Mata Hari. It would eventually lead to her death by firing squad on October 15, 1917.

"I don't think you should go," Trace blurted out.

Mata Hari stared incredulous. "What are you saying? I must go. Of course, I simply must go see Vadime. And don't you want to see Edward?"

"They won't let you see Captain Masloff."

"Who?"

"The French. You're from a neutral country."

"Then I'll get papers. I have contacts. They'll help me."

Trace shook her head, firmly. "No, Mata Hari."

"I don't understand you. What kind of a woman are you? I love Vadime. He needs me. Especially now, he needs me. He must be scared, and in pain. He'll need care and money. The Marquis gave me 3,000 francs. I asked for more, but he said times were difficult. So, I'll use some of that money to see that Vadime gets the very best of care."

Trace saw that it was useless, so she tried another approach. "Why don't I go for you? I'm sure Edward can help me get papers. His family is influential, and nobody knows me. I'm sure I could get to Vadime and help him. You can stay here—or even better—you could go to the Netherlands and, when Vadime is better, I'll bring him to you."

Mata Hari's mouth tightened, and her wary eyes looked Trace up and down with new suspicion. "What are you up to, Miss Rutland? What dangerous game are you playing?"

"Mata Hari, I'm just trying to protect you."

"Protect me from what? I'm Mata Hari. I'm known all over Europe. I have connections and contacts. I know military officers and public officials. They will help me. I have influence with these men. Many have been my lovers."

Trace saw the pride rise in Mata Hari's face as she straightened, lifting her imperious chin.

Mata Hari continued. "The officers all adore me. I have always said that an officer is another being, a sort of artist, living outdoors with sparkles on his arms, and in a seductive uniform. I have had many lovers, but it is the beautiful officers I love—brave men, ready for battle, always sweet and gallant. For me, the officer forms a race apart. I have never truly loved any but officers. Those officers will come to my aid now, Trace, you can be sure of it, especially when they see that I am out to help one of their own."

Trace felt desperation rise. Should she tell Mata Hari the truth? Was this the time for that? Was it now or never? Would she listen and believe? Trace had to try. She must. What did she have to lose? If she didn't try, history would play itself out again.

Trace bolstered her confidence with a lift of her chin. "Mata Hari, before the war, you performed several times before Crown Prince Wilhelm, eldest son of Kaiser Wilhelm II, who is now a senior German general on the Western Front." Mata Hari narrowed her eyes but stayed silent.

Trace breathed in uncertainty and nerves. "Mata Hari, the French will probably want you to spy on Prince Wilhelm in return for being allowed to see Vadime. Please refuse them. Please. It will be a trap that could lead to your death. You will meet a French Army Captain named Georges Ladoux. He is an expert in counter-espionage. When you apply for traveling permission as a neutral Dutch national and a Francophile, Ladoux will propose that you spy for France against Germany—that is, try to get information from Prince Wilhelm. Once you agree, Ladoux will allow you to visit Captain Masloff. You may be tempted to do this because you need money for the long-term medical care of Vadime, but please, resist the temptation. Don't do it."

Trace bored her eyes into Mata Hari. "Listen to me. Refuse to spy for France. Tell Ladoux no. Please."

Mata Hari's stare turned to ice. Her body went rigid. "So, you are a spy after all, Miss Rutland. I knew it. Now it all makes sense. How you got here, and all the other secrets."

Trace opened her mouth to protest, but Mata Hari held up the flat of her hand to stop her.

"Not another word, Miss Rutland. I don't know what side you're working for or what you're after, but I want you out of here just as soon as you can leave. I want no part of this. I am an artist and a performer, and I want no part of this twisted political business."

Trace ducked her head, resigned, defeated.

Mata Hari pivoted and strolled off aggressively down the pathway, leaving Trace in half shadow and half sunlight.

CHAPTER 14

Two days later, on a warm and cloudy summer afternoon, Trace arrived in Paris in a crowded train car. Outside, she found a cab, a black sputtering Renault, and she sat high on the back seat as it bumped along the cobbled streets toward 12, rue Vieille-du-Temple. She passed horse-drawn carriages and crowded canopied cafés spilling out onto the streets. Watchful policemen were mounted on magnificent horses, merging with the traffic. Trace took it all in with a startling wonder, as if she were watching an old colorized movie on the History Channel. It was magnificent and grand to see the soaring Paris monuments, the ornate architecture, the glorious arching fountains, and the well-dressed ladies strolling in aloof elegance, each in fine clothes, with no signs of the loose, casual attire of her time.

She watched the rambling, downcast soldiers, some on crutches, some with only one arm or one leg, evidence of the terrible war that was being fought only miles away. Her thoughts turned to Edward, and she wished she could call, text or email him. In the telegram he'd sent to Mata Hari about Vadime, he'd only given Trace a passing hello. Maybe he'd already cooled toward her.

Trace stared out the open window, thinking it would be comforting to see a familiar face in the strolling crowds. In this time and place, she did not know another living soul, other than Mata Hari, the Marquis, Vadime and Edward. It gave her a desperately lonely feeling to know she had no parents or friends, no one she could call or write; no one to trust for help, except perhaps Edward.

Fortunately, the Marquis had given her a letter of introduction and recommendation. Surely that would help her acquire a passport and thereby establish a legal identity in this time.

Trace stared, alert and curious, as men in dark suits and mustaches pranced about the streets, smoking cigars or cigarettes, pausing to purchase a newspaper at a corner kiosk, or to lift a boot onto a bootblack's carpet-covered box, allowing the shoeshine boy to go to work.

Trace had been forced to leave the chateau without the ring—the Mata Hari ring. Though she'd crept into Mata Hari's spacious room and searched for it when Mata Hari was out with the Marquis on a country drive, Trace couldn't find it. There had been so many trunks, and jewelry boxes, and letterboxes and hat boxes. She'd searched the chest of drawers, the closets, and the bathroom, but had come up empty.

Mata Hari could have put the ring anywhere. Not finding the ring meant that Trace was marooned in this time, with no hope of returning to her own time, to her own life. Trace felt like the loneliest girl in the world.

Mata Hari had not come to Trace's room to say goodbye, although the day before, she had graciously helped Trace pack a trunk with dresses, shoes, makeup and jewelry. When Trace had asked about Paris hotels, Mata Hari had quietly written down three reasonably priced ones. Trace had chosen The Hotel Caron de Beaumarchais because it was close to Notre-Dame, the Ile Saint Louis and the banks of the Seine. Boutiques and restaurants were also nearby, as were newspaper kiosks.

Trace checked into the 18th-century style hotel, with its spacious marble lobby, fine French style furniture, and center fountain featuring a gilded Diana the Huntress at the summit, her bow and arrow poised and ready to shoot.

Trace's hotel room, if not large, was elegant, with a square bedroom, clean bathroom and little living room. The windows had bronze draperies tied back with tasseled swags, and looked out on the street below, to a bakery, a boutique and a café. Trace raised a window to allow a refreshing breeze in to cool the stuffy rooms, but she wished there was an air-conditioner to turn on.

In the next few days, she would have to venture out to find cheaper lodgings, but for now, the hotel would provide her a sense of safety and comfort, which she badly needed. She would also need to find a job. Unlike Mata Hari, Trace did not want to be a "kept" woman, even though she was sure Edward would continue to give her money if she needed it, especially now that she was in Paris, where he'd wanted her to be.

After she'd settled in, she opened her trunk and arranged her dresses in the closet, and then stored her makeup and toiletries in the bathroom. Minutes later she was sitting at the ornately carved writing desk. She took a piece of cream colored hotel stationery from the desk drawer, and a brushed gold fountain pen, and started a letter to Edward. She decided to alter her normal, more casual writing style, and use a more formal style, more appropriate to this time. Having not written a letter by hand in years, Trace took her time, forming the letters with care and with a bit of a flourish.

Saturday, July 5th, 1916

Dear Edward:

I hope this letter finds you safe and well. I was so sorry to hear about Captain Masloff. I do hope he is recovering from his injuries. I am also hoping that you are not taking any unnecessary risks.

Forgive me for not writing to you before now. I have been confused and fatigued. Perhaps someday, I will be able to tell you the truth about how I came to the chateau. I hope, in time, we will be able to get to know each other and trust each other. I did enjoy spending time with you, Edward.

Mata Hari received your telegram and, as I'm sure you expected, she is leaving the chateau tomorrow morning and coming to Paris to stay at the Grand Hotel. Once settled, she hopes to get the necessary papers or traveling approval from the French military authorities, so she can visit Captain Masloff in Vittel. I don't think it will be easy for her since she is from a neutral country, and I hear the French are very strict about that kind of thing, but she is determined.

As you can see from the letterhead, I am in Paris, staying at The Hotel Caron de Beaumarchais. Since Mata Hari was leaving for Paris and then Vittel, I thought it best for me to leave as well. If you wrote me a letter addressed to the chateau, I probably will not receive it for some weeks. I do not plan to return to the chateau, nor do I believe Mata Hari will return. I did tell the butler, Fabrice, to forward all letters to me here at the hotel. I hope he will do so. Even if I move from here—which I intend to do as soon as I find more affordable lodgings—the front desk said they would hold my mail for a time, since I told them the letters will be coming from a soldier, who is fighting on the Front. They were very kind and reassuring.

I am also writing because I was hoping you would be granted a leave in the near future. Do you envision such a leave anytime soon? I would love to see Paris with you. I would love to spend more time with you, so do take care of yourself and come to Paris when you can. When I move, I will send you my new address.

Until then, Edward, I am sending you a kiss and many prayers that God will protect you as you fly over the Western Front.

Trace

Outside on the warm Paris streets, Trace felt out of place and vulnerable, like a stranger at a fancy vintage dress party. Everything and every person was strange and utterly captivating: the old cars with their squeaky horns; the ladies in long satin and chiffon dresses and elegant hats; the men sauntering in suits and ties, despite the heat, wearing various hat styles, from bowlers to fedoras to derby tweed flat caps.

The world of 1916 was distinctively different from her own time in countless ways. The people had a distinctive bearing—more erect and less casual, as if they took pride in the style and color of their clothes. Besides the obvious distinction of language and dress, there seemed a more patient resignation to time. Traffic moved more slowly, and there wasn't the intrusion of jet airplanes overhead, or the thumping, chopping blades of helicopters, or the humming sounds of generators and air-conditioners.

Trace strolled along the edge of the Seine, taking in the stately Notre-Dame-de-Paris Cathedral rising in the distance. She ambled past painters wearing berets, watched lovers on benches holding hands, some locked in an embrace, and smiled at shabbily dressed kids as they waved to the boats on the river. Had Paris changed much in over a hundred years?

Trace recalled a time in the future—2015—when she'd traveled to Paris with a girlfriend for a quick four-day vacation. Although many of the landmarks were the same, and her walk along the Seine at that time had been similar, this 1916 Paris was a world apart. It was more romantic in many ways, more formal and rustic to be sure, with nearly all the men smoking, the streets and sidewalks littered with cigarette butts, and the ever-present scent of bread, flowers and horse manure. And yet, even in this time of war, it was easy to see that Paris was a vibrant city bustling with life, art and pleasure.

Trace knew, from her reading of history, that it would all change in just a few short months, as the war intensified.

At war's end in 1919, signs of the Great War's impact would be everywhere. There would be an influx of desperate refugees fleeing the devastated regions in the north. There would be piles of rubble and boarded-up windows where German bombs had fallen, along with a gaping crater in the Tuileries rose garden. Along the Grand Boulevards, the rows of chestnuts would have gaps where trees had been cut for firewood.

And as Trace paused to take in the Cathedral of Notre-Dame, she knew it wouldn't be long before the great windows would be missing, their stained glass stored for safety and, in their place, pale yellow panes would wash the interior with a strange, eerie light.

Trace knew that even now, there were shortages of coal, milk, and bread, and that that would only increase. Trace had seen photos of flags of victory fluttering from the lampposts and windows, and she'd seen heart-wrenching photos of limbless men and discharged soldiers in frayed old army uniforms, begging for change on street corners.

The Paris women would put away their pretty clothes and, instead, they'd wear the dark clothes of mourning, because nearly all of them would have lost a son, a father, a husband or a brother.

Trace felt her spirits deflate, and her shoulders sagged. This was the price of knowing the future and being helpless to do anything to change it, short of something radical, like plotting someone's death, which Trace could never do.

Which brought her to her next thought. How could she travel to the Netherlands to see Nonnie? She'd have to find a way to get a passport.

Her unsteady thoughts shifted again—to Edward. As she wandered back toward the hotel, she saw an elderly woman pass, plodding along with a cane and a slight limp. She gave Trace a sweet, worried smile, as if she could read Trace's thoughts. Trace nodded and smiled back, wondering if Edward would survive the war, and as the sun broke through the clouds, Trace realized she missed Edward. She missed him a lot, and as she walked the busy streets, she wondered if he was right when he'd suggested that they had known each other in some past life. In some ways, it sounded possible. She had felt an immediate connection to him—a startling attraction, as if they were old lovers being united after a long absence. Before her time travel adventure, she would have thought the whole thing a New Age notion. Now, she wasn't so sure. Now, she wasn't so sure about anything. A quote from Shakespeare's Hamlet came to mind. "There are more things in heaven and earth, Horatio, than are dreamt of in your philosophy."

Suddenly ravenous, Trace spotted an outside café, smelling the bread and the coffee. Did single young women eat alone in cafés in 1916? She had no idea. Her eyes flitted about looking for an empty table, to see if there was a single woman eating alone. There wasn't. In her time, she loved eating alone in New York cafés, watching people furtively and overhearing conversations. But there were no women, of any age, eating alone in this café. Okay, fine, so be it, she was hungry. She'd start a fashion in Paris in 1916.

Trace saw men and women glance at her with curious speculation. She spotted an open table for two and went for it. As soon as she sat, more eyes fastened on her. Why were they all staring? It was a crowded café, after all. Weren't there other people and things to stare at besides her? Was it her clothes, or was it that she wasn't wearing a hat or gloves? Did she look that out of place? Did she look like someone who had dropped in from the future?

A silly thought arose. Trace recalled how she'd once perused YouTube videos posted by people who purported to be time travelers. There were two modern sisters who claimed that they had "time-slipped" back to the French Revolution. She didn't believe them.

Then there was a photograph from the early 1940s, in which a crowd was gawking at some event of immediate interest. In the middle of that crowd was a modern-looking hipster, wearing designer sunglasses from the late 1990s, and a shirt with a logo that wouldn't be manufactured until 1995. If that wasn't enough, the dude was also holding a mostly hidden cell phone in his left hand.

At the time, Trace had thought the stories entertaining but ridiculous. She hadn't believed any of them, just like the majority of people who had left negative comments.

Now, as she sat in a 1916 Paris café, she tried not to look self-conscious as she adjusted herself in the chair, awaiting the server, wishing she had her cell phone to hide her face in.

The waiter soon arrived, wearing a long white apron, a sad looking mustache, slicked back dark hair and wary little snake eyes. He grunted a "bonsoir," handed her a menu and waited for her order, his pad at the ready, his impatient pencil point tapping it.

Trace ordered onion soup, fromage and a coffee. Her French was not good, but good enough. The waiter understood her.

Trace sat back and watched the traffic for a time and then followed a high fashioned woman, in a flowery hat and stunning long dress, as she walked a proud, white poodle. Two old men with dusty, shapeless suits, sat on a bench, smoking and reading newspapers.

She was startled when a man stepped up to her, cleared his throat and offered a little bow. "Excusez-moi, madame, j'espère que je ne vous dérange pas?"

He was excusing himself, hoping he wasn't bothering her. Trace had always understood French much better than she spoke it. But this man spoke French with an accent of some kind. That she could tell.

"I don't speak French well, Monsieur. I'm an American."

His pleasant face lit up. "American! How nice."

He was a short man, dressed in a loose-fitting jacket, white shirt and wide dark tie. His black hair was long, falling across his broad forehead; his chin was good, his nose prominent; he held a pipe in one hand. Tucked under his arm was what appeared to be a sketchbook. He wasn't exactly handsome, but he was charismatic in an odd sort of way, his piercing eyes holding humor, depth and seduction. Trace figured the man was in his early to mid-thirties.

"I couldn't help but notice that you are alone," he said. "Are you expecting anyone?"

Trace's eyes shifted. Should she lie? "No. I am alone."

"In that case, would you permit me to sketch you?"

Trace admired the come-on line. It must be an old-school approach. This was much more interesting than a modern-day dating site.

"Why me?" Trace said, baiting him. She was flattered. People were watching them, with interest.

"Because you stand out. You caught my artist's eye right from the start."

She lowered her eyes to hide her pleasure.

"Allow me to introduce myself. I am Pablo Ruiz, although I am known by my friends and people who pay me as Picasso. Pablo Picasso."

Trace's eyes lifted, widened, and stared at the man in utter disbelief.

CHAPTER 15

Pablo Picasso sat opposite her, pulled a pencil from his inside jacket pocket, flipped open his sketchbook, and leafed through some pages until a blank one appeared. Then he went to work, the pencil dancing across the page. His intense gaze focused on the page for a time, then lifted sharply on her, his eyes, two dark pools exploring her hair, lips and eyes, his pencil scratching away, his face locked in stern concentration.

"What is your name?" Picasso asked.

"Trace, Tracey Rutland."

He lifted a dark eyebrow. "I like Trace. It has imagination, and it's direct. I like things that are direct."

Trace was aware of some of Picasso's more famous works, thanks to an art class she'd taken in college, but she couldn't recall creation dates. She believed that his most famous work, entitled Guernica, had been painted in the 1930s. Trace was sure that The Old Guitarist had been painted in the early 1900s, and she recalled that Picasso had painted it after the suicide of a close friend. Should she mention it?

She also was aware of Picasso's highly geometric and minimalist Cubist objects, with the occasional element of collage. She had difficulty relating to those paintings, finally conceding that she didn't have the necessary background to understand and appreciate them. Other dates and times of his works were a blur, like so many things from the past and the future.

When her soup arrived, along with some baguette, she hesitated, not knowing if her eating would spoil Picasso's sketch.

"Go ahead. Eat," he commanded, as he worked on.

So, Trace did eat. She was hungry.

"What is it?" he asked, quietly, as if talking to himself, not looking at her.

"What is what?" Trace asked, staring at this world-famous man, who had died sometime in the 1970s. Her mind still struggled to take in the reality of him.

"You," Picasso said, pointedly. "Yes, you. Am I to sketch your face, what's inside your face or what's behind it? You seem to be in pieces to me. Okay, I'll have to find you in pieces."

Trace stopped eating. "Pieces? What do you mean, in pieces?"

He didn't lift his eyes as the pencil jerked and skimmed across the page. "Painting is a blind man's profession, Trace. He paints not what he sees, but what he feels—what he tells himself about what he has seen. I'm not sure yet what I am seeing."

Trace didn't know what to say, so she didn't say anything. When her cheese arrived, she ate sparingly, feeling increasingly uncomfortable, as if she were under a microscope and the entire café was examining her.

"This is not my café, you know, Trace. I came here to meet my friend Sevuk Andranikian, but he did not show up. I usually meet friends in the Café de la Rotonde. Do you know it?"

"No…"

"It's in Montparnasse, at the corner of Boulevard du Montparnasse and Boulevard Raspail. You should come. Victor Libion, the founder, is a friend. You will meet many of my friends there, and maybe you'll meet Sevuk Andranikian. He is a professional friend to many bartenders, from Lisbon to London to Paris. Boire comme un trou—or better said, Sevuk drinks too much—but I love him like a brother. He lost all his family last year, when they were slaughtered by the Ottoman Empire. You could cheer him up. He loves mysterious, pretty girls. He also tries to paint but…to copy others is necessary, but to copy oneself is pathetic. Still, I love Sevuk. He is both rich and poor, both man and boy, both comic and tragic. How will he find his wholeness? His one? His completeness?"

Picasso shrugged, stopped abruptly and glanced up at her, as a thought struck. "You should come to my studio, so I can see you again, so I can put together your many pieces… or not. Maybe you're best in pieces. Many of us are, you know, broken up into pieces. This war is doing that very well. I'm sure you see it. Not outside so much, but inside, where the true reality lives. Lots of pieces. But then I think you know that, Trace."

No, Trace did not know that, but maybe she was learning.

"My studio is easy to find, Trace. It's on Rue Schoelcher."

"Mr. Picasso, I need a job," Trace blurted out.

He lifted an eyebrow. "No need for 'Mister,' Trace. Picasso is me. I am Picasso. What kind of job?"

"I don't know. I'm a dancer, singer. I can act."

"Ah yes, Trace. Yes. You perform. Of course, you must, with that flame of honey blonde hair, those startled eyes and those rose petal lips, which I'd love to touch with a feather."

Trace's eyes moved away from him. Was he flirting with her? Pablo Picasso?

He continued to work. "You could model, Trace. I know many artists. The theatre is now barren, with this raping war going on."

"Is the money good?"

"Good? Trace, this is Paris during a war. Artists are not rich. Anyway, money is a child trap. I'd like to live as a poor man with lots of money."

"I need money, Picasso."

"Okay, you need money. So, you model. You meet artists. Artists know people in the theatre. Artists need inspiration. Artists need mistresses."

Trace had just met this man and yet, in some strange way, she was comfortable with him. He was honest, blunt, seductive and childlike, with absolutely no pretensions. She'd never met anyone like him.

"Okay, so I'll model," Trace said.

She finished her lunch, while Picasso finished his sketch of her.

"Can I see it?" Trace asked.

Without a word, Picasso turned the sketchbook about, holding it up to the light.

Trace inclined forward to study the penciled sketch. Her hair was scattered and exaggerated, her face long, eyes wide apart. It was not a literal portrait, but she could see herself in it. It was remarkable. So like her and yet unlike her. On one side of her face was a fresh, young woman with a penetrating eye. On the other side was a face with lines, shadows, and a wide, fearful eye. One side was young, the other wizened and old. Trace was amazed—stunned to silence. Picasso had captured exactly what she was feeling—and had been feeling ever since she was a little girl—as well as the fear and vulnerability she'd felt since she'd arrived in 1916.

Picasso grinned mischievously. "There are so many realities, Trace, that in trying to encompass them all, one ends in darkness. That's why, when I sketch a face or paint a portrait, I must stop somewhere, in a sort of caricature. All portraiture is caricature."

He stood, closed his sketchbook and stared down at her, his dark eyes digging into her. Without another word, he reached into his pocket, pulled out a few francs and tossed them down on the table.

"Money, Trace, for your time as my model here today. Come and see me. You'll make more money. Perhaps we'll play with a few feathers around your mouth or your heart. Who knows?"

And then he was gone, sauntering off into the crowds under a late afternoon sun.

Trace spent another restless night, shifting, waking and pacing the room, anxious for morning to come so she could visit the American Embassy to begin the process of obtaining her passport. She'd dreamed of her daughter—Mata Hari's daughter, Nonnie—and Trace felt an increasing urgency—a burning need to see the girl, so that no matter what happened to Mata Hari, Trace could begin to heal and find some peace.

As Trace sat in the hotel's gold and blue dining room, finishing her coffee, she was surprised to see Mata Hari enter. She flirted girlishly with the gracious maître d' and followed him to Trace's table. As Mata Hari approached, her face fell into a grim, serious expression. Trace brushed her lips with her satin napkin and stood.

"Please sit down," Mata Hari said, with a quick wave of her hand, as the maître d' bowed and left. Trace returned to her seat and, without an invitation, Mata Hari sat opposite her, as an efficient waiter in a white coat and black bow tie arrived.

"Just coffee and a croissant," Mata Hari said.

The waiter nodded and glided away.

"Have you finished your breakfast, Trace?"

"Yes."

Mata Hari wore a chiffon dress, detailed in white beads, with white gloves and a matching broad white hat. Trace couldn't help but notice that the dress had three different overlapping layers, and all had to be buttoned, snapped, and hooked in just the right order. Talk about labor intensive.

"You should have a croissant," Mata Hari said. "They are excellent here—three parts butter to ten parts flour, or so the pastry chef, François Darroze, explained to me some time ago. He is off fighting in the war, you know, and I have recently heard that he was killed in some damned awful battle. Well, his croissants live on, don't they, and that is a fortunate thing for all of us."

This was not a joke, and Trace was again struck by Mata Hari's apparent lack of sensitivity. She could be warm and generous, but also cold and aloof.

Mata Hari went straight to business. "Trace, I am furiously working to receive my papers so that I can travel to Vittel. I want you to come with me."

Trace questioned Mata Hari with her eyes. "I don't understand. You asked me to leave the chateau."

"I responded in anger."

"Do you still think I'm a spy?"

"I don't care what you are. It doesn't matter to me now. I've changed my mind about the whole thing. I need a friend now, Trace, and despite what I said, I feel as though I can trust you. And, anyway, if you are spying for the British or the Americans, what of it? Maybe, somehow, you can help me get to Vittel to see poor Vadime."

"I can't help you," Trace stressed. "I can't even help myself right now."

"Okay, fine. Then let us help each other. Let's just say I need a traveling companion. Will you go with me?" she asked, her eyes imploring.

Trace stared down at the white tablecloth. "Is there any way I can talk you out of this, Mata Hari?"

"No, of course not. I must get to Vadime. Please do not start all that foolish talk again."

Trace looked up. "Have you heard from Edward?"

"Yes. He has visited Vadime two or three times. Poor Vadime has been partially blinded. He's depressed and sick." Mata Hari leaned forward. "I have contacted two former lovers for help with my papers, Jean Hallaure, a French intelligence officer, and Baron de Marguérie, a French diplomat. I'm waiting to hear back from them."

"And how is Edward?"

Mata Hari leaned back. "He told me to tell you that he'll be coming to Paris soon. He said he has arranged to send you more money, so you are not to worry about leaving the Hotel Caron de Beaumarchais. He also told me to tell you that he'll help you with your passport. As you know, his family has connections."

Trace made a small murmur of complaint, irritated at feeling helpless to support herself. Should she go to Picasso? If she did, she was sure he'd take it that she was prepared to sleep with him, or maybe even become his mistress. That was just too weird, and it was out of the question.

"What is the matter, Trace? Edward cares about you deeply. His family is very rich. He will take care of you. You are a very fortunate young woman."

Trace sighed. "Yes, it would seem so."

"Will you go with me to see Vadime, Trace? Please."

Trace stared directly at Mata Hari. There was no way Trace was going to get involved in Mata Hari's intrigues and eventual destruction. There was no way she was going to put her name out there for all the French officials to see and ponder over. After all, Trace had already been through all that, hadn't she?

"No, Mata Hari. I'm sorry, I can't go with you."

Mata Hari stared, soberly. "Then I'm sorry, Trace. I hope you won't be angry with me."

"Angry about what?"

"I assumed you'd come with me, so I forwarded your name to my two contacts, and I asked that they process traveling papers for both of us."

Trace felt a sudden, knifing threat. She felt an alarm go off in her head. She had no past. She didn't exist in

this time, and yet she was here. That would undoubtedly be a red flag. If Mata Hari thought she was a spy,
what would these paranoid, suspicious French officials
think?

It was too late. Trace's name was out there now.
Should she run? Where? She had no passport. She
had the Marquis' letter of recommendation, but how far
would that get her?

Trace grew cold with fear. Could Edward help her?
Could he get her to England somehow, and away from
all this?

CHAPTER 16

A little over a week later, Mata Hari and Trace were to meet again at the Café de la Rotonde, located on the corner of Boulevard du Montparnasse and Boulevard Raspail. While waiting for Mata Hari, Trace had glanced about, looking for Picasso, but she didn't see him. What she did see was a man wearing a dark suit and a dark bowler hat, seated at a table near the sidewalk, pretending to read a paper. Trace knew he was watching her. He had a blunt, impassive face and a sober expression. His beady bird-eyes shifted toward her a couple of times. He was not a very good policeman or detective, but his presence had an effect: Trace was fidgety and nervous.

Under cloudy skies, Trace sipped a coffee and nibbled on a pastry, pretending a French insouciance. She had spent her last few days wandering the city, visiting the American Embassy, and sitting in her room reading newspapers and novels, distracting her mind.

Unfortunately, the American Embassy had denied her request for a passport, despite Marquis de Beaufort's letter and Edward's British Embassy contact, Allister Chapman. They wanted more documentation, especially in this time of war. Of course, Trace had no documentation, and she'd told them her family had all been killed in America, and she was desperate to return home. No amount of pleading—or lying—had helped. For now, at least, Trace was stuck in Paris.

Edward had been true to his word. He had sent more money to the hotel—a lot of money—and even though she was not comfortable taking it, fearing it sealed her fate as Edward's mistress, she felt she had no other option at the present. So, she had come to the Café de la Rotonde, where she hoped to see Picasso. Trace did not want to visit his studio. She was not interested in becoming two men's mistresses, even if one was Pablo Picasso—but she did want his contacts—modeling contacts. She wanted to be independent and on her own. She was, after all, a modern woman, and not an early 20th-century Parisian woman, who had little choice but to take advantage of her looks for as long as they held out.

When Mata Hari arrived, Trace noticed the clumsy policeman glance over, his eyes alert, body stiff with recognition, like a wolf spotting his prey.

Mata Hari sat down heavily. Her face was flushed, her expression weary. Trace smelled her rich, smooth, heady perfume.

"I'm sorry I'm late, Trace. You have no idea what I have been through. These people are so rude and incompetent. My contact, Henry de Marguérie, helped get my travel request to Vittel approved by the Commissioner of Police, and I'm sure it has arrived at the military authority by now. I went to that so-called authority again today, but there is a different lieutenant every day. So I will have to go there again tomorrow morning to ask that they move on this, so we both get the papers we need. Vadime could be dying and I am not there. I am so tired and disgusted with all these démarches in the police office. I told them that if they need references, I'll ask Maitre Clunet to supply them. He is my lawyer, after all. He has known me for ten years and has had my marriage and divorce certificates in his hands. He knows everything about my whole existence. Why all this waiting? It is intolerable."

"If it's difficult for you, Mata Hari, it will be impossible for me without a passport."

Mata Hari gave a flick of her hand. "No. No. We will get you a passport. Anyway, they all know me. I'm famous. But there is something going on with them, and I don't like it."

Trace stole a quick peek at the policeman. His face was hidden in his newspaper. He'd removed his hat.

After Mata Hari ordered a steak frites and a glass of red Burgundy, Trace spotted Picasso and another taller man edging in from the street. She sat up.

"What is it?" Mata Hari asked.

"It's Picasso. Do you know him?"

Mata Hari shrugged, unimpressed. "I met him at a party once. He's short and I don't like his paintings. To me, his paintings are a muddle of shape and color. There is no reality in his work."

Picasso spotted Trace. He gave a little wave, tugged on his companion's coat, and they started over.

At the table, Picasso offered a little bow. His smile was small but assured.

"Trace and Mata Hari, I bid you a good day."

Trace knew what he was thinking. Since Mata Hari was a high-priced courtesan, surely Trace was too—guilty by association.

"My dear Picasso," Mata Hari said, offering her hand. He leaned and kissed it. Trace followed suit, and he kissed hers.

What would the game be? Trace wondered.

"Let me present my good friend, Sevuk Andranikian. Do not expect him to smile because he never smiles. In Armenian, his first name Sevuk means black, gloomy and sad. Isn't that right, Sevuk?"

Sevuk Andranikian shrugged a shoulder, resigned and bored. He was tall and thin, with sober intelligent eyes, a sad mouth and thinning hair. Perhaps he was closing in on 40 years old. "Gloomy is the way of this world these days, is it not?" he said slowly, in a thick accent, pronouncing every word carefully, so that he was easily understood.

"It certainly is gloomy," Mata Hari said. "This awful war has killed off all the fun."

Trace noticed Mata Hari's poor choice of the word "killed" but no one else seemed to notice or care.

Sevuk nodded his sad greeting to the women and then glanced about. "I need a cognac," he said. "And you, Picasso, must have your absinthe."

"May we join you?" Picasso asked the ladies.

Trace saw Mata Hari's meager smile, but her manners took over and she indicated toward the two vacant seats.

After the men ordered, they spoke of the gloomy gray day, of the gloomy war and the gloomy state of Paris. After the drinks were served, Trace watched an agile waiter hurry by, balancing three mugs of foaming beer on a circular tray. Mata Hari turned the conversation toward her travel problem. The men listened, patiently, nodded, drinking, smoking.

"And poor Trace here cannot even manage to get a passport."

Sevuk turned his unhappy eyes on Trace. "And why is that, mademoiselle? Why won't the officials grant you a passport?"

Picasso joined in. "And why don't you already have one, Trace?" he asked.

Trace inhaled a breath. "Let's just say, as you once said, Picasso, I am a woman in pieces."

"And what does that mean?" Mata Hari asked, searching faces. She gave a quick shake of her head. "On second thought, I don't want to know what it means."

"Passports are easy to come by in this market," Sevuk said, nonchalantly.

Trace perked up. "Easy?"

"Yes... For a price, of course."

Picasso laughed, pointing a finger at his friend. "Mr. Andranikian is also a man in pieces," he said. "And one of his pieces is money. He is never without lots of money."

"Money is also easy to obtain," Sevuk said.

Trace and Mata Hari perked up, all ears. Trace spoke, measuring her words and lowering her voice to a near conspiratorial whisper. "Is it something that can be done fast? Will it cost a lot of money?"

Picasso sipped his absinthe, his warm, dark eyes on Trace. "I believe you can afford Sevuk, Trace."

Trace didn't like Picasso's implication, but she ignored it, adjusting her gaze back to Sevuk. "Can you help me?"

Sevuk looked her over, speculatively. "Me personally? No. I am, how do you say in English, a connector. Or is it contractor?"

"A broker," Mata Hari tossed in.

Sevuk nodded, in recognition. "Yes, yes, a broker of sorts. That is what I am and what I do best."

"Can you help me with my traveling papers?" Mata Hari asked, anxiously.

"You, Mata Hari, no. You are being watched, you know."

Mata Hari stiffened, glancing about. "Watched? By whom? Where?"

"Don't look around, Mata Hari," Trace snapped. "Don't!"

Mata Hari glared at Sevuk. "What is all this?" she asked, irritated.

Sevuk was unfazed. He looked directly at Trace. "You...young lady, can be helped, but, as I said, for a price."

"Who is watching me?" Mata Hari persisted, her eyes holding sudden alarm.

Sevuk slid his gaze toward her. "The police, Mata Hari. Surely, you are aware of that."

"And how do you know this?" Mata Hari demanded.

Picasso leaned forward. "Sevuk is Armenian, Mata Hari. For years, the Armenians have been brutalized by the Turks. In 1914, when the Turks entered World War I on the side of Germany and the Austro-Hungarian Empire, Turkish military leaders argued that the Armenians were traitors."

Sevuk lowered his eyes onto the table, and when he spoke, his voice was filled with low anger and pain. "On April 24 of last year, the Armenian genocide began. On that terrible day, the Turkish government arrested and executed several hundred Armenian intellectuals. Soon after, ordinary Armenians were thrown out of their homes and sent on death marches through the Mesopotamian desert without food or water. The genocide continues. My entire family was killed. I alone escaped, thanks to a kind woman and her husband. I ran and hid for days, with killers after me. Now, I smell a policeman only a few feet away. I know their moves, their tactics. I know their evil, killing minds."

They sat in a troubling silence. Trace was thinking that not much had changed in the world, and that was depressing. Of course, none of the people sitting there knew the future as she did. They did not know of the crushing depression that would occur right after World War I, or the awful destruction and loss of life that would happen during World War II, or of the violent terrorism that would stun the world in her lifetime.

She decided to be bold. "Sevuk, I need a passport. I'll pay whatever I have to pay. Can you help me?"

He raised his watery, miserable eyes. "Yes...but we will not speak of it again until I contact you."

"When will that be?"

He shrugged. "Who knows? Now, let us drink and talk about life in better days to come. I mean, my friends, life must get better than this, no?"

They toasted and drank, and then fell into their own somber thoughts.

CHAPTER 17

Trace and Mata Hari arrived in the resort town of Vittel nearly two weeks later, on Wednesday, July 26th. Trace now had a passport, thanks to Sevuk Andranikian. Mata Hari had finally received her traveling papers, only two days before. Trace had asked Mata Hari how she received them, but she had refused to answer, saying it was none of Trace's business. She said that she'd done what she had to do to see her wounded lover.

For her part, Trace had met Sevuk near the Seine, a few days after they'd met at the café, and he'd handed her an address where she was instructed to go. She didn't hesitate. Sevuk told her to lose the policeman who was following her, and he gave her clear instructions how.

An hour later, Trace ducked into a certain fashionable women's shop just off the Champs-Élysées near the Arc de Triomphe, handed a piece of paper to a certain female sales clerk whom Sevuk had described, and then Trace was promptly escorted to a side room that led to a back door.

Trace exited the shop through the door to an alley-way. There, a big man with a grim expression, power-ful chest and massive arms was waiting, just as Sevuk had said he would be. With her heart pounding, the big man took her arm gently, as a lover would, and led her to the Avenue Victor Hugo. From there, they climbed into a taxi and started off to Montmartre, arriving at a little row house between a sad looking café and a brothel.

Trace was led up a dim narrow staircase into a sparsely furnished room, with a single unmade bed, a rickety chest of drawers and a small dining table.

"Wait here," the big man said, gruffly, and then he was gone. She stood rigid, feeling the saliva thick in her throat, hearing the toots of car horns outside, hear-ing coarse arguing voices next door.

Minutes later the door burst open, and Trace pivoted, making a surprised, fearful sound. A stocky man in a black coat and beret entered, camera in hand, suspicious dark eyes darting about the room. He was a sour, stern man, with a cigarette dangling from thin lips. He shut the door behind him and barked at her.

"Are you alone?" he said, in feisty French.

Trace nodded.

He looked her over with sullen pleasure. "We work fast. Stand against that wall, the gray one."

Clouds of cigarette smoke encircled his head as he puffed away, grunting commands, adjusting and check-ing the lens. Trace wondered if he'd make a grab for her, throw her onto the bed. His menacing eyes wan-dered there more than once. Her fingers tightened into fists.

He clicked away, mumbling at her to move from left to right. He was ugly, sinister and rude.

And then he said something in French she didn't understand. He stared hard at her for a moment, shook his head, and then, to her total relief, he left, slamming the door.

Trace had paid Sevuk a lot of money for the forged passport—more than half the money Edward had sent—but four days later, just as Sevuk had promised, the passport arrived at Trace's hotel in a manila folder marked PERSONAL.

Upstairs in her room, she impatiently tore open the envelope and tugged out the leather passport. When she saw the American Eagle and her photograph—a very flattering likeness—she smiled with relief and pleasure.

United States Of America Department Of State.
The Undersigned Secretary Of State Of
The United States Of America
Hereby Requests All Whom It May Concern
To Permit
The Citizen National Tracey Peyton Rutland,
To Pass Without Delay Or Hindrance, And
In Case Of Need, To Be Given
All Lawful Aid And Protection

The passport was dated April 1916, and there was a French stamp with the date May 16, 1916. All that remained to make it legal was Trace's signature. For the

first time since she'd arrived in 1916, Trace felt a crashing relief, as if all the windows and doors had been
flung open, and bright sunlight was streaming in. She
was free now. Free to travel wherever she wanted.
Free to travel to the Netherlands to see Nonnie.

Trace had agreed to travel with Mata Hari to Vittel
for two reasons: one, she wanted to see Edward, because she had missed him, and because she sensed
some mysterious connection with him that she wanted
to explore; and, two, she was sure Mata Hari carried the
ring that had somehow, miraculously and regrettably,
brought Trace to this time of 1916. Trace planned to
steal the sapphire ring at the first opportunity, travel to
De Steeg to see Nonnie, and then use the ring to return
to her own time—back to her own life.

But what about Edward? Could she tell him the
truth? Probably not. Would he believe her? Of course
not. She was still grappling with the weird truth of it
every day. But she could not stay in this time. She was
not born to it. As Picasso had said, she was in pieces
and she felt that she was in pieces, a little more each
day.

Would she ever be whole again? By the time she arrived back to her own time, would she have merged the
misshapen, interlocking pieces of her two lives and arranged them into a complete and healthy picture of herself? Was that the reason she had come here?

As she and Mata Hari traveled to Vittel on a crowded, smoke-filled, rattling train, Trace knew full well
how Mata Hari had finally managed to receive her papers. As was consistent with history, Captain Georges
Ladoux, the expert in counter-espionage, had agreed to
grant Mata Hari her traveling papers to see her lover,

Vadime, only if she agreed to spy for the French. Mata Hari had agreed. Of course she had.

It was a good thing that Sevuk was able to obtain a passport for Trace, because the French authorities had denied her any papers, whatsoever. She only hoped that Captain Ladoux hadn't flagged her as a possible spy by association with Mata Hari.

Trace knew about Captain Ladoux, and whenever she thought of him, it gave her shivers. Captain Georges Ladoux was a career army captain who had come out of St. Cyr, the West Point of France. He was a short, black-bearded man with a waxed mustache and brilliantined hair. He was also a protege of the overall commander of French forces. His job involved organizing counter-espionage—despite his modest rank of captain. The intelligence service at that time was in the embryonic stage, and Trace found it interesting that Ladoux, at 42, was still only a captain, despite a devastating war that offered rapid and easy promotions to fill dead-men's shoes. It was obvious to Trace that this man had a troubled military career. He'd been tucked away, and he knew it. He wanted to prove himself and, of course, he would prove himself, being the small, troubled man, he was.

But Mata Hari had refused to discuss with Trace anything about how she'd received the traveling papers. "I am going to see Vadime, and that is all that matters, Trace. I will not discuss any more about it."

Okay, so Mata Hari was acting according to history, and maybe there was no way to stop that, but Trace herself had free will, and she did not intend to get caught up in the intrigues, traps and tragedy that had befallen her as Mata Hari.

Trace had observed that she and Mata Hari had been followed onto the train. Two grim-faced men were in different seats and in separate compartments. They were not good detectives. Trace had spotted them easily, and maybe they wanted to be seen. Maybe that was all part of the threat.

These were the same two men who had been following Mata Hari around Paris as she taxied to her various restaurants, designer shops and hair salons, as she prepared to see Vadime. A separate policeman had been following Trace, although she didn't see him now, on the train.

A taxi was waiting for them as they exited the train at Vittel and, thankfully, Mata Hari had brought only two trunks and not her usual dozen or more. As Trace and Mata Hari bumped along the road that led into the spa and resort town, Trace gazed out the taxi window to see a grassy field with parked ambulances and brown hospital tents that held the wounded. She saw busy nurses, their white headscarves flapping in the wind as they entered and emerged from the tents.

The taxi suddenly lurched to a stop, stuttered forward and then pulled over to the shoulder of the road to allow four ambulances to pass. They were blocky, clumsy-looking vehicles, with green canvas on wood frames and a white circle with a bold red cross in the center. They were filled with the wounded from some battlefield and Trace noticed, with great interest, that one of the drivers was a woman.

An ambulance in front stopped, and a gray-clad nurse in a navy cape left the rear of an ambulance and waved another to pass. Trace surmised that those soldiers had the more serious wounds and needed immediate attention.

The two women in the taxi watched with sober, compassionate expressions as the ambulance turned onto the open field and bumped along the rutted ground toward the tents and waiting doctors. As the ambulances came to a stop, nurses and white coated orderlies rushed to help the soldiers, some borne on stretchers, others wearily stumbling along, figures in khaki, wrapped in blankets or coats, bandaged or splinted. Some were stiff with mud, or caked with blood and dust, salt and sweat. Trace felt sick to her stomach. Even from this distance, she could see that these men were young, but with old faces pinched in pain, shock and exhaustion.

Mata Hari fought a rising panic. At this horrible sight, she feared the worst for Vadime.

She leaned forward toward the driver.

"Can you get us out of here?" she snapped.

He shook his head, ignoring her. "Not until all these ambulances pass, unload the wounded and give us the all clear."

Mata Hari shook her head, discouraged and upset. "Before this damned war, Vittel attracted thousands of wealthy visitors. It had a casino, polo grounds and a race course. The waters here are soothing for the liver, kidneys and stomach. Look at it now. Look at these poor, beautiful men, broken and dying. God in heaven, it makes me so angry, Trace. So very angry at the violence and the waste caused by this intolerable war."

A half hour later, they arrived at the Hotel de Ville, where Vadime and other wounded officers were convalescing. Mata Hari and Trace entered the hotel lobby and handed over their papers to the cautious, imposing soldier. They waited nervously as he examined the papers in obsessive detail, looking up several times with a wary glance and an accusing manner when he saw Mata Hari. Obviously, this soldier was not a fan.

The entire hotel had been turned into a hospital, and highly trained Catholic nuns and orderlies moved about, pushing wheelchairs or accompanying the soldiers outside to sit in the sunshine.

When the women were finally permitted entry into the hotel, they approached a stern, bad-tempered nurse at the front desk who gave them a once-over of disapproval. The woman's narrowed eyes revealed that she recognized Mata Hari, and she was another who was not pleased to have this wanton woman in her hospital.

With an imperious, upturned chin, and after an adjustment of her extravagant hat made of gold and silver feathers, Mata Hari asked to see Captain Masloff. The nurse grunted a barely audible reply, telling her she would have to wait to be escorted.

An endless thirty minutes later, a weary, distracted orderly led Trace and Mata Hari down a long, red, carpeted corridor, through a side doorway and out across a spreading green lawn, where soldiers sat in wheelchairs or wicker chairs, or wandered under cool, shady trees.

Vadime sat relaxing in a wicker chair, dressed in his dark uniform, smoking a cigarette and reading a newspaper. When Mata Hari called to him, he dropped the paper to his lap, and his face lit up, revealing a black eyepatch over his left eye. He pushed up slowly, propping himself upright with a cane, as Mata Hari rushed to him, tears in her eyes. Trace watched them embrace and kiss, and she backed away to allow them privacy.

News of Mata Hari's arrival had spread, and curious soldiers had left the hotel to gather in whispering groups, their enquiring eyes watching as Mata Hari and Vadime strolled off through sunlight and shade toward a distant pond, Vadime with his cane, obviously favoring his right leg.

Trace had two hours before she was to meet Edward, if he was on time. His last telegram had warned that he might be late, or that he might not make it at all. Trace was escorted to a taxi and she motored off to the elegant and expensive Vittel Grand Hotel, where Mata Hari had insisted they stay. At the train station, Mata Hari had had the trunks, suitcases and hat boxes sent ahead to the hotel.

Trace checked at the hotel lobby desk, then climbed the wide, royal blue carpeted staircase to the second floor, where she was escorted to a well-appointed suite.

Once she was alone, she hurriedly unpacked some of her clothes, surprised at how nervous she was to see Edward again. She felt like a teenager about to go on her first date.

To distract her mind, she went to the tall windows that opened out on a beautiful view of the landscaped gardens, distant woods and wide blue sky, her mind again consumed with thoughts of being with Edward.

Although they had exchanged many letters over the last weeks, and Edward had declared to her that he was falling deeply in love, she had been restrained in her response. Nonetheless, she continued to feel a flowering affection for him. His letters had been heartfelt and tender, not frivolous or carefree, and they were filled with a kind of desperation. In his last letter, in which he had enclosed more money, he had written:

"I feel so lost these days, Trace. I'm so tired of flying and fighting; of watching my friends die; of living with my stomach in knots and my heart aching for another chance to see you and spend a glorious day with you. Yes, I know we have spent so little time together and we know so little about each other, but war and death, and the sterling thought of living my life with you, have all sharpened my desire to beat this awful war and stay alive. Having met you has lent imagination and a man's wonder at the romantic thought of loving you for all time. You have captured my heart, Trace, and forgive the Eton College schoolboy sentiment, and the Cambridge graduate who could write his feelings in Greek and Latin (although not so eloquently) but I'd rather say it in English, the simple way: I have simply fallen in love with you, Trace, and I don't care if we just met an hour ago or ten years ago.

Deep in the lonely night, I allow my excessive emotions to think of you as if you were already my wife, my lover and my friend. I silently kiss you and have conversations with you. Don't think me daft, Trace, just think kindly and lovingly towards me.

Please don't stop writing to me, dearest Trace. I would surely wither and die without your letters—your wonderful letters. I am so looking forward to seeing you again. I've had so many dreams about it—and about you. I just want to hold you, Trace, and never let you go. There are so many things I want to tell you.

Trace turned from the windows, allowing her hesitant eyes to rest on Mata Hari's trunk and luggage. Should she search for the ring? No, not now, not until after Mata Hari had unpacked. Still, Trace was tempted, once again pushing down an urgency that was always there: the ring could take her back to her own time.

What lay heavy on Trace's mind was that she was being followed, and she didn't like it. At Vittel, when she'd entered the taxi, she'd noticed a short, stubby man enter the taxi behind hers.

Unless she could get away from Mata Hari, and soon, she would undoubtedly get pulled into some police station for questioning. That could possibly lead to her undoing. She had no past. No past in this time meant she was undoubtedly a spy. Spies could be tried and shot.

A little over an hour later, as Trace lay resting on a button-tufted, emerald velvet sofa, she heard a knock on the door. Arising, adjusting her hair, her heart racing, she walked briskly across the deep carpet to the door. She swung it open to see a cupid-faced bellboy dressed in a royal blue uniform with polished brass buttons. He smiled and handed her a sealed envelope. With a flush of excitement, she opened it, completely unaware that the bellboy was politely waiting for his tip.

It was from Edward.

Your own doting flyer is downstairs, waiting to kiss you. Please come.

CHAPTER 18

Trace's eyes sparked as soon as she saw Edward in the hotel lobby. They quickly closed the distance between them and fell into each other's arms, remaining in an embrace as guests passed, watched and whispered. Later, as Trace and Edward sat in the hotel's stylish Tea Room, near windows that looked out on a wide green lawn, gentle flower gardens and splashing fountains, Edward stared at her with tired, worshiping eyes and a warm smile.

Trace noticed a softer shade of character in his face, as if his daily encounters with death had humbled him, matured him. He had aged, and there was a weary fatigue evident in his posture and speech.

On the white tablecloth, the silver tea service and porcelain cups were accompanied by little cakes and sandwiches artistically displayed. The palm court orchestra played genteel waltzes.

The couple didn't talk for a time. They sipped tea, silently studying each other with a new pleasure.

"I can't believe I'm actually here, looking at you, Trace," Edward said. "I've dreamed about it often enough."

Trace smiled warmly. "You look very tired, Edward. You must be so sick of war."

"Not now, Trace. Not here with you in this place. No talk about war and flying."

He looked about. "Here, it's all quite civilized, isn't it? It's actually quite jarring to be here like this, away from the flying and killing."

"Do you have to go back?"

He laughed a little. "No. Never. I've decided to steal you away and run off to South America or the United States. We'll live with your relatives. They'll love me."

Trace smiled, her eyes sharpening on him. "They'll definitely love you, Edward."

"And we'll live the life of our dreams."

Trace sighed. "A nice thought, Edward."

Edward rested his chin on a fist, gazing dreamily at her. "I know this is devilishly bad manners, elbow on the table, staring like a perfect lout, but I don't care. Trace, I have something I want to say, and I don't want you to say anything until I'm finished. Agreed?"

"No. You have to give me some idea of what you're going to say."

"So, you have no idea what is in my head—what has been in my head since I left you—which, by the way, seems like a year ago?"

She kept her eyes on him. "I have some idea."

"Trace, before I met you, I was living in a violent world that was resolute on destroying itself."

"I'd say it still is… and I'll further say that the world will continue to do so for a long time to come."

"Be that as it may. I was trapped in a world-weary struggle that was making me morose and cynical. I had deep suspicions about life, about dark human emotions and mankind's devious motives. I believed that the savage gods that rule civilized folk had gone to sleep or just stopped caring about what happened to the human race. But then… I met you."

Trace opened her mouth to speak, but Edward stopped her with a hand up.

"Let me say my piece, Trace, and then you can speak yours. Okay?"

Reluctantly, Trace agreed.

Edward straightened, smoothing out his uniform and adjusting his tie. He reached for her hand and, at his touch, she felt a quick current of thrilling emotion.

Their eyes met. "Trace, I feel liberated and free. Whenever I think of you, I feel happiness and optimism. I don't give a damn what happens to the human race. All I want is for us to be together. Therefore, I want us to get married, and as soon as possible."

As if on cue, the orchestra finished their set and the room dropped into silence.

Trace sat very still, her mind a blank.

Edward frowned. "You look surprised, Trace. Well, actually, you look a bit woozy. Didn't my letters convey my love for you?"

Trace blinked. Of course, she had imagined he'd say it, but imagining it is different from actually hearing it. And seeing Edward in the flesh, and being lost in his handsome, hopeful face as he sat there stiffly waiting for her answer, was something she couldn't have imagined.

"Everything in my life has led me to you, Trace. It has led me to this moment and to this time, and to this one lovely thing: you. I hate to sound like such a silly romantic fool, but all day and all night I hear the melody of you, and it enchants me, and it haunts me, and it thrills me. It's what keeps me alive, Trace."

Trace felt the weight of the moment, and she was moved by the poetry of his words. No man she'd ever dated before had been capable of such a flowery declaration of love.

Trace searched for the right words. "Edward, we don't really know each other. We've had no real, quality time together."

"Then we'll make up the time, loving each other."

"We've only just met. How can I say I'll marry you?"

"Because you feel what I feel, Trace. You know it, and you feel it, don't you? You felt our connection right from the beginning, didn't you? Yes, I know you did. What do I care about when we met? What does time have to do with anything, if you feel love so strongly in your heart? Time is just some imagined thing, Trace. Some arbitrary measurement that's just an illusion. What counts are feelings and emotions. What really counts is love. Don't you see?"

Trace felt embraced by Edward, surrounded by him, but she was torn and conflicted by confusion and passion. No matter what he said, and how persuasively he articulated it, the truth was, they didn't know each other. The truth was, they had just met and exchanged some letters.

Edward leaned in. "I can hear your mind working, Trace. Tell me, what you are thinking?"

If she said yes to Edward—if she married Edward— she would no doubt have to stay in this century and live in his vast and extravagant country home with his wealthy family. She would be expected to perform all the domestic duties women were required to do—with all the ceremony and polish they entailed—not that she knew exactly what those duties would be.

She would also be subjected to all the limitations of being a woman in this time, the silly beliefs, the many constraints. She would not be allowed to have a career, and chances were, she'd be tucked away like some ornament—loved, certainly—but also restricted.

Edward was inspecting her face, searching for an answer in her eyes and in her expression.

If Trace didn't marry Edward, would his disappointment weaken his resolve to live? How would she feel if he was killed in the next few days? Could she live with that?

"Don't you love me just a little, Trace?" Edward asked, in a small voice.

Trace did care for Edward. Even though they'd spent little time together, each word, each look had carried weight and purpose. She had definitely felt that. Each touch was new and exciting, yet breathlessly familiar. But was it love? Had she ever been in love before? No.

How could she say no to Edward, when he was about to return to war? How could she say yes?

She started to speak but faltered. She tried again. "Edward, what will your family say? They've never met me. I'm an American. I have no title, and no titled family, property or wealth. They'll want to know how we met—when we met. They'll be disappointed in you and hate me. It's all too fast, Edward. We must think this through carefully and rationally. It's just so... so fast."

Edward grinned. "Fast? My family hate you, Trace? Impossible. Once they meet you, like me, they'll fall in love with you. Anyway, I don't care that it's fast, and I don't give a damn what they or anyone else says about how I feel for you. My family lives in an entirely different world from me. I see death and dying every day. It sharpens my mind and my senses. It shows me how delicate and precious and fast life is. It shows me what is important. That's all that matters to me, Trace. Right now, you and I are all that matter to me. Will you marry me?" he said, his eyes twinkling with excitement and expectation.

Trace looked at him, taking him in fully, and silence fell between them.

Perhaps Edward was right. What was time anyway? Here she was in this place and time, being offered marriage to a handsome, rich guy, who obviously adored her. What the hell did it matter what time or place it was? Danger was all around. Uncertainty was everywhere, like a threat, and maybe it always had been. Life in her time, and in this time, were unstable and confused. So what if the whole thing seemed impossible? How nice it would be to have someone who loved her with such dedication and devotion.

And then there was the burning question. What if she turned him down and Edward was killed? She would be devastated, and she would blame herself for all time.

Trace slowly lifted her nervous eyes to his, still uncertain. "You will have to write to Miss Pemberton, Edward. You must. You're engaged to her."

He looked at her, meaningfully, folding his hands on the table. "I already have written to her, Trace. I wrote her two days after we met, and I broke off the engagement. After I met you, I knew there was nothing between Miss Pemberton and me. Nothing but friendship, that is. Now, finally, will you marry me, Trace?"

Trace swallowed.

"Trace, will you?" he said with restless, impatient energy.

Perhaps living in this time would not be so bad after all. Perhaps living on a beautiful estate and raising children with Edward would not be so bad. Actually, living a life with Edward and a family could work out—perhaps it would be a better fate than if she returned to her own time, where romance and marriage had become confusing, to say the least.

"And face it," she thought to herself. "It's not like you've ever met a man in your own time who even remotely turned you on as much as Edward does. Just looking at him makes you weak in the knees."

Trace's smile started small, then stalled. Edward leaned forward, waiting.

"If I say yes, Edward, will you promise me that we won't live with your family? Will you promise me that we will have our own home?"

"Of course we'll have our own home, Trace. I told you about it. It's a lovely place in Henley on Thames. You will love it. I promise you."

Trace inhaled a breath and let it out slowly, still fighting apprehension. "All right, Edward, then I will marry you. Yes."

Edward leapt up, circled the table, grabbed her shoulders and lifted her to her feet, holding her at arm's length.

"Hurrah, Trace! Hurrah!"

He pulled her into his arms for an embrace.

Startled heads turned. There were sour faces, happy faces and shy faces, all gawking at the couple with keen interest. Edward didn't care about propriety.

Their lips met, and a flicker of a kiss soon deepened and flowered, and Trace flushed with swelling desire, as Edward's strong arms pulled her tightly against him.

If nothing else, Trace thought, heat rushing to her face, the sex will be great.

CHAPTER 19

Trace and Edward were married three days later, on Saturday, July 29th, at St. Michael's Anglican Church, an old stone church about two miles from town. Twelve pilots from Edward's flying unit attended, along with six airplane mechanics and three of their French girlfriends. Mata Hari and Vadime were there, along with a few doctors, nurses, orderlies and officers, many of whom were anxious to catch a glimpse of Mata Hari.

When Mata Hari was told about Trace's and Edward's plans to marry, she'd once again come to the rescue. She was all hand-patting and efficiency, with a girlish excitement and energy that galvanized everyone.

She proudly presented Trace with a stupendous flowing dress made from fine cream cotton, trimmed in silk, with silver beads and long ruffled sleeves. The matching shoes fit tightly, and pinched Trace's toes, but the broad white silk hat with a plume of ostrich feathers was a definite standout.

When the first notes of the pipe organ swelled with The Wedding March, Captain Masloff and Trace linked arms and started down the aisle, Vadime still needing the aid of his cane to walk.

Edward's eyes shined with love and adoration as he watched his bride glide toward him, beaming, floating in a graceful radiance. Mata Hari had styled Trace's hair high, in cascades of long, easy curls, and with the hat tipped to one side, her hair gleamed under the soft candlelight.

Trace's heart opened fully when her misty eyes took in Edward in his crisp military uniform, standing tall and resplendent, his hand reaching out for her as she approached.

During the ceremony, she hovered in a kind of trance as the minister uttered the pretty, lofty words that would join the two for "as long as you both shall live." She remained calm and quiet as Edward produced the diamond ring he'd purchased only the day before, promising her he'd replace it with a 3.31-carat platinum ring, a family heirloom, when they traveled home to England. Tears stood in Trace's eyes as he gently slipped the ring on her finger and whispered, "Forever, Trace."

After they were pronounced man and wife, their lips brushed several times before Edward leaned in for a passionate kiss. Mata Hari wept, and the congregation seemed to hold its breath, as they waited for the newlyweds to break from their long embrace.

The reception was held at the glorious gold-leaf mirrored Hotel de Ville ballroom, where the chandeliers glistened, the champagne flowed, and the nine-piece orchestra thrilled the room with waltzes, tangos and the foxtrot.

Trace was delightfully impressed by Edward's skillful dancing. They circled the floor, all laughter and elegance, dipping and twirling to applause, tilting under the luster of chandelier light, Trace feeling the buzz of the Champagne.

As the party began to wind down, Trace and Edward swept from the ballroom to the awaiting carriage. The humid night air, the close, blinking stars, and a round, buttery moon made the night wildly romantic, as if it had been ordered especially for them.

And then the white enclosed carriage and the proud chestnut horse carried them away to intimacy, and toward a new, soon-to-be unwrapped life. They could only pray that their budding love would grow, and their life together would flower.

Trace and Edward sat close, hands clasped, as the single horse carriage trotted through the quiet, winding cobblestone streets, arriving at a quaint, three-story hotel on the outskirts of town. Here, they'd spend their two-day honeymoon. Edward had to be back at his unit, a subject they refused to discuss.

At the heavy mahogany front desk, Edward signed the leather register in the name Mr. and Mrs. Edward Bishop. The stout hotel matron grinned at them, showing gapped teeth. With a clasp of hands and emotional wet eyes, she said something in French that neither Edward nor Trace understood. They thanked her in French, and that excited her, starting another round of rapid-fire French that the couple couldn't comprehend.

The honeymoon suite was on the third floor. The concierge toted the bags up the stairs with a straining effort, cursing the out-of-order bird-nest elevator. Edward had offered to help the man, but he refused. He was small, spare and old, and he sighed a lot, muttering things in French that seemed like incantations to the gods asking for the strength to survive another day.

Edward shouldered open the heavy oak door, swept Trace up in his arms and carried her across the threshold, her eyes filled with laughter.

It was a wide room with an ancient four-poster bed, covered by a thick cream comforter and a scattering of fresh rose pedals, which Edward had ordered earlier. Trace squealed with pleasure, planting a wet kiss on his nose.

Back on her feet, she explored the swallow-you-up green quilted chair, the faded patterned rug, and the gleaming pine fireplace. Several potpourris placed about the room gave off fragrances of vanilla and rose.

On the center table were two large vases, both blooming with fresh flowers that Mata Hari had chosen. Trace skimmed her nose over them, inhaling the sweet, delicate scents.

Edward reached for Trace and pulled her close, staring at her completely and silently. He touched her cheek and, in a whisper, he said, "I love you with all my heart, Trace. We are going to have a wonderful life together. I promise."

They'd forgotten about the concierge. He cleared his throat and lowered the bags, speaking in English. "Do you like fire? More fire for you?"

"No thanks," Edward said, reaching into his pocket and drawing out some coins. He handed them to the thankful man. "Thank you, Monsieur. Everything is perfect. Thank you for all your assistance."

The man bobbed a bow. "Merci, Monsieur ..."

And then he was gone, closing the door softly behind him. The newlyweds were alone at last.

Edward placed his hands on his hips, examining the room. "I chose this old place because it seemed romantic somehow. Being the hopeless romantic that I am, I thought we'd remember it always: the frayed carpet, the broken elevator, the quaint furniture and..." His eyes strayed toward the bed. "The double bed."

Trace felt a sudden rush of love for Edward. Had a woman ever been so loved by a man? By a handsome and courageous man? By a good man?

Trace lifted a shoulder and slowly moved into him, parting her lips, holding him in her eyes. "I do love you, Edward."

Edward switched off the light and, in the firelight, they danced for a time to silent music, kissing, touching, working their way toward the bed, slowly undressing. Trace felt Edward's heat and stiff desire, and it made her high and wanting. All the questions, the ragged emotions, the confusion she'd felt since arriving in this time, soon melted away when Edward kissed her and made love to her.

Trace awoke deep into the night. Flickering firelight played on the walls and she heard the occasional crackle of burning wood. She smelled pine, and the hovering scent of fresh flowers. Edward must have built a new fire after she'd fallen asleep, and as she watched the dancing flames, she was gripped by fear. How much longer would Edward have to fly in this war and risk his life? It seemed unfair and impossible that he would have to leave her and fly against men who wanted to kill him. He was a good and a true man. A sweet and strong lover, and they had joined so easily, so tenderly, so profoundly. Love for him arose and expanded and filled every part of her. How had that happened? Where had it come from?

She turned to watch Edward sleep, partially covered by the comforter, his breathing soft, his hair askew, his eyes fluttering.

What was he dreaming? she thought. She watched him for a while, wonderingly, before gently leaving the bed and slipping into a creamy satin robe, another gift from Mata Hari.

Barefoot, she went to the fire and gazed at it, enchanted by the trembling flames. Folding her arms across her chest, she wandered to the window, parted the heavy curtains and stared out into the dark night.

A bright blue click of lightning crawled across the sky. There was a distant rumble of thunder, and as she lifted the window, a wet wind rushed in. She smelled rain.

Somewhere out in that volatile night world was her world—the world in the future—the world of her time. What was going on in that world? Had it stopped since she'd left, or was it rolling along, jet airplanes crossing the skies; cars and trucks racing along freeways; TVs, laptops, cellphones all active with communication; and the unending 24-hour news cycle beating out the events of the day? What were the new TV shows, the new movies, the new Broadway musicals? How were her family and friends? Well, none of them had been born yet. They didn't exist, did they? The future, her future, was so far away.

She watched fidgety veins of lightning flash, lighting up the world like flashbulbs. Thunder tumbled in closer, and soon the first drops of rain struck the window.

Minutes later, rain fell so hard it roared. The storm did not awaken Edward. Good, she wanted him to sleep. She'd seen the deep fatigue in his eyes as they'd danced, laughed and celebrated. She wanted him to sleep and erase the violent images of war and death. She wanted him to rest and forget that they would be separated in two days. She wanted his good and kind mind to heal.

As the rain pelted down, Trace stared, recalling the conversation they'd shared after that first delicious climax. Edward had kissed her hair and neck, traced her lips with a finger, and whispered lovely, romantic things. Things about forever.

"When I leave, you'll go home to England, Trace. You'll be safe there, and you'll have everything you'll want or need. I won't be able to get a leave for quite a while now. Things are really heating up again."

Trace had been gently startled by that. "Edward, I'm not going off and leaving you. I'll stay in Paris."

"No, Trace... It's not safe. It's not safe for you to stay with Mata Hari."

"What do you mean, Edward?" she asked, although she knew what he meant—of course she knew. She just didn't know that he knew.

"My dear one... There's talk about Mata Hari, and from more than just one source."

Trace pressed. "What kind of talk?"

Edward adjusted himself so that he was looking down at her. Edward had not yet built the new fire, and in the darkness, she could see only his silhouette.

"Trace, Mata Hari is not as popular or as young as she once was, and she's fallen out of favor with some very powerful people. She wants to marry Vadime.

She needs money and, worst of all, she is very naive about the realities of this war and espionage."

Trace lifted up. "Espionage?"

"Yes, Trace. I hear she may be spying for the Germans, as well as for the French. Now that may sound absurd to you, but I heard it from a reliable source—from my brother, Thomas, who works for British intelligence in London. Thomas said that just before Mata Hari traveled down here, she was approached by the Deuxième Bureau, France's external military intelligence agency, and was asked to spy on Germany. The only reason she was allowed to come and see Vadime is because she agreed to be a spy. But there's even more disturbing talk: that she is also spying for the Germans, and she's doing this because she needs money for her and Vadime. If she is spying for Germany, Trace, she's playing a very foolish and dangerous game."

"She's not, Edward. I know that for a fact. She is not spying for the Germans. She took money from them because she was broke, but she didn't take the spying seriously. If anything, she's spying for the Allies. For the French."

The room settled into silence, and she couldn't see Edward's expression. When Edward spoke, his voice was at a troubled whisper.

"And how do you know this? How do you know anything about this, Trace?"

Trace sagged back down, wishing she hadn't been so talkative. "Because I know, that's all."

"Did she tell you?"

"No... well, no, not exactly... Well, some things," Trace said, as an afterthought, to make her knowledge sound plausible.

"You're being evasive, Trace. Why? You're worrying me."

Trace reached up, wrapped a hand around Edward's neck and pulled him down for a kiss. Afterward, Edward rolled over on his back, and laid an arm across his forehead.

Trace lifted up on an elbow to look at him. "Edward, don't ask me to go to England to live with people I've never met, and who won't want me. I can't do it. We're married, and I am going to stay in Paris where I can be close to you."

Edward sighed. "Trace, part of what made me fall in love with you was your mystery. I felt it the first time we met—all the secrets you keep. Yes, that was very attractive. A mystery woman. You're a walking secret, a kind of riddle, a code that I can't crack. But now, things are different. We are married now, and I don't want anything to happen to you."

"Nothing's going to happen to me."

"Trace...sometimes I wonder if I know who you really are. I still don't know where you came from—and I don't believe a damned word about your performing with some traveling theatre group. Why can't you trust me and just tell me the truth about things? We are man and wife now, Trace. Why can't you tell me who you are?"

"Because I can't right now. I just can't. I told you we didn't know each other. I said we were getting married too fast."

"Stop it, Trace. We got married because we love each other."

Trace dropped onto her back with a heavy sigh. "Edward, you're going off to war and I don't know if I can bear it. What am I going to do while you're gone? I'll be worried sick every day, wondering how you are and where you are."

Edward sat up. "Let's not talk about it, Trace. Not tonight, of all nights. Tonight, there is no war. Tonight, I don't give a damn about your past or what you've done. I don't even care if you're a spy."

Trace sat up, sharply. "I'm not a spy, Edward."

"Fine. I don't care, but I do care that by your being with Mata Hari, you could be suspected of being a spy, as she is now. The French are very paranoid right now, Trace. They are shooting spies. The Allies are losing a lot of men—thousands of men in every battle—and they need scapegoats to save their careers and their own necks. I've even heard rumblings that some military divisions have begun to talk about mutiny. People in France and England want an end to this bloody war, and they are sick and tired of incompetent leaders. Trace, all I want is for you to be safe. That's why I want you to go to England, away from all this cloak and dagger business. You'll be safe there with my family, and I'll feel so much better about it. I'll come to you as soon as all this killing business is over, and we'll move into our own house. You'll love it, Trace. I promise you. Will you do that for me? Will you go to England?"

The storm had passed, and the fire was slowly dying when Trace turned from the window, her shoulders sagging. The quick breeze that blew in was cooler. She shivered and lowered the window.

She couldn't lie to Edward. She had finally told him she couldn't go to England. Not without him.

Edward had taken her declaration in silence, finally turning away from her and falling asleep.

Trace didn't tell him that as soon as he left for war, she had plans to travel to The Hague to see Louise Jeanne MacLeod—Nonnie—Mata Hari's daughter— Trace's daughter. Trace had to convince her to see a doctor so that she wouldn't die, either from a cerebral hemorrhage or from complications related to congenital syphilis, on August 10, 1919, at only 21 years of age.

But what about the Mata Hari ring? No matter what happened, Trace still needed that emerald ring, and she was determined to get it before she left for The Hague. With that ring, Trace would have the choice to stay in this time for as long as she wished, or to return to her own time, if things suddenly turned bad, or if something happened to Edward.

CHAPTER 20

Trace and Edward spent their two honeymoon days in glorious sunshine, exploring the countryside on bikes, picnicking on a mossy green hill, wading through clear, cold streams, and sharing stories of their childhood. It would have been ideal if Trace hadn't been required to be on guard, to make sure she gave no hint of her "other" identity. Any story she told had to be reset in the early twentieth century.

They avoided any talk about the war or the future. At night they dined locally, strolled under a gray marbled moon, and returned to their little nest to sip wine and make love, while the fireplace hissed and popped, and firelight played across the walls.

During those wandering days, Trace felt torment and ecstasy. She had fallen in love quickly, and her rich love had now deepened. It helped to heal and soothe her. Edward's kisses softened the anxiety of future and past, and chased away nightmares. His love had a transformative effect and, for a time, all the pieces that had been broken and scattered were mended and whole.

But the cruel knowledge that Edward would soon be flying again, fighting again, rushed the loving hours, and that was a torment. What would she do if he didn't return? She couldn't even think the word 'killed.' What would she do if he was taken from her? And what would she do if he did return? Could she continue to live a lie for the rest of her life here, constantly in fear that she would make a mistake and say something suspicious? If she managed to find the ring, could she persuade Edward to time travel with her to an uncertain future, where he would have no wealth and no social standing? And what if they had a child? There were no clear answers, no clear decisions, no clarity anywhere.

Edward left on Tuesday, August 1st, on an overcast day—a gloomy day that threatened rain, with moving gray clouds lowering to the tops of trees. The two lovers had returned by carriage to the Hotel de Ville, Edward forcing smiles and Trace struggling to hold back tears.

Edward held her close, looking skyward. "Not good flying weather," he said. "Lots of wind up there."

"Don't talk about flying, Edward. Not now."

"All right, my dear."

He looked at her softly and held her eyes. "Trace, I have cabled my parents and written them a long letter about my feelings for you, and about our marriage. I told them that if anything happens to me they are to ensure you are provided for."

"Edward, I don't want…"

Edward cut her off. "Shhhh. Let me finish. And they will provide for you. I have included all the particulars for your provision in my will, which I drew up the day before we were married, and I have sent copies to my solicitor and to my parents. Everything will be quite legal. You will never want for anything, Trace. As my wife, you will always have money, property and a comfortable home."

The tears streamed down Trace's cheeks, and she didn't bother to wipe them away.

"Nothing is going to happen to you, Edward, do you hear me? You are coming back to me," she said with a choking sob.

"Of course, my darling," he said, giving her a peck of a kiss. "Of course, I'm coming back. But this way, while I'm still flying, I'll know that you will be taken care of. I'll feel so much better knowing that, Trace."

Trace pulled a hanky from her purse and blotted her eyes.

"Do you know, Trace, that this is the first time I have seen you really cry? Small tears, yes, but these big ones, well..."

Trace turned away from him, aware that he was trying to lighten their parting.

"I get all splotchy when I cry. I look terrible. Listen to me, I sound like a whiny..." She stopped.

Edward gently turned her chin to face him. He grinned, playfully. "You're right, Trace, you do look awful when you cry."

Trace playfully slapped him on the arm, and he laughed.

As they left the carriage, Mata Hari and Vadime met them, their expressions sad. They all said their good-byes with hugs and kisses. Vadime grabbed Edward's shoulders firmly, and he held his friend at arm's length, staring with a solemn face. In a deep, determined voice, he said, "You be wise and strong up there, Edward. Don't try to be a hero."

"You mean like you, Vadime?"

"I must try to be a hero, Edward, for my Mata Hari. I'll be back in the fight in a month or so. So, look for me."

"No, you won't," Mata Hari said, sharply. "You will not fly again in those flimsy machines anymore. I forbid it."

Vadime released Edward, turned to Mata Hari and laughed. "Whatever you say, my sweetheart," and then he winked at Edward.

As Edward's car rolled away down the drive and curved around a grove of trees, disappearing into the haze of the day, a sick misery arose in Trace. Vadime and Mata Hari tried to comfort her, but she left them, walking off toward the little rippling duck pond, as an urgency built in her chest.

Trace circled the pond, watching two swans glide and drift, watching ducks paddle about lazily and then waddle up on the grass, flapping their wet wings.

She felt as though she were being pulled in all directions: the past, the present and the future. How would she ever manage to survive without Edward? He had simply opened her heart to a love she'd never believed existed.

Being back in her hotel suite with Mata Hari was painful. How she missed Edward already. Later that evening, she declined an invitation to dine with Mata Hari, Vadime and a Colonel Orlofsky, saying she had a headache and needed rest.

Lying on the settee, Trace pretended to be asleep when Mata Hari left for dinner. As soon as she was gone, Trace arose and hurried into Mata Hari's spacious bedroom, casting her eyes about, finally noticing that two trunks had been opened. A maid had placed lingerie in the chest of drawers and toiletries in the bathroom; had hung the gowns and dresses in the deep closet; and had arranged Mata Hari's many shoes neatly on the floor.

Trace's eyes fell on the second trunk that lay to the far side of the closet. She strolled over, casually, as if she were just looking around. The trunk had hardwood slats with patinated metal hardware, leather side handles and a metal reinforced bottom with tiny casters. Whenever she traveled, Mata Hari always placed her jewelry in this trunk and padlocked it. To Trace's relief, the padlock had been removed. Mata Hari had no doubt opened it to select her jewelry for the night.

Trace glanced around, guiltily, lowered to her knees and gripped the right leather handle. She tugged the trunk out and away from the closet onto the rich burgundy patterned carpet, inhaled a breath, grasped both sides of the trunk lid, and gently lifted it.

It was a remarkable site—a spectacular smorgasbord of jewelry, elaborate golden and bejeweled headdress, a beaded metallic bra and several sheer veils. There were shimmering earrings, necklaces, bracelets and armlets, all carefully packed in silver boxes or placed in red velvet pouches.

Trace swallowed, excitement building in her chest. Surely the ring was here. Where else would it be? She methodically began her search, lifting lids and opening pouches hopefully, her hands anxious, her heart racing. She peered inside each one, and then placed it aside. Minutes later, it was clear the ring wasn't there, and her eyes changed from hope to disappointment. Trace carefully replaced every item back in its proper place, lowered the trunk lid and shoved it back into the closet.

She stood and started back to the living room, pacing, thinking, planning and missing Edward. As she saw it, there were only three possibilities of where the ring might be. Mata Hari may have slipped it on for the night. She may have placed it in a safe or safe deposit box, or she could have given it to someone. Trace doubted that.

She crossed the room, entered her own bedroom and shut the door behind her. She sat on the end of the bed, lowered her head and closed her eyes. Perhaps it was time she resigned herself to living in this time and place, and accept the situation she was in. She should be grateful that she'd met Edward and been able to establish a new life for herself by marrying him—an impossible, irrational choice she should have never made, and yet, she didn't regret it. Not for one minute. She truly loved him.

But it was so very uncomfortable, not being able to divulge the truth about herself to the man she loved. It was as if she were a secret double agent, living a counterpoint reality: a married woman in 1916, and a single woman in 2018, lost in a time travel fog. There was no one to turn to or share her predicament with, and no obvious option to return to her own time.

Later that evening, when Mata Hari returned from dinner, Trace told her that she'd decided to travel to The Hague to see an old friend who was living there.

Mata Hari was immediately suspicious. She asked many questions, including why she wasn't following Edward's wishes and leaving for England. Trace deflected Mata Hari's curiosity by telling her she would travel to England after her visit to The Hague.

Mata Hari accepted what she said, but the look in her eyes revealed abiding skepticism.

CHAPTER 21

Trace arrived in The Hague by train at 3:45pm on Saturday, August 5th, 1916. She checked into the Hotel Paulez, located on the Short Corner Voorhout Lange Voorhout. It was a pleasant four-story hotel that Mata Hari had recommended. She'd stayed there herself the year before, while repairs were being done on her house nearby.

Mata Hari had also suggested that Trace could stay at her former house on Nieuwe Uitleg 16, now occupied by an old friend, Greta Janssen, but Trace decided on the hotel instead, not wanting to make yet another contact with someone who'd ask her about why she was there. Mata Hari had continued to voice suspicion about Trace's decision to go, and the morning Trace left, the women had briefly argued.

"What business do you have there, Trace?"

"I told you, I have a friend who asked me to come."

"Why do I question that? Why do I not believe you?" Mata Hari asked, as they sat for afternoon tea in the Tea Room with Vadime.

"Perhaps you should join her, my sweet?" Vadime said.

Mata Hari turned away with a shake of her head. "I have no reason to return to The Hague. I don't have the best of memories of that place."

Vadime turned somber as he puffed on a cigar. "My dear Mata Hari, I will have to return to flying sorties next week. Instead of returning to Paris, why not join Trace in The Hague?"

Mata Hari leaned forward, her face filled with an agony of concern. "You do not need to go back to that awful war, Vadime. Return to Paris with me. Leave this terrible place."

"You know I can't do that, my dear. I am a soldier and a pilot. Let us not argue about this anymore."

Mata Hari turned her sharp, penetrating gaze to Trace. "Does Edward know you are going to The Hague, Trace?"

Trace lifted her teacup to her lips, paused, and sipped. After she replaced the cup on the ornate floral saucer, she faced Mata Hari with a sturdy confidence, the only way one could argue with Mata Hari.

"Yes, I told him."

"You must trouble him greatly," Mata Hari said, turning away with another shake of her head.

Trace was irritated. "Instead of telling me what I should do, Mata Hari, you should think about what you are doing. You should leave France, altogether, until after the war. You should return to The Netherlands and stay there."

"Why do you keep pestering me about this, Trace? I don't understand you."

"Because you are in danger."

"I am not. It's preposterous. I am Mata Hari. What can possibly happen to me? You should be traveling to England, as Edward has requested. Why do you disobey his wishes and travel to The Hague? Why don't you listen to your husband?"

Trace stayed silent.

Vadime lifted an eyebrow. "What kind of danger, Trace?" he asked, his interest piqued.

Trace considered her words carefully. "Mata Hari is being watched by Captain Georges Ladoux's men."

Mata Hari flicked a dismissive hand. "He is nothing, that little man. He is a silly, peacock-strutting Frenchman."

Trace settled back with a sigh. "Mata Hari, you need to take this whole situation seriously. As the war has progressed, there has been a shift in French moral values. You know this. You've read about it in the papers and heard about it in the theatres. Let's be honest: you are not as popular as you were before the war. These French officers, and many of the French public, now distrust foreigners, and they're becoming more—for lack of a better word—moral."

Vadime spoke up. "Who is this man, Ladoux?" he asked, looking from one lady to the other. "What is all this about, my dear?"

Trace decided to come out with it. "Vadime, Captain Georges Ladoux works in French counter-espionage, and he agreed to grant Mata Hari her traveling papers to come here, but only if she agreed to spy for the French."

Vadime sat up. "What? Spy? Is this true, my dear?"

Mata Hari sighed, audibly. "It is nothing, Vadime. This Captain Ladoux is nothing. A nobody."

Trace continued. "Captain Ladoux believes France is riddled with foreign spies and he's out to destroy their network. He wants attention-grabbing cases to prove his worth to his superiors and to the French public."

Trace stared hard at Vadime. "Frankly put, he regards Mata Hari as little more than a prostitute, and he thinks she may be a German spy."

Vadime's jaw tightened. His eyes hardened. "This is all so ridiculous. It is an insult to Mata Hari."

Mata Hari laughed. "Ladoux is such an ugly little man, Vadime. He has nothing on me, and he never will."

Mata Hari pushed her chair back and stood up. "I've had enough of this. I'm going now. I will see you off tomorrow, Trace. Come Vadime."

As Vadime left with Mata Hari, he glanced back over his shoulder at Trace and shrugged.

Trace settled into her elegant room at the Hotel Paulez and eased down onto a blue patterned velvet loveseat, shutting her eyes and listening to the quiet murmur of the city sounds outside her window. Moments later, she reached for her purse, retrieved Edward's latest letter and reread sections, feeling a new swelling of love for him; feeling that pulsing anxiety that every day he flirted with death and could be snatched away from her. She leaned back and read.

The weather has been bad, with high winds and rain. We've been unable to fly. In this weather, I feel so dreadful for the soldiers in those muddy, vile trenches.

They die of so many things: bullets, disease, despair. When will this terrible, hellish war end, Trace, so I can return to you and our cozy little room with its firelight and wine?

Being married to you makes things better and it makes them worse at the same time. I miss the scent and the look of you—the breath of you—those sleepy morning eyes looking back at me with love. And it just plain hurts not being with you. It is an agony I have never experienced, which can only be eliminated by being with you. But you keep me going, Trace, as I knew you would, once you became my wife.

My darling, forgive my English persistence, but I implore you once again to please consider leaving Paris for England. Yes, I heard from my parents. Understandably, they were shocked by our sudden marriage—especially my mother. But Trace, they want you to come. Yes, they want to meet you. Of course, I told them how incomparable you are. How mysterious you are, and how beautiful you are. I will send them our wedding photo as soon as I receive them. They will see how properly and wonderfully in love we are, and how absolutely ravishing my wife is.

On a positive note, we have a mascot—a black and white mutt dog that wandered onto the field the other day. I've named him Ricky-Ticky, after a flyer, Rick Thackery, who was shot down and killed about two weeks ago. Being the daft Brit boys we are, we nicknamed him Ricky-Ticky, instead of Ricky-Thackery. What a great chap he was, Trace, and he really wanted to meet you. He was from Brighton. Have you heard of it?

Got to go, darling girl. Forgive the cheap paper, but it's all I could find in this bloody place. Sending you all my love and many kisses. Looking forward to seeing you.

Your English Bloke...

Edward

Saturday evening, Trace walked through the city that seemed hauntingly familiar and, of course, it should have seemed familiar, from her life as Mata Hari/Margaretha. Young Margaretha had moved to The Hague to live with her uncle when she was 16. At that time, The Hague was a city full of colonial officials who had returned from service in the Dutch East Indies, modern-day Indonesia. In 1885, at the age of eighteen, Margaretha saw a newspaper ad that had been posted by her future husband, Captain Rudolf John MacLeod, who was searching for a wife.

As Trace walked along tree-lined streets, passing busy cafes, in a swelling August heat, she recalled her feelings at that time. At 18, she was bored, miserable, and desperate for romantic adventure, so she answered the newspaper advertisement, and enclosed a photo of herself. The article had said that Rudolf was looking to meet and marry, "a girl of pleasant character."

Marriage seemed like a first-class ticket to a better life. Margaretha knew that officers in the Indies lived in large houses and had many servants.

Trace could hear the faint voice of Margaretha in her head. "I wanted to live like a butterfly in the sun."

She and Captain Rudolf John MacLeod ("Johnny") were engaged in March of 1895 and married on July 11, 1895. He was 20 years older than she.

After walking nearly two miles, Trace found a taxi. She sat staring out the window into the sunlight, passing canals, streetcars, flower vendors and parks. When the taxi bounced along cobblestones, entering a neighborhood of stylish old row houses, clean streets and a park with flower gardens and fountains, Trace sat up, awake, aware that she had seen all these places before. This had once been her home.

As she had planned to do, Trace traveled to Nieuwe Uitleg 16, the home of Mata Hari's friend, Greta Janssen. When Trace handed Greta a letter of introduction by Mata Hari, Trace was welcomed in. There, she spent a pleasant two hours sipping tea and eating cakes and sharing stories about Mata Hari. Greta was a tall, thin, free-thinking woman, who believed that Mata Hari was years ahead of her time.

"She will go down in the history books," Greta said, emphatically. "You can bet on that. She will show that women can make a noise in this world too. Not just the men."

When Trace mentioned that she was off to visit Nonnie the following day, Greta was supportive and enthusiastic. She offered Trace a letter of introduction for Captain MacLeod, saying she'd need one if she was to be accepted.

As Trace lay awake that night, she felt as though she were on the verge of a great journey that could possibly change her life forever. She was about to travel to De Steeg to see her daughter, Nonnie, and her husband from her past life as Mata Hari.

As she awoke the next morning, Trace felt a cut of pain. Did she really want to do this?

CHAPTER 22

On Sunday morning, Trace packed a canvas bag with clothes and toiletries, enough for two nights. She hired a car and started off to find Rudolf John Mac-Leod's house, which was over two hours away in De Steeg, Gelderland. The car was expensive, but she had plenty of money, thanks to Edward. Since she hadn't spent money on new clothes or on an expensive hotel room, as Edward had requested she do, she was comfortable spending the money on a journey to De Steeg.

Another reason for taking the car concerned the trains. They ran infrequently. Also, if she was being followed, her shadow would be easier to spot in a car, and perhaps easier to lose.

When Trace had left the hotel, she'd cautiously glanced around to see if she was being followed. She didn't see anyone, but she couldn't be certain.

As the black touring car left The Hague and drove west along tree-lined roads, golden grain-waving fields, past streams and green farmland, Trace felt the same aching pain she'd been feeling ever since she'd decided on this trip. She'd come a long way to see Non—many miles and many years, and she could only hope that her flimsy plan, her acting, and her practiced dialogue would gain her entry into the MacLeod house.

When the car entered De Steeg, driving along Hoofdstraat under a canopy of arching trees, her throat tightened. An image formed in her mind—vague at first—then, as if bubbling up from a clear pool, she saw it: an old postcard she'd sent to Nonnie in 1915:

Dear Nonnie. I'm dying to see you again. I always try so hard to, but it never works. Will you do me the great pleasure of seeing me? That's the only thing that I desire from you.

But Non hadn't gone to see her, despite the many postcards her mother had sent her from all over Europe, all ending with "Love Mama." Perhaps MacLeod had kept them from her; perhaps her daughter had never even seen them.

As Mata Hari, Trace recalled writing hundreds of letters, sometimes six a day. In Trace's world, with all the social media, Mata Hari would have been a frantic e-mailer and Twitterer. Her letters told everything about who she was, and the kinds of moods she was in. Interestingly, in this life, Trace was not so open about her own moods, preferring to keep her feelings guarded. She wondered if it was directly related to the life she'd lived as Mata Hari.

The car turned left onto a dirt road and bucketed along past a fenced-in field under heavy trees, until it arrived at a two-story modest house nestled under a cluster of majestic trees. The car stopped, and the driver swiveled around, speaking in English. "Madam, we have arrived."

She nodded. How she wished she could have taken a yoga or dance class that morning. After so many years of dance lessons, her body missed the movement, the expression, the relaxation it gave her.

She paid the driver, asked him to wait, and then she stepped out into the quiet day, hearing birdsong, noticing the play of insects in the manicured flower garden, where startling red roses burned the air around them. There was golden light falling on a distant pond and a boy with a long fishing pole wandering its shores, a hat pulled low over his forehead to keep out the glare of sun.

What a lovely place to raise a child, Trace thought, wanting to impress this moment on her mind; wanting to recall every detail accurately. She stared at the house where Nonnie lived—the house where Trace was about to meet her former husband—her husband from another life.

When Non stared into Trace's eyes, would she intuit something unusual—something familiar? Would Trace? Trace's chest tightened, her pulse raced, and sweat beads formed above her upper lip. She gently blotted her mouth with a hanky.

Every cell in her body became alert, heightened by memory and remorse. Every buried memory awakened and chastised her for what she had done to her daughter in this time, so long ago—yet so bizarrely here in the present. A past that had been frozen—now a present that could thaw that past, if she handled the situation just right. Now, she had a second chance. Perhaps this was the primary reason she had been thrust back into time.

Trace took a step forward and stopped. More memories flooded in—fresh and vivid and terrible from a long time ago. She had been awarded legal custody of Non, but with MacLeod withholding financial support, it was a struggle to keep her Non. After she lost the battle with the Dutch government for a share of MacLeod's military pension, she had headed for Paris, leaving Non with family friends, fulling intending to bring Non with her once she got on her feet.

What could she do? She needed money, and so she explored her options as a lady's companion and a teacher of German conversation and the piano. She took rooms, not at the Grand Hotel, but at an English guesthouse in the 14th arrondissement, and they were very austere. They were not extravagant and had no real conveniences.

But then everything changed. Then came the allure and excitement of fame, and the money and the men— those lovely officers. They became like a drug to her, and she lost control. She had made so many bad choices. And then everything went crazy and spun away into confusion and terror, until the day she was executed.

Trace didn't move for a time, as memory shook everything lose again. She couldn't stop the stampeding memories, and God, how she wished she could.

In her mind's eyes, she saw five police inspectors and their superior enter her room at the Élysée Palace Hotel and arrest her on charges of "espionage, complicity and intelligence with the enemy."

She saw herself on trial for being a German spy. She was dressed in a tricorn hat, a dark-blue coat and a low-cut frock, unaware at that time that she was actually fighting for her life, as she faced a jury of seven officers, who would later send her to the firing squad.

And then, in another scene, she saw little Nonnie running toward her, arms outstretched, her face lit up with joy at seeing her Mama again. Trace staggered, grabbing for the wrought iron gate for support. It took minutes to gather herself and shake off the past...the future... the present. The taxi driver emerged from the car, concerned, waiting.

Inside the house, a curtain parted, and a shadow face peered out. She moved toward the front door on wobbly legs. She must go through with this. Trace paused before the two-story brick building with a wrought iron gate. A pair of trees framed stone circular steps that led to a black panel door with a center knob and a single brass knocker.

She hoped someone in the house spoke English. She climbed the steps, lifted the knocker and rapped gently on the door. She waited, feeling sweat trickle down her back, feeling her left eye twitch.

Moments later, a middle-aged woman with a stern, pudgy face, wearing a white day dress and maid's cap, stared back at her with cool, steady eyes.

Trace swallowed. "Hello... do you speak English?"

The woman's eyes narrowed. "Yes..."

"I am Mrs. Tracey Bishop. I was hoping I could speak with Captain MacLeod."

The woman's eyebrows lifted in suspicion. Her voice, already low and clipped, thickened with a heavy accent. "And what is your business with Captain MacLeod?"

Trace had prepared for this. "It is about his daughter, Louise Jeanne."

The woman blinked, thought about it, thought about it some more, and grunted.

"Wait. I will see if he will speak with you."

The maid closed the door and, as it clicked shut, Trace inhaled a breath and waited, her nerves frayed, the anticipation boiling inside her.

When the door swung open and Captain Rudolf MacLeod, Johnny, stood glaring, an avalanche of emotion and memory crashed down on top of her.

He stood stiffly in his dark suit, as if at attention, his eyebrows thick, the full bushy mustache streaked with gray and turned up at the ends. His bullet bald head seemed belligerent, his eyes hard with accusation.

Trace was transfixed. Frozen for a moment. Stabbed by fascination, wonder and terror. She had been married to this man for seven years—seven miserable years. She'd lived through his drunken rages, felt his blows on her body and face, and endured his shouting abuses.

"What do you want?" he asked, brusquely. "What is this about you wanting to see my daughter? Who are you?" he demanded.

His English was remarkably good, but his accent made it sound aggressive and Germanic. Trace fought for poise and a steady voice. She had to make her case, for Nonnie's sake. For her sake. Trace lifted her chin in an appearance of confidence, but she kept her voice soft and pleasing.

"Captain MacLeod, I am a music teacher. I have heard from a friend that your daughter plays the guitar and the piano. I wish to offer my services to you."

He frowned. "She has a music teacher."

"Yes, Captain MacLeod, but I also teach singing, and I have heard that your daughter wishes to improve her voice."

He considered that. "Who sent you?"

"Greta Janssen, sir. She lives in The Hague. I have a letter of introduction from her. I have sung in New York, Chicago and Paris. I can offer your daughter a variety of both American and European styles and, I assure you, sir, my services are reasonable."

"Sung where? In theatres where rich men wait for women outside the theatre doors?"

"Oh, no, Captain MacLeod," Trace lied. She knew, of course, the history of American theatre. She knew about the "stage-door Johnnies" who routinely lingered around stage doors wanting to meet women. They paid handsomely for sexual relationships.

"No, Captain MacLeod. I sang in churches, and for literary and social gatherings, and at universities."

"Where is this letter of recommendation?"

Trace fumbled in her purse until she found the envelope. She handed it to the Captain. He opened the flap, drew out the folded page and snapped it open. He read, one eyebrow arched, his expression dark.

Trace saw that Captain MacLeod had already made up his mind to say no. But then he looked at her again, studying her, curiously. He narrowed his eyes on her and seemed to see her for the first time. This is what Trace had hoped for, was praying for—that he was seeing something in Trace that he couldn't quite put a finger on, but something familiar.

"What is your name?"

"Mrs. Tracey Bishop."

"Where is your husband?"

"He's a pilot, flying for the Allies in France." Trace knew that Captain MacLeod respected military men. "He is also a captain, sir. His name is Captain Edward Bishop."

"He's a captain, you say?"

"Yes, sir."

Captain MacLeod stared with a new interest. "...You'll excuse me, young woman, but have we met someplace before?"

Trace wanted to say, you bet we have, but instead, she said, "Not that I am aware of, Captain MacLeod."

Trace could almost see the wheels and gears of his mind turning and working. He twirled the end of his mustache as his eyes wandered, and he looked out into the sunshine, suddenly lost in memory. A moment later, his eyes settled on her again.

"Do you know who I am, Mrs. Bishop?"

"I am aware, sir, that you were once married to the woman known as Mata Hari."

His mouth twitched at the mention of her name. His eyes hardened.

"Why did you specifically choose my daughter to give lessons to? Surely, there are plenty of young girls in The Hague to whom you can teach music? If you are seeking notoriety or something more sinister, I can assure you that you will get nowhere with me."

His booming voice brought back soul memory and images of domestic quarrels and physical fights.

"Captain MacLeod, I heard that your daughter is musically talented. I want to be away from cities, away from people and away from war. When my friend, Greta, told me about this place, so quiet and peaceful, she also mentioned your daughter. She had seen her play

the piano at the young women's concert. I simply
thought it would be pleasant to be in this place for a
time and teach your daughter what I have learned."
As he stared at Trace, his eyes softened. At times,
he looked puzzled and preoccupied and she wondered if
he was fully listening to her.
Trace continued. "I communicated my wishes to my
husband, Edward, and he agreed that I should occupy
myself with satisfying work, but just for a few weeks—
just until late September or so. By then, Edward will
have a long leave and we will travel to his home in
England."
Captain MacLeod continued staring at Trace, and
she was sure she saw desire rising in his eyes. "Where
are you living?"
Trace had called the night before and booked a
room, anticipating that she may have to stay the night.
"I'm staying at the Hotel Quisisana."
Captain MacLeod lifted an eyebrow in approval.
"It's a good hotel. A fine place. Yes. To be frank with
you, Mrs. Bishop, I need to think about this. This
whole thing seems odd and quite irregular to me. However, it might be good for Non," he qualified, "that is
for Juana-Luisa. If you meet her, you can call her by
that name. Anyway, she gets bored here and she does
love her music, and she spends a lot of time practicing.
She wants to be a teacher, you know. She also has an
interest in America and Americans. Just the other day
she was asking me about America. I have never been,
you know."
Trace breathed in her nerves.

"All right then, come by tomorrow at 4pm sharp. I'll give you my answer then. I don't promise anything, you understand?"

Trace gave him a little bow. "Yes, Captain Mac-Leod. Thank you. I will see you tomorrow at 4pm."

CHAPTER 23

Trace spent a restless night in her soft feather bed, fighting the sheets, as warm night air blew in from open windows. Toward dawn, she finally burrowed into a deep sleep, her fleeting dreams filled with Broadway dances, Nonnie's girlish laughter, beckoning fingers, and Edward's soft kisses. She'd dreamt that she and Edward were on a picnic, food, flowers and wine spread out on a wide, checkered blanket under golden sunlight. She'd tilted her mouth up and Edward had kissed it, thrilling her, awakening an early morning longing for him.

She arose still sleepy, pulled on loose pants, tied back her hair and practiced some yoga stretches and simple dance routines, to help ease her ragged nerves, to get the kinks out of her neck, and to relax her tense muscles.

She ate a light breakfast in the dining room while reading The Times, and walked the manicured hotel grounds, her thoughts crowded with thoughts of Edward and Nonnie.

At 4pm sharp, she was knocking on Captain Mac-Leod's front door. He opened the door, dressed in a dark brown suit and tie and, although he didn't smile at her, his eyes were friendly.

He stepped aside. "Please come in, Mrs. Bishop." Trace took a fast, supportive breath and entered a polished foyer. Captain MacLeod closed the door behind them.

"Please forgive my bad manners yesterday, Mrs. Bishop, for not inviting you in. I am very protective of my daughter, her being the daughter of that infamous woman, Margaretha." He looked down with distaste. "I refuse to use her ridiculous stage name. Anyway, we have had curiosity seekers and reporters wanting to speak with Non. I refused them all, of course, and will continue to do so."

Captain MacLeod indicated toward a room off to the right, and Trace followed him across a thick, blue-patterned carpet onto dark wood floors that led to a wide wooden staircase. The Captain proudly offered a tour of several large rooms, including a living room with a decorative fireplace and heavy furniture, and a music room with a black baby grand piano, a tufted velvet sofa and club chairs. Old maps of Europe were framed and hung on the rose-colored walls. A cheerful drawing room had a semi-antique rug, card tables, floor to ceiling bookshelves and open windows that looked out on groves of trees and gently rolling fields.

The house was clean, somewhat austere, and as silent as a convent.

As they were returning to the music room, Captain MacLeod turned, stood upright and looked at her, resettling his shoulders and arching his eyebrows.

"Mrs. Bishop, my daughter will be down to meet you shortly. I want it made quite clear that she will be the one to agree, or not agree, to this arrangement. Is that understood?"

"Yes. Of course," Trace said, managing a tight smile.

Trace and Captain MacLeod sat stiffly in the music room, sipping tea that the sullen maid had delivered. Trace could feel the Captain's eyes steal toward her, but she pretended to be occupied with some old battle maps that she thought would have been hung more appropriately in the drawing room. They were peculiarly out of place in this room.

When Trace heard soft footfalls on the staircase, she sat bolt upright, hearing her heart thud in her ears.

"That will be Non. You may address her by her birth name, Juana-Luisa."

Trace set her teacup aside and stood, waiting, trembling, as the footsteps drew closer. The Captain also arose and waited, his hands locked behind his back, his head lifted in pride.

Juana-Luisa entered the room somewhat meekly, dressed in a simple white blouse and a dark skirt, with a raised hemline to the ankle. The shoes were a kind of low heeled clog.

Trace tried to swallow away a lump, but she failed. Juana-Luisa stood tall and beautiful, with an appearance that resembled her mother's. In many ways, Trace thought this lovely young woman was even more beautiful than Mata Hari had ever been. Non had a natural sensuality, a kind of gentle magnetism and mature poise, with smooth creamy skin and a pretty mouth. Her gleaming, raven black hair was combed back conservatively and tied behind into a bun, but it did not look matronly on her.

Non's dark blue and observant eyes seemed to take in everything with a nervous glance. When she gave a quick respectful bow to her father, he nodded back, keenly aware of his daughter's polish and charming allure.

And then Trace felt Juana-Luisa give her a few seconds of appraisal, and all of Trace's thoughts stalled. Was there any recognition in Non's eyes? Did she sense a thread, a mother-daughter bond between them?

Non approached Trace, presenting a gentle hand to shake. "Hello, I'm Juana-Luisa," she said with a friendly smile, with hardly any accent.

Trace took the hand softly, and when their hands touched, it was electric. Trace was lost in a thicket of emotion, and she struggled to find her voice.

"I'm... I'm, Mrs. Tracey Bishop... Friends call me Trace."

Non held her smile. "Trace... I've never heard that name. Is it American?"

"Yes... it is."

"Where in America are you from?"

"Kentucky. Lexington, Kentucky."

Non brightened, her eyes lighting up. "I've read about Kentucky. It's known for horses and for the Kentucky Derby, isn't that right?"

Trace nodded with some surprise. "Yes, you're right."

"Is Lexington near where they hold the Kentucky Derby?"

"It's not far. About an hour and a half away... maybe a little more."

Captain MacLeod spoke up. "Anneke brought tea, Non. Shall I pour you a cup?"

Non turned her head, distractedly. "No thank you, father."

Non indicated toward Trace's chair. "Please sit down, Mrs. Bishop."

Trace did, and the Captain offered Non the chair opposite Trace. They all sat, and Non placed her hands in her lap, gently twisting them.

"My father said you sang in New York, Mrs. Bishop."

Trace noticed Non had not called her by her first name. Of course, Trace thought. This was a much more formal time. No young woman called an older one by her first name.

"Yes...Various women's clubs and churches."

"Have you lived there, in New York?"

"Yes, for a few years."

Non's eyes changed, becoming thoughtful. "I'd love to go someday. I've heard so many delightful things about New York and America."

"I hope you can come," Trace said.

Captain MacLeod spoke up. "Non is about to receive her teaching certificate. She studies in Leiden."

"Congratulations, Juana-Louise. And what will you be teaching?"

"Kindergarten. I hope to teach in Velp, which isn't far away. I can take a streetcar to the school."

Non was visibly eager to hear more about America, asking question after question. Finally, the Captain cleared his throat and suggested that the two women move to the piano and begin the audition.

Trace was not the best pianist, but she had taken eight years of lessons and she could read music, if it wasn't too difficult. She sat on the piano stool, adjusting it to her comfort, as Non stood by. Both women were fighting nerves.

"What would you like to sing?" Trace asked Non.

"I'm a soprano, Mrs. Bishop. I'd love to sing Vilja from the operetta Die Lustige Witwe, that is, The Merry Widow. I'm sure you know it."

Trace smiled nervously. She'd heard the song, but had never sung it, and had never played it. She had seen the great opera star Renée Fleming sing the title role at the Metropolitan Opera in 2015, but she didn't know who wrote it.

"Oh... Yes. That's a lovely piece."

The Captain cleared his throat again, and his right eyebrow lifted in a soft rebuke. "You know, Non, that The Merry Widow was written by Franz Lehár."

Non looked at her father apologetically. "I know, father."

Trace had no idea what the issue was.

The Captain narrowed his eyes on Trace. "Of course, Mrs. Bishop, you know that Franz Lehár is an Austro-Hungarian composer."

Trace wished she'd studied more World War I history. Fortunately, she'd lived in this time long enough to know that Austro-Hungary, along with the Ottoman Empire and Bulgaria, were fighting against the Allies, who were Britain, France, Russia, Italy and the United States. Trace had also learned that World War I began when Archduke Ferdinand, of Austria-Hungary, was assassinated by a Serb in 1914.

Non was holding the sheet music in her hand. "I know, father, but it is such a beautiful piece and I feel it will give Mrs. Bishop a true rendering of my voice. May I please sing it, father?"

Captain MacLeod's lips tightened, but his eyes softened.

"And we are a neutral country, aren't we, father?" Non concluded.

"We may be neutral, but I have no love for Austro-Hungary, Non."

There was a brief silence, while Trace witnessed the power Non had over her father.

He gave his lovely daughter a brief smile. "All right, Non. Just this once. All right. Sing it for Mrs. Bishop."

Trace took the sheet music and placed it before her. When she saw what key it was in, she wanted to heave out a sigh of relief. The music was in the key of F major, which meant it contained only one flat, which meant Trace could play it.

Trace relaxed her shoulders and began to play, though her hands were shaky and clammy. Surprisingly, the piano keys felt sure and solid under her fingers, and the fine instrument was tuned to perfection. The touch was light, and the notes sang out, filling the room.

Non eased into the aria in a feathery light voice that was both warm and ethereal. As the aria progressed, Non's voice revealed a natural and stylish line, along with a dark moody touch that was surprising in a young woman. Toward the end of the piece, she managed to lighten the quality and resonance of the top notes, until by the final A natural, her voice lingered, then gradually fell away into a kind of breathy, romantic diminuendo.

When she finished, and the last of the music had faded into silence, Captain MacLeod rose to his feet, applauding enthusiastically. "Brava, Non. Brava!"

Trace, too, applauded, impressed and moved by her daughter's artistic voice. Without being aware of it, her eyes had filled with tears.

How could she have been such a fool? As Mata Hari, how could she have left this treasure of a girl for money and officers? Why hadn't she had the courage to hold onto this beauty at all costs? Why had she been so selfish?

Non bowed, demurely, and looked at Trace, shyly, for approval. "Do you have any suggestions or comments, Mrs. Bishop?"

"You have a lovely voice, Miss MacLeod. Truly, it is an exceptional instrument and your technique is good. I compliment your teachers."

"Please call me Juana-Luisa, Mrs. Bishop."

"All right. I'll offer only one little tip—something I learned from my teacher in New York. Be aware of your chin. Tilting your chin an inch higher or lower can adversely affect the quality of a note. Also, it can color the sound. But be careful, it can also push the note a little sharp or a little flat."

Non was excited by the suggestion, and she asked Trace to play a few bars of Vilja, so she could try it out. After singing six measures, trying the new suggestion and hearing the effect, Non broke into a sunny smile.

"Yes, I see, Mrs. Bishop. I can feel and hear the difference."

Captain MacLeod applauded again. "Yes. Yes! I hear the difference. Brava, ladies. Well done, Mrs. Bishop."

Trace and Nonnie spent the next half hour singing and practicing scales, while Trace offered suggestions on breathing, and singing on the breath.

An hour later, Captain MacLeod escorted Trace to the front door. He shook her hand, staring deeply into her eyes. Trace felt his attraction, and he held her hand much too long. If it was agreed she would give Non singing lessons, would Captain MacLeod make a pass at her?

His eyes sharpened on her, as Trace slowly retrieved her hand.

"Mrs. Bishop, you have given us a delightful afternoon. Non is already very fond of you. Non and I would love for you to come and give her singing lessons. When can you begin?"

CHAPTER 24

On Saturday, September the 9th, nearly four weeks later, Trace and Non took a break from their music lessons and went walking arm in arm, in lush afternoon sun. They strolled leisurely through a shady grove of English Oaks, out along a dirt path which led to a small duck pond.

They had bonded quickly, becoming close friends and confidants, laughing easily, sharing philosophies, hopes and wishes. Both looked forward to the twice-weekly lessons, and they reveled in each other's company, which exhilarated Trace. Every day spent with Non was a soul restorative day. It was as if, after a lifetime, deep inner wounds were finally being healed. Some of the aching emptiness and guilt Trace had felt since childhood were steadily melting away.

Each time Trace gazed into Non's eyes, she was nearly overcome by an infinity of love—by a mother's love, longing and hope that her daughter would find true love and happiness, and never know the sharp pain of abandonment.

It was on that day that Trace decided to ask Non about her mother, about Mata Hari. Trace had tossed a pebble into the pond, and she watched the rippling circle expand out and glisten in the sun.

"Do you ever think of your mother, Juana-Luisa?"

Non became thoughtful. "Yes. Yes, I think of her often. Do you know that when I go to school, I carry my lunch in a Mata Hari biscuit tin? Her image is on so many things. It's not like I can ignore her. Yes, I do think of her. I think, what is she truly like? I've read so many things, both bad and good."

Trace turned to Non. "Bad and good things?"

Non sighed. "I can't talk about my mother the way I'd like to. I have heard so many rumors about her life in Paris, but every time I ask my father about what happened, he gets terribly vague and upset. I know she wrote him once, asking for permission for us to meet, but the meeting never occurred. I don't know why."

"Maybe you could still meet her? Arrange another meeting?"

Juana-Luisa turned sullen. "Do you know that some months ago, my mother and I were both living in The Hague at the same time? I'd heard that she was living there, and I was curious, and I guess a little scared too. I was living with relatives, and so I got up the courage to go see her."

Trace picked up another pebble and tossed it into the pond. "What happened?"

"I walked by the house. There were no men around, but there were lovely curtains in front of the windows."

Non toed the ground. "I didn't go to the door. I kept on walking."

"Why didn't you go in, Juana-Luisa? You could
have met her. Talked to her. I'm sure she would have
loved to see you."

Non shrugged. "I don't know. Maybe I was scared
she didn't want to see me. What if she turned me
away? What if she was with somebody? A man? I
don't know."

"I'm sorry…" Trace said, her voice tight in her
throat. "I am so very sorry."

Non linked her arm in Trace's, examining her cloudy
face. "You have no need to be sorry, Trace. You've
done nothing to be sorry for."

Trace looked at Non, tenderly. "She did love you,
you know. Your mother loved you very much. She
just couldn't get out of herself. She was all locked up
in her own self-importance and her silly, ridiculous career, and her own selfishness. But she did love you,
Nonnie. She did, very much."

Non studied Trace carefully. "You've never called
me Nonnie before, Trace."

Trace grimaced, realizing she'd blurted out her
thoughts without editing them, as she often did. She'd
been overcome, both by love and guilt.

"I'm sorry, Juana-Luisa. I said too much."

"You spoke about my mother in the past tense,
Trace. Is she all right? Has something happened to
her?"

"No, no. Nothing has happened."

"Have you met my mother? Do you know her?"

This was going all wrong. Trace wished she'd kept
her big mouth shut. She decided to deflect the question.
"Juana-Luisa, I know you weren't feeling well last

week. Did you see a doctor? Do you have a good doctor?"

"You're changing the subject, Trace. Why?"

"Because I want you to go see a good doctor. The best doctor in the Netherlands."

Non stepped back, concerned. "Trace, you're frightening me. You seem changed today."

Trace grappled for words. "I'm sorry, Nonnie, I mean, Juana-Luisa." Trace searched for excuses and found a real one. She quickly gathered her thoughts.

Three weeks ago, Trace had moved all her things from The Hague to the Hotel Quisisana in De Steeg, and she'd written Edward about it, including her new address. His letters were coming less frequently, and when they did arrive, she sensed an undertone of emotional distance. She worried about his mental state. Was he suffering from battle fatigue or depression? Could he be questioning their marriage? Trace missed social media, where they could have easily kept in touch by texting and emailing and posting photos on Instagram or Facebook.

"I'm worried about Edward," Trace said, in a low voice.

"Worried? Has something happened to your husband?"

"No, not exactly. It's just that his letters aren't the same. He seems distant. Not like himself. There used to be such life and humor in his letters. I'm worried about him."

Non turned her head. "I hope you won't be leaving soon, Trace."

Trace tugged Non closer. "I don't know... I plan to stay another three weeks, unless I hear from him and he tells me he can get away from that awful war. I sent him a letter earlier today, begging him to write and tell me how he is as soon as possible, or maybe even send a telegram."

Non lowered her head. "You must miss him terribly."

"Yes, I do miss him, very much."

"If you must leave, you will come back, won't you?"

"Of course. Of course, I'll come back, and I'll bring Edward. I'd love for the two of you to meet. You'll love him, and he will adore you. I just know it."

Non shined with happiness.

Minutes later, Captain MacLeod came walking toward them. Trace hoped she didn't show her bitter disappointment. He nearly always appeared whenever she and Non were alone, obviously growing increasingly jealous of the time they spent together. Whenever he came near, it was as though a cloud were covering the sun.

"You two ladies must be telling secrets again. Perhaps you could let me in on them?"

"No secrets, father. Just women talk. It wouldn't be of any interest to you."

He rested his ready, sparkling eyes on Trace. "You must stay to dinner tonight, Mrs. Bishop."

Trace had always declined his offer, not wanting to spend any time with the man. She was intent on discouraging any advances, which she feared would happen if they were alone.

"Thank you, Captain MacLeod, but I..."

He held up a hand. "I will not take no for an answer this time, Mrs. Bishop, and I'm sure Non would love for you to stay."

"Oh yes, Trace. You must stay to dinner."

After dinner, as Trace had feared, Non excused herself and went upstairs to rest, stating that she wasn't feeling well. To Trace, this by itself was distressful enough, but to also be left alone with Captain Mac-Leod, who'd been drinking heavily, was doubly upsetting. The Captain's eyes were glassy, his voice wandering, his face shiny from the booze.

After Non had left, the candelabra between the Captain and herself gave off a warm glow that contradicted Trace's sudden gloomy change of mood. Sitting opposite the Captain at the oak table, Trace looked at him with concern. During dinner, she had seen the change in Juana-Luisa's color—from a healthy glow to a sickly pallor.

"Is she often like this?"

He, too, seemed distressed. "Not often. Sometimes. It comes and goes. She's really quite healthy."

Trace knew better. "Has she seen a doctor recently?"

The Captain's expression turned dark, his eyes brooding, an angry thought drawing him up from the table. He reached for a cigar, snagged a match and lit the thing, puffing, blowing plumes of gray smoke toward the ceiling. He waved a dismissive hand.

"Doctors are frauds, thieves and killers. It was a doctor who killed my son when he was just a baby, my little Norman. That damned doctor nearly killed Non as well, not that their bitch of a mother was of any help. But I will not continue with this conversation, only to say that I despise doctors. Most should be shot. Anyway, Non is a strong girl, and a very resilient girl. She will be fine. Rest is what she needs. I always tell her to rest, rest, and get more rest. She works too hard on her studies. She is much stronger than most women... Yes, stronger every day."

It was obvious that he was trying to convince himself. Trace tried to mask her doubt and annoyance. She fought to control a sudden eruption of rage, a near volcanic anger that was shooting up, from deep within her soul. It was a raw, remembered anger directed at this clueless, ignorant man, and it was an anger at whatever energy or force had trapped her here in this time and place.

If she was helpless to change the past—improve it—then what in the hell was she doing here? What was the point?

If Juana-Luisa didn't get a doctor's care—an expert doctor's care—she would die in 1919 from a cerebral hemorrhage, brought on by complications of syphilis. Syphilis her father had contracted from one of his whores. How could she ever forgive this drunken, violent, empty shell of a man?

"Are you quite all right, Mrs. Bishop?" the Captain said, moving toward her. "You seem to have lost your good mood. We must try to get it back. We are alone now, and I want us to become very good friends. I want you to trust in me and confide in me, like you do with Non. Perhaps I can drop by your hotel one day and we can talk and learn each other's secrets."

When he laid a heavy hand on her shoulder and began to caress it, Trace's hands went to fists. Acid began pumping in her stomach.

He lowered his voice to a near whisper, but it still carried strength.

"I am still a good and strong soldier, Mrs. Bishop. I think I would surprise you, if you gave me the chance. Yes, I could make you happy, and satisfy you in many ways."

She felt his hot gaze travel her body, and it sickened her. She felt an old buried hatred, and she felt a new boiling hatred. Her eyes fell on a serrated steak knife, lying before her. How easy it would be to grab the thing and plunge it into his chest, again and again, until he was dead. How she would love to do that.

The Captain continued his booze-induced blurry talk. "I am most touched by your concern for Non, Trace, if I may call you that, but don't be worried. Believe me. I know her. She will be fine. She is quite strong. But you and I, we are a different matter. You are a very appealing woman, Mrs. Bishop."

Intoxicated by rage and disgust, Trace squeezed her eyes shut, fighting for control of her emotions. She must control them, for Nonnie's sake, for her own sake.

This time, she had to choose a different path from the one she had chosen as Mata Hari. She had to control her mouth and her boiling fury. She had to swallow her rage and sacrifice her need to express it for something greater—for her infinite love for Nonnie.

Isn't that why she had come here? To face the wrongs of her past? To choose another way, a better way, to make better decisions? To establish a strong, healthy relationship with Nonnie? Right here and now, she could finally begin to stop the guilty tears that had filled so many of her nightmares since her childhood; the awful dreams of abandoning her daughter, and of living a silly, indulgent selfish life that had sent her to her death.

She had succeeded in being with Nonnie now, and no matter what happened in the future, she could always hold fast to the memories of her daughter's lovely smile, her lilting singing voice and her vanilla scent, hovering in the soft summer air.

One false move or one wrong word could threaten everything.

Trace took in a breath and sweetened her voice. "Captain MacLeod, how can a woman not be flattered by your kind words? You have been so generous to me during the past few weeks, and I will never forget it."

She paused, gauging his response. He hadn't remove his hand from her shoulder.

Slowly, she turned her head toward him, smiling. "How I wish you and Edward could meet. I know you two would get along very well. He would love this house, and especially those framed military maps."

She saw Captain MacLeod's face change. He slowly released her shoulder, but he didn't move away. When he spoke, his voice was low, holding some irritation, even as it returned to formality.

"You are most fortunate, Mrs. Bishop, to have a soldier as a husband. They make the best husbands, you know. Yes, the very best."

Trace watched as he squared his shoulders. "I, too, would serve again if it weren't for certain health issues."

He cleared his throat. Trace exhaled in silent relief as he started back to the far side of the table. "Of course, I must be here for Non. I cannot be away from her."

Trace nodded in agreement. "Of course you must be near her, Captain. Juana-Luisa is a fine, lovely girl.

And I'm sure she needs you now more than ever, as she grows fully into a woman."

He stood behind his chair, her words helping to restore some of his pride. "Yes, yes, quite right, Mrs. Bishop."

Trace seized the moment and stood. "Thank you, Captain, for a delicious dinner. Please give my compliments to your very talented cook. I hope you'll excuse me, but it's getting late, and I must return to the hotel to write a letter to Edward. As you can imagine, he waits for my letters impatiently."

"Of course he does, Mrs. Bishop. Letters from home keep a soldier living and fighting. I'll have my caretaker, Hans, take you back to your hotel."

The sour maid, Anneke, appeared from nowhere and opened the front door, staring at Trace with a grim expression.

Trace paused on the threshold, glancing toward the stairs. "Captain, please give my regards to Juana-Luisa and tell her I hope she feels better in the morning."

He snapped to attention. "Yes, I will, Mrs. Bishop. Good night then."

In the backseat of the car, as Trace was driven off into the night, she had the uncomfortable feeling that, despite her best efforts, Captain MacLeod had taken offense. Of course he had; he was not one who could easily accept rejection.

Trace decided she would send a note to Nonnie the very next morning, inquiring about her health. She could not bear to think of not seeing her daughter again.

CHAPTER 25

Two days later, Trace's hotel room telephone rang. It was 10 in the morning. Who could be calling? She left the bathroom and picked up the heavy black handset receiver.

"Hello…"

"This is the hotel operator, Mrs. Bishop," the male voice said. "A Miss MacLeod is in the lobby and she wishes to see you."

Trace brightened. "I'll be right down."

Five minutes later, Trace embraced Nonnie in the hotel lobby, and after they were seated on a pink couch with carved cherubs, Nonnie took Trace's hand.

"Father doesn't know I'm here."

Trace struggled to remain calm. "What has happened?"

"I read your note, but only after I pleaded with father to let me see it. He wasn't going to let me."

"Why not?" Trace asked.

"I don't know. He's been drinking heavily again. He's fallen back into his dark moods. After I read your note, he told me he was going to terminate our music lessons."

"But why?" Trace asked, suddenly alarmed. "What happened?"

"I don't know, but I had to come see you. I told him I was going into Velp. Trace, he is so changed since Sunday night when we had dinner. Did you two have an argument or disagreement?"

Trace sighed. She couldn't tell Nonnie the truth, that she had basically shot her father down, although politely. "No, we parted amicably. Everything was fine."

Nonnie looked away, distressed. "When I told him I would not give up my lessons with you, he flew into a rage. I thought he was going to slap me. He said I'd never see you again, that you were just another opportunist."

Trace held Nonnie's hands. "Listen to me, Nonnie. Forgive me, but I'm going to call you Nonnie. Listen, I don't want to come between you and your father."

Nonnie's voice broke with emotion. "You're not going to leave me, are you, Trace? Please say no."

"Of course I'm not going to leave you. We'll work something out. Maybe you can come to Paris with me, or England, when Edward and I move there."

"My father would never let me go."

"Let's never say never, Nonnie. We'll work it out. Just let this blow over and we'll make some plans. You're 18 years old now. You're a grown woman. You'll be able to choose for yourself what kind of life you want to live."

Nonnie looked deeply into Trace's eyes, hers brimming with tears. "Forgive me, Trace, but I feel so close to you. You've been such a good friend. I was hoping we could travel to America together."

Trace felt a sinking feeling, but she forced a smile. "Anything is possible, Nonnie. Let's just stay calm until your father is in a better mood. I'm sure he'll change his mind about the music lessons, and everything will return to the way it was. Until then, I have no plans to leave, so I'll be here. In the meantime, if you can get away now and then, come by and we'll spend time together."

Feeling reassured, Nonnie nodded and then drew Trace in for a hug. "I'm so glad you came into my life, Trace."

Trace felt the sudden sweetness of the moment turn sour. Something told her Captain MacLeod would never relent. He'd never let her give Nonnie music lessons again. What was she going to do?

The next morning, on Tuesday, September 12, Trace's plans were shattered. She awoke when she heard a light knock on her door. She sat upright, feeling blunted and worried about Nonnie. She'd had a little too much wine at dinner the night before. She pushed out of bed and staggered to the door.

"Yes... Who is it?"

"A telegram for you, Mrs. Bishop."

Trace sighed as she opened the door a few inches and squinted a look. The bellhop slipped the telegram to her through the narrow space.

Looking with blurry eyes, she took the telegram and studied it. "I'll tip you later... if that's all right?"

The bellhop gave a little bow, touched two fingers to the bill of his blue cap and retreated.

Trace blundered over to the draperies, drawing them back enough for a stream of sunlight to enter and illuminate the telegram. She slumped down into a chair, turned the envelope over in her hand, staring numbly, postponing the inevitable. Finally, with effort, she slid a thumb along the seam and opened it. Retrieving it, she gave a little shake of the page, tilting it toward the light. It was dated Monday, September 11th, 1916.

COME AT ONCE TO PARIS. EDWARD SICK. HE'S ASKING FOR YOU. BRITISH RED CROSS HOSPITAL NO.8 PARIS
MATA HARI

Stunned, Trace dropped the page.

A little over an hour later, she was packed and at the front desk paying her bill. She slid an envelope addressed to Juana-Luisa MacLeod toward the desk clerk and asked him to post it for her. The bellhop had already deposited her bags in the waiting cab, and she was anxious to leave.

As she thanked the front desk clerk and paused to tip the bellhop, she turned unsteadily, noticing a man staring at her from just inside the hotel entrance. He was a tall, erect man in his forties, with a somber, beseeching expression, and nervous eyes.

Trace started forward, head down, ignoring him, the cab waiting at the curb. As she passed the man, he spoke to her in a loud whisper.

"Mrs. Bishop?"

Trace stopped and ventured a look.

"Yes...?"

"Can we talk?"

"I'm leaving. I'm in a hurry. I don't know you."

"Just for a few minutes... Please. It is important."
His accent sounded German.

Trace glanced about, self-consciously. The desk
clerk was watching. So was the bellhop.

She lowered her voice, not meeting his gaze. "What
do you want?"

From inside his tweed jacket pocket, he produced an
envelope. "Will you please give this to Mata Hari?"

Startled, she shot him a look.

"Please. It is very important."

A shiver of cold fear crawled up her spine. "No, I
won't," she said, exiting the hotel for the car. He followed, limping, and as the cab driver opened the door
for her and Trace ducked into the back seat, the man
stopped short, only a few feet away, his wounded eyes
drawing her in.

The brawny, flat-nosed cab driver gave the man a
belligerent once-over. "Can I help you, sir?" he asked,
fist on his hips.

The man thrust out the envelope. "Please, Mrs.
Bishop. You'll be saving lives. Many lives."

The cab driver looked at Trace for instructions.
"Shall I send him off, Madam?"

Trace was conflicted. The man touched her in some
inexplicable way. There was a deep sadness about him,
as if something had been broken inside. She thought of
Sevuk Andranikian. Against her better judgment, she
nodded. The man rushed forward, handing off the little
envelope through the open window. She took it.

"God bless you, Mrs. Bishop."

And then he was gone, limping off toward a grove of
trees.

The train was delayed leaving The Hague, and Trace spent anxious minutes shifting in her seat, frequently asking the irritable conductor for updates. When the train finally got underway, it stopped in Brussels to pick up more passengers. From there it was slow, crowded and smoke-filled. It went thundering along toward France, its shrill, moaning whistle fitting the passengers' melancholy moods.

At the French border, surly, stony-eyed soldiers barked orders, and checked papers and passports. When Trace presented hers, one particularly sinister-looking soldier glared at her.

"Where are you going?" he asked in French.

"Paris."

"Why?"

She fumbled her French but managed to say, "To see my wounded husband in the hospital. He's a flyer."

He returned her passport, winking a flirtatious smile. "Of course, you are, Madam American," he said in English. "Of course, he's your husband. I know about you women Americans."

She turned away, disgusted. The war is making animals of us all, she thought.

The train made unscheduled stops, picking up wounded, bandaged soldiers, their young faces ashen, pinched with pain. They were being attended to by Red Cross nurses who also looked war weary. At various local stops, additional wounded soldiers boarded and sat with low chins and sloping shoulders, their vacant eyes staring off into remote distances.

"One of these soldiers could be Edward," Trace whispered to herself.

As the train entered the outskirts of Paris, Trace allowed only brief thoughts of Edward, and every time she thought of him, she felt a jagged pain of fear and foreboding. She'd been traveling for nearly eight hours, and she'd only eaten some bread, cheese and coffee in The Hague train station. As hungry as she was, she couldn't even think about stopping for food until she saw Edward.

Mata Hari had sent the telegram over a day ago. How long had Edward been ill? What kind of illness? Was it serious? Was he conscious? Had he been wounded? Would he know her? And then there was the worst thought of all: Was he still alive?

Trace exited the train at the Montparnasse station and wandered for ten minutes before she found a taxi. She asked the driver in English if he knew where the British Red Cross Hospital Number Eight was located.

He shrugged, and she repeated the question in French.

"Oui, Madam, it's at the Baltic and Corn Exchange."

Inside the taxi, Trace shut her eyes and lulled her head back, listening to the hum of traffic, the squeaky horns, the rattle of street carts. She prayed to God that she would find Edward alive.

"Madam…" the driver said, twisting around to face her. "We are here."

Trace sat up, eyes open, blinking. She must have drifted off to sleep.

Trace paid and exited. She faced a gated arched entrance, flanked by 12-foot stone walls. As she approached the gate, two British soldiers emerged from a guard booth. They checked her passport and listened, sympathetically, as she told them she was there to see Captain Edward Bishop.

Inside, a stocky, square-jawed soldier escorted her up a flight of stairs, across a brown marble polished floor, under a high vaulted ceiling and circular windows, to a wide lobby desk. A pleasant, round-faced woman in her 30s, wearing a nurse's cap and a full white nursing uniform with the Red Cross badge printed on her brassard, lifted her eyes from a clipboard.

Trace gave her all the pertinent information about Edward, trying not to sound frightened, irritable or impatient.

The nurse looked Trace over with some interest.

"Are you feeling well, Mrs. Bishop?"

Trace was jarred by the question. "Feeling well? Yes. Fine. May I please see my husband?"

"Very well. You look quite pale. Can I get you some tea and bread?"

"No, thank you. I just want to see my husband."

A thin orderly appeared, dressed in a white jacket. He escorted Trace up a flight of circular white marble stairs, their footfalls echoing in the muted silence. Halfway down a long broad hallway, Trace followed the orderly left, into a room that held fifteen single beds, all lined against the back wall, under tall windows that let in good light. Trace stood there, the blood pounding in her temples, her eyes darting about, seeking Edward.

The orderly nodded forward, and Trace swallowed back panic as she moved across the hospital ward. She passed men with drawn faces, anxious looks, and rigid muscles where bullets had struck. There were the multiple wounded, their bodies having been riddled with large or small shell fragments. Some of their limbs were in Thomas's splints due to multiple compound fractures. Others had stumps of torn-off limbs.

Five nurses were active, some quietly speaking with the soldiers, some dressing wounds, others scribbling notes in charts. All five nurses became alert when they saw Trace approach Edward's bed, fourth from the left. Trace didn't realize she was holding her breath until she shuddered, feeling light-headed, weaving unsteadily toward him.

There he was. Her handsome Edward. She stared down at him. He lay in partial shadow under a sheet, drawn up to his chin. He had changed. His handsome face was pallid, worn and thin. He had aged. His damp hair, combed back from his sweaty brow, had thinned.

"Edward…" Trace whispered, fighting back tears. If he awakened, he did not need to see her crying.

A young nurse was suddenly at her side. "Are you Mrs. Bishop?" she asked, softly, in a British accent.

Trace looked at her with weary, startled eyes. "What's the matter with him?"

The nurse folded her hands at her waist, her kind eyes placid. "Mrs. Bishop, I'm Nurse Benningfield. Your husband was found two miles from his airfield, still seated in his airplane. His air machine had been severely damaged, but he had managed to land it, with only minor injuries. When help arrived, Captain Bishop could not move, and he could not speak. It took a long time before he was coaxed out of the cockpit. He was taken to a local field hospital and examined. He had minor cuts and bruises, and a bullet had grazed his shoulder, but other than that he was physically okay. But he didn't respond to questioning, and he would not speak. He just stared. Unfortunately, while he was there, he caught pneumonia."

Trace took in the gravity of the nurse's words, her mind steadying with an effort. Trace knew that in 1916, there were no antibiotics to fight pneumonia. Edward's body would have to fight it off.

Nurse Benningfield continued. "He was moved here five days ago."

"Why wasn't I called? Why has it taken so long?"

"We didn't know where you were, Mrs. Bishop. Edward did speak your name now and then, but he didn't say how to get in touch with you. Finally, a flyer mate of his, a Captain Masloff, learned what had happened to Captain Bishop, and he was instrumental in your husband being admitted here."

Trace stared beyond Nurse Benningfield, her mind in turmoil. When she spoke, it was as if she were in a trance. "Edward has PTSD. He just couldn't fly anymore. Don't you see? He just couldn't go on. That's why he couldn't move or speak. He has PTSD."

"I beg your pardon, Mrs. Bishop. I'm afraid I don't know what PTSD is."

Trace looked beyond the nurse, her eyes unblinking. "Post-traumatic stress disorder."

"I'm unfamiliar with that, Mrs. Bishop."

"Of course you are, nurse," Trace said, sadly. "Of course you are, because it won't be recognized until sometime in the 1980s. I don't know exactly when."

Trace's voice tried to speak, faltered, and then started again, each word trembling out of her mouth. "You see, Edward has been in combat for months and months. He has seen death and dying constantly. He has seen friends die in fiery crashes; he has seen soldiers on the ground die by the thousands. Edward is mentally, emotionally and spiritually exhausted. Don't you see? He can't give anymore. He can't do anymore. He can't fly anymore. He has done enough for this stupid, pointless war."

Trace exhaled a frustrated breath, folding her arms tightly against her chest, resting her sad eyes on Edward. "Edward is tired and sick... He needs to go home."

Nurse Benningfield looked on with sorrow and compassion. She lowered her eyes and spoke at a near whisper. "He's a strong young man, Mrs. Bishop. We're optimistic."

Trace shook her head, glancing away toward the exit, determination rising. "Okay, I need to get Edward out of here. I need to get him home to England. I need to get him out of here as soon as possible."

Nurse Benningfield avoided Trace's eyes. "I don't think he's ready to be moved, Mrs. Bishop. He's too weak. He needs care and rest. Much rest."

"I've got to get him out of here," Trace said, her voice filled with stress and urgency.

Nurse Benningfield saw that in Trace's current state, there was no reasoning with her. "Okay, Mrs. Bishop, I will need to speak with Nurse Beckworth, the head nurse.

"Can you take me to her, please? Can you take me now?"

"Yes... if you wish."

"Do you know if my husband's family has been contacted?"

"Yes, I believe so. I'm not positive about that, but that is the protocol."

Trace peeled back the sheet and took hold of Edward's cold, clammy hand. She gently squeezed it. "It's all right, Edward, my darling. You just sleep now. I'm going to take you home."

Head Nurse Beckworth was a big-boned, matronly woman, whose graying hair was pulled back into a tight bun. She sat in a small, clean, windowless office on the third floor, behind a walnut desk that was stacked with papers in wire in/out baskets. She wore a darker color uniform, which Trace assumed indicated a higher rank.

After Nurse Benningfield explained Trace's request, she left, leaving Nurse Beckworth and Trace in a brief silence. The nurse made a steeple of her hands and leveled her full gaze on Trace.

"Mrs. Bishop, we contacted Sir Alfred Bishop, some three days ago. We have yet to receive a response, which isn't unusual, with the war raging on and communication often breaking down. We have tried to call as well, but we have been unable to manage a workable line."

Trace came right to the point. "I want to take Edward home to England."

"Mrs. Bishop, Captain Bishop is very ill. He should not be moved."

"But he would be..."

Nurse Beckworth interrupted. "...In my medical opinion, he needs professional care and plenty of rest."

"If I can make him understand that he's going home; if he can see me and believe me, I'm sure he'll recover much more quickly."

Nurse Beckworth kept her solemn eyes on Trace. "I'm going to be frank, Mrs. Bishop. Captain Bishop is weak. Very weak. If he is made to travel in his current condition, I believe he will die."

Trace closed her eyes, covering them with a trembling hand. Her voice took on a resigned quality, a strained, sad sound. "How are you treating his pneumonia?"

"With anti-pneumococcal serum. I'm going to be straight with you, Mrs. Bishop. So far, he is not responding. I wish I could say otherwise, but I don't want to lie to you. Not in these times."

They sat in a moody, swelling silence.

Finally, Trace lifted her head, removing her hand from her wet eyes. "Has Mata Hari been by to see Captain Bishop?"

Nurse Beckworth didn't blink, but Trace saw a hint of displeasure in her eyes.

"Yes, she was here, along with a Captain Masloff, who was responsible for getting your husband admitted."

"Okay, Nurse Beckworth. Thank you. But when Edward improves, I am going to take him home."

Nurse Beckworth turned aside, as if to ward off an attack she knew was coming.

"Mrs. Bishop, the Army will have to approve it. Captain Bishop has not been discharged and, as of now, his commanding officer is expecting him back at his unit as soon as he recovers."

Trace jumped to her feet, blood rising to her cheeks. "That's complete bullshit! It's absolutely insane. What's the matter with you people? Haven't you learned anything about war, and brutality, and what it does to a man? Edward will never go back to that goddamned war. Never. Over my dead body!"

Trace's outburst and raw language startled Nurse Beckworth. She stared down at her desk, unsure of how to respond.

Trace shivered from hunger, fatigue and rage. She no longer cared what she said or what these people in 1916 thought of her.

Trace massaged her warm forehead and lowered her voice. "Nurse Beckworth, I am sorry. I'm... I'm just lost, you see. I'm just lost, and I don't know what to do, and I'm afraid Edward is dying. You see, I can't let Edward die. He can't die. I can't let him die. I'm just so lost..."

CHAPTER 26

After Trace slumped out of Nurse Beckworth's office, and before she exited the hospital, she visited Edward again. He continued to sleep soundly, but his breath was labored and his face damp. A nurse was close by to monitor him. Trace couldn't bear to watch him, her funny, tender lover, lying there like that.

Outside, she wandered into a corner Bistro, and sat near the front window. The waiter was old, grumpy and stooped, the bread stale, and the meat, supposed to be chicken, was drowning in a thin, tasteless sauce. The entire world seemed lost in an endless nightmare.

Everything was changing in Paris as the war took its toll on soldiers and civilians alike. It was almost as if fate had lowered a heavy cloud of despair over the city. From the next table to her left, two grumbling men wearing berets complained about how incompetent the French generals were. She understood enough French to hear them say that the military leaders and politicians should negotiate a peace with the Germans and put an end to the misery of war.

Trace sat, sipping a second glass of red wine, feeling hollow, fighting an irrepressible grief and loneliness, too fatigued to think or feel anything remotely uplifting or positive.

By the time she returned to the hospital, it was nearly dark. The guards at the entrance had changed, and the new on-duty soldiers double-checked her passport, their wary eyes scrutinizing her. She waited, impatiently, as they discussed something about her passport.

"I told you, my husband is Captain Edward Bishop. May I please go see him? I was here earlier."

Inside, Trace returned to Edward's room. A nurse brought a chair and Trace sat heavily, every bone in her body tired, every muscle aching, her head pounding.

How she longed to take Edward back to their little honeymoon cottage, build a pine fire and fall asleep next to him, as the scent-filled room and the shadowy flames licked at the walls.

Trace awakened with a jolt. She had fallen asleep and dreamt that Edward had called her name. She sat up, alert, listening, the lights in the ward muted, a raspy snore coming from a bed nearby.

"Trace..." Edward's rusty, whispery voice said.

Trace shot to her feet. Even in the dim light she saw his eyes were open. She saw light playing in them.

"Edward..."

"Yes... it's your old English bloke."

She leaned and kissed his hot, damp forehead. "Oh, God, you scared me."

He struggled to speak. "Can't get rid of me, Trace girl."

"Don't talk, Edward. Save your strength."

He coughed, a low hacking cough. Trace pulled a handkerchief from her purse and wiped the saliva from his mouth.

"Attractive... huh, Mrs. Bishop?"

"Don't talk, Edward. Please don't talk. Rest, my darling."

"Got to," he said, rolling his head toward her. "Trace... so sorry about the letters. Couldn't write much. Mind couldn't find words. I couldn't sleep. Couldn't think. Couldn't keep my airplane in the air. Bad. Things got bad, Trace."

"You're fine now, Edward. I'm going to get you home to England. You'll be fine once you're home. Do you hear me? I'm going to get you home to England."

His sallow face was upturned toward hers, his eyes warming on her. "My God, but you're beautiful."

"Edward, listen. The hospital has called your family. I'm sure they'll be here soon."

Edward's mouth fell into a frown. He worked to pull his weak, trembling arm from under the sheet. He reached for her hand. She took it, pressing it to her chest.

"Trace...I'm very, very sick. I know it. I feel it."

"No, you're getting better, Edward. The nurses said so. I spoke to a doctor, who said you'd had a touch of pneumonia, but that you're improving."

His eyes stared into distances. "I've seen so much death, Trace. I know that bastard so well. I have lived with him, talked to him, cursed him. I've seen him come for all my friends. All my friends are dead, Trace, except for good old Vadime. And he is nearly blind. I saw death coming for me. I did. I saw him, a

251

big black, shadowy specter. But the odd thing about it is, he was smiling at me. But he's coming."

"No, he's not. Don't talk like that, Edward. Stop it, you're scaring me."

He coughed again, a deep aching cough that racked his body. His face wadded up in pain. Trace glanced about, looking for a nurse. One saw her and hurried over, a nurse she hadn't seen before. On the opposite side of the bed, the nurse stooped and felt Edward's forehead. Her eyes lifted with concern.

"He's burning up with fever. Captain Bishop needs to rest, Mrs. Bishop. I think you should go. I need to call the doctor."

"Yes, call the doctor. Hurry!" Trace said.

"No," Edward demanded, with another cough. "No... Stay, Trace. No doctor. I've got to talk to you."

The nurse hesitated.

Edward rolled his head toward the nurse.

"Alone...please, let me be alone with my wife."

The nurse paused, nodded and faded away into darkness.

Edward squeezed Trace's hand. "Trace...something in me is broken... The war..."

"No, Edward... No... You're going to be all right. You're getting better. I'm going to get you to England. You'll be home with your family. Think about that. Picture that. Imagine you and me at home in the warm sunlight. Picture it, Edward. You'll be home and I'll be there with you, darling. We'll plan our life together, and..."

He cut her off. "Listen to me, darling. Please. I can't fight anymore. I'm all fought out, you see."

"You don't have to fight anymore, Edward. You'll never have to go back to that damned war. Never. I'm going to take you away from here, as far away as I can. I'm taking you home."

"Trace...sit with me... Sit, please. I'm so sleepy. I'm so tired. Will you just sit with me?"

"Of course I'll sit with you, my darling."

Still holding his hand, she sat on the edge of his bed. He smiled up at her, tenderly. "Such a lucky bloke am I, Tracey Bishop." He grinned. "So strange. You... I don't know who you are or where you came from, but I'm so glad you married me... an old broken-down pilot."

"Don't talk anymore, Edward. Please just rest. I'll be here. I'm not going anywhere. Sleep now."

He nodded, coughed again. "Good... Good. Then I'll just sleep for a few minutes...just a few minutes."

His eyes fluttered, he took in a little breath, and drifted off to sleep.

Minutes later, a tall British doctor came by. He took Edward's temperature, felt his pulse, and looked grimly at the nurse.

Trace stood up, twisting her hands. "What is it, doctor?"

"You're Mrs. Bishop?"

"Yes..."

"I'm Dr. Slater. You should go now. You look as though you could use some rest yourself. When was the last time you slept? You look utterly exhausted."

"I'm not leaving him," Trace said firmly.

"Look... I need to administer additional medication. Captain Bishop needs sleep. He hasn't defeated this pneumonia."

"I'm staying."

Resigned, Dr. Slater received the syringe from the nurse, tapped it a couple of times and then injected it into Edward's right arm. Dr. Slater straightened, fixing his eyes on Trace.

"Nurse Callen will stay with you, if you wish."

"Thank you, but no. I'll stay with him."

After the doctor and nurse were gone, Trace eased down into the chair, still clutching Edward's hand. Minutes later, she was overcome by waves of exhaustion and she nodded off.

At some point, deep in the night, she awakened with a start. In the faint light, she saw Edward staring at her. He opened his mouth to speak but nothing came out.

She leaned forward. "Edward? Are you all right? Do you need anything?"

His voice was a faint whisper, as he struggled to speak.

Trace grew uneasy. Frightened. "Edward?"

"Love, I love you..." he managed, with a weak squeeze of her hand.

Trace stood up. "Edward?" she said, her pulse quickening.

He looked deeply into her eyes and for a moment, she saw him fight—fight to keep his eyes open—fight to speak—fight to stay with her.

Her voice shook with emotion as she frantically glanced about for help. "Nurse.... Nurse!"

Men stirred in their beds. Some lifted up and looked over.

In a raspy whisper, Edward said, "...Always... Trace... Always..."

Trace stared at him in helpless agony as his gritty eyes struggled to hold on to the world. But they gradually gave way, fading into an easy surrender; into a kind of glory. As Trace held her breath, she saw the soft, playful loving light go out of his eyes, like the blowing out of a candle, and Edward's big hand, that she was still clasping, fell limp and cold.

Trace bent beside him, her eyes welling up. "Edward... No, no, Edward. Don't leave me. Please don't leave me..."

But he was gone. His eyes were still, vacant, staring into the depths of oblivion.

Trace's eyes were scrunched in pain, her cheeks covered with tears. She struggled to control sobs.

Finally, mechanically, she stared into the darkness, seeing nothing. Drained and disoriented, she meandered out of the hospital, into the night, with no direction in mind.

CHAPTER 27

Trace awoke in darkness with a pounding headache, twisted in her blankets. She stared into the blackness for a time, lost to time and place, and then returned to sleep.

She was awakened by the clanging of church bells nearby, and by daylight leaking into her room. Where was she? With effort, she sat up, casting her slitted, blurry eyes about the small spare room, with its leaning night table and tarnished chest of drawers, holding a chipped porcelain face bowl and water pitcher. Her ancient bed was a squeaky, lumpy thing that had fought her all night.

The single window was mostly covered by dingy, gray, billowing curtains, the breeze rushing in cool and wet. As the bells dwindled away, she heard street noises and muffled voices. She heard the tap of early morning rain on the window.

She was in some hotel. Which one? She strained to recall. It took a minute. Oh yes, it was a small, basic hotel, the Beau Séjour on La Rue Lepic in Montmartre. That's right, after Edward's death, she had stumbled out of the hospital, ignoring a nurse calling after her, and somehow found a taxi. She'd asked the driver to take her to Montmartre, where she'd ended up at a café she couldn't remember.

She'd had too much to drink on an empty stomach: Pernods and maybe even a brandy. She'd drunk to help kill the pain of Edward's death, to wash away her loneliness and to escape from this awful time of 1916. Eventually, two young British soldiers began talking to her. They reminded her of Edward and she'd alternated between crying and laughing as they tried to cheer her up, although she couldn't recall exactly what they'd laughed about.

One of the soldiers had said she was very drunk and suggested she stay at the Beau Séjour, loosely translated as the "Beautiful Stay," which was close by.

So here she was, with a foul sticky mouth, stiff back, and a shattering, bloody headache. What day was it? She had no idea.

She propped up a pillow and leaned against it, sighed and soon fell back to sleep.

Her growling stomach woke her. It clawed and scraped with hunger, and she'd never been so thirsty. Her lazy, sleepy eyes found the water pitcher, and with a nauseous effort, she managed to stand and stagger over to pour a glassful. She tossed back the metallic tasting water in three gulps, poured another glass and drank and then poured another.

She flounced back onto the bed and teetered before landing on her back, staring up at the cracked ceiling and chipped yellow paint. With closed eyes, she began to think and remember. With scarcely the strength to move, she forced herself to plan her next move.

First and foremost, she must go see Mata Hari and demand the ring. Trace had to return to her own time. She was finished here in this time. Her life here had been a disaster, a nightmare, and there was no need to remain. If Mata Hari refused Trace the ring, Trace would simply tell her the truth. What did she have to lose? She couldn't remain in this place and time any longer.

A minute later, a disturbing thought arose: Mata Hari would not be in Paris. She had gone. By now, Mata Hari had set off from Paris to Belgium, via Spain, ostensibly to seduce German officers and provide secrets to the French.

In Madrid, she will seduce–or so she will think—the German intelligence attaché, Arnold Kalle, and she will give him a series of mostly worthless fake pieces of gossip about the French conduct of the war. In return, he will give Mata Hari some vague pieces of German information, which she will send to the French.

Secretly, and without Mata Hari knowing, in January 1917, Major Kalle will transmit radio messages to Berlin describing the helpful activities of a German spy, code-named H-21, whose biography would make it perfectly clear that Agent H-21 was Mata Hari.

Major Kalle will know that the French know Agent H-21 is Mata Hari. Major Kalle's intention? To punish Mata Hari for taking German money in return for useless and bogus information. The French will use this to help convict her and, finally, to stand her before a firing squad.

When Mata Hari returns to Paris in February 1917 and books a room in the Elysée Palace Hotel, a French judge and a dozen police officers will barge into Suite

113 of that luxurious hotel on the Champs Elysées, and they will arrest Mata Hari. She will not take her arrest seriously, and she will even hand out chocolates in a German helmet while smiling and flirting with the policemen. Months later, only days before she is to die, Mata Hari will finally see that her charms and flirtations, which have always worked miracles in the past, will no longer have any effect on these men. She will be executed.

Trace forced herself to leave the bed. For a time, she paced, nibbling her nails, and fighting back an aggressive sorrow.

Painful and agonizing thoughts of Edward's death stabbed at her. She had purposely left him in that hospital because she knew his family would come and take him home, where he belonged. Yes, he belonged to them now. They were his history. They held close and personal memories of him. They had borne all his trials and joys and they would mourn and weep his loss for the rest of their lives.

But leaving him, and walking away like that, had been one of the hardest things she'd ever done. She had been in no mental or emotional shape to meet Edward's family, and she did not feel a part of the Bishop family, despite the brief marriage. She did not feel she deserved the Bishops' money or property, and she was sure Edward's family would feel the same way, especially now that he was dead.

After she'd watched him die, she seemed to fall, sink and drown in bottomless grief. She wished she were religious and could busy her hands with rosary beads, distract her mind with a mantra, or throw herself onto the altar of any church. The truth was, she felt as though she were tumbling into a mental breakdown, black, cold and eternal.

Her love for Edward had come in a thrilling rush, and it struck with such an impact that it had startled, awakened and exhilarated her—making her believe in the magic of love.

The impossible, staggering thought of his being gone forever seemed a treacherous act of a God who lacked any reasonable compassion. What would she do without his warm, rich love, his boyish humor and enthusiasm; his all-encompassing love for her?

She moved to the window, parted the thin curtains and peered out into the cloudy, rainy day, at the foggy bistros and cafés and the people strolling by under black umbrellas, the scuffle of their footsteps sounding like a threat. The day hung heavy over the streets, the autumn air chilled her; her circling, brittle thoughts mocked her, her life in the future beckoned to her. What would she do now for money? She had very little left. How she longed to leap from that window and fly away—to flee this time of 1916.

Later, Trace sat slumped in a café booth over a plate of cheese, over-ripe fruit and a cup of coffee. She was oblivious to the people who came and went, the muted conversations about the lousy weather, and the ever-present cursing of the war and the deprivations it had caused.

Before her lay a daily paper on the marble top, left by a previous patron. An article caught her eye and she slid the paper toward her and began to read. It took several careful readings before the French became clear, and the story revealed itself.

The article reported that a French cavalry unit dressed in red caps, blue feathers, glossy black boots and polished brass buckles, had bravely ridden their horses into battle, armed with only lances, against German machine guns. Of the nearly two hundred who charged, not one of the cavalry survived. The writer blasted the political leaders, the commanders and the generals for their clumsy, incompetent prosecution of the war, and for the senseless deaths of nearly 900 soldiers every day.

Trace slid the paper aside. What insanity this war is, she thought, and in her time in the future, she'd known so little about the sacrifices people made in World War I.

At first, she didn't hear the voice standing over her and, when her swollen red eyes slowly lifted to the sound, she saw three men, one standing directly next to her and two behind. They were policemen.

The man who spoke to her had a little mustache, a thin face and bleak narrowed eyes. The two policemen behind him were stiff and somber.

Outside, rain tumbled down.

"Are you Mrs. Tracey Rutland Bishop?" the mustached policeman asked, in nearly perfect English.

A tremor shook her. In a small voice, she said, "Yes..."

"Will you come with me, please?"

Oddly, the first thing Trace thought was, Bad things come in threes... First was having to leave Nonnie, then Edward's death, and now this, whatever it was, and it couldn't be good.

"What's this about?" Trace said, in an automatic response.

"That is not for me to say, Mrs. Bishop. Will you please come with me?"

A sick misery arose in her. "May I pay my bill, please?"

He nodded. "By all means."

Outside, a policeman held an umbrella for her as she climbed aboard the car that had POLICE printed on its side in bold yellow.

They drove through the rainy, gaslit streets, slicing through the morning mist, rolling along the wide cobblestoned boulevards. Trace was sitting next to the very upright officer who had arrested her, while the other two sat in front, one as the driver.

Trace shut out thoughts and emotions. She did not have the strength to speculate. She would have to save what little energy she had to confront what was ahead.

CHAPTER 28

Captain Georges Ladoux's office was airless and spare, located at the Central Directorate of the Judicial Police at 36, quai des Orfèvres. Captain Ladoux was short and stockier than Trace recalled, with a square face, a broad black mustache, and a severe manner. He glared accusingly at Trace from across his desk. She sat on a hard, wooden, uncomfortable upright chair.

Of course, Trace knew that Captain Ladoux was head of the Deuxième Bureau, French military intelligence. She knew everything about him, and she knew she was in serious trouble.

"Do you know who I am, Mrs. Bishop?" he said in a thick accent, pronouncing her name as Beeship.

"Yes…"

He then continued as if he hadn't heard her. "I am Captain Georges Ladoux, an intelligence officer charged with organizing counter-espionage against the Germans."

Trace took in a breath, sat on the edge of her seat, and smoothed out her dress, one made of gold and pastel colored threads, with a spray of pastel rose buds and velvet foliage. The long sleeves matched the front, and the dress lay around her in graceful folds.

She'd purchased the dress for Edward, just before they were married, and she wore it now in his memory. Edward had complimented her in it. He had kissed her, passionately, and he had adroitly helped her out of it one delightful afternoon before he'd returned to war.

"First, let me offer my condolences over the death of your husband."

Trace nodded, silently, her face impassive. He didn't give a damn about Edward's death, and she knew it.

To say that the moment held catastrophic possibilities was a gross understatement. To say she was scared to death of this corrupt and evil man was also an understatement. To realize that she had been flung back into time to find herself in the very same horrifying situation she'd found herself in, in a past life, was debilitating and devastating.

But this time, she was not Mata Hari, she was Trace. Despite her fear and the present danger that the moment presented, Trace felt a steely obstinacy and a burning resolve to fight back. She would not ignore the danger, as Mata Hari had, nor assume she could use her feminine charms to escape it. She was going to face the challenge, no matter what the cost.

Captain Ladoux was the product of an age when women were not only subservient to men, they were also at their mercy. Any woman who didn't play by their rules—obedience, marriage, bearing children and keeping a home—was suspect. Men controlled the money. Men controlled the politics. Men controlled the military. Men had careers. Men had mistresses. Men had power. Women had to be pliant, understanding and longsuffering.

Trace was a product of her time, despite her memories of being Mata Hari. She sat as erect as a soldier, feeling as combative as a soldier.

"You weren't married very long, were you, Mrs. Bishop?" he said, flatly, shaping the inference to hint at something more important.

"The war took care of that. It makes one wonder if thousands of men have died needlessly because of military incompetence."

He bristled, sitting straighter, lifting his head in offense, his eyes turning cold on her.

"You, madam, should learn to curb your tongue."

"Why am I here, Captain Ladoux? Why haven't you contacted the American Embassy?"

The muscles in his face tightened. He reached down, picked up Trace's passport and held it high, shaking it. "Your passport is a fake, Mrs. Bishop."

Trace didn't flinch. "You still haven't answered my question, Captain Ladoux. Why haven't you contacted the American Embassy? I am an American citizen, and thus I am entitled to all the protection that the United States government offers."

"You do not ask questions here!" he shouted. "I ask the questions and you answer them. Do you understand?"

"I will answer, sir, when I have a United States representative here with me."

He slammed a fist down hard on the desk. "You are spying for the Germans, Mrs. Bishop. You are not entitled to anything. Do you understand?"

She kept her voice even. "Forgive me, Captain Ladoux, but I am not a spy of any kind, and your charge is utterly and absolutely ridiculous."

He shot up, his face flushing red with anger, his voice gritty and threatening. "Do not insult my intelligence, Mrs. Bishop. Do not insult me, Mrs. Bishop. The charges before you are serious, and they are conclusive. Make no mistake about that."

Trace's stomach knotted. What conclusive evidence could he have?

She struggled to keep her nerves out of her voice. "And what is this evidence you have, Captain Ladoux? Present it. Show it to me."

He eased back down in his chair, his mouth tight, his eyes bold with accusation. He opened the top drawer of his desk and took out a small square envelope. He tossed it on the desk before her, squinting back at her with an animal suspicion.

When Trace's eyes fell on it, she felt the fire of panic. It was the envelope the limping man had given her at the hotel in De Steeg. The envelope he had asked her to give to Mata Hari. Trace had forgotten all about it. Where had Captain Ladoux found it?

"Mrs. Bishop, two nights ago, the night your husband died, you took a taxi to Montparnasse. You exited that taxi and entered Café La Coupole. While there, you were observed talking with two British soldiers. I suggest, Mrs. Bishop, that you became quite drunk, perhaps to drown out your pain over your husband's death, perhaps because this is your habit. In any case, one of those soldiers thought it was bizarre that you spoke of things, like the future, and how the war would end. You seemed to have a lot of knowledge about the war, Mrs. Bishop, and this soldier found it disturbing. He said you spoke about Mata Hari and, more interestingly, you spoke about me, and how I would be tried as a double agent."

Trace nearly collapsed in shock, defeat and anguish. Why had she been so stupid? She often rattled on when she'd drunk too much, but now she couldn't recall what she had said. Her only memory was of a fiery outburst about Edward not being released from the damned war long before his PTSD took hold.

Trace managed to sit tall, her face not betraying the earthquake that was going on inside her—her inner crumbling state.

Captain Ladoux held up the envelope. "Mrs. Bishop, this little envelope dropped to the floor from your coat. One of the British soldiers found it after you left. Those two honorable British soldiers did the right thing, Mrs. Bishop. They handed this note over to the French police."

Trace stared hard, not moving, as Captain Ladoux continued, looking smug and confident, enjoying his trap.

"For your information, Mrs. Bishop, the man who gave you this is working for French Intelligence. The note is of no real importance here, except that it confirms that you and Mata Hari are spying for the Germans."

"I didn't open the note. I had no idea what was inside."

"Mrs. Bishop, we have suspected you for some time. You have aroused our suspicions during your and Mata Hari's travels in and out of the war zone. For your further information, Mrs. Bishop, I have contacted the

U.S. Embassy, and have inquired about you. They have no record of you whatsoever, and they stated quite conclusively that they did not issue you this passport, nor any other passport. So far, we have been unable to learn anything about your past—where you came from, how you got here or why you came to France. But I suggest to you that you are most likely a spy, recruited, trained, and operating out of Antwerp, in occupied Belgium, as part of the espionage network run by the infamous Elsbeth Schragmuller, better known as Fraulein Doktor, one of the more shadowy figures in German Intelligence."

Trace's face was blank with shock. "What? I am not. I've never even heard of the woman. You don't know what you're talking about."

"It won't do you any good to deny it, Mrs. Bishop. This is a very serious charge. Very serious indeed."

Captain Ladoux stood, squaring his shoulders, as if ready to pass sentence. "As such, I hereby inform you that you are under arrest for espionage against France. You will be escorted to Saint-Lazare, a prison for women, where you will remain until you can be interrogated further at the Palais de Justice, by the investigating magistrate, Pierre Bouchardon."

Trace was as still as a statue. Her eyes shifted down and away; an icy chill arose that nearly stopped her heart.

CHAPTER 29

At the Prison Saint-Lazare for women, Trace was cruelly placed in solitary confinement in a padded suicide cell, under 24-hour supervision. The cell was dark and dank, and smelled of mold and human waste.

Saint-Lazare had originally been built in the twelfth century as a leper colony, and it became a prison five centuries later. Since it stood on the boundary of marshland on the banks of the Seine, the prison was notoriously cold and damp.

Within days, Trace became deathly ill and was taken to the infirmary, where she was slowly nursed back to moderate health. She was then assigned cell number 12; ironically, the same cell Mata Hari would occupy after her arrest in January 1917.

Trace's cell was dusky and close, and like most cells, it was populated by fleas, lice, bedbugs, cockroaches and the occasional rat. The lavatory was a metal bucket, and her washing had to be done with the single bowl of cold water she received every morning. The food was minimal and of poor quality: bad coffee, stale bread and thin soup with tired vegetables. A small portion of meat was served once a week.

Trace soon developed a chronic cough and was placed under the care of Soeur Leonide, the venerable superior of the Soeurs de Marie-Joseph, who staffed the prison. As such, a nun arrived twice a day to check her medical condition and pray for her.

Trace spent most of her time in bed, beating away the bugs, struggling for sleep and sanity. She developed a body rash that never went away. She lost track of time and was never told when she would be interrogated by the investigating magistrate, Pierre Bouchardon. It finally became evident to her that Captain Ladoux's plan was simply to leave her in prison to rot and die. After all, who would know? Obviously, no one had come for her—not Mata Hari or Captain Vadime, and they were the only people she knew. In 1916, she was a nobody who had arrived from nowhere. She had no discernable background and no family; therefore, she would not be missed when she died.

Over the next few weeks, she grew rail thin, exposing sharp cheekbones. Her eyes sank into her ashen face. She forced herself to eat, although she had no appetite.

While Trace slipped in and out of sleep, she pondered her fate. Why had she returned to this time? What had been the purpose? To rot and die in prison so far away from her own time and place that no one in either time would ever know what had happened to her?

On one drowning day, a nun brought Trace a mirror. She stared into it. Her whole face was a ruin, her short hair a tangled nest, her eyes filled with wide madness.

As the days passed and she grew increasingly frail and listless, she began to lose all hope. She often spoke to Edward, her lips moving soundlessly. There were times she felt his kiss and heard his warm voice, encouraging her to take heart, and never give up. Nonnie, too, often appeared in Trace's vague and wandering dreams, her daughter's face springing up into Trace's consciousness like a blessing. She relived those delightful days in the sunny piano room in De Steeg, as she and Nonnie sang and laughed and sometimes danced a waltz, whirling about the room, happiness all about them.

Trace longed to write Nonnie, but she had neither the strength nor the will to do so. And, anyway, what would she say? "Here I am, Nonnie, rotting away in Saint-Lazare Prison, accused of being a spy." If Captain MacLeod saw the letter, and he certainly would, there would be no hope of ever seeing Nonnie again.

As the days and nights blurred by, Trace comforted herself with the grateful thoughts that despite her dire circumstances and certain death, being with Nonnie had made it all worthwhile. Edward's love and their brief marriage had made it all worthwhile.

On one aggressively cold morning, Trace awoke, shivering. Every muscle seemed to ache, her teeth chattered, and her stomach was a boiling knot of agony. In that broken, shattering moment, she glanced up through swollen, slitted eyes and saw the first light of morning streaming in from a high narrow window. She couldn't pull her eyes from it, even though her eyes burned and twitched. The light poured in and formed a yellow column of light, bright, sturdy and constant. Suddenly, something in Trace awakened: a memory, a stirring of desire. Her breath deepened. Tears filled her eyes. She did not want to die. She wanted to live! She wanted to see her family and friends. She wanted to sing again, to feel her body move in time with music; she wanted to dance with a chorus and feel the exaltation that follows a curtain call.

In a flash, she realized she had to act, she had to do something. No one had come to help her, and no one would—not unless she took action now. She had to contact the one person who might be able to help.

Trace forced her heavy body up onto her feet, her legs rubbery, her head reeling. She leaned over the bed, inhaling deep breaths, willing new strength to enter her body.

When the cell door opened, Trace angled her body toward it. Sister Constantine entered, a young, pious woman, who had never looked Trace in the eye.

Sister Constantine froze when she saw Trace struggling to stand.

"What are you doing up, Mrs. Bishop? You must lie down. You are sick, very sick."

"No," Trace said so sharply that Sister Constantine flinched.

Trace lowered her voice, speaking slowly and deliberately. "Sister Constantine, I want to dictate a letter to you, and you must promise me that it will be delivered."

Sister Constantine's expression turned fearful, and she whispered. "I don't think I can do that, Mrs. Bishop. It's not allowed."

Trace stared at the woman with pleading eyes. "If you do not help me, Sister, I will die, and I am sure that God does not want me to die. I am innocent of all charges, and it is in your power to save my life. Not in the angels' and not in God's. It is in your power to save me. Please help. You are my last hope."

Trembling, Sister Constantine bowed, making the sign of the cross.

CHAPTER 30

Sir Alfred Kenyon Bishop was a tall, straight, balding man, who possessed a tenacious personality and a regal air of authority. He had that stiff-upper-lip quality that many British are known for, and he was also known for his shrewd, calculating intelligence and quick, biting wit. His legs were long, his gait assured and his eyes lively and observant.

At 58 years old, he was a member of the Liberal Party and had been a respected member of Parliament since he was 52. He enjoyed a close relationship with David Lloyd George, who was the current War Minister and who, in December 1916, would become Prime Minister of England.

Sir Alfred was led down the long, gray, polished hallways of the Judicial Police station by a uniformed police sergeant, and ushered into Captain Ladoux's office. As Sir Alfred entered, the door was closed promptly and quietly behind him.

Captain Ladoux lifted his eyes coolly and fixed them on Sir Alfred, watching as the man shouldered out of his cashmere overcoat and draped it over his arm.

"Good morning, Captain Ladoux," Sir Alfred said cordially. "It is a cold, miserable morning, and I hear we may have some snow."

Captain Ladoux nodded, indicating toward the chair before his desk. "Please be seated, Sir Alfred."

The men did not shake hands and Captain Ladoux did not offer to take Sir Alfred's coat. Sir Alfred sat, glancing around Captain Ladoux's office, noticing the bookshelves overflowing with old books, and the desk cluttered with papers.

"I shall get right to the point, Captain Ladoux. As you were informed by my messenger yesterday, Thursday, November 5th, I am here to kindly request the immediate release of my daughter-in-law, Mrs. Tracey Rutland Bishop, from the Saint-Lazare prison, where she has been held since September 17th."

Captain Ladoux folded his hands and lifted his chin. "I could have saved you a trip, Sir Alfred. I'm afraid that what you request is quite impossible."

Sir Alfred crossed his long legs. "Oh, come now, Captain Ladoux, it is not impossible at all. A simple signed release from you and from the Magistrate, Pierre Bouchardon, will certainly do the trick, I should think."

Captain Ladoux remained still, his jaw set. "Sir Alfred, I can appreciate your position and your many…let us say… official political connections. However, Mrs. Bishop has been arrested for spying for Germany against France. That is a very serious offense, and one that cannot be so easily disregarded or dismissed."

Alfred's voice deepened, his eyes taking on some fire. "Captain Ladoux, I have reviewed all the evidence you have against Mrs. Bishop, and so has my son, Thomas, who works for British Intelligence, along with a number of his colleagues. We have examined this so-called evidence and concluded, quite frankly, that you have no real evidence at all against Mrs. Bishop."

"So you say, Sir Alfred... but this is France, and not England."

"Shall we examine the evidence, Captain Ladoux? You have a note that was given to Mrs. Bishop by one of your planted agents in De Steeg, that was to be delivered to Mata Hari. You deem that as proof that she was somehow working with Mata Hari, who is now supposed to be some kind of double agent. Now as to whether Mata Hari is, or is not, a double agent is of no concern to me. Captain Ladoux, what you did to Mrs. Bishop was blatant entrapment. The note contains no damning information regarding Mrs. Bishop whatsoever. Frankly, I am at a loss, and quite baffled, as to how you can use that little note as any evidence at all. Your further evidence states, quite astonishingly, that my daughter-law was likely a spy recruited, trained, and operating out of Antwerp, in occupied Belgium. Ostensibly, she was involved in a German espionage network run by Elsbeth Schragmuller, better known as the Fraulein Doktor. This accusation is, first of all, baseless, and secondly, completely absurd. You have no shred of proof at all, Captain Ladoux. You maintain that because Mrs. Bishop's origins cannot be traced to any one family, country or locale, this must mean she is a German spy. I am told, Captain Ladoux, from the nuns who are praying for her soul at this moment, that Mrs. Bishop cannot even speak German."

Captain Ladoux leaned back in his chair, offering a little triumphant smile.

"My regrets, Sir Alfred, that you deem French intelligence so inferior to British Intelligence. But I can assure you that we have all the evidence we need, not only to convict Mrs. Bishop, but also to have her brought before a firing squad. Whether you like it or not, Sir Alfred, we are at war and Mrs. Bishop has spied against France. I can assure you, sir, she will be tried, found guilty, and executed."

Sir Alfred let out a weary sigh. "Captain Ladoux... your theatrics are impressive."

Captain Ladoux bristled at the obvious insult.

Sir Alfred stared at him, his eyes flinty. "In 1913, I had the honor and privilege of having President Poincaré as my personal guest at Bishop Manor in England. Last evening, I dined once again with your good and honorable President, Raymond Poincaré, at the Hotel Lutetia. We spoke at length about Mrs. Bishop and, as such, I presented him with the entire tenuous evidence you have assembled against her. I told him of my son Edward's sacrifice for the Allies, and for France in particular. I told him that Edward had been married in France, and that he had died in France. I told him that my son loved and respected the French and had the greatest admiration and respect for French culture and French justice. Captain Ladoux, I told him that Edward's wife, my daughter-in-law, Mrs. Tracey Peyton Rutland Bishop, was rotting away in Saint-Lazare Prison, falsely accused of being a German spy."

Captain Ladoux's body stiffened, his face went rigid. His nervous eyes began to shift, as he adjusted himself in his chair.

Sir Alfred's voice took on an edge. As he uncrossed his legs, his eyes moved from accusation to contempt, to anger. "I told President Poincaré that it took me over a month to learn where my daughter-in-law was, because the French military, French intelligence and the French police made it practically impossible. I was finally able to learn of my daughter-in-law's whereabouts thanks to a letter she wrote to me, and then managed to have delivered to the British Embassy, just five days ago. I relayed to President Poincaré my disappointment, regret and bewilderment at such incompetent and unfortunate behavior from such a respected and honored agency of France."

Sir Alfred slipped a hand inside his black, woolen suit jacket and drew out an envelope. He stood, pulling himself to full height, his eyes flat and hard. He paused for effect and then, deliberately, Sir Alfred placed the envelope on the Captain's desk.

Captain Ladoux's eyes grudgingly slid down to view the envelope, as the silence stood between the two men.

"Captain Ladoux, I have lost my son. I do not intend to lose my daughter-in-law because you, sir, are obviously incompetent at finding the true enemies of France, a great country and true ally to England in this terrible war. That is a letter from President Poincaré, instructing you, personally, to release Mrs. Tracey Rutland Bishop from the Saint-Lazare prison immediately. Please read the letter carefully, sir, if you wish."

Captain Ladoux's face turned crimson with rage, his eyes not lifting from the envelope to meet Sir Alfred's.

"I'm sure I do not need to read it, Sir Alfred," he said, in short, clipped, angry words.

"As you wish, Captain Ladoux. Then I trust that President Poincaré's orders will be carried out to the letter, and that Mrs. Bishop will be released immediately?"

Captain Ladoux gazed up at Sir Alfred, his eyes flaming. "Yes... Of course it will be done."

"Excellent, Captain. I will have a car waiting at the main building on rue Saint-Denis. Oh, and please ensure that Mrs. Bishop's passport is returned to her. Thank you, Captain Ladoux. Good day."

After Sir Alfred closed the door, leaving Captain Ladoux alone in his quiet fury, he slammed a fist down hard on the desk and shouted, "Va te faire enculer, bâtard anglais!"

CHAPTER 31

Trace was lying on cool clean sheets, covered by a woolen blanket, in a quiet, private hospital room. As her eyes fluttered open, she stared in perplexed reflection. There were fresh flowers beside her bed, giving off a glorious scent, and through the curtained window she turned her head to see a far meadow covered with snow.

Where was she? She made an effort to sit up, but she was too weak. She lay there, feeling a dragging resistance. Her bones felt hollow. Her body numb, lifeless.

Was the stench from that prison gone—the stench that had permeated her hair, her clothes, her skin?

The scent of rose and vanilla answered her question, and the warm, comfortable bed soon caressed her back into a delicious sleep.

When she awoke next, a single light glowed from a table at her bedside. Outside, it was dark, the curtains pulled. When she heard a soft, deep voice, she slowly rolled her head toward the sound.

"How do you feel?"

Her foggy eyes searched the dimly lighted room. Someone rose from a chair, and a tall shadow approached the foot of her bed. She narrowed her eyes to see a man, dressed impeccably, in a dark suit and dark tie. His face was kind, his smile warm.

Trace swallowed twice before she could speak. "Where am I?"

"You are in a private hospital, north of Paris."

Had she returned to her own time. "Paris? What day and year is it?"

"It is Tuesday, November the tenth, 1916."

Trace closed her eyes in disappointment.

"Are you feeling better?"

"Yes... Not so strong yet... but better."

She opened her eyes. "You're the man who came for me, aren't you? Are you Mr. Bishop, Edward's father?"

"Yes. I'm Alfred Bishop. I received your letter and I am so pleased you wrote to me."

Trace fixed her eyes on him. "Thank you for coming..."

He moved to the left side of her bed, offering a little smile of reassurance. "Of course I came. I would have come sooner if I had known where you were."

Trace didn't speak for a moment. Her mind whirled and worked to snap all the pieces together. "Yes...Edward's father."

"I returned to Paris to find you after we buried Edward in England."

She looked at him slowly, carefully. "You came looking for me?"

"Yes. Of course."

She shut her eyes, tears forming, and then she turned away, letting them trickle down her cheeks.

"Is there anything I can get you, Mrs. Bishop? Anything at all?"

She shook her head. "Thank you... Thank you for getting me out of there. I thought I was going to die."

"You still need care. And rest. When the doctors say you are ready, I would like to take you to England. If you are agreeable, of course."

She turned to face him. "England?"

"Yes. It is best that you leave France... the sooner the better."

She knew exactly what he meant.

"Do you have any plans to travel anywhere else, when you are recovered?" Sir Alfred asked.

"No. None. I have nowhere to go."

Trace saw a flicker of relief in his eyes. "Then I hope you will return to England with me, when you are ready and able."

Trace looked at him earnestly. "I am so sorry about Edward... your son."

"Thank you. Edward wrote to us about you. He was emphatic that I promise to protect you and take care of you."

Trace turned away again, feeling an unbearable sorrow. "I loved your son very much, Mr. Bishop. It happened so fast... I mean our love for each other. I don't know, maybe it was the war that sped everything up. Maybe it was a thousand things. Maybe that's why I came here to this time. I don't know."

"Came from where, Mrs. Bishop?"

"Please call me Trace."

"If you wish, Trace. All right."

"Edward was a very special man, and I will never forget him."

She tried to hold back the tears that continued to run down her cheeks. Sir Alfred removed a handkerchief from his pocket and blotted the flow.

"Everything is going to improve now, Trace... We must begin anew. We must think of the future now. I know it is what Edward would want us to do. So, while you continue to recover, I want you to consider not only returning to England with me, but also remaining there and making it your home. As I'm sure Edward told you, he provided handsomely for you in his will, both in money and property. As I said, I made a solemn oath to my son that I would always look after you, and that is what I will do, if you will permit it. My wife, daughter and Edward's brother are all looking forward to meeting you and welcoming you into our family. You don't have to decide now, Trace, but please consider it. Just give it some thought. Meanwhile, get plenty of rest, and if there is anything you need or want, please let me or the nurse know, and you shall have it."

Trace couldn't stop the tears. After all she'd been through—after the losses and the cold dark nights— after all the mounting anxiety, uncertainty and confusion, the hopeless life in Saint-Lazare Prison, she couldn't possibly stop the flow of tears. And now, lying there, taking in Edward's father's kindness, warmth and generosity, she couldn't stop them.

Sir Alfred remained by her side, drying her tears, until she drifted into a deep sleep. And then he sat, a quiet shadow, his hands folded, head bowed, wondering who this pretty, young woman was, where she had come from, and what he was to do with her.

CHAPTER 32

Bishop Manor was a striking, three-story, Georgian-style manor house that sat on nearly 34 acres in a quiet, rural area, with fenced pastures and eye-catching hedged gardens and fountains.

Trace sat in the rear seat with Sir Alfred, being chauffeured in a 1916 Napier motor carriage that Sir Alfred proudly stated was manufactured in Acton, West London.

While Alfred talked, Trace stared out the window with childish wonder, as they continued past old trees, rolling meadows, and stone field walls. The magnificence of Bishop Manor soon came into full view, the slate roof, soaring columns and substantial balustrades, revealing a classic elegance, a world far beyond anything she could have ever imagined.

Trace's full attention was focused on the impressive house, the gardens, the manicured hedges, and the pond, and she only half-listened as Alfred rambled on about the car.

"Trace, I find that I like the automobile more than I would have ever believed. I still love my horses, of course, but I must admit that I enjoy the look, the feel, and the smell of this new machine. It seems manly and masculine somehow."

The car rumbled ahead, turned into the gated entry and advanced across the winding crushed stone driveway, flanked on either side by tall, majestic trees.

Sir Alfred pointed, enthusiastically, as they advanced toward the stone courtyard.

"Over there, Trace, is farmland, and additional flower gardens. See the Coach House and pond? And a little further on—just past those trees—is a graceful stone cottage. That cottage is yours, my dear, the one Edward left you in his will. It includes a garden, private meadows, and woodlands, with walking and riding trails. I hope you can ride a horse, Trace."

She looked at him, turning her hand this way and that, as if to say, "More or less."

Sir Alfred continued. "Well, don't you worry about that. I'll teach you to ride. Later, we can take a stroll over and I'll show it all to you. It's a magnificent piece of property."

His voice dropped a little. "If you wish, once you have settled in, I'll walk you to the family cemetery, where Edward is buried."

Trace turned away, unsure. "Yes, I'd like that."

Sir Alfred forced a brighter tone. "Of course, this is the end of November, Trace, and things look rather brown now, but in the spring, this whole area explodes with color and beauty. You will love it."

Trace eased back in her leather seat, and looked again at Bishop Manor, nearly overcome. "It's so big, Sir Alfred."

He laughed, taking her hand. They had become very good friends in a short amount of time. They'd laughed and cried, and as Trace had grown stronger, they'd walked the hospital paths in prayerful silence after sharing stories and loving memories of Edward. When Sir Alfred had asked where she'd come from and how she'd arrived in Paris, Trace had been evasive. "I'll tell you everything someday," she'd said, "when the time is right."

Sir Alfred followed Trace's eyes as she explored the manor and land.

"Yes, Trace, I'm afraid it is all much too big."

Sir Alfred turned thoughtful. "It has twelve bedrooms, ten bathrooms, six reception rooms, a grand hall, two libraries and my study, where I can escape from the world and get away from it all. But the war has changed everything, Trace. Houses like this one won't be around much longer, or at least the families who own and run them won't be around. Who can afford them? I've already had to sell off some of the land. Look at the great house, Trace. It is a relic from another time and place, like me. At least that's how I feel sometimes."

Trace turned to him with fondness, linking her arm in his. "Sir Alfred, believe it or not, I know what you mean about feeling like you're from another time and place."

"Do you, my dear?"

"Yes, Sir Alfred, I do indeed. "

"And stop calling me, Sir Alfred, Trace. You are family now. You're my new daughter."

"I like calling you Sir Alfred. It suits you and your regal bearing. If anyone should be called Sir Alfred, it's you."

He laughed, squeezing her hand. "You always cheer me, Trace. It is so easy to see why Edward fell in love with you."

They were close to the circular courtyard now, and the Bishop family and servants were standing at the entrance of the Manor, in lines, opposite each other. The entire scene made her think of the popular TV series, Downton Abby.

"They're waiting for us, Trace, ready to welcome you. There's my wife, Gwendolyn, my daughter Bryanne, and my son Thomas."

Trace was buzzed with excitement and anxiety as the car drew up to the entrance and came to a bouncing stop. A tall, silver-headed butler, in a dark suit and white tie, leaned, opened the door, and offered Sir Alfred a cordial greeting as he exited.

"Good to see you again, Sir Alfred," he said.

"And you, Charles, thank you. All is well, I trust?"

"Yes, Sir Alfred. All is quite well."

Trace inhaled a bracing breath and reached for Sir Alfred's hand as he helped her from the car.

Would they think she was good enough for Edward? Pretty enough? Smart enough? What would they expect of her? Would they ask about Edward? Of course, they would.

Sir Alfred led Trace to his family and introduced her, first to his wife.

"Trace, this is my wife, Lady Gwendolyn."

Trace immediately saw that Edward had inherited his mother's forehead and sharp nose. She was a thin, elegant, middle-aged woman, with graying stylish hair, who radiated class and polish. She offered Trace a gracious hand, and when she spoke, her voice was smoothly mellifluent.

"We are so pleased that you have come to us, Mrs. Bishop."

"Thank you, Lady Gwendolyn. I am so happy to meet you," Trace said, feeling a chilling wind whip her hair about. She raked it back in place.

"And I to meet you, Mrs. Bishop. We have heard so many delightful things about you, and we so look forward to getting to know you."

Trace felt Lady Gwendolyn's expert, watchful eyes perform a quick assessment of her face, hair and stature. Did she approve? Trace wondered.

Sir Alfred had told Trace that his daughter, Bryanne, was the eldest child, now thirty-two years old. Her husband, a doctor, was working at a field hospital somewhere in France.

Bryanne was attractive, but not an especially pretty woman, being rather full in the hips, with a long neck, close-set eyes and a tight button of a mouth. But her hazel eyes were lovely, as was her glossy chestnut hair, formed in tight curls. Her smile was genuine, and Trace sensed a keen intelligence behind the reserved expression.

"Happy you have come, Mrs. Bishop," she said, formally. "We have been looking forward to this for many days."

Trace took her warm hand. "I am very happy to be here," Trace said.

Thomas Bishop was dressed in his brown military officer's uniform. He was 28 years old, and he did not look like Edward. He had short black hair and wore black-rimmed glasses that made him look both professorial and older than his years. Thomas was shorter than Edward, his features not as refined, and he presented a rather awkward demeanor, as if meeting new people were not easy or preferred. He did not meet Trace's eyes as they shook hands limply.

"You are most welcome at Bishop Manor, Mrs. Bishop," he said, stiffly. "I hope you will find us pleasant, and our home both welcoming and comfortable."

"Thank you, Thomas, I'm sure I will."

Sir Alfred introduced Trace to Charles, the head butler, and then he rubbed his hands together, looking skyward. "Let's get out of this cold wind and gather around a cozy fire with some tea. Trace, Bryanne will show you to your room, where you can freshen up before we have our tea in the corner drawing room, which I will take you to now."

Inside, Trace saw layers of distinctive crown moldings, artistically carved plaster, and rounded doors. Strolling down dark wood corridors, she noted lighted gilded framed oil paintings of seascapes, landscapes and portraits of 18th and 19th-century men, looking solemnly out at the world with confidence and a challenge.

On a brief tour of the house, Trace passed under the high ceilings of spacious rooms, including a ballroom, an airy family room, and a grand dining room, seating up to twenty-five.

There were twelve fireplaces; hardwood floors; richly carpeted bedrooms, dens and drawing rooms; and French doors that opened to covered terraces with panoramic views of rolling meadows, sculpted hedges with walkways, and a distant forest.

Bryanne ushered Trace upstairs to her luxurious bedroom, and they were soon followed by a stocky house steward, who carried Trace's leather bags and trunk, containing new dresses, lingerie and toiletries, all of which she'd purchased in Paris only a few days before.

After Bryanne and the steward retreated, Trace took in her room, all nerves and excitement. It was stylish and lavish, decorated in burgundy, gray and white, with a glowing fireplace that warmed the room. Her canopied bed immediately caught her eye, and she wished she could flop down onto the thick creamy comforter and sleep for days. She'd still not fully recovered from her illness and ordeal at the prison, and the trip to England had been an exhausting one.

But the Bishop family was waiting in the drawing room, seated around a generous natural stone fireplace, waiting for her to begin afternoon tea. Waiting for her to tell them about herself, and surely about Edward.

Trace turned in a circle, amazed and dizzy from the day, and from the last few months. What a stark change this room was—this house was—from Saint-Lazare Prison. She shivered when she realized, again, how close to death she had been. If she had not written Sir Alfred and if he had not come for her, she would have surely died by now. Dear Alfred. He'd been the perfect gentleman, the perfect father-in-law, and the perfect friend when she'd needed one the most. How would she ever be able to repay him?

As Trace descended the wide mahogany staircase to the first floor, her eyes were busy, her thoughts circling around Edward's memory. He'd grown up in this house, knew the portraits, the rooms and the land. It had all been a part of him, and it had helped to make him the quality person he had been.

She imagined him there beside her, linking arms, strolling down the stairs, smiling that silly boyish grin that always warmed her and stirred her to want him. And then she ached for him.

Approaching the drawing room, she heard muffled voices coming from inside, and she fought a mounting dread of what was to come. She was all this family had left of Edward's last months. She had been his love, the one true witness to his mind and his heart. It was she who had heard his last, dying words.

The family stood when Trace entered, and that made her feel even more out of place. She wasn't royalty, after all. Sir Alfred motioned for her to sit next to him in a burgundy leather chair, a comfortable distance from the roaring fire.

After the under butler, Saunders, served them tea in rose china cups with golden rims, they all sat rather awkwardly, searching for the right pitch of conversation.

Lady Gwendolyn was the first to speak. "How was the weather in Paris, Mrs. Bishop?"

Trace lowered her cup to her saucer and lowered her voice. "Lady Gwendolyn, perhaps you should all call me Trace or Tracey. I know Trace is an uncommon name, but where I'm from, it is not so unusual."

Lady Gwendolyn gave a faint smile. "Very well, my dear, if that is what you wish."

Sir Alfred spoke up, hoping to lighten the mood. "Trace insists on calling me Sir Alfred, however. She thinks I look regal."

"And so you do look regal, father," Bryanne said. Trace smiled and then answered Lady Gwendolyn. "As to Paris, Lady Gwendolyn, it was gently snowing when we left, and it was quite cold."

"I trust your journey was a pleasant one...Trace," Bryanne said, haltingly, as if she were trying out the name.

"Yes, it was, thank you," Trace said.

"Trace is being kind," Sir Alfred said. "It was not an especially pleasant journey, and it hasn't been ever since that damned war began. The trains are slow, stopping every fifteen minutes or so, there are no private railcars, and the food is an abomination. But this is war, and everyone is making great sacrifices. Paris and France are suffering greatly. Frankly, I found Paris damned depressing, and I thought I would never hear myself say that."

Thomas stared down at his tea. "I heard there were more Zeppelin raids over Paris, father. From our last report, there were forty fatalities."

"Yes," Sir Alfred said, with a sorrowful shake of his head. "Trace and I were in the hospital, just north of Paris, when that one occurred. A very sad business it was. Women and children were some of the unfortunate victims. It's monstrous what these Huns are doing. Absolutely monstrous."

Lady Gwendolyn gently cleared her throat, endeavoring to bring the conversation back to a more agreeable tone.

"The weather here has been quite pleasant until yesterday. Bryanne and I were able to take a walk in the gardens, wearing only light shawls."

Bryanne spoke up. "Yes, mother is so right. But then last night, winter returned, and I had to call Saunders to make up three more fires."

Thomas seemed preoccupied. "Trace, are you fully recovered from your distressing ordeal? I was completely overcome with outrage at the way the French intelligence treated you. It was quite unfair and unnecessary. They did not have one shred of evidence against you. I read the complaint many times. It was beastly what they did to you."

Lady Gwendolyn and Bryanne noticeably stiffened. Sir Alfred turned his soft attention to Trace.

"Quite right you are, Thomas. They were using Trace as a scapegoat for the French military leaders' incompetence. I dare say, they'll be finding additional poor innocent souls to parade around and execute as spies, so the French population will believe they are killing the people who are responsible for their losses. The French people are plenty mad at the daily casualty list, and rightly so."

Lady Gwendolyn's voice was clear, and at a near whisper. "We do hope you are recovered, Trace, from your dreadful tribulation."

"Yes, thank you, I am much improved, thanks to Sir Alfred, and thanks to you all. It is so good to be here."

Sir Alfred nodded, pursed his lips, folded his hands across his belly and looked toward the ceiling. "I know we are all beating about the bush here. I am aware that we would love to hear from Trace about Edward and his last days. Trace and I have had some rather long talks on the matter. But today, I believe we should let Trace have a good rest before dinner, and then let us see how she feels about sharing her thoughts, impressions and words about Edward."

Trace spoke up. "If I may, Sir Alfred, I would like to say something about Edward."

The room dropped into silence, only the crackling fire filling the silence.

Trace gathered herself before speaking. "Edward loved you all very much, and he said so many times. He often spoke of you, individually, with fondness and humor. He loved this house, and so longed to return to it, and to all of you. I'm telling you this because, while we were on our honeymoon in France, I told him, in a rather inspired moment, that I hoped to meet his family someday. He brightened and smiled with such pleasure. He said, 'They are all the best of souls, with the best of humor, and the kindest of hearts.'"

Lady Gwendolyn blinked rapidly, as if tears were close. When she spoke, she fought to maintain her cool dignity. "Thank you, Trace. Thank you so much for sharing our Edward's thoughts."

She was the first to rise, her face suddenly pale. Sir Alfred's eyes held sadness. Everyone stood as Lady Gwendolyn retreated, handkerchief flowing from her hand.

Trace did not attend dinner that night, having had a kind of relapse. When she arrived back in her room, she'd stumbled and grabbed for one of the bedposts for support. Perhaps it was seeing Lady Gwendolyn's suffering face and Sir Alfred's red-rimmed eyes. Perhaps it was the sudden impact of knowing she'd never be able to return to her own time. She knew she'd never find the Mata Hari ring now. She was lost, and she was trapped in this time for the rest of her life.

And then the bleakness, and the grief, and the ice-cold memories shifted within her, and she lost breath, and wilted to the floor.

Bryanne found her an hour later. Frantic, she called for Sir Alfred and Charles.

Trace remained in bed for the next two days. The family physician, Dr. Felix Chambers, attended her, feeding her soup and tea, constantly monitoring her fluctuating temperature.

On the third day of her illness, the Bishop family waited in the drawing room, all raw nerves, anxiously awaiting Dr. Chambers' update.

Sir Alfred paced with locked hands behind his back. Lady Gwendolyn stared gloomily into the fire, and Bryanne sat in the corner reading, although she wasn't absorbing the words on the page. Thomas had returned to London, to continue with his war work.

"When will this terrible war end, Sir Alfred?" Lady Gwendolyn said. "I just can't bear much more of this awful agony."

"I don't know, my dear," Sir Alfred said, mournfully. "I just don't know."

They settled into their private thoughts.

"I miss Edward so much, Alfred," Lady Gwendolyn said, her voice shaking. "I don't know how I shall bear it having Trace here."

Sir Alfred gave her a side glance of surprise, but he said nothing.

CHAPTER 33

By the time Christmas arrived, Trace was stronger mentally and physically, but she still fought a weary spirit. Edward was always on her mind, especially living in the house where he had been born and raised. Thoughts of Nonnie were also with her day and night. Three times she had tried to compose a letter to the girl, but each time, she'd concluded that the tone and style were all wrong. In one, she'd suggested they meet. In another, she'd suggested that Nonnie visit her in England. In the third, Trace hadn't mentioned meeting at all. She was conflicted and on edge.

She also wasn't looking forward to Sir Alfred's and Lady Gwendolyn's traditional Christmas Eve party. She would have to meet and be judged by so many strangers. At first, the family showed little interest in the party, but Sir Alfred convinced everyone that Edward would have wanted them to continue their traditions. At least it was going to be a modest affair because of the war and Edward's death.

For a time, the party preparations seemed to cheer the family, even Lady Gwendolyn, whose struggles with depression and grief seemed to age her right before Trace's eyes. But the holly and the ivy, and the mistletoe, and the Christmas trees in the drawing room, parlor and ballroom, all lifted Lady Gwendolyn's mood, and she fussed and busied herself with the details of the decorations and the menu.

Trace had found that it was not easy to be around the woman, who subtly gave off the vibes that somehow Trace was to blame for her son's death. But Trace realized the issue was something else after she overheard Lady Gwendolyn and Bryanne in the drawing room one Sunday afternoon, speaking in little whispers about how they both wished Edward had returned home to marry Elizabeth Ashley Pemberton. They were not unkind to Trace, but their formal manners and lack of warmth did wear on her, and she grew anxious to leave Bishop Manor.

Sir Alfred was solicitous of her, and even fawning, something Lady Gwendolyn and Bryanne observed with mild irritation. Did they think his attention to Trace was romantic? Yes, she thought so, but she knew better. Sir Alfred and Trace had spent a lot of time together while she was recovering. He'd spoken candidly about Edward and his own life, sharing stories of triumph as well as regrets, and they had shared tears over many things. They had become friends.

Trace also knew that Sir Alfred saw her as the last connection to his son, and it was clear that he approved of her. He made a point of saying so to his wife, something Trace overheard one afternoon. Nonetheless, Trace had resigned herself to the reality that Lady Gwendolyn would never really approve of her, for whatever reason.

On Christmas Eve, the guests began arriving at 6pm, the men dressed formally in tuxedos and white ties, the women adorned in extravagant displays of emerald and burgundy-colored satin gowns, or bustle dresses in cream and light peach silk. Their hats were lavish Edwardian styles, some broad-brimmed with feathers, some made of silk crêpe with veils, and one that stood out from the rest, boasted an extravagant blue ostrich plume. All the women wore shimmering jewels that sparkled and glinted in the light.

Trace wore a black, full-length mourning dress, crafted in Edwardian style, with a lace collar and black laces. Sir Alfred had suggested she purchase the dress while they were in Paris. Trace felt that she looked a little like Morticia Addams from the movie The Addams Family, but she was assured her dress was stylish and appropriate.

Trace's hair, cut short in prison, had lengthened, and with the help of Bryanne's lady's maid, it was arranged up, designed in careful, artistic curls. Trace had gained weight and, even though she wasn't overly fond of the gown, she knew she looked pretty at least.

As the guests entered and were announced, Sir Alfred and Lady Gwendolyn stood in the great hall, smiling their greetings, while Trace remained behind, standing next to a demure Bryanne, who wore a conservative black satin gown and black satin hat with feathers.

A reluctant and nervous Thomas was dressed in his brown woolen captain's uniform, with a tunic and straight legged trousers, and a stiff peaked cap tucked neatly under his arm. Trace had not seen much of Thomas since she'd arrived. He spent most of his time in London, working in secret, which seemed to suit his personality.

He leaned toward Trace's ear and whispered. "I despise these bloody parties. Edward loved them."

Trace gave him a quick glance and a smile. "Yes, Edward loved parties."

"Did you know that Elizabeth Ashley Pemberton has been invited, and that she accepted?"

Trace kept her pleasant demeanor, but inside, she felt a twist of tension. "No, I didn't know."

"She's not so bad, really," Thomas whispered. "Not Edward's type, but not so bad a girl. More my type, I think. I dare say, she is not so fond of these parties either. She's rather bookish, having a particular fondness for Dickens, Christmas crackers, and Walkers shortbread, which, incidentally, so do I."

Trace kept her eyes focused ahead, nodding and smiling at the guests, who were commenting on the pine garlands strung along the crown molding, and the 10-foot Christmas tree, aglow with lights and decorated with paper chains. The lengths of colored paper were stuck together with a paste made from flour and water, and they had been created by the children of the servants.

Lights from the sparkling multi-teared chandeliers added a shiny glitter, and made the world seem as though they were all stirring about, like bubbles, within a glass of champagne.

From lofty distances came music from a string quartet, playing waltzes, Haydn and Mozart. Trace longed to dance, and she wished to dance with Edward. Yes, he would have loved this party.

When Elizabeth Ashley Pemberton entered with her father, a distinguished white-haired man with a ruddy complexion and impressive handlebar mustache, Trace lowered her eyes and grabbed a breath. Bryanne was given the unpleasant task of introducing Trace and Miss Pemberton. Miss Pemberton was a thin, fragile-looking girl in her late twenties, with dark thin hair, an upturned regal nose, and large blue eyes that seemed lost in a kind of lofty wonder.

Miss Pemberton offered Trace a sweet, worried smile. "I am so happy we can meet at last, Mrs. Bishop," she said in a light, feathery voice. "I have heard so many pleasant things about you."

The two ladies held limp hands, briefly, as if hands were fragile and could break.

Trace said, "It is my pleasure, Miss Pemberton. I am so glad you could come."

"Thank you," Miss Pemberton said, as her smile faded, and her eyes filled with a dreary, dreamy melancholy. "I am so sorry, Mrs. Bishop, for your loss. I am sure this has not been an easy time for you, nor for the entire Bishop family. Please accept my deepest condolences. Edward was a dear man and a good, agreeable friend. If at any time you wish companionship, please consider my company, Mrs. Bishop. I do not live so very far away, and near our home at Gatewood, there are several lovely gardens and woodlands to stroll in for exercise and restorative contemplation."

Trace perceived that Miss Pemberton's offer was genuine, and she was touched by it.

"Thank you, Miss Pemberton. You are very kind."

Miss Pemberton took Trace's hand again. "We have all felt Edward's passing very keenly, Mrs. Bishop. These have been difficult days for us all."

After she had drifted away, Thomas leaned in again. "Like I said, not a bad girl at all. Between you and me, Trace, I don't think she was in love with Edward."

Trace turned slightly, her lips close to his ear, so he could hear her whispering voice. "And you, Thomas, are you in love with Miss Pemberton, and her Dickens, Christmas crackers and Walkers shortbread?"

After a startled moment, Thomas grinned with a boyishness that reminded her of Edward.

"I can see why Edward fell in love with you, Mrs. Bishop. As my old Scottish grandmother used to say, "Yair a cheeky lass, me darlin'.""

In the grand dining room, Trace was relieved to be seated next to Thomas, who kept her entertained with irreverent stories about the Bishops' various colorful neighbors. They feasted on roast turkey, beef, goose and vegetables, along with mince pies made of meat, fruit and spice. Trace especially liked the colorful dishes filled with candied fruits. They sipped red and white wine, and they finished the meal with plum pudding and a glass of fine Port.

The Christmas Eve party moved to the ballroom at 9:30, and it was soon alive and soaring with waltzes and the delicious aroma of pine, spice and vanilla.

Trace watched the dancers from the sidelines as they took turns around the floor, whirling in delightful motion, rounding the space. Her dancer's spirit lifted as she imagined joining them. For the first time in months, she smiled freely, watching the blurring elegant room blossom in celebration.

Thomas drew up to Trace. "I can see it in your eyes that you'd like to be out there dancing, Trace. Do you dance well?"

"I like to think so. Yes, I would like to dance, but not here and not tonight. I think Edward is missed. I hear it in conversation. I can feel it in the rooms."

Thomas nodded. "Yes, Edward was always the life of the party, and everyone loved him."

"Were you jealous of Edward?"

Thomas smiled. "No, Trace. Oddly enough, we were very close. He was always very supportive of me, and we were different kinds of men. He an extrovert and me, well, I like my privacy. Edward and I got along very well, and I miss him greatly."

Trace sought to change the subject. "You should go dance with Miss Pemberton, Thomas."

"Not proper, Trace, just as it isn't proper for you to dance because you're in mourning. We all know the rules, Mrs. Bishop. I must wait for the appropriate time. Everyone in this room knew Edward and Miss Pemberton were engaged."

Trace looked around. "I wonder what all of Edward's friends think about me and our sudden marriage?"

"I dare say some were surprised. Some no doubt disapproved. But on the whole, this war has changed all of us, and it is changing society and the way we look at the world. I think most now see you, Mrs. Bishop, as a lovely girl, and if Edward loved you and married you, then, in time, they will accept you."

Trace looked at Thomas and smiled. "As we say where I come from, you're a cool dude, Thomas."

Thomas grinned. "Cool? I like that expression. A cool dude," he said, repeating it with a shake of his head. "It sounds very slang and delightfully informal, doesn't it? But I like it. I must try it on the chaps at the war office."

"And I still say that Miss Pemberton would love to dance with you."

"A rebel you are, Trace. A true rebel, and I approve. Perhaps I shall dance with Miss Pemberton and see if the room shatters into disapproval."

When the musicians took an intermission, a young soldier scrambled up onto the stage, slid in behind the piano, and began to play O Come All Ye Faithful. With punch glasses raised, the room erupted into boisterous song.

Around 11:00, Charles entered the ballroom and walked purposefully across the floor to Sir Alfred. Sir Alfred bent toward the butler to hear his message, and Trace watched Sir Alfred's expression move from mild surprise to concern. He thanked Charles and stepped over to Trace.

"Well, my dear, it seems you have a visitor."

"Me? How can that be? Are you sure?"

"Charles said a Captain Vadime Masloff is waiting for you in the drawing room. He wants to speak with you."

Trace was stunned. "Vadime?" For nearly five weeks, she'd successfully shut out thoughts of Mata Hari and Vadime. How had he found her? What did he want?

Lady Gwendolyn drew up, her expression curious. "Is everything all right, Alfred?"

"Yes, I believe so. Trace has a visitor."

Lady Gwendolyn grew anxious. "Do we know who it is?"

"A friend," Trace said, evasively. She did not want Lady Gwendolyn to accompany her.

Sir Alfred rested his tender eyes on Trace. "You suddenly look a bit pale, my dear. Would you like me to come along?"

Trace considered it. "Yes, Sir Alfred. Yes, I would."

They left Lady Gwendolyn staring after them, worried.

CHAPTER 34

Vadime was standing before the fireplace, hands locked behind his back. He turned sharply when Sir Alfred and Trace entered. After Sir Alfred closed the doors behind them, Trace introduced the two men. Vadime, wearing an impeccable royal blue uniform and high black boots polished to a fine gloss, offered Trace a courtly bow and a handshake to Sir Alfred.

"Good evening, Mrs. Bishop," he said in his thick Russian accent. "Forgive me for arriving so late. I hope I am not intruding."

Trace took a few steps forward. "What are you doing here, Captain Vadime? How did you know I was here?"

He gave her a quick, tight smile as he glanced about at the extravagantly decorated room. He indicated with the sweep of his arm. "If I may say so, Sir Alfred, your home is impressive. I am glad to see that you, Mrs. Bishop, are looking so well."

Trace stood in a tense, guarded silence. She wasn't sure she wanted to know why he had come.

"Captain Masloff, Trace said you knew my son."

"Yes, Sir Alfred. Captain Bishop and I were good friends and we flew many sorties together. They called us the modern knights," Vadime said, with a reflective smile. "But those days are gone now for us. Yes, those days are over."

Captain Masloff stared pointedly at Sir Alfred. "Your son was a good man, sir. The best man I ever knew, and the finest pilot I ever flew with. I say that in all honesty, Sir Alfred. I say that truthfully and from my heart. You should be very proud of your son. We flyers loved him as our brother."

Sir Alfred's mouth firmed up, and he stared at Vadime with gratitude. "Thank you, Captain Masloff. Thank you for your friendship to my son. If there is ever anything you need, I hope you will let me know."

Captain Masloff snapped a bow. "You are most kind, Sir Alfred. Thank you."

They stood in a respectful silence for a time, before Sir Alfred glanced back toward the door.

"I will go now and leave you two alone. I am sure you have private issues to discuss."

After Sir Alfred's footsteps faded, Trace offered Vadime a chair. He declined. Instead, he stood stiffly, and Trace wondered if his leg pained him.

"As to how I knew you were here, Mrs. Bishop, that was easy. I was flying with the French, and the word about you spread very quickly. At first, I didn't know you were in Saint-Lazare Prison, and neither did Mata Hari. But then we heard that Sir Alfred had come for you. That is news that moves fast, Mrs. Bishop."

Trace gestured toward the black eyepatch over his left eye. "And how is your eye, Captain Vadime?"

He shrugged. "That eye is blind, Mrs. Bishop. Yes, it is, and always will be. No matter. It is not a serious thing."

"But how can you fly with a blind eye?"

He gave her a sad smile. "I am not to fly any longer. Flying is over for me. It is over for my good friend, Edward, and it is over for me." He tapped his right leg and smiled, ruefully. "My leg, too, is not so good. I'm afraid I am an old man before my time, Mrs. Bishop."

Trace stared into the fire. "I'm so sorry, Vadime."

"May I smoke, Mrs. Bishop?"

"Of course."

Captain Vadime removed a cigarette from his silver cigarette case, a gift from Mata Hari, placed it between his lips and found a match on the table. He struck the match and cupped a hand to light his long cigarette, blowing a feather of smoke toward the high ceiling.

"And how is Mata Hari, Captain Vadime?"

He slipped a hand inside his tunic, like Napoleon, staring at his cigarette as he spoke. "Mata Hari is in Madrid. She will return to Paris in January."

Trace felt a restless stirring. "Why doesn't she go to the Netherlands, Vadime? Can't you convince her?"

"She will not, Trace. Yes, I have tried to tell her that. She is in danger."

"I know she's in danger. Captain Ladoux of French Intelligence is out to trap her, and he will trap her, just as he trapped me."

Captain Vadime nodded, sadly. "I, too, tried to warn her. So she told me she needed money for me. Can you imagine her doing these things for money, to give to me?"

He shook his head and took a long drag from his cigarette. "I must go to Russia now."

"Russia? Why?"

His single eye widened. "Why? Surely, you know what is going on in Russia, Mrs. Bishop. Haven't you heard that my country has had many hardships, with riots and rebellions? With Czar Nicholas away at the front, there is no authority. He is not a military leader, you know. Russia has fallen into chaos. Its people and its soldiers are rebelling against these hard times. I must go and do what I can for my poor country. I fear, Mrs. Bishop, that things have gone too far. I fear, Mrs. Bishop, that the entire world is coming apart. Will any of us survive it?"

He turned, and angrily flicked his cigarette into the fire. "Mata Hari has pleaded with me to stay in France and wait for her, but I cannot. I must go and help my country. Maybe I will fight and be killed, but I must go and help, and do what I can for my family and for my country. Yes, I must do this, or I am not a soldier, not a man, and not a good Russian."

He scratched his cheek, his troubled eye moving for a time. It finally settled on Trace.

"You know, Trace, Mrs. Bishop, I loved Edward like a brother. Yes, I did love him that way. He was my good and true friend. He was a good and true soldier, who would fly into a storm of enemy planes, no matter what the danger. He never said no to any mission, and he could have. He was a... what is the word... Okay, I don't know this word..."

"Inspiration?" Trace said.

Vadime jabbed a sharp finger at her in recognition. "Yes. Inspiration he was. Edward was brave, and he was, as you say, an inspiration to all who fly and fight over France."

Trace looked down and away, releasing a sigh.

"Why have you come, Vadime? If you are on your way to Russia, why have you come all this way to see me?"

Vadime nodded, staring down at the rich gray, blue and burgundy patterns of the carpet.

"When I saw Mata Hari last, just before she was leaving for Spain, she handed me something to give to you. She was very insistent that you receive this. She said, 'Give this to Trace, and make sure you give it to her as soon as you can.'"

He paused, lifting a hand to the right pocket of his tunic. He released the polished brass button, reached in and tugged out a red velvet cloth, wrapped by a gold elastic band.

Trace watched him closely, breath trapped in her throat.

"Mrs. Bishop, Mata Hari said she had a dream about you some weeks ago. She said in that dream you begged her for this. For this ring. She said it was the same ring you were wearing when she first saw you in the chateau back in late June."

As Vadime slowly unwrapped it, Trace's wide, round eyes fell on the velvet cloth. Vadime dramatically lifted his hand and presented the ring, holding it into the light.

Trace was transfixed, staring. There it was—alive—glittering emerald magic.

Vadime bowed, offering it to her. "Mata Hari said she wanted you to have it. It is her gift to you. Call it a Christmas gift."

Trace stared at the ring, feeling the magnetic pull of it as it emanated a strange beckoning energy.

"You may have it," Vadime said, waiting for Trace to accept it.

Holding Vadime's stare, she reached, gently taking the cloth with the ring at its center.

"It seems to hold much value for you, Mrs. Bishop."

"Yes, it does. Will you please thank Mata Hari for me, Captain Vadime?"

"I will write to her. I will tell her. Perhaps you will write her too, Mrs. Bishop? She was fond of you, you know. A bit frightened of you, for reasons I don't understand, but very fond."

Trace reached for his hand, and she held it for a while. They said nothing, as the silence lengthened, and they thought of old times.

When Vadime was leaving, Charles held Vadime's greatcoat, and Trace helped him shoulder into it. They shook hands once more.

"Take care of yourself, Captain Vadime."

He clicked his boots together and snapped a crisp salute. "It has been a great pleasure knowing you, Mrs. Bishop. Я верю в тебя, which in Russian means... I believe in you. You will be fine... yes?"

Trace stepped outside under a light snowfall and waved, as he drove away in a waddling old car, with exhaust puffing out clouds of smoke. After the car had faded into the snowy night, Trace turned back to the house to see Sir Alfred waiting for her.

Charles closed the door behind them, bowed to Sir Alfred, and started back toward the ballroom.

"Is everything all right, my dear?" he asked with apprehension.

Trace clasped the wrapped ring tightly in her right hand. "Yes...He's leaving for Russia. He stopped by to say goodbye, and to offer his respects and condolences. He was Mata Hari's true love, you know."
Sir Alfred studied Trace. "Was he? And do you know Mata Hari, Trace?"
Trace avoided his eyes, smiling to herself. "Yes, Sir Alfred, I know her."
"Thomas tells me that she is heading into a world of trouble. She seems to be involved in some sort of spying for the Germans and the French."
"Yes... I've heard that too."
"I'm afraid our unpleasant friend, Captain Ladoux, is out to trap her."
Trace could feel an inner darkness forming. She willfully pushed it away. She didn't want to be living in this time, when Mata Hari was about to be arrested and shot for treason. Would the ring she was holding take her home?
"Yes, I'm afraid so."
"I hope, my dear, that you will not return to France to see her."
"No, I will not. I have other things to think about."
Sir Alfred offered her his arm and she linked hers in his. "Well, don't think too hard, Trace. I have come to the startling conclusion of late that thinking is highly overrated. On the other hand, dancing and a good glass of Port are just the right way to go."
Trace laughed a little. "Yes, I like that. But if we dance, won't people talk?"

"Yes, of course, they will talk, Trace, and gossip for days. I say, let them. Edward would want us to dance... especially now, at Christmas. So, let us have one turn around the ballroom floor, Mrs. Bishop, and enjoy ourselves."

CHAPTER 35

After Christmas, Trace spent most of the next two days in her room, saying the party had been wonderful but exhausting, and she needed rest. Thomas and Sir Alfred went to London, Thomas to work, and Sir Alfred to attend Parliamentary business. Trace was composing a letter to Nonnie, determined to finish and mail it before the New Year. Now that Trace had the ring, everything had changed, and she was excited by all the possibilities.

She began the letter by apologizing to Non for not writing sooner, and then proceeded to tell her about Edward's death and her own long illness. Trace did not mention anything about her time in Saint-Lazare Prison or how she'd wound up in England. She wrote briskly and enthusiastically, every cell in her body alive with the possibility of seeing Non again. In the final paragraph, she was very direct.

My dearest Nonnie, I must see you again. Will it be possible for you to come to England for a visit? If that is not an option, then I will come to you, if you wish it. Please let me know how you are and if our meeting is possible. I have missed you greatly, and long to hear your voice and walk with you again. Please write as soon as you can and let me know your thoughts.

Yours, affectionately,

Trace

P.S. I hope your father is well. Please give him my warmest regards.

On December 30th, Sir Alfred returned from London and invited Trace to walk with him through the woodland paths which led to the quaint, Tudor-style stone house Edward had willed to her. She admired its textured stone exterior walls and dark brown window frames. This house was hers if she wanted it. She'd visited it only once before, not venturing in or even exploring the area, finding it too depressing.

When she and Sir Alfred arrived at the house, it was an overcast, gray winter day, with low moving clouds. The estate manager, Colin, had opened the house, and had built a comfortable fire in the deep stone fireplace.

Trace entered with reverence, passing through the quiet Victorian decorated rooms somberly, recalling conversations she and Edward had shared. The firelight reminded her of their fireplace in that little hotel room in France, where the world and the war had seemed so far away, where their new love was fresh and filled with hope.

As she took in the rooms, Edward's presence seemed to fill the spaces; every stone, every floorboard, and every cross beam.

"He loved this house, Trace," Sir Alfred said, warming himself by the fire. "Before he left for the war, he spent much time here, reading and walking the grounds. He preferred this little house to Bishop Manor."

Trace did not want to linger, and when she told Sir Alfred she was ready to leave, he seemed surprised and a bit wounded.

"You don't like the house?" he asked.

They stood outside in a blowing wind that pushed heavy clay clouds across the sky and rattled the bare limbs of trees.

"It's lovely, Sir Alfred. I can see why Edward loved it so much, but I couldn't live here. I feel Edward everywhere in it."

Sir Alfred turned away, gazing sightlessly toward the pond. "My dear, we have to move on with our lives. We must let Edward go and begin anew. That is what he would have wanted. I wish that Gwen could do the same. She seems to have fallen into an even greater depression, and I don't know what to do for her. She keeps telling me that she sees Edward calling to her in her dreams."

While they strolled the paths back to Bishop Manor, Trace gathered her courage, working to keep her voice from quivering.

"I'm going to be leaving soon, Sir Alfred."

He stopped short, his head whipping around, eyes boring into her as he tried to understand. "Leaving... Leaving to where? Why?"

Trace pinched the collar of her coat at her neck. "I want to go home. It's time I went home."

"Home? But this is your home now, Trace. Edward has left you money and property. I've seen to every legal matter—every detail—and I can assure you that you will live well for the rest of your life, Trace. You will not want for anything. If you don't like the house, then fine, we'll find you another house. That is easily done.

There are many comfortable homes nearby. Maybe you want to move to London. Of course, you're still a young woman, and you want to meet people your own age. Perhaps you find Bishop Manor too sedate for your taste. Very well, we can arrange a move to London."

Trace watched his mind working, spinning out a desperate litany of alternatives, hoping to change her mind. Sir Alfred continued.

"And then, in time, you'll meet someone—someone you can love again, and you will move on with your life, and you will have a family and friends and... My dear, there is no reason for you to leave."

Trace reached for his forearm and squeezed it. "Sir Alfred...I want to go home. I've been away a long time."

He licked his lips, shifting his eyes toward the Manor house, then back to Trace.

"Home to America then?"

Ever since Trace had received the Mata Hari ring from Vadime, she'd spent hours agonizing over how she would break the news to Sir Alfred. He'd become a father to her, and she knew he had come to love her like a daughter. She did not want to leave him—everything and everyone else, yes—but not Sir Alfred.

She also wanted to tell him the truth—the complete truth—but she couldn't find the right vocabulary. How could she tell him her impossible story? Without the right approach and the precise words, Sir Alfred would never be able to comprehend all that had happened to her.

"Yes, Sir Alfred, home to America."

He nodded, shoving his hands into his overcoat pockets. "I see," he said wearily, his breath smoking. Trace noticed the crown of his balding head was pink from the cold. "We should get inside, Sir Alfred. It's cold out here."

As they drew up to the house, Sir Alfred's eyes held a weary misery. At the entrance, he paused, as a new idea struck.

"All right, Trace. Travel to America. Yes, return to America and visit your family, of course, my dear, that would be the right and proper thing to do. But then come back to us. Spend as much time as you need in America, and then come back home to England."

Trace looked at him with love. "Sir Alfred... you know how much you mean to me. Without you—without all you've done for me—I wouldn't be here. I'd be dead..."

"None of that matters now, my dear. You are here now, and this is your true home, no matter where you were born. England and Bishop Manor are your home," he said, with creeping desperation rising in his voice.

Trace couldn't bear to see Sir Alfred's anguish.

"We don't have to discuss this now, Sir Alfred. We have time."

Inside the house, Charles took their coats. and as they moved toward the staircase, Trace stopped, looking him full in the eyes.

"I don't want the money, Sir Alfred. I don't deserve it, just as I don't deserve or want the house. Edward and I knew each other for only a short time. As a married couple, we spent only a few days together. They were wonderful days—and all the time I spent with

Edward, and wrote to Edward, and received his letters
were happy times; the best times."

Her eyes lighted at the memory. "I guess that's what
war does to lovers. It heightens everything; intensifies
everything. I was in love with Edward, despite the brief
time, Sir Alfred, but I don't want anything from your
family. I don't want anything for loving Edward."

Sir Alfred gave her a small twist of a sad smile.
"You, my dear, were no doubt one of the best things
that ever happened to my son. However, I insist you
keep the money. It was Edward's wish, and he was not
an impulsive man, or an irresponsible one."

Trace took a few steps closer to Sir Alfred. "Thank
you for all your kindnesses. I love you, Sir Alfred. I
want you to remember that, no matter what happens."

He nodded, tears glistening in his eyes, and he
turned away to hide them. "I'll just go... I'll just go for
some tea. Yes, a good hot cup of tea sounds just about
right. I'll see you later, my dear."

Trace watched him shamble away toward the drawing room.

CHAPTER 36

The Bishops were to attend a New Year's Eve party at the Prescotts' Court Mansion, about ten miles away. Trace declined the invitation, explaining that she needed to begin packing for her journey to America, and since she wasn't acquainted with the Prescott family, she wouldn't be missed.

Lady Gwendolyn had also declined, to the surprise and concern of Sir Alfred, Bryanne and Thomas. It was the first time—indeed the only time—Lady Gwendolyn had ever turned down such an invitation. It just wasn't done.

When Sir Alfred looked in on his wife a day earlier, she was in bed, with the draperies pulled against the winter sunlight. Sir Alfred eased down on the edge of his wife's bed and gently stroked her hair.

"Have the spooks returned, my dear girl?"

"I'm afraid so, Alfred. I cannot possibly attend the party at the Prescotts'. Will you forgive me?"

"I shall do my very best to forgive you," he said, jokingly.

"I have sent a note with my apologies, conveying to Lady Prescott that I am quite ill."

"Shall I stay with you, Gwen?"

She took his hand and kissed it. "No, Alfred. You must go. We both can't be discourteous. We shall be drummed out of society, and you will lose your position in Parliament."

"Not such a bad thing, these days, my dear."

Gwen smiled up lovingly at her husband. "I don't believe Lady Mary is all that fond of me anyway, and it is obvious that she lights up like a spring day whenever you're around, Alfred."

"Don't be silly, my dear. She is a calculating woman who only desires favor for her husband. She has grand designs for him, you know. She wants me to put in a good word with Lloyd George."

"And you will, won't you, Alfred?"

"Perhaps... Perhaps. John Prescott is a crashing bore, but we will need all the help we can get as we try to end this war. He is a pliable man, even if he is in constant pursuit of an intelligent thought. Listen to me go on. I've become supercilious and insufferable."

Alfred's eyes wandered the room.

"You seem preoccupied these days, Alfred. Is it because Trace is leaving us?"

Alfred lowered her hand and stood, slipping his hands into his trouser pockets.

"I'm sorry you never warmed to her, Gwen. I had hoped you would become good friends."

"Oh, it's not so much about warming to her, Alfred, I just don't believe Edward was really in love with the girl. It was all too fast for true love. How could they have truly fallen in love in such a short time? I'm sure

Edward was infatuated, because she is certainly a pretty girl and, I dare say, a likable and intelligent one, but love… well—and then for Edward to leave her so much money and that house, that's been in our family for generations."

"She doesn't want the money or the house, Gwen. And she doesn't intend to return to England or Bishop Manor."

Lady Gwendolyn sat up and propped her back up against a pillow. "Alfred, would you mind parting the drapes a little? Perhaps some sunlight would be pleasant after all."

Sir Alfred did so, and weak sunlight brightened the room. Alfred returned to his wife, again easing down on the edge of her bed. Lady Gwendolyn studied her husband's long face.

"Do you believe her, Alfred? Do you truly believe she does not want the money or the house?"

"She does not…and as I said, I am certain she will not return to us and, yes, I am sad about it."

Lady Gwendolyn stared ahead. "Alfred, I know you have grown fond of her, and you must know that I greatly admire what you did for the girl, pulling strings to release her from that ghastly prison. Of course, you know how much I admire and love you for that."

"If you had seen Trace after she was released from that dungeon of a prison, Gwen, your heart would have shattered into rage and compassion. My God, those people are barbarians. She had red splotches on her face, arms and legs, bitten by fleas and bedbugs. She was rail thin, her skin as white as chalk. They had snipped off her beautiful hair and left her there to die. Why even the nuns had nearly stopped their visits, believing her close to death. I'd never seen such wild and fearful eyes in a woman. She wept in my arms, Gwen. She wept and held me so tightly, and thanked me repeatedly for helping her. Yes, dearest Gwen, I am fond of Trace. Yes, I will miss her greatly."

Gwen gripped her husband's hand. "Alfred, what you did for her was the right and moral thing to do. Yes, of course, the Christian thing to do, and I am thankful to God that she survived and has blossomed here at Bishop Manor. But, well... I have just never felt that the girl belongs here."

"I don't know what you mean, Gwen," Sir Alfred answered, his voice cracking with emotion. "Edward loved her, and he charged us to take care of her in the event he did not survive the war. Those were his last wishes. Our son's last request. It is our duty now to carry out his wishes."

"Edward was not well, Alfred. You read the reports the Army sent us. He had become ill... His last letters to us were vague and wandering. I don't think he knew what he was doing when he married the girl. Perhaps Trace took advantage of him in some way."

Alfred pushed up to his feet, his eyes fired up. "Gwen, that is not fair, and you know it. Edward's letters, before he stopped flying, were filled with admiration, praise and love for Trace. He said it was she who kept him alive, she who gave him the will to keep going when he was at his wit's end. He was certainly well enough of mind when he courted and married Trace Rutland. I just don't know or understand why you have never warmed to Trace, but..." He threw up his hands and sighed. "I still believe that we should..."

Lady Gwendolyn interrupted, "...Alfred, hear me out. I have thought long and hard about Trace. I have prayed for guidance. It's just that I have never met anyone like her."

"For pity sake, Gwen, she's an American."

Lady Gwendolyn held his eyes, as if willing him to understand. "I have met Americans, Alfred. I know several American women, thanks to this horrendous war and the war work we have done together. But Trace is different somehow. She moves differently, she thinks differently, she acts differently."

Lady Gwendolyn scratched her head, struggling to find the right words. "I cannot quite grasp what it is I feel exactly. I guess it is my silly woman's intuition, as all you men like to say. But Trace is unusual, and you must have noticed that, Alfred. Whenever I am around her, I feel as though she occupies a different space than I, or even a different time. As ridiculous as it sounds, there are times when I feel I can see right through her, almost as if she's not really here. It is quite disconcerting."

Alfred turned away, with a shake of his head. "You do say the damnedest things sometimes, my dear."

They remained in silence for a time before he leaned and kissed her warm cheek. He lay a gentle hand on her forehead, and the back of his hand against her hot cheek. "You do feel warm, Gwen. Shall I send for the doctor?"

"No, no. I'm fine. Alfred, forgive me for saying this, and I do not wish to sound like a shrew, and I certainly do not wish to be unkind to the girl, but I am sure I will feel better once Trace is gone."

Sir Alfred held his tongue, although there were many things he wanted to say in Trace's defense.

On New Year's Eve, Trace began packing her trunk, her stomach twisted into knots and a murmuring anxiety making her hands shake. She was anxious to hear from Nonnie. She'd hoped a telegram from her would arrive right away, but none did.

Trace did not know for certain whether the ring would return her to her own time, and if it did not, then what? The Mata Hari ring lay on the bed before her, its deep emerald gloss emanating a soft, hypnotic glow. If she stared into it long enough, she noticed that she dropped into a sleepy relaxed state, as if she were slipping away under quiet rippling waves.

Over the last few days, she'd often stopped what she was doing and returned to her room to stare at the ring in fear, speculation and fascination. Would its power send her forward in time, to her previous life? A life that now seemed a misty dream, a fanciful world of cell phones, the internet, nuclear weapons, passenger jets that shot across the sky, and cultural realities that this world of 1916—soon-to-be 1917—could have never imagined.

This time—this world—was her real world now and had been her real world for six months; the faces, the relationships, the deaths, the events, all that had happened to her, these were her world, and a quivering part of her had grown comfortable and accustomed to it.

Except for the war, there was much to admire about this world: it was simpler, gracious, cultural and, at least on the surface, genteel. With the money and property she'd inherited, she could indeed live a very good life, either here or in London.

She had fought doubts about returning to her world. But she'd also had sleepless nights, when she'd risen from her bed, switched on the lamp and gazed into the ring, greatly tempted to try out its magic.

But she couldn't do that. She couldn't simply vanish into thin air. How would it affect Sir Alfred? What would be the outcome? The police would be called to investigate; questions would be asked, and the entire Bishop family would be thrown into an ugly, unwanted publicity and sorrow. They'd had enough distress. And then there was Nonnie.

On January 10, a letter finally arrived from Nonnie. Being told by Trace that she was expecting a letter from De Steeg or The Hague, Charles brought the letter to Trace's room right away.

Trace closed herself in her room, holding the letter; staring at the letter. She crossed the room to the mahogany upholstered chair and sat. She listened to the sound of her own breath, coming in and out. Trace knew this letter could be life-changing. When Trace looked at Nonnie's elegant handwriting, she felt a swelling love warm her chest. Finally, she opened the envelope and retrieved the letter, written on a heavy cream bond, the words written in a beautiful calligraphy hand.

Dear Mrs. Bishop:

Trace's shoulders dropped. Why the formal Mrs. Bishop and not Trace?

I was so pleased to receive your letter. It had been so long since I'd heard from you, and I had been worried that something unfortunate had happened. Now, I learn that something dreadful did occur. Please accept my heartfelt condolences over the death of your hus-

*band. How terrible war is. How miserable to read of
the many soldiers' deaths in the newspapers. I have
wept for you, my dear friend. I have wept over your
loss.*

*To also learn that you have been deathly ill has al-
so truly disturbed me. When I hadn't received news
from you, I had imagined dire things. How I wish I
could have attended you, my dearest friend. I am so
happy to hear that you are now fully recovered and that
you are living with your husband's family in England.
That news has helped soothe my nerves.*

*I'm afraid I have some rather unfortunate news of
my own. My father has taken ill and, even though doctors attend him regularly, he has not appreciably improved. He remains in bed, unable to walk. He also
has difficulty eating. The doctors and I have tried to
persuade him to abstain from imbibing, but so far, he
refuses to listen. As you can imagine, I am quite worried and sad.*

*I'm sure you understand, Mrs. Bishop, that I can-
not possibly leave my father at this time. In addition, I
have been offered a job teaching kindergarten children
in Velp. I start in one week. My father insists that I go.
He says it will help him improve; therefore, I will begin
my life as a teacher, just as my mother did. I find it
strange, but teaching is what I love.*

*So, as you can see, it seems our lives are moving in
different directions. Dear Trace, I wish I could invite
you for a visit, but my father has never recovered his
favor for you, ever since that night you dined with us. I
do not know what occurred, and I won't ask, but it is
quite clear that my father does not wish me to see you*

again. It makes me sad, of course, Mrs. Bishop, but I must obey my father. He means everything to me, and he needs me now, more than ever.

Please know that the time we spent together was a golden time and one that I will never forget. You lifted me up and gave me support, affection and love. What greater gifts can one receive?

Perhaps, Trace, at some time in the future, we will meet again. I'm sure of it. Until then, dear friend, I leave you with just a portion of one of my favorite Shakespeare sonnets, which reminds me of our friendship:

SONNET 29

HAPLY I THINK ON THEE, AND THEN MY STATE,

LIKE TO THE LARK AT BREAK OF DAY ARISING

FROM SULLEN EARTH, SINGS HYMNS AT
HEAVEN'S GATE.

You will always be my treasured friend, whose presence lifted my spirits when they most needed lifting. Every time I sing, I think of you, dear Trace.

With fond affection and love,

Juana-Luisa MacLeod

CHAPTER 37

Trace accepted Nonnie's decision. She had to, didn't she? But she was touched by and grateful for her affectionate words. For the rest of her life, she would remember and celebrate the time she'd had with Nonnie. She would be grateful that, for some mysterious reason, she had been granted the grace and privilege of seeing her lovely daughter once more and, this time, they were able to part lovingly, with full hearts. What more could she ask for? Trace realized that she couldn't change the past for Nonnie and Mata Hari, but she had been able to change herself. She had been able to love Edward. She had been able to love Nonnie. What greater gifts were there?

Trace booked a hotel room in Southampton, disappointed that the first passage she could get to North America was on a cargo ship, sailing to New York on January 22, 1917. For the most part, since 1914, passenger ships were nearly non-existent, having been requisitioned by the British government and used as transport ships for troops and supplies to support the war effort.

Trace had been lucky to find a cargo ship and to book a private cabin. Of course, she would never board the ship, that is, unless the Mata Hari ring was impotent and had no real power to return her to 2018. Until then, she had to pretend her voyage would indeed occur on January 22, and she would have to wait, not something she liked.

On the afternoon of January 17th, over tea, Trace finally relayed her travel plans to Sir Alfred. He grew noticeably nervous as he listened, despairing that she had booked passage on a merchant ship, afraid it would be sunk by a torpedo or a mine, just as the sister ship to the Titanic, the Britannic, had been sunk less than two months before, in November, 1916.

He tried to persuade her to stay in England, at least until after the war.

"Trace, I fear you put yourself in great peril. Look what happened to the Britannic, a hospital ship carrying 1066 souls. You read the account in the papers. It was sailing in the Aegean Sea when it was rocked by a massive explosion, surely from a mine or a torpedo. Fortunately, only 30 perished, but it is too dangerous for you to make such a crossing right now. We are hopeful the war will be over soon. Please wait until then to return home. What is the hurry?"

"I'll be fine, Sir Alfred. Stop worrying. I have to go. I must go."

They argued for another ten minutes before Sir Alfred finally admitted defeat.

"All right then, I will travel with you to Southampton to see you off. That, of course, I must do."

"No, Sir Alfred. I have traveled alone many times in my life, and I will be fine. You have a lot of work to do, especially now that Lloyd George has become Prime Minister. You're needed in London, Sir Alfred, more than ever. You must not come with me."

He stood with his back to the fireplace, saucer and teacup in hand, worry lines on his tired face. "Trace, I shall never forgive myself if anything happens to you."

Trace lay her cup and saucer aside, got to her feet and crossed to him, looking up at him tenderly. "Sir Alfred, I'm going to be all right. I promise you."

"Like you can promise such a thing in this unscrupulous and capricious world."

"You must relax, Sir Alfred. You must let me go."

He sipped his tea absently. "Well, anyway, you will write to your old friend, won't you, Trace?"

Trace had thought about this, although she had never been able to come up with a satisfying answer. How do you write to someone when you live a hundred years into the future, and they have been dead for many years? It was an insurmountable problem.

Trace took in a little breath, running a hand through her hair, which had thickened and returned to its original luster.

"You will write, won't you, Trace?" Sir Alfred repeated, almost at a pleading whisper, appraising her guarded expression.

"Yes, of course I'll write, Sir Alfred."

She turned and started back to her chair and sat. They were quiet for a time, as they sipped their tea.

"Is Lady Gwendolyn feeling better?" Trace asked.

"Yes, although she still stays in her room. I wanted her to join us for tea, but she regretfully declined. I am sorry, Trace."

"Don't be. Once I'm gone, I'm sure her health will improve."

"Why would you say such a thing, Trace?"

"Please, Sir Alfred. After all the confessions you and I have had these last few weeks; and those confidential talks we had when I was in the hospital. A woman knows things."

He screwed up his lips and shook his head. "A woman is a puzzle and a trial sometimes, Trace. I wish I could say otherwise, but I find it increasingly so."

Trace laughed a little. "So we are, Sir Alfred. So we are, indeed."

Sir Alfred rested his warm eyes on Trace. "How I regret Edward's death, my dear. How I wish you two could have lived here in love and harmony. I could have spent the rest of my years playing with and spoiling my grandchildren."

The room receded into a heavy silence.

CHAPTER 38

On January 20th, a gray, misty morning, Trace left Bishop Manor for the last time. Thomas had returned from London to see her off, and Trace was surprised and grateful to see him one last time.

Bryanna and Lady Gwendolyn presented pleasant faces, while Sir Alfred struggled to hide his sadness. Charles sheltered Trace from the cold mist with a black umbrella, as she hugged Sir Alfred, kissing him on both cheeks, her eyes wet and his red. His stiff upper lip was quivering.

"You will write to your old friend, won't you, Trace? Send me your address and I will certainly write to you. I want to hear everything you are up to."

Trace was choked with feeling as she touched his cheek, staring into his kind, searching eyes. "Yes, I will write to you, Sir Alfred, and I will tell you things that will amaze and astound you. Things you will never believe."

He chuckled. "I hope that is true, my dear Trace. An old man likes to be astounded now and then. It keeps his blood warm and his heart ticking, you know."

Lady Gwendolyn looked on with keen interest, silently wishing Trace happiness, and yet privately thanking God that she was leaving.

Thomas embraced Trace warmly, his eyes soft on her. "Return at any time, dear Trace, and we will throw you the party of parties."

Trace winked at him. "When you sat and spoke at length with Miss Pemberton at the Christmas party, no one seemed to disapprove, and the world is still spinning around. I think the lady is smitten, Thomas."

He smiled. "All in good time, Trace. All in good time."

Bryanne extended a mechanical hand and wished Trace luck and every happiness.

As the car putted off and the family remained in a single line, waving, Trace twisted around and waved back until they grew smaller and smaller, finally fading into ghosts in the gray, foggy mist.

As Trace settled into her seat, she shut her eyes, recalling her final visit to Edward's grave the day before. The sun had slid in and out of clouds, at times bathing the peaceful family cemetery in golden light, at times blanketing the world in shades of gray. There was a quick, chilling wind.

Trace had knelt before the grave, bowed her head in prayer, and placed a bouquet of flowers she'd found at the local greenhouse that morning. Edward's marker was a towering obelisk gravestone, with a cross at the crown, and angels with curled wings on either side, their pious faces gazing heavenward. The inscription read:

CAPTAIN EDWARD KENYON BISHOP
BORN AUGUST 6, 1891
DIED SEPTEMBER 14, 1916
BELOVED SON OF SIR ALFRED KENYON
BISHOP
AND
LADY GWENDOLYN ANNE BISHOP

WORTHY IS THE LAMB, WHO WAS SLAIN, TO RECEIVE POWER AND

WEALTH WISDOM AND STRENGTH AND HONOR AND GLORY AND PRAISE!

It was early the next evening, January 21st, when Trace wearily checked into the five-story South Western Hotel in Southampton. It was a very Victorian structure, built of yellow brick, with chocolate trim, and turrets shooting into the sky.

After her bags and trunk were delivered to her third-floor room, Trace collapsed on the large upholstered panel bed and shut her eyes. It had been a long day and an arduous trip, with her train being delayed in London. She'd spent the night in a London hotel and caught a rerouted train the next morning, finally completing her journey to Southampton.

She managed to eat a modest dinner in the club car, while ignoring several British soldiers, who were casting flirty, lusty eyes her way. They looked like boys, fresh out of high school, frisky and confident. She hoped they were not on their way to some front to be slaughtered.

During the train ride across the foggy, unraveling countryside, Trace mentally began to compose her letter to Sir Alfred. She started it several times, erased it, and started again, eventually finding the right pitch and tone.

In her hotel room, Trace sat at a mahogany ball-and-claw-foot writing desk, a flickering oil lamp beside her. She removed a piece of hotel bond paper and a brushed gold pen from the drawer, and she began to write. After several smudged words, Trace finally found the right way to use the odd little pen, and she wrote swiftly, feeling emotional.

Dearest Sir Alfred:

There are no words to express all the love, gratitude and emotion I feel in my heart. When I saw your shocked and kind face as I stumbled out of that prison, squinting against the bright light and in a delirious state, I wasn't sure who you were. No one had told me, not the nuns or the guards. Certainly not Captain Ladoux, who had come by my cell one last time to look at me with disgust and loathing. He actually spat at me. I truly fear for Mata Hari. She will meet him soon, and there's nothing I can do about that.

You were my savior, Sir Alfred, and when I felt your kind presence in the room or saw your large shadow sitting close by, you were my guardian angel, my protector.

And then there were the talks we had about Edward. How we both cried our eyes out. I was honored that you shared so much of your life with me—your memories, your regrets, your hopes and wishes. You had asked me for my life story—for my regrets and wishes. I told you I didn't want to recall anything about my past, that I just wanted to get away from that prison and France, and never go back. Remember when the nightmares and my screaming awoke you? You calmed me and soothed me; you were so kind and loving. How I needed that. How that healed me more than anything else.

Remember, I told you how lucky Edward was to have you as a father? And how he'd often said how much he loved and admired you and his mother, Lady Gwendolyn? I wanted to tell her that so many times—I wanted to explain things to her—but I could see she was not comfortable in my presence. I hope you will tell her these things that Edward said, and thank her again for all her kindnesses.

Now, Sir Alfred, I am going to tell you about my past—or rather about my future. I am only telling you now because I will never be able to write to you again, and it hurts me deeply to have to tell you that. Sir Alfred, you will never hear from me again, so I must tell you the truth, whether you believe me or not. You deserve to know the whole truth.

There is no easy way to tell you my story, so I'm just going to come out with it.

Sir Alfred, I am not from your time. Again, I was not born in your time. I came to this time as a time traveler from the future. I know that sounds crazy. But please read on.

Why did it happen? How? It was a bizarre twist of fate, or an anomaly, or something I don't understand and probably never will. Anyway, I did come to this time—your time of 1916-1917—from the future. To be exact: I came from the year 2018.

I can see your face now, Sir Alfred. It is filled with confusion, disbelief and alarm. You might even be laughing, believing that this is some kind of joke. It is not a joke, I can assure you.

I could have told you many things about the future that you would have found to be both wondrous and disturbing. I could have said so many things, but I didn't, and I won't now, except to tell you these few things that will happen. The Great War or World War I—as it will be called—because there will be a World War II beginning in Europe in 1939... Anyway, The Great War will not end until November of 1918, and the peace treaty will be signed in Versailles.

Also, Mata Hari will be executed on October 15, 1917. All her appeals will come to nothing. No one will be able to save her, as you saved me. That is all I'll say about that. If you doubt what I am writing, just wait, and then perhaps you'll believe me.

I never told Edward these things. Perhaps I would have in time, but our time together was always so short, and I wanted to enjoy all of it, without any intrusions, and believe me, it would have been an intrusion. I wanted Edward to enjoy all the time we had together, and I believe he did.

Why did I time travel to the past? I believe it was to meet Edward and fall in love. I had never fallen in love before. I had never met a man who touched me so deeply in so many infinite ways. I also came to reunite with a young girl who had haunted my dreams for years. I came to reconcile my relationship with her. Also, I came to see myself as I was in the past, to learn from that and then to grow to be a better woman, a bet-

ter person. I hope and believe I have succeeded. But without your help, Sir Alfred, I would not have survived. Thank you, dear friend.

I am hoping to return to my time, Sir Alfred, and if it all goes well, I should be there soon. If not, well, I will still make my way home to America and try to find my great-grandparents. That will be strange, but if it comes to that, then I will be in touch, and perhaps I will return to Bishop Manor someday. But don't count on it. I fully intend to vanish from your world forever.

Just know and believe me, Sir Alfred, when I tell you that I will never forget you, and I will hold you in my heart for the rest of my life and perhaps beyond. Who knows, we may meet again in another time and place. The world truly is a strange, beguiling place, isn't it, Sir Alfred, my good and truest friend?

You will always be in my thoughts and prayers.

With love,
Tracey Peyton Rutland Bishop
Southampton, England
January 21, 1917

Trace posted the letter downstairs with the friendly hotel clerk, and then promptly returned to her room, flushed with a mounting anticipation. Inside, she bolted the door, hurried to the desk and removed another sheet of paper. She sat and dashed off a final quick note.

To Whom It May Concern:

I, Tracey Rutland Bishop, had to leave town suddenly. I am fine, of sound mind, and I am in no danger. Please give all my items herein to charity.

Yours sincerely,
Tracey Rutland Bishop

With every task completed, there was only one thing left to do.

Breathing in her nerves, Trace opened her purse and gingerly removed the red velvet cloth that held Mata Hari's ring. The Victorian mantel clock ticked away in the loud silence of the room, as Trace carefully loosened the strings, allowing the velvet sides to fall away, revealing the awaiting emerald ring, its center shining with tiny fires. She glanced at the mantel clock. It was 12:35am, January 21, 1917.

Outside, she heard the clop of a horse's hooves on the cobbles, and a squeal of wind rounding the hotel. She lay the velvety cloth on the desktop, the ring between two fingers, ready, so close to her left-hand fourth finger.

She hesitated, willing her galloping pulse to calm and settle. There was no use to wait any longer. Her decision was made. It was now or never. With a sudden inhalation, hand trembling, she slipped the ring onto her finger.

Instantly, the hair on the back of her neck stood up, as the air around her begin to shimmer, like heat on a hot, summer day. There was a tickle across her skin, as if feathers were brushing her face, her neck, her chest. Bursting blue glittering dots appeared and twirled about her in a dazzling display of motion and color.

Trace stared rapt, as a flash of light—like a flash-bulb—exploded, blinding her for a time. She heard bells—deep throated bells—to her right, her left, and high above. The floor beneath her shifted and moved, as a rumbling, whirling wind whipped her hair, scattering her skirt. It flapped around her legs.

Suddenly, the room was pitched into darkness, and Trace couldn't tell if she was looking up, down or sideways. Helplessly disoriented, she reached. She fell, falling, plunging down, heart pounding. She was flung on wild currents, feeling that pit-of-the-stomach sensation of freefall, completely at the mercy of motion.

A whooshing wind slammed into her, pitching her head-over-heels, and she screamed as she was sucked into a tunnel of golden blue light, and hurled away into spinning stars and blurring lights.

Voices called her name—sirens wailed, explosions and bursting flares sailed by, cries for help and ghost-like figures reached, and faces flew by.

She passed through freezing curtains of rain, darted over towering snow-capped mountain peaks, and drifted over moon-drenched lakes. There were more loud bells, and chimes, and distant ethereal music, and choirs singing in entrancing dissonances.

As she raced toward a green shimmering wall, Trace flung out her arms to brace for impact. With eyes wide in terror, she crashed through a gooey, watery wall, screaming, tumbling, lost and cold, plunging down into an ocean of darkness.

CHAPTER 39

Trace was trembling violently—afraid she'd shake apart and fall into pieces. The pounding in her ears was loud in the silence, but her feet were planted on something solid—a plush carpet? A warm breath of air began to still her chattering teeth. Her first thought was "Where am I?"

Thank God, the world had stopped spinning, her stomach had stopped churning. All was quiet, dead still. With effort, she allowed her eyes to adjust to the murky darkness, as vague images and shapes slowly began to emerge.

As her shuddering subsided, she heard hurried steps descending stairs. She caught a quick breath, and held it, waiting, every sense on alert, eyes struggling to pierce through the dim light.

A ghostly figure loomed ahead, like an apparition. She stared, peering. The figure stood tall and still in the open library doors. The room and reality gradually seeped back into her senses, and she opened her mouth to speak, but had no voice.

"Trace? Trace, is that you?" he said, in quiet apprehension.

Trace stiffened at his voice. The silhouette slowly advanced into the room toward her. From outside, a garden light leaked in from the slightly parted draperies, just enough to reveal the man's face. Trace gasped.

"Sir Alfred?" she said, the words catching in her tight throat.

"Trace...No. It's Cyrano. Cyrano Wallace. You're here... You've returned."

Trace's strangled thoughts and bold, staring eyes struggled to make sense of what she was hearing and seeing. She felt fragmented and displaced—she was an echo, reverberating, and pieces of herself seemed to be swirling about her head. Other parts of herself still seemed trapped in other worlds.

To her utter shock, she watched the image of Sir Alfred slowly recede and melt away into darkness, as a blue shimmering image of Cyrano Wallace emerged.

"Trace, are you all right?" Cyrano asked. "How do you feel?"

Trace stood mute for a time, unable to process, while she observed Cyrano's ephemeral vibrations smooth and flatline into the form of the man before her, Cyrano Wallace.

Beating nerves strained her voice. "Where....? Where am I?"

He cleared his throat. "You're in my home, in the Berkshires."

"The Berkshires?" she asked, searching the room. She slowly began to recognize that she was standing in Cyrano Wallace's library. She recalled now. Yes, she remembered this room.

Her moving, startled eyes took in the room, finally coming to rest on Cyrano Wallace's Mata Hari collection: the Chinese marble sculpture, the ornate opera glasses, the two fur necklets, the silver cutlery and the old French francs. In the hazy light, Trace took in the Mata Hari painting, revealing the exposed woman's beguiling body and warm, bewitching eyes.

Trace struggled to anchor herself, looking down to examine her body. She still wore her 1917 gray velvet suit, with the flared skirt and coat flared below the waist. Her dark blue buttoned ankle boots were clean and polished, showing no signs of the time travel.

Inevitably, her eyes lowered onto the ring—the Mata Hari ring—and Trace still felt the force of its power—its mysterious, and awesome, and terrible magic.

She was finished with it. She wanted no more of it. Deliberately, she gripped the ring, wriggled it from her finger, and enclosed it in a tight fist, as if to squeeze the life from it.

Trace worked to make a keen appraisal of the room, her eyes sharpening, her head clearing. Once again, she leveled her eyes on the display table and the Mata Hari collection. Resolutely, she relaxed her fist and moved unsteadily toward the table. With trembling effort, she stopped, staring down. In one firm motion, she returned the ring to its rightful place in the collection, immediately backing away, as the glowing ring seemed to be watching her with its single, beseeching eye. Trace felt its dark, beckoning allure, its silent siren call, and she turned away from it. Turned her back on it, forever.

Cyrano had been watching with a strange curiosity, catching her spooked eyes as she looked at him.

"I am so tired, Mr. Wallace. So very tired and ex-hausted. Can I sleep somewhere for a while? I must sleep."

It was snowing when Trace awakened in her soft, luxurious canopied bed. With a yawn and a stretch, she sat up to watch feathery flakes drift past her window. She felt a lift when she turned to the bedside digital clock to see it was 8:13am. Yes, a digital clock. It was true. She had returned to her own time. How long had she slept? She had no idea what month or day it was, although it had to be winter if it was snowing.

She eased back, feeling a crashing relief and deep gratitude that she had returned home to complete her life in this time, and not in 1917. She felt lighter, freer, younger. She felt the giddy urge to leap up and dance, grab big chunks of the day, and live her new life to the fullest. She was reborn, vital, and she was curious. What had happened since she'd left this time, arriving in France in June 1916? How much time had passed?

She shut her eyes, as a kind of test. Yes, the old im-ages returned: Mata Hari, Vadime, Captain Ladoux, Nonnie and Edward. But they were vague and fading, and Trace had slept well, with no bad dreams, and no nightmares.

She tossed back the warm comforter, admiring the cream-colored satin nightgown Cyrano had provided for her last night. He mentioned that he'd bought it for Constance two Christmases ago.

Trace belted the matching robe, found some cozy slippers and made her way downstairs to the formal dining room that she easily recalled, as if she'd seen it only yesterday.

Cyrano sat alone, quietly, a cup of coffee before him. When Trace entered, he pushed back his chair and stood, studying her carefully.

"Good morning, Trace."

"Good morning, Cyrano."

"Coffee?"

"Yes... Love some."

Cyrano stepped to his left, held her chair, and she sat.

"I have given my butler, Andrew, the day off, so I'm afraid you're going to be stuck with me, and my bad cooking and clumsy service."

He left through a side door, soon returning with a pot of coffee and a porcelain cup and saucer. After the coffee was poured, he sat the pot on a warmer and stood to her side.

"Feeling better?"

Trace put a fist to a yawn. "Yes... Much better, thank you. This coffee just might save my life."

"Hungry?"

"I'm a slow morning person. Maybe later. Thank you."

"Very well," Cyrano said, returning to his chair and sitting.

They sipped the coffee in silence for a time, each searching for the right words to begin the conversation.

"We're supposed to get about five inches of snow," Cyrano said, looking toward the windows.

Through the picture window, Trace watched the play of the snowflakes soar and drift.

"I love the snow," she said, dreamily.

"How's the coffee?" Cyrano asked.

"Good. Very good."

"It's the one thing in the kitchen I do well. I'm not bad at scrambled eggs either. I was often the breakfast chef when Constance was alive."

In the light of day, Trace took her first good look at Cyrano. Again, she felt that strange, unsettling feeling she'd had the night before—that Cyrano not only reminded her of Sir Alfred, but that he resembled him in many ways, the mouth, the eyes, and the way he moved his head in conversation when listening. It was an uneasy feeling, and difficult to put into thought or words. It was as if Cyrano was floating on the surface of the water, and Sir Alfred lay just beneath its clear, rippling surface.

Trace assumed it was just an obvious after-effect of time traveling, as she must still be hovering between two worlds, not yet fully present in either. Would it pass?

"You're looking at me strangely, Trace." Cyrano said. "Are you sure you're feeling okay?"

She glanced away, breaking her little trance. "I'm sorry, Cyrano. I'm not quite myself yet. I'm not totally... well, here, I think."

Cyrano waited for more. He didn't want to rush her, but he was boiling with an anxious curiosity, longing to hear her story.

A moment later, Trace asked, "What day and year is it?"

"Monday, January 22, 2018."

Trace shot him a look. "But... how could it be? How long was I gone? You saw me, well, disappear, right?"

"Yes. You simply vanished into a kind of blue misty fog, which lingered in the room for about ten minutes. I searched everywhere for you, and I had Andrew search for you. You simply vanished. That was early yesterday, Sunday morning, January 21st. You were gone an entire day. As you can imagine, I was alarmed. I didn't know quite what to do. Should I call the police? Should I call your parents? Should I call a medium? I was greatly relieved when I saw you standing there this morning."

"How did you know to come downstairs? How did you know I had returned?"

"I was asleep, and suddenly I felt your presence. I woke up. It was one of the weirdest things that has ever happened to me, but then… this whole situation has been, to put it mildly, very strange and somewhat upsetting."

"When I appeared this morning, what time was it?"

"Around one o'clock."

They heard a howling wind, and Trace swiveled around to watch the snow being blown into a chaotic frenzy.

"Can you tell me, Trace? I mean to say," Cyrano said, fumbling his words, "well, are you ready to tell me what happened to you?"

Trace faced him, thinking again how uncanny it was that he reminded her so much of Sir Alfred. It relaxed her, made the moment seem familiar and pleasant.

"Would you mind making me those scrambled eggs, Cyrano? While I eat I'll tell you everything."

He nearly leaped to his feet, his face brightening. "Of course, I'll scramble the eggs. I'll be back in a few minutes."

At the side door, he paused, turning back to her. "Trace, I want you to have a complete physical with my doctor. I'll make the appointment for tomorrow morning, if that's all right with you."

And then it struck her. That sounded so much like Sir Alfred. The pitch and timbre of the voice; the sensitivity, the concern. She gave him a long, penetrating appraisal, looking deeply into his soul, parting the waters, so to speak, to peer down into the depths of a deep, murky lake.

In that pulsing silence, her inner vision cleared, and she was able to see—to truly see—and a cool shiver raced up her spine.

Trace watched in stunned fascination as Sir Alfred took a few steps toward her.

"Trace? Trace, what's the matter? What has happened?"

Sir Alfred's figure rippled, faded and dissolved back into Cyrano Wallace.

Cyrano was quiet, straining to understand.

Trace knew now, without any doubt. She was no longer caught between two worlds. She had arrived back into this one, and she was anchored here.

But her time travel journey had bestowed a bizarre gift—a psychic gift. She could see beneath the waters into the past—at least she could see into Cyrano's past. She saw beyond the veil of this reality to see who Cyrano had been in his past life.

Trace spoke in a dazed wonder, in an unsettling whisper. "Cyrano...You were Sir Alfred Kenyon Bishop. In your previous life on Earth, you were Sir Alfred Kenyon Bishop."

Cyrano stared, mystified.

They sat at the kitchen table, staring into the middle distance. Snow continued falling, and the wind wheezed around the house, as the hallway grandfather clock bonged eleven times.

Trace had just finished telling Cyrano her entire time travel story, leaving nothing out, and he'd sat in anxious attention through it all.

She'd finished the eggs, toast and coffee long ago, and she pushed her plate aside. They remained silent for minutes, as Cyrano struggled to process the story. Trace held his eyes to gauge his reaction.

Finally, he mechanically reached for his napkin and blotted his damp forehead. He was noticeably troubled, his eyes moving around the room, as if searching for reason, as if wishing to rerun the minutes back, so he could return to the solid reality he had lived in for 70 years. But there was no going back. That world was gone now—shattered—and this new world, whatever it was, distressed and troubled him.

He breathed out a long, sibilant sigh, refusing to meet Trace's eyes.

"You do believe me, don't you, Cyrano?"

He pursed his lips, blinking. "Well, I don't know. Perhaps you should call me Sir Alfred?"

Trace gave him a questioning glance, then looked away. "Then you don't believe me, or anything that happened?

Cyrano folded his hands, his eyes coming to hers. "That's the problem, Trace. I do indeed believe you. How can I not? I saw you vanish before my eyes, and then reappear like some ghost. And some part of me knew you were about to return. I have to believe you, even if I don't want to believe you. It's all very distressing. Yes, Constance believed in all this occult business, but I never took it all that seriously. I mean, how can anyone believe in such things, unless they actually experience it? It's fantastic. It's upsetting. It's just, I don't know, unbelievable."

He shoved his chair back and stood. "I need something. I need time. Yes, I need time to think about all this, Trace. For God's sake, I need a drink."

Cyrano left the room abruptly, and Trace slumped in her chair. Minutes later he was back with two crystal rocks glasses filled with an amber liquid. He handed a glass to Trace.

"What is it?"

"A 25-year-old single malt Scotch. I know it's only a little after eleven in the morning, but I need it, and you deserve it. Drink it down in a swallow. This is not the time to sip."

He raised his glass and they clinked. "Well, here's to old friends. And I mean old friends," he said, with a humor that helped relax Trace's nerves. They both chuckled, and then tossed back the Scotch.

Cyrano stared at her, pointing a finger. "I have a confession to make, Trace. When I first saw you standing there in the library the first time, something inside me shifted. You looked and felt so familiar to me. I didn't admit it to myself then, but I truly felt like I knew you, or had known you. It was a good feeling, a warm feeling. It was a feeling of recognition, of meeting an old friend after so many years apart. Did you feel it?"

Trace stared down at the empty glass, already feeling a comfortable buzz from the Scotch. "I don't know. I was so fixated on that Mata Hari collection. I was so hell-bent on slipping on that ring. Nothing else seemed to matter."

"Well, I'll have to get used to all this occult business, I suppose. I'll have to admit that, at the very least, we are quite comfortable together. I can't deny my feelings."

Trace met his eyes. "I can't say I feel bad about it, Cyrano. I hated leaving Sir Alfred behind. He... You saved my life. He became a second father to me, my only father in that time."

Cyrano threw up his hands. "Okay, then. Now that we are good and old friends, Trace, I hope you will come to see me from time to time. You could even stay here with me, if you like, and make this your home."

Trace smiled. "I will certainly come, Cyrano, and I'd love to stay, but I am an actress, or at least I was an actress, and I have to work in the City. I haven't even thought about that—any of it. I believe I'm supposed to begin rehearsals on a new show in February."

"Then stay at my Park Avenue condo, Trace. It has three bedrooms. I was about to sell the place, but I'll keep it now. You might as well live there. It will be empty most of the time. Go ahead, move your things in right away. It's got everything you need—all the conveniences and a 24-hour doorman, of course. For that matter, as I think about it, I can come down and join you sometimes. We can go to the theatre, the opera, the galleries, the best restaurants. We can do whatever we want to do. And if you have a boyfriend, bring him along. The more the merrier."

They stared into each other's eyes. Finally, Trace went to him, burying her head in his shoulder. He slowly, hesitantly, wrapped her in his arms, and they remained there for long minutes, old friends reunited.

CHAPTER 40

Back in New York, Trace hurled herself into her previous schedule of dance classes, auditions, voice coaching and yoga. She may have been gone for only a day in this time, but in the seven months she had spent in 1916, she had danced and sung little, except when she was with Nonnie. She was surprised how much flexibility and technique she'd lost. Every dance class felt as though she were moving underwater, her voice felt thin and brittle, and her first yoga classes left her feeling stiff and sore.

By the first week in February, when she began rehearsals for the new Broadway show musical, Daydreams, she'd nearly returned to the fit, thin body she'd had before her time travel adventure.

Upon returning to her time, what she'd found most remarkable was that the world had continued on without her, as if nothing ever happened. None of her friends or family members, nor her agent, had missed her because, of course, she'd only been gone for a day. They had simply experienced their usual day, while she had been through what seemed to be years.

The energy, sights and sounds of modern New York City had been jarring at first, but she'd slowly readjusted, and she soon fell into all the familiar rhythms.

During rehearsals, Cyrano did come to the city, and they attended several Broadway shows, as well as performances of the New York Philharmonic and the Metropolitan Opera. They seldom talked about Trace's journey, making a pact between them to focus only on the present.

"The past is dead, thank God," Trace said, during one of their many dinners in the theatre district.

"Are you still having nightmares?" Cyrano asked.

"Interesting that you should ask. No. I haven't had one nightmare about Mata Hari or my past life since I returned. I sleep soundly, better than I ever have before."

Cyrano raised his wine glass and they touched. "Then perhaps it was all for the best, Trace. Perhaps it was a good thing."

Trace paused to consider his words. "I still have flashbacks sometimes, and there are times I can look at a person and see who they were in their past life. Like, for instance, the director of Daydreams. A few weeks ago, I saw that, in a past life, he had been a she. That was startling."

Cyrano's eyes widened. "Really?"

Trace continued. "But in the last few days, I've noticed that I don't see these things quite so clearly anymore. They're getting fuzzy and out of focus."

"Is that a good thing?" Cyrano asked.

"Yes, it's a good thing. I don't want to know about the past anymore. I'm very happy now, with you in my life, and with my new show. I'm happy being here and now. I don't care who I was, or what I did, or who anybody was. That part of my life is over."

Cyrano raised his wine glass. "Then let's toast to the here and now."

And they did.

Daydreams was in rehearsal for seven weeks and opened on March 22nd, to excellent reviews. Although Trace was the second lead, she received a glowing review from the New York Times.

Trace Rutland, as Emmeline Jones, was dramatically entertaining, funny and fetching in her 19th-century emerald gown, and proud head piled high with artistic blonde corkscrew curls that bounced about her face. Even in the comic scenes, Ms. Rutland sang with depth and color, and her voice, rich, like a full-bodied wine, easily reached the far corners of the theatre. Her dancing was fluid, graceful and exotic, and as she weaves webs of subtle seduction around her feckless lover, William Wells, the audience is also caught and captivated by her ineffable allure and charm, as noted by the standing ovation Ms. Rutland received at curtain call.

The night of the opening, Cyrano threw a lavish party for Trace and the entire cast, and it was one of the most memorable nights of Trace's life, filled with dancing, singing, Champagne and good friends.

During the following weeks, Trace fell into her old disciplined life of performing eight shows a week and spending Mondays, the one night the theatre was dark, sequestered in her apartment, sleeping and resting her voice. Despite Cyrano's invitation to live in his Park Avenue condo, Trace had decided to remain in her West Side one-bedroom apartment. She felt more at home there.

On a warm, sun-drenched Monday during the second week in May, New York was bursting with color and new life. Trace felt the call of the day, and she escaped her sun-starved apartment to bathe in glorious sunshine. She ambled along the carriage path in Riverside Park, taking in the riot of colors and breathing in the scented island gardens, watching the dog walkers, the lovers and the joggers.

Plugged into earphones, and tuned to her favorite playlist, she wandered, listening to a combination of old rock and current Indy selections. She had no destination in mind, and that was part of the joy—doing nothing, with no appointments to keep. Before her, lay a dazzling spring day, opening in bouquets of yellow, white and red.

She was listening to The Shins' song Name for You, feeling the soft spring air, feeling light and happy, and touched by spring fever.

It was after she'd shut her eyes that it happened. She was strolling, bopping, and singing, weaving about in a little improvised dance.

The sudden impact to her left shoulder stunned her. Her eyes shot open as she back-pedaled, arms wheeling, body struggling for balance. She tumbled backward, landing on her ass, earbuds jerked from her ears, cellphone flying.

Disoriented and startled, she stared dumbly, taking in a sharp inbreath. A guy cut into her vision, standing there, staring down at her with worried interest.

"I'm so sorry," he said, reaching for her. "Are you all right? Can I help you up?"

Trace struggled to catch her breath. He'd punched the wind from her lungs. "Why did you run into me?"

"I'm sorry…I'm really sorry about that."

Trace took in his blue and white jogging shorts and blue T-shirt. His hair was cut short, but stylishly spiked into a peak. He was nice looking enough. Well, no, that wasn't exactly right. He was actually very good looking. Thick hair, blue eyes, good shoulders, flat stomach. He held a cell phone and dangling earbuds.

"Did you hurt anything? Are you okay?" he asked.

Trace sighed, rubbed her scratch-up elbow and glanced around. Five people were hovering about, looking on with interest.

"I'm okay," Trace said. "You scared the life out of me, running into me like that."

She turned, stretched an arm and reached for her cell phone.

She frowned at the cracked cell screen. She'd just had it replaced.

He extended a hand, she grabbed hold of it, and he pulled her to her feet. She brushed herself off, still noticeably upset at the damaged cellphone screen.

"… And I just had that fixed."

He noticed. "I'm sorry. I can pay to fix it. No problem. Happy to do that."

She shook her head. She heaved out a sigh. "No, forget it. It's not that important."

"I had just closed my eyes for a minute," he said, guiltily. "I was listening to some music. I didn't know anyone else was close."

"Well I was close," Trace said, not mentioning to him that her eyes were also closed. "I mean, you shouldn't close your eyes when you're jogging."

He looked contrite. "No, of course not. I am truly sorry."

Trace looked him over again, with increasing interest. He was very attractive, at least four inches taller than she, and his eyes held a particular kind of fascination that seemed to draw her in. They were pools of blue, and in the clear morning sun, she saw gold in the irises. Yes, they were appealing and captivating. He was appealing and captivating, and it was Spring, and she'd only been on one date since she'd returned from 1917, and that was more of a friendship date than an actual "date-date."

"Are you sure you're all right?" he asked.

Trace softened. "Yeah, sure. I'm okay. I may never walk again, but other than that I'm okay."

He grinned, a shy grin that Trace found quite charming.

She thought, how could a guy who is so hot-looking be so shy? Trace warmed to him.

"Did you hurt yourself?" she asked.

"Oh... Well, just my shoulder, a little. It's okay. I mean, I'm a man, you know. I can take it," he said, with a playful wink.

The curious little crowd shrank away, leaving Trace and the guy alone.

He glanced about, shifting nervously from his left foot to his right. "Okay, well, if you're okay, I guess I'll see you around then."

"See me is definitely the right word," Trace said, lightly. "Make sure you keep those eyes open and you do see me."

He laughed. "Yeah... Okay. Will do."

And then he was off. Trace placed her hands on her hips, turning in disappointment to watch his sexy jogging figure retreat into the dazzling light of day.

"You could have given me your name," she mumbled, rubbing her sore elbow.

A week later, on Monday morning, Trace was asleep on the couch, a book cracked open on her chest, a half-drunk cup of coffee on the floor beside her, and an intoxicating breeze billowing across her face from an open window.

The "Ding Dong" from her doorbell jerked her awake and she sat up, squinting a look toward the door.

"Yes," she said, in a scratchy voice. "Yeah... Who is it?"

Another ring. Trace pushed up, wiggled her toes into slippers, shuffled over to the door and peered through the peephole, fish-eye lens. Her neck stiffened in recognition. She jerked back with surprise, then grinned with sudden pleasure.

Fumbling with the door chain lock, Trace finally opened the door. Standing before her was the same good-looking guy who had slammed into her only a week ago in Riverside Park.

He stiffened in surprise. "Oh. It's you...?"

"Yeah... Me. Is that okay?"

He shrugged. "Oh, yeah. Sure."

"And there you are, again. Thank God you're not jogging," Trace said, with a little flirtatious grin. "I'd have to duck, or run, or something."

He blushed. "Yeah... Again, sorry about that."

Trace nodded toward the Macy's package he held.

"Is that a peace offering present for me?"

"Oh, no... Well, actually, no. I live upstairs, in apartment 42. You're in 22. The delivery guy mistakenly left it by my door."

"You live upstairs?"

"Yes."

"How come I've never seen you? I've been living here for two years."

"I only moved in about three weeks ago. By the way, I hope you're okay... I mean about the other day. Any bruises?"

Trace sharpened her eyes on him. Yes, she liked what she saw. She liked it very much: clean jaw, spiked black hair, dancing blue eyes, and a killer shy smile that she suspected he used effectively as seduction. She didn't really believe he was all that shy. She thought that this hot guy knew how to disarm and seduce, and she liked it. She liked his supposed technique, and she decided to use a bit of her own technique.

"I do have some bruises, actually. Want to see?"

The shy grin faded into a mischievous smile that nearly melted her. "Maybe I could make them better."

She presented a coy smile. "Are you a doctor?"

"No, a personal trainer. Personal, being the catchword."

Trace lifted an impressed eyebrow. No wonder he was in such good shape. She imagined hard, rippling muscles under that blue cotton shirt.

"Personal, huh?"

"Yeah."

"East Side clients?"

"Some..."

"Movie stars?"

"Only one."

"Would I know him, her?"

"Her. Yep. What do you do?"

"Actress. Dancer."

"Starving?"

"Not for a while. I eat rather well. I'm actually gaining weight and, incidentally, I was considering looking around for a personal trainer."

His right eyebrow arched. He shrugged his right shoulder. "Well, it must be fate then. I mean, here we are meeting again, and I am, as it turns out, a personal trainer."

"Is that package heavy?" Trace asked, pointing.

"No. Would you like me to bring it inside?"

She stood aside. "Why not?"

Inside, he set the box down on the kitchen counter, while casting his eyes around her apartment, nodding in approval. "Nice. I like the layout. A one bedroom?"

"Yep. Yours?"

"Yeah... Same kind of layout, but I see you have that bay window and window seat. Mine doesn't have that. Good storage?"

"Not bad," Trace said. "I've added some closet space in the hallway over there."

Trace felt instantly comfortable with this guy. He had an easy, approachable energy that was disarming. She loved his unstated humor.

"Should we give names?" she asked.

"Blake Farrington."

Trace bobbed her eyebrows. "Impressive. Regal sounding, Farrington. I bet you have a flashy middle name too."

"I wouldn't call it flashy. Kind of ordinary."

"I'll be the judge…"

"It's Edward. Blake Edward Farrington."

Trace's eyes widened. "Edward? Your middle name is Edward?"

"Yes. Yes, and I know my entire name sounds aloof and arrogant but, then, my grandfather was a barrister, that is, a lawyer, in England. Anyway, what's your name?"

Trace was lost in a thought. "Trace Rutland."

"I detect the hint of a southern accent."

"Lexington, Kentucky. And where are you from?"

"Born and raised in West Hartford, Connecticut. Points of interest—the Mark Twain House, and yes, I've been in the house several times. There is also the Talcott Mountain State Park, a nature sanctuary with beautiful panoramic views."

"Sounds like a lovely place to grow up."

"What is Trace short for, Tracey?"

"Yes."

"Well, then, Trace, would you like to take a little walk with me and my dog? Maybe we could find an outside café somewhere and have lunch. It's a perfect day for it."

Trace, smiled, folding her arms. "Yes… I would love to take a walk and meet your dog. What's his or her name?"

"It's a he… His name is Ricky-Ticky."

Trace froze, her thoughts racing, circling, remembering. "What?" she said, in a startled whisper.

"What…what?"

"What did you say your dog's name was?"

Blake saw her face fall into sudden alarm. "Not was. Is. His name is Ricky-Ticky."

Trace turned from him, eyes searching the air, remembering, recalling an old letter.

"Who names a dog Ricky-Ticky?"

"What's wrong with it?"

Trace shut her eyes, willing the old letter to bubble
up from the depths of memory—the letter she'd received from Edward, back in 1916. Yes, he'd written
about a dog—a dog that had become their unit's mascot. She'd read that letter so many times she'd memo-
rized it. Even though her psychic powers had faded,
Edward's letter was still there, branded in her brain.
She recalled a part of it—the part about the dog.

On a positive note, we have a mascot—a black and
white mutt dog that wandered onto the field the other
day. I've named him Ricky-Ticky, after an English flyer, Rick Thackery, who was shot down and killed about
two weeks ago.

"Is something wrong?" Blake asked.

Trace opened her eyes, staring at him hard, peering
down into the depths of his very soul. Didn't she know
this man?

When she spoke, her voice was hushed, body still.
"No, nothing's wrong. Your dog's name... It's not a
normal dog's name, is it? I mean, it's unusual. Where
did you get that name? The name Ricky-Ticky?"

He shrugged. "I don't know. I saw the dog, I mean
he's just a black and white mutt I found at an animal
shelter downtown. I don't know, I looked at him and
the name just came tumbling out of my mouth. Is there
a problem with it?"

Trace stared. She couldn't pull her eyes from Blake.
"How old are you, Blake?"

He was a bit taken aback by her sudden serious questions. "How old? Thirty-two."

"Do you fly? Do you have a pilot's license?"

"Trace... what is this? No, I'm not a pilot. I don't like to fly. In fact, I avoid it at all costs. It just makes me kind of nauseous to even think about it. I know it sounds a little crazy, but whenever I have to fly, I always think there's some airplane up there, hiding in the clouds, out to get me. I prefer driving or taking boats or trains. What is all this?"

Trace's eyes glazed over—became distant, roaming the scenes of the past, seeing 1916 Paris, smelling the fresh bread wafting out from the bakeries; strolling past the crowded cafes; sipping tea with Edward in the Tea Room at the Hotel de Ville.

When her eyes finally cleared, she gazed up at Blake, and her features slowly brightened. She took a few steps toward him, her eyes exploring his, as she worked to pierce the screen of the present and see into the past as she had successfully done with Cyrano—to peer deep into the waters of Blake's past life. But she saw nothing. She couldn't break through, even though she sensed a connection. A recognition. A reconnection.

Trace lifted her shoulders and slowly let them settle, as she exhaled an easy breath.

When she spoke, her voice was calm and even. "Blake...I would love to take that walk and have lunch. Yes, I'd like that very much. And I'm very excited to meet Ricky-Ticky. I've heard about him, you know. A long time ago, I read all about him in a letter."

EPILOGUE
OCTOBER
SIXTEEN MONTHS LATER

When Natalie Mary Farrington was placed into Trace's arms, she cried. Blake and Cyrano were standing on either side of Trace's hospital bed, gazing down with tender expressions.

Trace kissed her newly born baby daughter on the forehead and cheeks, whispering words of love. Natalie's pinched eyes struggled to focus, as she made fussy little sounds.

"Welcome to the world, little punkin. She's a beauty, isn't she?" Trace said.

"She looks like you," Blake said.

Trace glanced up. "Do you think so?"

Cyrano spoke up. "Yes... Blake's right. She has your forehead and your mouth, Trace. No doubt about that."

Trace took her daughter's little hand and stroked it with a thumb, staring lovingly, as she reviewed the past, hectic months. She and Blake had fallen in love so easily and so fast. To her, it was as if they'd picked up where they'd left off back in 1916, and after a few weeks of dating, Blake had simply said, "I feel like I've known you before. Do you feel the same way?"

Trace had not told him about her time travel experiences. All that would come later, or maybe not at all. Time, as they say, would tell.

On December 15th, Trace and Blake were married at the Romanesque Episcopal Church in Lenox, Massachusetts, Cyrano's church, where over two hundred guests attended. Cyrano worked tirelessly with Trace to ensure that every detail was taken care of, pestering the florists, the minister, the organist and the caterers.

As a result, Trace and Blake drifted through their magical wedding day with kisses and laughter.

The reception was held some miles away at a grand ballroom, where Trace and Blake sipped Champagne and danced the night away to the big band sounds of the 1940s, 1950s and 1960s.

They honeymooned for three weeks, in Rome, Venice and the Amalfi Coast, spending Christmas in Venice. After they returned to New York, Trace began rehearsals for a new musical, and Blake received a lucrative opportunity to work at an exclusive East Side Spa.

Cyrano insisted that they live in his Park Avenue condo, and they agreed only if he'd accept the same amount of rent they were paying for their two Upper West Side apartments.

When Trace realized she was pregnant, she, Blake and Cyrano hit the town in a celebration that lasted into the wee hours of the morning, dining in Chelsea and consuming copious amounts of sparkling apple cider and alcohol-free rosé.

Whatever had happened in the past no longer mattered to Trace. Her nightmares as the doomed Mata Hari faded and then finally ceased completely. Trace became happily immersed and occupied with her new life. Thanks to her time travel journey, she'd been purged of the old demons, the nightmares and the guilt. She was living her life in the present—as the New Ager's say—she was living in the Now. And it was the Now and the life of her dreams. She had a great marriage, a fabulous career, more friends than she could count, and a lovely baby girl, the new love of her life.

Two weeks after Trace returned home with Natalie, Cyrano dropped in, carrying a package. Trace helped him out of his coat, kissed him on the cheek and accompanied him into the living room. He remained quiet about the package, as they entered the spacious room that opened into a wall of windows that offered a glorious view of the flaming trees of Central Park, and the distant towers of Manhattan.

Trace had placed Natalie in her crib, and arranged it facing out to the world. She cooed and clapped and reached, and when Cyrano drifted by to give his adopted granddaughter a kiss, she smiled up at him and giggled.

"Hello, my beauty," he said. "Hello, love of my life."

He turned to Trace, still holding the package. "I take it Blake is out working to get New York in good physical shape. From what I hear in the news these days, we can all use it."

"Yes, he just took on four new clients: two corporate CEOs and their wives. He's getting quite the name. Did he tell you that he wants to open his own studio?"

"Yes, and I told him that I thought it was an excellent idea. Perhaps I'll even become a client. I've put on some weight this summer, and the holidays are coming."

Trace stared curiously at the package. "Is that for me?" she said, smiling, batting her eyes.

Cyrano grinned broadly. "Yes, but before I bestow this gift upon you, I want to make a statement."

Trace nodded, crossing her arms. "A statement. Well, sir, I am all ears."

"Yesterday, my entire Mata Hari collection, including the lost Mata Hari ring, was shipped off to the Fries Museum in Leeuwarden, Netherlands. You will never have to worry about seeing that damned ring again."

Trace jerked a nod. "Good. I'm glad it's gone. I hope that ring is kept under lock and key forever."

Cyrano nodded. "Well said, Trace. Now that that bit of news has been concluded, let's move on."

"I know that grin, Cyrano. It's your affluent grin. Whatever is in that package is expensive."

He presented it to her. "Take it. It is yours, and Natalie's. It will be a very good investment for her someday. Open it, immediately. I can't wait to get your reaction."

Trace gingerly unwrapped the brown paper.

"Be careful, Trace. It's breakable."

As she peeled back the last of the paper, she saw a pencil sketch, in a silver frame. She held it up into the light, staring, transfixed.

"Do you like it, Trace?" Cyrano asked, eagerly, hands clasped together. "Do you?"

She nodded, keeping her eyes on the sketch. "Yes... Yes, I like it very much."

"It's a Picasso. A sketch by Picasso. See, there's his signature. But, here's the thing. Doesn't it look like you? When I saw it at auction, I nearly fainted dead away. Look at it," Cyrano said, pointing. "Picasso did that sketch outside a Paris café in 1916. Isn't it a remarkable resemblance of you, Trace?"

A slow smile of remembrance came over her. Yes, she recalled that day very well. She recalled Picasso, and she remembered exactly what he had said to her, as if it were only yesterday.

"Am I to sketch your face, what's inside your face or what's behind it? You seem to be in pieces to me. Okay, I'll have to find you in pieces."

She was no longer in pieces. Those fragments of pain, fear and terror had all been washed away, replaced by the rich wholeness of love.

Cyrano stepped back, his face animated. "Trace, were you there? Did you meet Pablo Picasso in 1916? Is that you in the sketch? Please tell me."

Trace handed the framed sketch back to him, her eyes clear and present. She turned to focus on Natalie. She went to her, reached and stroked her daughter's soft peachy cheek with a finger, smiling down at her, feeling a sweet, blooming and infinite love that dwelled far beyond any sense of time and place.

She whispered, "I love you, little Nonnie."

And then Trace turned back to Cyrano. "Yes, Cyrano that's me in the sketch, but it's just a fragment of the woman I once was, a long time ago. A very long time ago."

THANK YOU

Thank you for taking the time to read *The Lost Mata Hari Ring*. If you enjoyed it, please consider telling your friends or posting a short review. Word of mouth is an author's best friend and it is much appreciated.
Thank you,

Elyse Douglas

Other novels by Elyse Douglas that you might enjoy:

The Sequel to *The Christmas Eve Letter*:

The Christmas Eve Daughter A Time Travel Novel (Book 2)

The Christmas Eve Letter A Time Travel Novel (Book 1)

The Summer Letters

The Other Side of Summer

The Christmas Diary

The Christmas Women

Christmas for Juliet

Christmas Ever After

The Christmas Town A Time Travel Novel

www.elysedouglas.com

Made in the USA
Coppell, TX
18 January 2020